STRAIGHT CIRCLES

STRAIGHT CIRCLES

by

Jackie Bateman

ANVIL PRESS / CANADA

Anvil Press Publishers Inc.
P.O. Box 3008, Main Post Office
Vancouver, B.C. V6B 3X5 CANADA
www.anvilpress.com

Library and Archives Canada Cataloguing in Publication

Bateman, Jackie, 1970-, author
    Straight circles / Jackie Bateman. -- First edition.

ISBN 978-1-77214-114-6 (softcover)

    I. Title.

PS8603.A8385S77 2018   C813'.6   C2018-901376-1

Printed and bound in Canada
Cover design by Rayola Graphic Design
Cover Photograph: spxChrome
Author photo by Rachel Pick
Interior by HeimatHouse
Represented in Canada by Publishers Group Canada
Distributed by Raincoast Books

Canadä

The publisher gratefully acknowledges the financial assistance of the Canada Council for the Arts, the Canada Book Fund, and the Province of British Columbia through the B.C. Arts Council and the Book Publishing Tax Credit.

To my stars,
George and Poppy.

Thirst

I was an animal hide left out in the midday sun, cracking and shrinking.
I was a withered bundle of dry twigs ready for the fire.
I had lizard's eyes; I had no tears left.
I was a desert.

There was no life left in me, no blood, nothing flowing. All the liquids had evaporated, leaving my poor auld body with nothing but skin and bone and dried-up dreams. The camera was alive next to me, humming. Him: watching, someplace else, while I shrivelled. I stared into the lens; I couldn't help myself. I saw darkness and the glint of my reflection in miniature. I saw my own sorry soul with nothing left to hold it back. And then I was away.

CHAPTER ONE

Haste Ye Back

L izzy shifted in the cramped seat, her knees brushing against the old man opposite. The last time she'd sat on this train, she was a teenage runaway, travelling in the opposite direction. If she'd known then that she wouldn't be going back to Scotland for nearly twenty years, she might not have left. Now she was a new version of herself, but the darkness of her youth had settled inside her, blurry fragments of the past that wouldn't shift out of her mind easily. Over the years those memories had buried their way deep, and they were slowly waking.

A woman, her face flushed and damp, piled into the carriage as the platform guard's whistle blew. 'Sorry, is anyone sitting there?' She pointed at one of the few seats without a pre-booked ticket wedged into the cracks.

Lizzy heard some muttering as she looked across. It was a young guy with DJ headphones on, a hefty sports bag on the seat next to him.

'Can I sit there?' The woman persisted, wiping her brow.

The man pretended not to notice her, fiddling with his volume button.

Lizzy leaned across, motioning at him to take off his headphones. 'Does your bag have a ticket?'

'What? No.' He pulled the bag to his feet and turned to look out the window.

'Then I suppose that seat's free.' She smiled at the woman, who mouthed a thank you.

As they tumbled out of King's Cross, the judders of the carriage made ripples through Lizzy's stomach. There was a family on the platform waving, holding tissues, and shouting goodbyes. Alfie had wanted to come with her, but she hadn't let him, not even to see her off at the station. He had too much to do, she'd told him, but the truth was she wanted to go solo, to be alone on this journey back to where it all started.

Graffiti covered the dirty walls; cans and wrappers littered the side of the tracks. London was all she knew. It didn't feel like she was going home, but to some place in a fuzzy cloud, full of strangers. Lizzy put one hand on her belly and felt the softness of the new life growing inside her. It was early days—eleven weeks—not yet an alien straining at her cardigan, or billowing out her blouse. The sight of a heavily pregnant woman had always made her turn away, but before long she'd be one of them.

She glanced at the blank faces around the carriage. The secret of it amongst strangers. It was like being removed from earth, looking down on mortals. But she was no angel. She should feel glowing and radiant, like the magazines said, but instead there was a thick fog, pressing. Her skin felt like plastic covered in a film of grease. And there was a place deep inside, maybe in her womb, that ached. It reminded her every day of new life, but also of other lives lost.

She squeezed the place below her navel, pinching the skin.

The elderly man opposite leaned forward, as if he were going to tell her a secret of his own.

'Nice work getting the seat for that lady, by the way, doll. Now the excitement's over, I'll most likely sleep. Don't mind my snoring.'

His eyes were milky, two cloudy windows into silver-haired age.

She spread out her hands on the table, stretching her fingers to compensate for the cramped legroom.

'I might have a snooze myself. I'll try not to dribble.'

'You do that, lassie. We'll be a couple of wee sloths, on our way to dreamland,' he whispered.

'See you there,' she said.

The man's accent was light and friendly, and it gave her a pang of sadness. As a teenager she'd tried so hard to lose it. Anxious not to be found in London, she'd had to blend in. She wondered if it would ever come back to her own tongue, like a long-lost friend.

This trip back to Dalbegie would take all the buried slivers of her childhood and piece them together. It was where she'd grown up, then plunged into adolescence, a tense world. Her yearning to return had started as a dull ache, a seed of a thing, that had recently grown into a fierce need to delve into the shadows, to go back to the place she'd escaped from all those years ago. It was time to move on, and the only way to do that was to go back.

She needed to find out what had happened to her mother.

Lizzy pulled out a book and tried to concentrate on the back cover. She'd always enjoyed a love story and this one seemed a good old tear-jerker, but she couldn't seem to take in the words. Her mind wanted to wander and jump. She turned it over. The cover image was a woman staring into the distance. Fluffy clouds. At the horizon, a young farmer, naked from the waist up, digging. She wondered if stories like that ever happened in real life, with the happily ever after. Fat chance.

Alfie had transferred all her old CDs onto her iPod, so she could have the soundtrack to her old life while she was visiting, like a back-drop. It was all his idea, and she loved it. She popped in her earbuds and settled back into her seat, closing her eyes to *Standing on a Beach* by The Cure. It seemed a bit cheaty to play the singles album, but it had all her old favourites, "10:15 Saturday Night" and "Charlotte Sometimes," and so she didn't care about the naffness of a compilation.

"Boys Don't Cry."

They did though, didn't they? She'd seen them on the street, heads folded into knees, filthy sleeves wiping wet eyes. Simon had cried when she left him, just before the accident. The streets had killed him. Dalbegie wouldn't be the same, because it wouldn't have Simon.

It would be a long and winding journey. First this train to Edinburgh; then another train to Inverness; then finally a bus to Dalbegie that stopped at loads of places along the way. Alfie had checked online and the bus still seemed to run at night. She'd hoped Auntie Maureen might pick her up from Inverness Station, but there had been no offers. So Lizzy would take the final leg on the bus; no bad thing because she could gather her thoughts without the strain of conversation with a relative she hadn't seen in donkey's years. And she'd have time to get used to being back where she came from.

As the inspector took her ticket, she ran through the phone call she'd made some weeks earlier, after plenty of deliberation and encouragement from Alfie. It wasn't difficult to get hold of Maureen, as she was still at the same address in that small town. When Lizzy spoke to her, Maureen sounded familiar, in that hazy way that memory pulls small details back from the dead.

'Auntie Maureen. It's me, Lizzy.' There had been silence at first, apart from telly voices in the background, a generic, low noise. 'Is that you? I'm sorry I haven't been in touch. I just wanted you to know that I'm okay. I'm in London.'

'My god. Is it really you, my Lauren's wee girl? You sound so different, so English. You'll be all grown up now. Oh my wee darlin'. I thought you were dead, so I did, gone forever, just like your ma, god rest her soul. When will I get to see you? Are you all right?'

'I'm fine. I'm almost thirty.'

'My god, that makes me feel like an auld wifie. Have you been in London all this time? Terrible place. I sent your uncle Brian to Edinburgh to look for you, all those years ago. And Glasgow as well. It was partly his fault that you were gone, what with him leaving us like that.

How was I to cope with four boys and a teenage girl? It wasn't easy for me, you know? Still isn't.'

Lizzy couldn't help but smile. Some things never changed. Everything had always been about Auntie Maureen. 'I know. It was terrible for you.'

Outside, the city began to blur as the train picked up speed. Across the aisle a young girl was colouring with chunky felt pens, chocolate milk spilled on her dress. She couldn't remember being that age, just a kid, with nothing to worry about. There was never a time when Lizzy didn't feel uncomfortable. Her world had been threatening and murky, and she'd been lured in by all the wrong people. *Scum.*

The grey, wet concrete of the city was gradually replaced by patches of green in suburbia. Back gardens with washing lines and plastic slides. Rectangles of drudgery. She didn't want to be one of those mums with stuff everywhere, the cheap crap that no kid ever seemed to play with. Her own childhood had been tight, stripped away. When she fled Dalbegie, she'd left with nothing but the clothes she was wearing; there were no photos, letters, or old stuffed toys to keep her memories strong. A notion of a face, the soft tone of a voice, and the trace of her mother's shadowy figure were all she had. Kids needed love and attention. Basic stuff.

What would she find back in Scotland? Her worst fear, the one that was overriding all else, was looking at an old photograph of Mum and it not matching up with the picture in her head. But it had to be done, before her face faded altogether. It was important, to keep the family history alive, with another generation on its way. She forced herself to think the words: *my baby.*

That morning, Alfie had held her tight, both hands on her belly, and whispered into her hair, 'When you get there, you'll know where you're from. But don't forget you both belong here, now. With me.' His face had been freshly shaven, the minty smell of his shaving foam lingering even now. It made her pine for him already.

ɔⅼɔ ɔⅼɔ ɔⅼɔ

Lizzy stepped into Dalbegie Station: a small, concrete shelter with two bus parks. The winding roads and the too-slow bus with a thousand stops had turned her stomach. She bent forward and held the back of her knees. Another bus had already parked there for the night, engine clicking, oil dripping on the concrete. She straightened and felt grateful for the chill air and damp on her face. It smelled so different, fresh and airy, after the heaviness of the city. Some pigeons were huddled underneath one of the awnings, piles of droppings underneath. This was the terminus, and she was the only one left; everyone else had disappeared into the night at various places along the way. She turned to the driver and raised her hand in thanks.

The driver nodded. 'Are you okay, there?'

'I'm fine, thanks. Just having a stretch.'

'You have a good night, darlin', and mind yourself.' He gave her a wave, walking off into the dimly lit street ahead. His footsteps tapped for a time, then everything was still.

She pulled out the map she'd printed from the B&B owners' email, and held it up to a streetlight. They'd told her it wasn't too far from the bus station, a short walk. She could just about manage it, before collapsing into bed. Maureen had wanted Lizzy to stay at her place, but the idea of all that talking hadn't been appealing. And the B&B was cheap. It was booked up for ten days and they would no doubt fly by, although Lizzy was sure by the end of it she'd be ready to come back home, to Alfie, and her job managing Step Inside. She could do the work with her eyes shut, but she liked the daily banter with the others. 'Quality shoes, crap staff,' she'd say when one of them skived or forgot to tidy up after a customer. It would be good to have a break from it all, though.

She pulled at the straps on her rucksack and set off. The houses along the pockmarked street had their curtains drawn, silhouettes moving here and there. They were identical, the rows of brick endless, featureless. She didn't recognize the place, or feel anything for it. Her boots clacking on the pavement was the only sound, save for the odd muffled voice coming from people's tellies. On the next street was a twee-looking house on the end of the row, with a wrought-iron sign outside bearing the comforting words, 'Welcome to Dalbegie Inn.'

But it wasn't comforting to be back and feel nothing. She'd been dreaming of this place for so long. But then dreams are dreams.

She knocked and waited, glancing behind her.

There were voices inside and some fussing around with the chain before the door opened. A middle-aged woman appeared, wearing an apron covered with flour and stains, and a pair of pink slippers. She looked confused.

'You must be Tilda.' Lizzy offered her hand.

'Of course. I didn't forget you.' Tilda wiped her hand on her apron and took Lizzy's. 'I expect you're as tired as anything, wee soul, standing out there in the freezing cold.' She stepped back and motioned inside. 'Come in, dear.'

'Thanks. The journey ended up longer than I thought.' Lizzy went in, and as a blanket of warm air wrapped itself around her she realized how cold she was. Tilda shivered.

'Baltic out there, so it is. I've put you in the second room on the left. I'll bring up a hot chocolate and some biscuits. Would you like a wee nip to go with it?' She wound her hands around each other, looking over her shoulder as if there was someone there.

'No nip, thanks. But a hot chocolate would be lovely.'

'Right you are.' She disappeared down the hallway.

Lizzy trudged up the stairs, ancient and creaky with a strip of faded red carpet running up the middle. There was a series of old black-and-white framed photos on the wall, of horses and carriages, rivers and hill-sides. She wondered if any of them had meaning for the owners, from family history, or if they'd been bought to look the part. At the top she went into room number two and sat on the bed. She texted Alfie to let him know she'd arrived safely, and that she'd call him in the morning.

He texted back straightaway: 'Nice one. Sleep tight.'

She imagined him watching the cricket or the golf, happy now he'd heard from her. Or in the pub with his mates, more like. Either way, he was such a worry-guts.

The bedsprings squeaked. The room was warm and spotless, the decor pink and white. There was a large telly on metal brackets in the corner. She'd need that for company. She had her own bathroom, thank god. The place was quiet too, except for a voice in the distance. It was getting louder now, a man shouting. Lizzy went to the window and pulled back the curtains and the nets behind them. The man was stag-gering up the road, a silhouette in the streetlight, singing so loud she could even make out the words:

'See the sleeping Scotsman, strong and handsome built,

Wonder if it's true what they dinnae wear in they kilt...'

He was wasted, his voice hoarse and slurry, stumbling off the pave-ment into the gutter and back again. She chuckled. Where'd she heard that song before?

'Oh, don't mind him, that's just old Taff MacGonagall,' Tilda said behind her. She brought in a mug and a plate of chocolate digestives and set them down on the bedside table. 'He's harmless, which is more than can be said for some of them.'

'Is there a pub near here?'

'Aye, we've the Dalbegie Dram not far from here, towards the High Street. It used to be all right in there, but now it's got a mite rough. Do you like a wee drink, Lizzy?'

'I do, but I'm off the booze at the moment. That hot chocolate looks delicious, though, thanks.' She picked up the drink and cradled it in her hands. *The Dalbegie Dram.* Last time she was here, she'd been too young to go to the pub. Sneaky tinnies and half-covered fags in the bushes were all they had at that age.

'Can I ask you a question, darlin'?' Tilda twisted her apron string around her finger.

'Of course.'

'You seem like a nice wee lassie, well-spoken and everything. All the way from London. What is it you're doing all the way up here? Sorry if that seems nosy, but me and Ken, we were wondering. The guests we normally get are uncles and cousins of folk we know here, too big or too many of them to fit into their family's houses.'

'I'm from here, originally. I've come back to see what family I've got left. I've been away seventeen years. Seems like a long time, now I've said it out loud.'

'Away with you. From Dalbegie? I'd never have known. You must have left when you were very young, just a wean. Who are your folks?' Tilda was whispering, as if their conversation was classified.

'I was thirteen when I ran away. My parents were Lauren and Rob Finning. Lauren, my mum, isn't alive any more though, and my dad lives in Yorkshire as far as I know. I've come up to see my aunt Maureen and the rest of the family. Find my roots, and see the place.'

She wouldn't tell her the rest. No point letting the world know her main reason for coming.

Tilda sat down on the bed, and it wobbled around, creaking and complaining. 'Lauren Finning. Of course I know her name; everyone 'round here would. She's the one that disappeared. Seems like yesterday. I'm sorry, darlin', about your mum. Did they never find out what happened? I always thought . . . well.'

'No, they never did.' Lizzy sighed. Her back was aching, and she put her hands to it. She didn't want to talk about it all right now.

Tilda got up quickly and went to the door.

'Just listen to me prattling on. I'll let you have a good night's sleep and we'll see you in the morning. You're the only one staying; it's a nice quiet September.'

'I will, thanks. What time's breakfast?'

'I'll get your breakfast whenever you get up. You take your time.'

The door shut and Lizzy took her mug back to the window. The shouting man, Taff MacSomebody, had reached the far end of the road. Out of the shadows another man appeared, taller and bigger. The two bodies merged together, and she couldn't quite tell if they were walking along with their arms around each other for support, or if the bigger one was pulling, dragging even. Either way, Taff had got quieter. They disappeared into the night, their footsteps muffled.

She put her cheek against the glass and the cold seeped in. She heard a sharp cry. The singing stopped. Lizzy strained to see anything, but they were too far away. The quiet hummed at her, but she couldn't worry about everyone else. Alfie was always telling her that, as if his worrying was acceptable and hers wasn't.

She pulled away from the window and as she turned around a flash went off like a camera's. A hand came at her, and an angry voice barked, indecipherable. It was there, and then it was gone again. She blinked, her legs shaking. It was a spark making itself known. There were men she had suffered in this place, all their voices merging, becoming one beast. She'd never understood the true meaning of the word 'flashback' before. But it was powerful, the demons surfacing in a blaze of light. She caught her breath, eyes adjusting. Then she clenched her muscles tight and pushed them away.

She locked the door. Leaving the curtains open, she turned off the lights and lay on the bed. This was something familiar, looking up at the sky to find her star. It was what she did when it was needed.

There was another shout outside, abrupt, followed by a single scream. Lizzy pulled the sides of the pillow up to cover her ears, and pressed.

There it was, the star, shifted from where she was used to seeing it, brighter than the others. It seemed bigger than usual. Closer.

I've done it, Mum. I'm back to where it all started.

Your star's bright tonight. And here's a thing. I'm sure I can feel you more than ever, now that I'm in Scotland. It sounds daft, but it's true. This is where you left the world, and so the spirit of you feels solid, like this is where you've been all this time. It means a lot, to know that you're with me, because these next few days are going to be tough. All the bad is going to start flooding back. I'll be brave, promise.

Would she ever feel as close to her own child? Even the idea of it seemed far away. For now, she'd ignore the future and what was to come. Focus on what she once had. Everyone at the time had speculated endlessly about what had happened to her mum, just like Tilda had. She ran away with another man, or got back with her dad, or got thrown in the river. The police never found a thing. The gossip and theories weren't good enough for Lizzy now. This new version of herself would ask more questions, overturn everything, and see the place through fresh eyes.

She'd get to the bottom of it all if it killed her.

CHAPTER TWO

Lizzy's Star

We're all proud of where we come from. If we're Irish living in Canada, if we're Danish living in England, if we're Scottish living anyplace else, it's all the same thing. To go back is to feel just right, like we're stepping into some old comfy slippers and everyone else is wearing them too.

Come to mind, it's to feel a bit out of sorts as well, like there's a black cloak waiting to wrap itself where it isn't wanted.

But anyways, there's a tug of a place, weak or strong, that never goes away, even if a bad thing happened there, in our town, or in the house where we grew up. We might have escaped from that early piece of our lives, and ach away, isn't it better where we are now? But that tug is still there, you know?

There's a thing your Granny Mac used to say, Lizzy: 'A clean shirt'll do ye.' It means you're not that long in the world; you could only have the one more change of clothes, the one more bag of laundry, before you'll be deid. So get on. If there's a message you've to give someone, a past you've to look to, it's to be done before it's too late.

And there you are.

I'd given up hope of seeing you again, but you're here, a static ball of electricity. You've come back, Lizzy, back to where the tug is coming from—we'll see if you can't get it to stop pulling at you. Crackling and sparkling, so you are. There's a tunnel swooping down from me to you, like an energy force. I reckon it's the umbilical cord back again, but this time it's empty of blood vessels and all those nutrients. Instead it's just a winding spirit of a thing connecting us. I'm here for you Lizzy, more than ever, some might say. In the face of things I was more useless alive than I am dead. What good is a mother when she doesn't protect her wean? There's no point to her.

My wee girl. It's your hair that makes you look the same. You're all soft, blonde and saintly. I mind when you used to sit on my lap, me getting all the knots out of those curls. I still know the feel of you, so light, bones sticking out. There was nothing of you. If I could hold you again, just once, I'd die the same way, all over again. I could do it. It'd be worth it.

There's tiny laugh lines about your eyes now; you'll be wiser than I was, I hope. You're looking up at the stars. I used to talk to Granny Mac that way. I know exactly how it feels, to need the closeness, the soul of someone, when they're not with you anymore. I told my ma everything when she lived a spitting distance away, but I fair spilled my heart when she was gone. What I couldn't know then was how it felt to be the spirit, the person looking down. Until now, it's all been a clarty mess, a blurred sense of things, and I can often rest and just 'be.' I'm not solid, but a soaring bubble, like a liquid or a gas, boundless and fluid. I've been everywhere and nowhere, catching snippets of this and that.

But now I've got a clear view. And it's because of you.

It's like I'm looking down the wrong end of a telescope. I can feel myself again, the floaty parts tightening, as my heart pulls everything together. This is the best and the worst it's ever been. I can see you, but I can't sit next to you, put your feet on my lap, or stroke your cheek. It's like torture, the animal instinct of a mother being denied.

But what are you doing here, my wee darling?

I'm glad you're in Dalbegie, back to your roots. But I'm feared for you, Lizzy. You need to mind yourself because this place is full of monsters, out to drag you down with them. It's just a wee town, but it's a dark place, battered and bored, houses sprawling out like they're trying to get away from the middle of it. Folk try to tempt you into things, and it takes a strong person to turn away. But you know all that, because you lived through it when you were twelve, thirteen, the most difficult years of a girl's life. Some of the wrong 'uns might be long gone, your posse from the old days. But you've not been back for such a long time, and a place can get to you when you're not looking. Be wary, Lizzy.

Bad things happened to you because of me. Everything's my fault, because I left you to stand up to the beasties on your own.

If I hadn't gone out that night.

If I'd stayed in with you, no secrets.

If I hadn't gone stupid over that man and what I'd like to do with him.

If, if, if. Then we'd still be together. There's nothing can be done about it all now. I hope you don't think you can solve anything. The past isn't for changing.

I know the B&B, Tilda's place. You're in safe hands with her, at least. She's a funny one, anxious, but she has a good heart. Looking well, so she is, more than I can say for her other half. I'm surprised Ken's still about, what with the drinking and the smoking. I expect he's making a nuisance of himself. He never was much help to Tilda, I don't mind saying. That man is all string vest and no substance, just like a lot of men around Dalbegie. A waste of space, a drinker. But Lizzy, you're going to fall asleep on that pink bed soon, dregs of cocoa left in the cup on the nightstand. Whatever happens, I'm looking forward to seeing the world through your eyes, being close to you.

Will you go to our old house on Bryant Road? It was our home together, where we carried on living, just the two of us, after your dad went and shacked up with that woman. It was the best time of my life, not being feared of him coming home, not having to tiptoe about the place. Things were simple. We'd have our fish suppers on our laps in front of the telly, and I'd plait your hair before bed. We painted the front door green. I'll bet it's a different colour now. I imagine you'll go there, how could you not? But don't expect much. Houses are only homes when you're living in them.

Part of me wants to shout at you, shake your shoulders, to warn you away. Another part wants you to stay right here, forever. I'm sending vibrations your way, waves of caution. I hope they get to you, because I can feel myself melting, slipping now, as you're dropping off. Your arms are placed firmly across your front, fingers entwined, protecting. I can tell there's something important to look after in there.

Call it a mother's intuition.

CHAPTER THREE

Oliver's Fringes

The Edinburgh nights were lengthening, the air turning fresh. I was noticing the seagulls again. It wasn't that they'd journeyed anywhere else, but rather their noise had been drowned out by the season: the chatter and bustle, taxi engines and bagpipes. I didn't especially enjoy their screams, but it was a relief that the background crackle had cleared and I could think again. They screeched my name, the seagulls, *O-li-ver,* reminding me that summer was coming to an end, giving me a nudge. It was time to move on.

Scotland had been my home for many years, ever since I left stinking London, with its abundance of places to hide but too few corners to be alone. I split my time between Edinburgh and Dalbegie, aside from the odd trip back to London to check on things, and a short stint in Bangkok. That debauched, damp episode in Thailand had followed a hiccup with my online and face-to-face followers. My client list, faithful and stable for so long, had taken a knock. Two of my members died, and one joined a religious sect and slipped sideways. My income took a downturn, and so for two years I reaped the benefits of cheap-thrill Southeast Asia, quite unashamedly.

I shouldn't need to apologize for what I did there, and so I won't. Thousands of Western men flock there, taking advantage, milking every last drop of privilege they possess. It's like death taking its final, hot breath, when people will pay for anything that will keep them feeling alive—globally offensive, I grant you, but not necessarily shocking. We've read those kinds of stories time and time again. Nothing's new. There I was, one of thousands, facilitating my own pleasures. It was a tiny pinprick of illegal activity amongst a gaping universe of wrong.

And yet afterwards I felt a little dirtier, a smaller man. No better than the rest. I was glad to return to Scotland, to my homeland, where the ratio of bad to good was tilted in favour of the good—where I was special.

It had been a short yet eventful summer, culminating in the Edinburgh Fringe Festival, an odious affair where has-been comedians and eager, inexperienced actors tried to impress the crowds of weary residents and overly enthusiastic tourists. *You'll laugh until you drop. Five stars.* It almost always rained. Although I despised hordes of people congregating in one place, I had stayed close to the events so that I could take advantage of the impressionable. I felt almost spontaneous for the first time in years. I had never truly enjoyed things that came too easily, even when in an artless mood, but for some reason I'd taken to more brazen abductions: grasping and pushing, bushes and open air. The thrill of a premeditated chase had grown less stimulating over the years, as I'd done it so many times. There was nothing clever about it anymore. Murder had become as commonplace as grievous bodily harm, or domestic violence, blending into the background with the rest of the smudged newsprint. For years the authentic had been merging with reality television, the blundered news. Nothing was real and yet everything was believable.

And so I returned to where I first began, to the pleasurable existence of an opportunist. The delayed gratification of holding back, of studying one's prey for nuances and habits, was getting to be rather a bore.

But I started to make mistakes. Perhaps I had become too complacent, overly confident after so many years of not getting caught. It was a dangerous thing to believe I was somehow immune, even subconsciously. No one is invincible. Even when nothing is real.

It was the last night of the Fringe Festival, a big bash going on at the Assembly Rooms, the crowds walking George Street, many suffering the cold and having a drink in one of the temporary open-air bars. The smells of cologne, cigarettes, and hairspray filled the overly expectant air. I perused Rose Street, parallel to the festival action, a somewhat more sordid mile of pubs and edgy cafés with antiquity and charm. I preferred it to fancier George Street. This had character, with hidden corners for inebriated potentials. A new Italian restaurant had opened on the street, fronted by a celebrity chef. It was one of those spaces that had pendulum bar lighting and square booths. I had begun to despise anyone who dined there, endorsing its grotesque contemporary out-fitting, giving money to the new kid in town.

I loitered near the entrance, watching couples going in, glowering at their high heels and golden handbags, sneering at dress shirts with overly large collars and cuff details. I didn't have a plan, but my anger was welling, and I decided to retire to the disused doorway opposite. Perhaps I would follow a group of women, wait until one strayed. But I was so wrapped up in rage that I didn't notice the policeman walking towards me until he was but a few feet away. By that time it was almost dark, the streetlamp making his silver badge glint.

'We've had a complaint,' he said. 'What are you doing there, sir?'

I gathered myself. My scalp was itching underneath my tweed walking hat and I scratched at it, stalling for time. It had been so long since I'd been challenged that my mind emptied as I struggled to assemble the right words.

The policeman came closer.

'Can I ask what you're doing?' He was old enough to have that weary look about him, the one that meant he'd seen it all.

You haven't seen anything that I haven't already done.

I cleared my throat.

'I'm waiting for someone. A woman,' I said. 'We're meeting here and we're going to have dinner.' I smoothed down the front of my shirt. It was a good fit, white and crisp, and I would have been better dressed than any of the upstarts inside that place, eating overpriced tortellini.

'You've been here a wee while,' he said. 'Do you think she's coming?'

'Perhaps not.'

'Well I think you should move on. The look on your face is scaring the clientele. You look like you're going to murder someone, son. Move on, now.'

I had no answer to that. For a split second I wondered if he could read my mind. But of course he couldn't. I was losing my touch, my social awareness. I'd never exactly been a conversationalist, and admittedly I'd had less and less contact with people over the years. I must have frowned, or looked aggressive, or somehow contorted my face so that he misconstrued it for confrontation.

'Let's go,' he said, and pulled at my arm.

I flinched. He was gentle enough, hardly forceful, but his touch was electrifying. I found physical contact with men abhorrent. I had harboured a resentment towards other people's germs for most of my life, but I dealt with it badly by backing up against the wall, inside the doorway. It was an unfortunate kneejerk, creating further suspicion.

'Get out of there, or I'll have to make you come out.' The policeman was pressing a button on his walkie-talkie, an outsized contraption that looked like it belonged in another decade.

I decided not to say anything further, to comply. I couldn't risk drawing attention to myself, least of all being taken to a police station and investigated. I had once been in prison, a good number of years ago, and I couldn't have that dragged up again. My face was burning, the skin under my chin tender and rather raw from a meticulous second shave I'd given myself that afternoon, and I had to focus on calming myself down. I resented the buzzword 'mindful' as a prefix for anything— mindful walking, mindful eating, mindful meditation—but decided to perform a few mindful actions nonetheless. I moved slowly, my feet shuffling forward, and my hands in clear view. I tried to draw the corners of my mouth upwards into a smile, and I blinked purposefully, as if my eyelids were heavy. Gradually I drew myself out of the doorway and into the narrow street to face the policeman. I gave him an exaggerated nod in compliance, raised my palms, mindfully of course, and turned away. Voices were crackling into his walkie-talkie, indecipherable and unpleasant sounding. No doubt he was feeling self-righteous, the big man, getting rid of the unpleasantness that was causing customers in the restaurant to feel uneasy while they buttered their ciabatta.

I strolled to the end of Rose Street, as casually as I could muster, shaking my head as if to say, 'good gracious, what a to-do about nothing.' When I turned the corner, I quickened my pace to get lost in the crowd and let the steam out. It hissed from every part of my body, but the release had little effect. The quicker I walked, the more annoyed I became, for letting the situation get to me, for losing my cool. I rarely lost control. My shoulder banged into a woman standing on the edge of the pavement, and she tutted infuriatingly in my direction. My apartment was some distance to walk to, all the way back down Dundas Street, but I slowed my pace to let my nerves settle. I asked myself if I had been in the city too long. Although it was no London or Bangkok, it was all getting under my skin: the density of the buildings, the people, the traffic, the constant whine.

I needed my retreat once more. It was time, just like the seagulls were insisting. I had enjoyed spring and summer in Edinburgh, but I was more than ready, as usual, to transfer to Dalbegie for the cleansing and bracing autumn.

When I got back, I poured myself three fingers of The Macallan 12 Years Old and sat in my bay window overlooking the distant hills. Their tops were barely discernible against the night sky, but the shadows were soothing, the outline clean and crisp. The smooth burn of the drink settled my stomach, taking my mind away from the policeman. I held Bird in my palm, soft and reassuring, my pocket friend that I'd picked up years ago at the National History Museum. She was a pale-yellow Meadowlark, not much more than a stuffed toy, but she reminded me of a girl I knew, a long-time infatuation. Her stoic expression, the delicate contours of her body, mirrored someone I had once obsessively observed, and still thought about from time to time. There was a period when she was in my thoughts every hour, every day.

She would never leave me.

My sanctuary was not far. For the rest of the year—the most wind-blown, bitter part—I would return to Dalbegie in the Highlands, for my quiet withdrawal. I would hide away, on the usual pretense of working as a web writer, showing my face here and there, a few of the local people laughingly pleased to see me again. It had become my holiday home, without the burden of having to 'relax' with other people. I'd been half-living there for some twenty years, and yet I couldn't call anyone more than an acquaintance. Perfect. The wind would howl outside my window, the rain pelting against the stone wall and the iron gate, but it didn't matter because I would be largely house bound and hiding, logging my exploits, searching online for things that were invisible to most casual observers. And I'd been developing a new idea, one that would allow me to remain hidden whilst delving into other people's minds. I was going to become one of the faceless thousands who belong to a forum, commenting here and there on other people's misfortunes and problems, subtly gathering information that could lead to a more exhilarating interaction. There was a site I'd had my eye on for some time, one that focussed on depression and anxiety, full of downtrodden women, young unemployed, angst-filled teens, and people with relationship issues. I would join under a pseudonym, feigning a disheartening situation, and become a real part of the suicidal family.

Was I merely acting as a pathetic internet troll, hiding behind the online façade? I liked to think I was better than that; I didn't make idle inflammatory comments for my own immediate pleasures. Rather, I exposed and exploited other people's problems and needs, waiting for one perfect strategic moment to lunge in for the kill.

When I was truly isolated, my ideas became more pronounced and increasingly prolific. They came up at night, swirling around my head, clashing together, merging. I felt original in Dalbegie, a new person with fresh ways of seeing. I craved it then, the paradoxical anonymity and closeness of a small town. Everyone knew my business, or so they believed. There wasn't a soul there who could ever know what I did, and who I really was. I had become an enigma, and the locals were used to that, to my quiet presence in the background. It was all part of my charm.

CHAPTER FOUR

Helen's Manky Cats

Helen hurried away from the store, a heavy plastic bag in each hand, the handles cutting into her palms. The owner of the mini-mart had given her a stony stare as she left. Perhaps he'd witnessed what had happened in the cereal aisle. That idiotic blonde woman had dropped her basket of groceries but couldn't bend down to pick up the stray cans because she had one of those annoying baby carriers strapped to her body, the baby dribbling down the front of it, kicking its legs like an alien bursting out of its mother's rib cage. Helen had kicked the cans, scattering them further, one or two of them disappearing underneath the shelving units. The act had made her feel better, her annoyance released. Perhaps the stupid bitch had complained.

She should have kicked her baby too.

Helen made her way home. The owner would forget about it eventually. She'd been a good customer over the years, never grumbling herself, not even when his yoghurts were going out of date.

The street was nearly empty, with everyone inside for dinner, or away in town for the scrap end of the festival. Some would be starting the evening with a drink in the Porty or the Frog. Everything was about drinking in Edinburgh. Nothing was about drinking for Helen, especially not the social aspect of it, the hours of speculating and slurring, camaraderie and backslapping. Her brother Steve would be down the pub by now, supping a pint with the boys, chatting and laughing like he did. Waste of time.

She trudged into her street, hundreds of TO LET signs flickering overhead. There were so many that it was distracting, the orange glow of them. This part of Leith had become a ghost town, a dead place. Everyone had moved out or sold up. What was the tipping point of this area's downfall—the economy? The crime crisis? The immigrant issue, perhaps. There had been so many violent incidents that maybe people simply couldn't stand the knots in their stomachs anymore. Her interest was curiosity, nothing more. Helen had a cheap place to stay amidst the quiet. No matter there was no one else about.

'Spare some change, wee darlin'?'

The homeless guy was sitting on the pavement outside the offie as usual, a dirty blanket wrapped around his shoulders. His hair was matted, his fingerless gloves coated in grime. They weren't unlike her own, she noted, although she could at least afford the launderette. She should go there soon, fill a bag with clothes from her bedroom floor, perhaps throw in her coat on a gentle wash. The pockets were lined with crumbs, the cuffs rimmed with black. It was her old favourite, that grey coat, one of the few things that still fit her, although the buttons were straining now.

Helen ignored him. She could get rid of him, clean up the streets, but there wasn't much of a challenge in that anymore. She wasn't a vigilante, a do-gooder. Let him be.

Mind you, no one noticed when a homeless waster disappeared. It was safe meat. And it had been a while since her last piece of the action.

The old woman from the flat opposite was coming up the street towards her now, shoulders hunched over a shopping bag with wheels. Helen studied it. It had plenty of room for the heavy stuff she got from the hardware store. It might be an idea to get one; her arms were not as strong as they used to be. But it would make her an old woman, and Helen wasn't ready for that yet, not in her fifties. There was too much ahead of her.

The woman raised her hand in greeting, although she must know by now that she wouldn't get one back.

'Hello, there,' the woman croaked as they crossed paths.

Helen pushed the outside door, lock broken long ago, and entered the tenement stairway. The air inside seemed colder than out, the musty smell of neglect circling the threshold. She wiped at the cobwebs on the end of the banister with her elbow, and set about climbing the stair. Eighteen steps to the first floor, then spiral round and another twenty to the second, but she'd never curse them, for they formed an extra barrier against the world. When she was inside her flat, it was a haven. She put her key in the lock and turned. Inside would be warm.

This used to be their mother's place, cluttered with glass ornaments and lavender knick-knacks in the day. The only thing left was a vase of fake flowers in the middle of the coffee table, drooping with dust now. They were symbolic, Steve once said, of Ma's life. Helen had kept them around for him. No difference to her. The rest she'd put in bin bags and taken them to the skip at the building site off Leith Links. No point keeping clothes, hair brushes, ornaments and the like. Even picture frames complicated a place, made it someone else's. Steve had taken the photographs out to keep. Helen wasn't in any of them in any case. She hadn't grown up there, being the estranged twin.

Mother had given her away. The superfluous baby. No need to cling to memories that she wasn't a part of.

She set the bags on the kitchen counter and held the kettle under the tap. A cup of tea and a biscuit would put her right until night came. It wouldn't be until darkness wrapped around the city that her appetite would surge. And tonight she'd feed it, go out there a scavenger. It had been too long. She stretched her arms up, her top straining at the seams. It had shrunk in the dryer, or else she had grown again. She bent to peer through the serving hatch to the living room. Rain had begun to patter against the bay window, the raindrops making streaks down the glass, winding their way from top left to bottom right, falling with the wind. Down they went, carving out nature's path. Where would the rain take her that night? To the depths of the old town, perhaps, where hidden stairways and shadowy nooks were waiting. There was plenty to devour there.

✧ ✧ ✧

The clock ticked its way into her conscious mind, pulling her back into the room. Helen sat up, her back aching from being slumped in the armchair. The rain had stopped, the sky black, most of the stars hidden behind a wall of cloud. A chunk of time had passed, the room much darker than when she sat down. She glanced at her watch. Almost nine o'clock, it was.

She switched on the lamp and her eyes fell on the scuffed wallpaper around the window frame, its shine dulled. She wondered what was underneath, if there would be bare brick or many more layers of paper from the generations even before Mother. There might be floral patterns or flocks of birds, stained and skew.

Her stomach rumbled. The bags of groceries were still on the countertop and she unpacked them, throwing the tins into the small cupboard overhead and stuffing the half-spoiled ready meals into the freezer. The fridge door held the milk and butter; a box of eggs lay sideways on the shelf. The rest of it was almost bare, the sides smudged with brown sauce. She took the can opener from the drawer. It was a bit rusty but it still worked. She'd have beans on toast.

Her mind reawakened as the smell of burned toast filled the air alongside the anticipation of what the night would bring.

Quiet. And release.

cʌɔ cʌɔ cʌɔ

The Cat Rescue had her on a regular early shift. Helen started at seven a.m., and she walked there on autopilot, with sleep in her eyes and a headache threatening to burst her brain open. She'd slept dead and had struggled to get out of bed. At least the place was close by, teetering on the outskirts of Leith. The fresh, chill air woke her up. She'd brought a cereal bar with her, and black coffee in a travel mug. She'd sip at it while she worked, and the dull pain would gradually subside.

She regarded the building ahead, a regal front to the pristine animal housing behind. In the mornings she opened up alone, trusted now. She got out her keys and entered through the main entrance. Sue, the warden, would be asleep upstairs. Sue ran the place, but she seemed to spend more and more time online: advertising the cats for homes, signing up volunteers, and of course looking for donations. Sue was one of the few people Helen could tolerate. They shared a connection with animals over people. They spoke only when they had to; there was nothing worse than needless chatter.

She went through to the pens. Back in the nineties when Helen did her community service, the place was tiny and straightforward to manage. Two or three volunteers could handle the cleaning. Now it had grown into an enterprise, more controlled and segregated. Each cat had its own sleeping shelf, scratching post, litter-tray 'zone' and even a special pillow. There were heated areas, places to socialize, and nooks to hide away. These animals had more than the homeless on the street; they were fed and healthy with friends and lots of attention. Meaning more work to clean up after them.

She had two hours to herself before Sue would appear, and when the other care staff breezed in, followed by the volunteers arriving with the usual levels of trepidation. There were sixty-eight cats that week, all hungry, in need of fresh water, and often new blankets or pillows due to soiling and stress. The pens needed washing out and vacuuming. Some of the cats would have fleas. It was a full-time job, and one that Helen excelled at.

The work could take all morning, depending on how many volunteers they had and whether any of the cats needed to go to the vet. But by lunchtime, everything would be spotless in time for visitors to view the animals, and for staff to go out looking for strays. Helen never stayed for the visitors, preferring to roam the streets, the alleys, the winding side roads of the Lothians, picking up maverick moggies and bringing them back yowling in a cage. Sue understood this about her, and let Helen have her pick of jobs now, after so many years of graft.

The Cat Rescue was where she met Oliver, when they first became a team. He had a streak in him that she recognized almost at once, a similar darkness that she had in her. He'd put on industrial-strength rubber gloves to clean the cages, like a chronic germaphobe.

'Don't ruin your nails, will you,' she'd said, and he'd looked at her with a mix of hate and admiration.

They were the same breed, the two of them. They'd always have a bond.

She went into the feeding room and pulled out the cat food, a stack of bowls, and a large metal scoop from the cupboard. Counting out sixty-eight, she readied the bowls in rows across the counter. Sue knew all the names of the cats and never forgot any of them. Helen didn't know any. They were animals, with sharp teeth and claws, and giving them names made them more human. But they were better than human: simpler. They didn't ask for names, so she didn't care to use them.

At ten o'clock, when the place was bustling with eager helpers talking to the cats, scraping and scrubbing, Helen sat in the staff room alone for her tea break. The main benefit of starting early meant her break was earlier than everyone else's, as was her lunch break and the end of her shift. Less need for interaction. She looked at the corkboard on the wall, paper notices pinned to it. Things for sale, yoga classes, guitar lessons. Little pointless messages, dotted around in all colours, sad and unnecessary.

She took off her shoes, and put her feet up on the footstool. All the hours standing had given her varicose veins, and they were throbbing a little. There was one in particular on her right shin that looked like it could burst out at any moment. She pulled up her trouser leg and regarded the blue of it. Her skin was pink and flabby in contrast.

One of the younger volunteers came into the room and Helen pushed down the staticky fabric of her slacks and sat back in the chair.

He stood in front of her, palms together.

'Excuse me, but do you know where I can find the other vacuums?'

Helen sized him up. He looked no more than eighteen. He couldn't have been one of the reprobates on community service; more likely he was one of the posh school-leavers on a gap year, dipping in and out of 'worthy' jobs before joining the backpacker cliché and flying to somewhere in Southeast Asia. All no doubt paid for by Daddy. His sweater was cashmere; Helen was sure of it. It was burgundy, and that spelled sumptuousness and a lack of creativity. *Burgundy*. She mulled the word around in her mind. Some called it 'wine-coloured,' but they were bourgeois imbeciles.

'Hello? Do you know where the vacuums are kept?' He ran his fingers through his consciously-styled mess of hair.

'What's your name?'

She studied the remnants of her tea. She'd made it too weak.

'Hugo.'

Of course it was. There was a hole in the big toe of her sock. She should cut her toenails soon; they were getting sharp. Come to mind, she should get her hair cut too. It had been a few months and she liked it bowl cut on her jawline. Hair got in the way of things.

The boy, Hugo, asked her one more time. *Where were the vacuums?* She shrugged and he went away at last. *Ask Daddy*, she thought.

She imagined waiting for Hugo after work, and following him home. He would no doubt live with his parents in the New Town, or more likely Murrayfield, maybe even the best end of Morningside. They would have iron railings outside their house, on a curved crescent, with pale stone and greenery. His dear mama would have his dinner ready.

Now that dinner would grow cold.

CHAPTER FIVE

Lizzy's Green Door

There were framed pictures covering Maureen's mantel-piece, the silver glinting, beckoning. Lizzy felt her heart rush. Her mum's face would be in there somewhere. She tried to settle, to be calm. She'd have a look at them all when she was ready. She shouldn't have come here on her first morning. It was too soon.

She turned away and pretended the photos weren't calling out to her. Maureen's place was much the same as it was before, minus the plastic baby toys strewn about the floor and the spilled milk or juice on every surface. It was all coming back to Lizzy now, the chaos of four young boys when she moved in with them, after her mum disappeared. She'd spent hours clearing up, feeding, helping out. Sometimes she'd felt like a maid. Now, there were old newspapers all over the dark wood table, and the windows were streaked with grime. Next to the telly were piles of video games and a scrambled mess of consoles. Older-boy mess. The house smelled of dust mixed with sweat, the carpets and rugs infused with years of sports socks and polyester slippers. Lizzy rubbed her nose. The pregnancy was giving her a keen sense of smell, unfortunately. And now her stomach was rumbling. The baby making itself known again.

At last, Maureen came through with a tray, everything clanking together. She'd been fussing around in the kitchen for ages.

'Look at you, sat there like you've never been away. The spit of your mum, so you are, apart from the hair. Hers was mousey, and a bit lank, but you've been blessed. You got it from your dad, I suppose, which doesn't seem right, him with that hair, what with his ugly temper.'

Lizzy regarded her aunt's own hair, greying and pulled back into a low ponytail. Her face was bloated and pallid, two round patches of pink blush on her cheeks.

Maureen carried on, setting the tray down on the pile of newspapers.

'Oh Lizzy, I can't believe you're here, after all this time. We all thought we'd lost you, gone off with that boy Simon and his skanky ma's boyfriend. What was his name? Oh, he was horrible.'

'Roy.'

Lizzy leaned forward and helped herself to a mug of tea before it fell off the tray, holding it up to Maureen briefly in thanks. She felt a chill at the sound of his name, and an image came to her of his yellow-streaked hair, that pikey pager that he used to carry around with him all the time. He must have been one of the last people on earth to have a pager.

'That was it. Roy. A bad egg if I ever saw one. So did you manage to give him the slip? Where did he go all these years?' Maureen slurped at her tea, although it was still almost boiling. She smoothed down her skirt, too tight for her, the zip bulging at the side.

What was she talking about? He was dead.

'I heard Roy got run over in the street here in Dalbegie, that he got himself killed.'

Maureen shook her head.

'There was never any road accident here. I'd know if there was. He disappeared, same time as you did.'

'We didn't leave with him, far from it. We were getting away from him. Roy had beat Simon up pretty bad. He'd sent us to Edinburgh on a drug drop-off. Our train into Waverley station was late so we missed the contact, and we were terrified he'd kill us for botching the job. Eventually we decided to do a runner, and we never saw him again.'

She left out the part when they opened Roy's package and found wads of cash. You never knew who would want it back. It had kept them alive, that money, but it was long gone.

Maureen gazed out the window, slurping her tea.

'Simon's ma was in a state, she was. She didn't get much sympathy, mind. A lot of folk blamed her for being a terrible mother, pushing Simon away with her drink and her drug problems, and letting that Roy run him wild. I don't blame Simon for wanting to get away from her. But you, Lizzy, you had all of us, the family. What made you go?'

'Roy made us sell his drugs. He beat Simon. I'd been missing Mum so bad. Dad didn't want me. I don't know what else to say, Maureen. I felt like I had nothing.' Lizzy leaned back and stared at the ceiling.

'My god, I had no idea about any of that. I was up to my neck in it, what with all the boys. Your mother would have done her melt, with all that going on. There's still a lot of it about, you know. The drugs. What's it all about? Sniffing powder, stabbing yourself with a needle. Bloody stupid if you ask me. Waste of money.'

'So Roy could still be alive?'

Lizzy shivered as she took a stick of shortbread from the chipped plate on the table. She imagined herself getting fatter every week, growing a rubber ring around her middle like Maureen's. She wondered if Maureen talked even if there was no one around to listen.

'Well if he is, he's somewhere else, thank god. He was trouble. Let's hope he got himself lost, or better still, locked up.'

Maureen went off on one about her sons still being in the house, eating everything, the price of bread and milk these days. Billy, the oldest, was the only one who'd moved out. He lived with his girlfriend in Inverness, working the building sites. The others were all at home: the twins Kai and Kane, plus Noah, the youngest at eighteen, the only one who had managed to stay in school until the end. They were all out looking for work. Noah hadn't managed to pass enough exams to get to college, but seemed to think he deserved a better job than the rest of them.

'Any job would be better than nae job,' she said.

'And what about Uncle Brian?' Lizzy plucked up the courage to ask. When he left them, he gave Maureen an awful letter that had made her cry all night. 'Is he still about?'

Maureen scowled, as if he were in the room.

'The boys needed their father, and he up and went, with only himself to think about. He still spends half his life in the pub. I didn't realize what a help you were to me, Lizzy. When you disappeared as well, I struggled. I'd lost your mum, your uncle Brian, then you. Four boys I had to cope with, all on my own. Imagine.'

'It's not easy being on your own.' Lizzy had been without either of her parents since she was thirteen. 'But at least the boys had you.'

'Well.' Maureen looked at her, the realization seeming to kick in at last. 'You're not wrong, there. They had their mother. Now, have you seen your dad?'

'I haven't been in touch with him since I left here. Haven't you heard from him?' Lizzy helped herself to another biscuit. She picked at the tassels on the embroidered arm of the sofa, encrusted together.

'You don't know, do you?' Maureen was staring at her.

Lizzy held her biscuit mid-air.

'Know what?'

Maureen gulped the remains of her tea, and slammed her mug on the table. The tray rattled and a biscuit slid on the carpet. She picked it up and nibbled at it, wiping a piece of fluff from one side.

'He came back here, brought some woman with him. Oh, Lizzy. They're living in your old house. The deed was in his name, so he took it over. I don't see him if I can help it. Never liked the man, I'm sorry to say. But sometimes he's difficult to miss, big brute that he is.'

He was here in Dalbegie. Her dad.

Lizzy stood up.

'I've got to go.'

Maureen brushed the crumbs from her chest onto the carpet.

'But we've so much to catch up on. You've hardly told me a thing. I want to know about this Alfie of yours. English, is he? Well. I'm sure he's not as bad as some.'

Lizzy grabbed her jacket from the back of a chair. As she turned, her eyes rested on one of the photo frames on the mantelpiece. She didn't mean to look, but it leapt out at her. *Mum.* She held onto the chair.

'I feel a bit funny, Maureen. I need to go back and lie down.'

'Yes, you must rest after that kind of a journey, and all this excitement. Wee soul, look at you, always were a skinny belinky. You need feeding up. Come back later, for your tea. The boys can't wait to see you.' Maureen picked up the frame. 'Looking at this, were you? It's a lovely one of your mum and our ma, the famous Granny Mac. I've got plenty more upstairs. I'll dig them all out for you.' She held it out, arm stretched in front of her, as if she couldn't see it properly unless it was miles away.

Lizzy fumbled with her jacket.

'It's hard, to see her again. When I ran away, I went with nothing.'

Maureen lowered her arm. 'Oh my god, I wasn't thinking. You won't have seen your mum's face in years. It must be terrible strange for you. Here, I'll put this in a wee bag for you, and you can take it with you. Look at it in your own time.' She rummaged in a drawer in the hallway, and produced a ScotMid plastic bag, ripped at the handle. She put the frame into it, and wrapped it all up. 'There. Take that, and we'll see you later, eh?'

'Thanks.'

Lizzy was trembling as she took it. The package was warm, alive. The frame must have been sitting close to the radiator. She made her way to the front door. 'Maybe I'll come by tomorrow for my tea instead. Is that okay?'

'Ach, that's fine. You take your time. It's strange for you.' Maureen stood on the doorstep and waved. 'Cheerio, Lizzy. Mind how you go.'

The icy air cut into her. She pulled her coat against the gusts of wind lifting and jerking. It whistled faintly, making her shiver. She walked past the rows of semi-detached houses, some front gardens raked and pruned, others a mess of weeds. There was a caravan parked alongside them, dirty white. Someone had drawn an unhappy face in the grime on one side, with the words *I can't see.*

Once she was well away, Lizzy took out the street map to work out where she was in relation to the big red star that she'd previously marked: number 20 Bryant Road, with its green door and all those potted plants on the neat doorstep. She'd been desperate to go, but her dad lived there now, sidled in, and it was ruined. She could feel the weight of her mum's photo on her back. It wasn't heavy, but it was there, tapping against her with every step, as if warning her to turn around. 'Back, back, back,' it said, with every tap.

But he was her blood and she should face him. Her dad was the first person she should question.

As Lizzy came closer to the house, the idea of him grew more intense, the physical bulk of him, his angry shouting part of her earliest memories. He used to come up to see her once a year, at Christmas, after he'd moved away. He'd take her out in the car, and they'd talk while he drove around aimlessly. They'd have lunch at a fast-food place, him awkwardly handing over an inappropriate present that was too young for her. She'd outgrown him even before she turned thirteen. He hadn't deserved her love, and yet she had adored him despite everything. But she was just a kid then. *Screw him.*

But still she walked towards the house.

She wished she'd worn her scarf. The temperature was about ten degrees lower than it was when she left London. A plastic bag fluttered across the pavement in front of her and into the gutter. The streets were the same as back home though, filthy and littered. An image flashed again, a lightning bolt, and she stopped, pushing her thumbs against her eye sockets, trying to get it out. A pale arm. A string of swear words. Roy would never have given up trying to find them, to get his precious money back. If he wasn't here, then where?

She bypassed the High Street and took the back way, thinking of Alfie and his dimpled grin to calm her mind. She'd called him first thing that morning, just before he left to catch the early train into town. Alfie had done well with his job as an assistant manager in a large electronics store on the Tottenham Court Road. A born salesman, his boss once said, all gab.

'How's the B&B, then? All frills and limp bacon, is it?' Alfie had shouted into the phone. She'd tried to get him to tone it down over the years, but had given up. It was what he did.

'The bathroom's avocado. Chintzy chic. Good luck with the meeting today. Have you got the grey suit on? Did you iron your shirt this morning?' Lizzy couldn't stop herself nagging. He had his first managers' meeting at head office and she wanted him to do well, to shine with the big boys. He'd finally earned some recognition, after all the hours he'd worked.

'Yeah, yeah. It'll be fine. I'll have them all wrapped around my little finger as soon as look at them. Don't worry about me. You be careful, though. I know what you're like. Don't think you're the next Miss Marple. See your family, take what crops up, and then get back down here with your old Alfie. I miss you, and you only just left.'

Had he guessed what she was up to?

'It feels weird, being here,' she said. 'But the air smells good. I miss you too. I'll talk to you tomorrow. Don't forget to check between your teeth.'

'Mind you don't trip on them shoe boxes. Look after the lump. See you, darlin'.'

He always ribbed her about having big feet. He felt so far away, a different world to this place. Already his London accent stuck out, now she was back in Scotland. She sounded just like him, though.

And then she was there. The Bryant Road sign was stuck on a low fence, with black graffiti scribbled on it. A woman with a pram came hurtling around the corner, almost banging the thing into her, its wheels covered with wet leaves. She had a cigarette hanging between her pursed lips. The baby was crying. Lizzy stepped into the gutter out of the way, but the woman didn't acknowledge her.

'You're welcome,' Lizzy said.

The woman sneered back, her face set hard. Lizzy felt a fleeting sensation of dread that she breathed away. Motherhood couldn't be that bad, could it?

She stepped back onto the wet pavement. Her old house was almost halfway down, on the right-hand side. Her best friend Molly had lived somewhere on the other side of the road. She used to cross over to pick her up on the way to school, in the early days, anyway, before she started bunking off. She half ran, her heart thumping—wanting to get there before she changed her mind. There were no people about, curtains still drawn. Some folk would be in their beds all day, unemployed, bored. Tired of it all.

There it was, number 20, a brick semi-detached with a rotting, lopsided fence. She stopped in front of it, catching her breath. It seemed tiny. The door was still green, although the paint was flaking to show the old brown colour underneath. The plants on the doorstep were gone, replaced with a sisal mat and an iron shoe scraper. The small garden up front was an overgrown mess, with a broken gnome on its side at the far end. It wouldn't take much love to tidy it up.

She should knock on the door. Have done with it.

Lizzy's back was sweating what with the rucksack on top of her jacket. Mum would hate to see this place all run down. Lizzy looked up at the bedroom windows and wondered if anyone was in. The curtains were closed, no lights on behind them.

The tears were coming. *Sod him.* She wouldn't let him get to her. She needed to prepare, to brace herself, so that when she saw his face she'd be the strongest she could be. She turned away and began the walk back. Another day.

She kept a look out for Molly's house, couldn't remember the number, but she'd know it when she saw it. Back then, a lot of time was spent there, if only to be away from *him.*

'Hey!' a man shouted behind her.

Leaves swirled on the ground by her feet. A mini tornado. Lizzy looked back and saw a heavy, balding man with his hands on the gate. *Oh shit; was it him?* She picked up her pace, shoulders hunched to hide her face. Her hair was blowing about and she cursed herself for not tying it up or wearing a hat. She was easy to recognize.

'Hey! Is that you?' he shouted again. The gate was whining open.

Bugger. She ran. Her legs were aching, the rucksack pulling, but she didn't stop running all the way back to the B&B. The sound of his footsteps had long gone when she arrived at Tilda's, but that voice. It was her dad, all right. She pressed her hands on the outside wall of the house and got her breath back.

Now she couldn't take him by surprise. What would he think about her coming back after so long? He might be angry, or pleased, wounded maybe. Either way, she'd give *him* a hard time. He was the one who had left in the first place, rejecting her.

He'd beaten her mum for years, over and over. That was enough to never forgive.

Perhaps he came back and killed her that night, just because she'd finally stood up to him.

She went inside. Tilda wasn't around, and she darted up the stairs to her room, thankful for the quiet. She lay on the bed, knees curled up, and watched the black clouds gathering. The bedspread was cold on her skin and she grabbed a cardigan from the chair and put it under her head, pulling one of the soft sleeves around her neck. The radiator was ticking, so hopefully the heating was coming on. Her belly was squished up, full, yet growling as if it were empty. This baby was sucking up everything she had, and it was only the size of a fig. Figs had always given her a bad stomach.

The police had questioned her dad at the time, but he'd had lots of alibis to say he hadn't left Yorkshire. He was a top suspect amongst every gossip in town, even though they'd proven nothing. She'd never thought him capable, before.

But there was someone else. That man Oliver had lived in Dalbegie too, in the white cottage opposite the newsagents, where her mum used to work. He was her last drop-off for Roy, before she ran away with Simon. He'd asked her inside and given her ten quid. His house had been stark, cold, and smelled of disinfectant. She might have forgotten all about their brief encounter, but a couple of years later she ran into him in a back alley in London.

He'd been following her, and watching her life unravel. He was the one who told her that Roy was dead, run over. He knew things about her. Maybe he knew something everyone else didn't.

The picture Maureen gave her was still in her rucksack. She pulled it out and set it face down on the dresser. Mum had behaved strangely in the weeks before she disappeared, giggling and soppy, taking long baths. Molly had reckoned she was in love.

Lizzy went to the window and looked down the street in the direction of the newsagents. She leaned her forehead against the glass, the condensation damp on her skin, and ran her fingers across it, making streaks in the mist. When she'd booked her train ticket, she'd fantasized about marching around the town, demanding answers, like a crusader seeking the truth. She'd be a real-life TV detective looking for clues, probing every corner of the place.

Now she was here, her energy was sapped, her sense of dread growing. She pulled back the duvet and climbed into her cocoon. She'd have to confront her dad, visit the old house, and dredge up the years when they were all together. If he got angry, she wouldn't be able to handle it. The anger should be hers, and there were a lot of things left unsaid. She glanced at the frame with her mum inside it. She'd find the strength and the words somehow, for her.

I'll get to him. And I'll give him a piece. I know what you'd like me to say, and I'll say it. I'll throw the words at his face. It won't bring you back, but I'll give it to him straight, full circle.

CHAPTER SIX

Oliver's Rainbow

I put up my collar and braved the bracing wind that had come from nowhere. Typically, the Edinburgh skies were clear one minute and tumultuous the next. The usual damp had been replaced momentarily by a cleaner, icier swirl from the north, and I lowered my face to stop it cutting into my cheeks. My new boots needed wearing in, the leather hard and squeaky, and I began the climb up Dundas Street rather gingerly. No matter. Soon I would be leaving the wet cobblestone city, to venture back to where the land was flat, rolling, and wild. Edinburgh was only half my life.

I rubbed my bare wrist. I kept my father's watch at the Dalbegie cottage. It would be waiting for me on the little round table next to my armchair, its strap threadbare from time and use. I always looked forward to the journey north, to that little town full of small minds, but this time my feelings were marred by a sense of failure, that I was sheepishly running away. The attention I'd received from the policeman on Rose Street threw me, even though it had come to nothing. I was a dirty man on the street found loitering with intent, no better than a common criminal. It was vulgar.

Was I losing my touch? Was I incapable of being brazen and spontaneous without being crass? I needed to make amends to myself, and be more productive.

I passed the antique shop halfway up the street and found myself glaring at the owner, who was standing at the window. He waved, then watched while I passed. I buried my hands in my pockets and pretended not to notice, although I could sense his burning stare, and I felt exposed. Was he curious about me for some reason?

Some youths bounced past me and I envied their energy as they laughed and shoved their way up the hill. My knees had begun to ache as they often did, ever since I'd entered the wrong half of my fifties. With each year that passed, my body would slowly crumble.

I crossed George Street, then made my way to Princes Street. It had become a sea of windows plastered with crass sale and discount signs, every store desperate for customers. It used to be a pleasant walk, with the castle as a backdrop, the occasional bagpipers making their melancholy wails. Now it was marred by cheap and tacky wares, by delinquents wearing back-to-front sports caps and tracksuits. I hurried along to Leith Walk, where I had arranged to meet up with one of my acquaintances, a long-standing member of my circle. She had followed me for years, a faithful yet wily feline, stretching out her claws once in a while to keep me on my toes. She would unwittingly help to rectify my sense of worthlessness that day.

I made my way up the long stretch of road towards the Cat Rescue, where we'd once worked together, rather fresh faced, at the beginning of our turbulent partnership. Much had happened since then, but I knew I could still rely on her for kicks. I could do spur-of-the-moment with her; I could be barefaced. And whenever we'd done anything together, we'd never been caught. I needed a boost, and this time I would let her push me. Whatever she wanted to do, I'd go with it, whether I liked the sound of it or not.

After miles of circumnavigating boarded-up storefronts, staggering daytime drunks and middle-aged shoppers, I sat on the crumbling stones that made some semblance of a wall outside the centre. The whole place was in disarray, the front of the original building a mess of cracks and ivy, stained brick, and seagull droppings. I studied the front garden, long grass ridden with moss and dirt patches. I cleaned my nails with my Swiss Army classic, trying to take my mind off the mess until Helen appeared, her squat figure emerging before me like Mr. Benn popping out of his changing room, dressed as an old Greek maid.

'Oliver,' she stated. She was a woman of few words. Not a bad thing.

'Helen. Shall we perform a joint 'operation' this afternoon? I thought we could see what reprobates we can find, high on life, and short on brains.' I stood almost two heads taller than her. But I was only half as wide.

She scratched her plump thigh, her nails audibly snagging the cheap material of her snug trousers. 'It's been a while. Let's do Arthur's Seat.'

We walked to the bus stop in silence, occasionally stealing glances at each other. Yes, I knew she was looking at me just as much as I was at her. We were wary, you see, and that kept things interesting. Years after our community service stint, she tried to steal from me. I almost admired her for it. Helen had been part of my face-to-flesh ventures at The Audacious in London. It was a set up in which twelve members would come in the dead of night to my hidden vault in Soho and watch while one of life's victims got hurt. Helen was one of only two women that attended, enjoying things that most women would find abhorrent. But then came that unexpected blip in our relationship, the thieving, and it affected my trust for her, if not my regard.

She had tried to steal my girl. But that was in the past. Thirteen years ago, to be precise, not that I was counting.

'I'm going away again, until the spring,' I told her as we boarded the bus that would take us most of the way to Arthur's Seat. 'It's time for my hibernation.'

She had put up her hood to protect her thatched head from a smattering of misty rain, and she pulled it back down as we found two seats together. Her hairy mole was visible, taunting me with its black, repugnant presence. I averted my eyes, thankful we were on the move, and that I could face forwards.

'Back to the Highlands like usual?' She was gazing out the window, looking uninterested. I knew that look.

'My second home,' I said. 'It's time for me to hunker down. I need the respite. Do you ever feel the urge to go someplace else?'

'Not really,' she said.

She never moved around if she didn't have to. Or should I say she never moved far from me. Helen was a parasite, feeding off my ventures. Even when we lived in London, she had sucked my blood hard, taking advantage of my passions, my desires. I'd been watching my long-standing, favourite subject for some time. My Lizzy in the big city. Over time I shifted back and forth between my twin roles as predator and protector; I wanted her as prey and yet made sure she was safe from all the lowlife in Soho and beyond. Eventually, and some might say surprisingly, Helen decided she wanted her too, no doubt for some one-upmanship reason of her own.

But she wasn't quick or clever enough to take the prize.

At first I wanted to rid the world of Helen's dumpy little soul, for daring to attempt to take what was mine. But then I realised that she was simply trying to impress; that to her, an abduction initially desired by me would win my acclaim. I, the duped, would present her a figurative trophy in recognition of her cunning.

She was half-right. I didn't reward her efforts, but I didn't strangle her to death either. Just halfway.

When we arrived at Holyrood Park, we alighted the bus quickly, a buzz of anticipation between us. We fell into step, stealthy on the wet ground. Helen pushed ahead, and I followed her towards the lesser-used trail, favoured by more ambitious hikers seeking a better view. She liked to take the lead once in a while, her small way of showing me that she could be in charge; that I could follow for once. I let her do it, enjoying her strength, knowing that in any case I would retain the upper hand. She couldn't beat me, and she knew it.

When she followed Lizzy that day, I was following her.

When she put the needle into Lizzy's neck, I was watching, and when she pulled her into the gap between the terraced houses of south London, I was waiting.

I pounced on her, wrapped a piece of short rope around her thick neck. She floundered, her sticky hand groping in her coat pocket for another needle, but I was too powerful for her, too aware of what she was capable. Her face reddened and her legs stopped kicking. I could have squeezed the last breath from her so easily, but in the end I didn't.

Instead I released her, and whispered into her greasy ear, 'You can't take what's mine. Do you understand?'

She gasped and clutched at her throat. Then she nodded her respect and disappeared, clumsy shoes scuffing on the pavement. Her devious plan hadn't worked, and I was left to deal with a half-doped Lizzy for my own means. Not that I was going to take advantage of her, and use someone else's botched-up plans. Helen had made an error, that was all, and I had forgiven it because Lizzy had fallen into my hands once more. Fate would see to it that she would always end up with me.

Now, I regarded Helen's dirty boots, her sumo-wrestler build, as she climbed up the grassy hill in front, wheezing a little now with the effort. The sounds of cars on wet tarmac and the chatter of children near the car park grew distant. We were entering another world together, our needs merging.

I paused. 'Isn't this a tad exposed?'

She shrugged. 'No one'll be around if they've any sense.'

The tall grasses swished, wind rattling across the hillside like some god was shaking a sheet of corrugated iron. This was our alliance at its best.

She paused just over the first hump, the pungent aroma of Edinburgh hops enveloping us. Then she clicked her fingers. Already she'd seen someone worthy of our attention: a lone, sinewy hiker in the distance, making his way up the peak to the outlook. There weren't many hours left of daylight, and a smattering of walkers and tourists were already heading back down the hill. A dog barked and ran like a bullet to the bottom. She was right; everyone was going home. I pulled at my collar and felt for my knife. We'd have our last hours of fun before I left the city behind. We surged towards pleasure, a force field pulling us in tandem.

ঔ঵ঔ ঔ঵ঔ ঔ঵ঔ

The view over the city was wondrous when the sun began to plummet. A cluster of distant clouds had decided to part, just so, and there was an orange glow on Edinburgh Castle, majestic and alive. I felt like a soldier coming home from war, setting eyes on home after many years away. Walkers had long gone down the hill, back to fireplaces, the smell of roasting meat, or a pub crowd perhaps. What was it that other people did? Perhaps I romanticized other people's lives when I was feeling settled, loosened.

Helen stood a few metres in front of me, a triangle in silhouette against the sky. She was wheezing, her shoulders moving up and down. In one hand she carried her hammer, the wooden handle pointing down, and in the other a bottle of water. When she got home she would need to scrub her implements as well as her own splattered self, crimson underneath the coat, which she had taken off while we had our fun together. For old time's sake. Or for auld lang syne, as they say.

Behind us, hidden amongst the yellow-green grasses and a significant cluster of errant rocks, was our hiker. I strangled him until unconsciousness took him. Then the evil little goblin got to him, playing with his fragility, breaking him. She always did have a fascination for bones. He woke, fainted, and woke again, shining eyes falling not on his torturer but on the sideline observer. Perhaps he thought he might be pitied by me. Or perhaps he was trying to figure out why I was watching. Then death took him, no doubt a relief, before he was folded up and thrown into the wild.

There's a Latin expression, *ad lucem*. It means *to the light*. A glow from the heavens plunged down, bathing the area where he lay. I swore I could see all the colours of the rainbow resting atop the grasses, glistening magic. His soul would rise above us, entering another universe, a better place perhaps. We were left on firm ground, overlooking the top of the city, at all the cobbles and tenement blocks. Two simple needs met. We were dual conductors of an orchestra; one made up not of musicians, but from a kaleidoscope of shards of glass and shades of darkness.

It was the first and last time we performed in perfect synchronicity.

I scurried away, craving the closeness of brick walls, alcoves, and crevices in which to hide. We had worked together, but we were different creatures. I turned to wave good bye, but Helen was lost in her own multihued world, her eyes closed and chest heaving. The hammer dropped from her hand into the undergrowth.

The sun dropped behind a tower and below the horizon. The shadows became one flat mass, and a chill gripped my limbs as all the colours faded. There was no gold at the end of a rainbow, but an empty place full of nothing. The elation had given way to anticlimax. There was nothing there for me now. It was time to go.

CHAPTER SEVEN

Helen Flips a Coin

Helen folded the *Edinburgh Evening News* in half and threw it by the front door for garbage. Some things never changed. The world was determined to subordinate women in every way possible, and as usual they assumed women were incapable of the evils of men. The front-page headline landed face up, taunting her:

Arthur's Seat Killer Strikes

'He' had thrown the unidentified body of the hiker, male, aged 34, into the scrub. 'He' had struck once before, a few months previously.

It hadn't bothered her before when she was assumed to be a man, but for some reason it was starting to get to her, the sexism and misinformation of the press. They were idiots. The police had already put out a warning not to hike alone, and they repeated the caution. Helen knew that no one would listen to this ridiculous advice. Most folk liked to walk alone, didn't they? The whole point of hiking was to get away from everything. And it was all the better for her.

Breakfast. She scratched at the back of her neck, itchy with grease. She promised herself she'd wash her hair later. It was a pain as there was no shower, just a bath, so she had to use a jug. She'd become old-fashioned like Mother. She put a couple of pieces of bread in the toaster and shuffled around in the cupboard for condiments. There was a spoonful of marmalade left, and some jam with a touch of mould on one side from where she'd stuck in a buttery knife. She'd scrape off the circles of green and it would taste fine. Her fingers got sticky from taking off the lid, months-old congealed jam around its edges. She wiped them on her T-shirt.

Women had it in them to be powerful aggressors. She was showing them all, but no one was paying attention.

Helen turned to the tiny window over the sink and drew a hammer in the grimy steam as she waited for the toaster to pop. Oliver knew her capabilities, but even he was smug in his ways, with his big words and his lofty presence. He'd followed her lead up Arthur's Seat, quite happy to watch while she took control. He liked to watch in the old days too. She had her own ventures now, outside of his ego. She had long been a valued member of his 'circle,' but she didn't need it, the comfort of a drawn line to sit inside. His line. Helen spent more time outside of Oliver's perimeter these days, forming her own shapes in the world.

She sketched on the window mist, adding clenched fingers at the bottom of the hammer. The glass squeaked in protest while she drew. Drips of condensation ran down from the outline and onto the sill. She wiped them up with a finger and sucked at it.

℞ ℞ ℞

Sue was hovering near the front door of the Centre. 'We're a couple of people short today.'

'Oh.' Helen stood in the hallway, unsure whether to push ahead and take off her coat.

Sue craned her neck as if there were someone behind Helen. 'Are you all right to do some extra cleaning, and skip some of the streets you were going to search this afternoon?'

'Yes, fine.'

'That's great, you're a doll.' Sue put her hand on Helen's shoulder and squeezed it gently. Then she ran it down her back. 'I can always rely on you, can't I?'

Helen baulked at the contact and backed away. 'Yes. Although I might take some time off soon.'

Sue smoothed down her hair, although it was cropped and grey, nothing much of it. 'I'll be sure to have staffed up by then, Helen. You haven't had a day off in months. You need a proper break, I know.'

Helen studied her coat buttons as she undid them, dangling on threads, some of them. She'd get as much of the work done as she could before ten, when the others came. Sue shouldn't have touched her like that, but she was a good boss so Helen would let it go. She wondered if Hugo's parents would have the decency to let Sue know that Hugo wasn't going to be at work. He wouldn't ever be back, but they didn't know it yet. She thought of a rhyme and repeated it inside her mind while she put her things in the cloakroom and set to work putting out the cat bowls.

Hugo, You-go, Blue-toe, Clue-no.

They might find Hugo, or they might not. If they did, they might think 'he' had done it. She smiled faintly.

Helen mucked out Hugo's cats first, so she wouldn't have to work alongside the other volunteers when they showed up. The first cage stank; two kittens with their mother, who didn't seem to be very good at licking up all their shit. *What mother was?* Her own had got rid of her as soon as she was born, couldn't cope with two babies. Just as well she was dead now, not obliged to make up for it by offering simpering apologies. They couldn't afford two, she'd said; it was Helen's dad that had insisted on giving one of them away. Mother had claimed she'd wanted to keep them both; she had thought about Helen every day since. *Blah, blah. Excuses.*

Helen put the cats in the lower part of the pen and scrubbed the upper walls, her rubber gloves up to her elbows. She scraped at the ceiling and the upper platform, brown-scum soap dripping onto her gloved hands. She'd been the unlucky one supposedly, the one they chose to give away. It wasn't her brother Steve's fault, blundering fool that he was, even though he was always apologizing. If they'd picked him to go, he might not have survived the care system; she was the strong one, even now. She was the lucky baby, in a way, for she'd grown up independent with an ingrained sense of survival. So far, Steve had spent his life drinking down the Porty with his pals while getting on the wrong side of the local drug dealers and living his life in fear of them. His answer to everything was to run away. Hers was to stand up to it.

One of the kittens was mewing, patting its paw on her leg. She regarded its furry ears, the tiny nose. She had been just as small, when she was handed over to the authorities. Only a few hours old.

The smell subsided, taken over by cleaning sprays, and Helen went to empty the bucket into the drain outside. Her back was aching. She could take a week off, maybe even two. There were plenty of things she could do with that time away from work. Replenish. Admittedly she had a tendency to lose the hours, to fester in bed and peruse the internet and eat Tunnock's Teacakes. But she could make sure she used the time productively, perhaps impress Oliver with her full potential. But how, exactly? She thought of Mother's old bed, soft and enveloping, and it spoke to her in a whisper. *Lie down, won't you? Don't bother yourself with it all.* But there was 'he' getting all the glory. Perhaps next time she'd paint her fingernails bright pink and leave traces of colour in the body's skin. That would throw the police, and make everyone think. She regarded her hands, cracked and stubby. She'd never worn nail polish in her life. Better to remain under the radar, an invisible middle-aged woman, innocuous and bland.

In the old mystery books, it was often the person you least expected that had committed the crime. It was funny how that basic premise had never been picked up on in real life. Shame on them. But why should she leave clues to be found? Let them wallow in their own ignorance.

⸱⸱⸱ ⸱⸱⸱ ⸱⸱⸱

She sat on a bench near the old Parish Church, overlooking Edinburgh Castle. Helen's fingers were numb, her face frozen. She'd been slumped forward, her neck stiff and sore. Why was she there? Why hadn't she put on her gloves and hat? It was Baltic, the wind whistling along King's Stables Road. She stood up and clapped her hands together, breathing mist, with a vague recollection of where she was going, and what she'd intended to do. The Meadows had a network of pathways across it. She was going to head down there, must have been side-tracked. She couldn't go now; she was immobilized from the cold.

She made her way back up towards Princes Street, facing away from the Castle and its towering grandeur. Her legs wouldn't move as fast as she wanted them to, and her feet scuffed on the ground every time she took a step. She'd go home, get a fish supper on the way. A man wearing a trilby hat touched his brim. Perhaps he thought she would appreciate it, his silly act of good manners. She scowled at the next person, and the next, lest they try to enforce their false respect on her. If they knew.

By the time she got back to the flat, her knees were killing her, although the fish supper from Bill's Plaice, wrapped in swaths of white paper, had warmed her hands during the last ten minutes of the walk. The smell of it grew more pungent as she entered the stair, salt and sauce, batter and grease filling the damp air. She tramped up, feeling for the key in her coat pocket, but didn't need it in the end, as the flat door was slightly ajar. Steve. He had his own key, and a habit of turning up when he felt like it. He used to live there, with 'Ma,' and although Helen had taken the place over after she died, Steve still felt like it was his too.

She pushed the front door with her foot. One glance told her he'd been asleep in the living room for some time, feet up on one arm of the sofa, his skinny legs too long for it, and a line of drool on one cheek. He was snoring. She grabbed a plate from the kitchen and sat on the armchair facing him, her coat still on. She slowly unwrapped the fish supper, careful not to make the paper crackle, and began to eat with her fingers, quickly, before he woke up.

She studied him. He was getting quite bald and scrawny. They didn't look even remotely related, let alone like twins. She leaned forward to get a closer look. Was that a cut on his knuckles? He'd been in a fight. Helen had got rid of his main enemy, years ago, but he continued to wind folk up. And she carried on cleaning up his mess, not that he appreciated it. Said she was 'weirdy.'

When the last chip was eaten, she crashed the plate down on the coffee table. The fake tulips shook, and Steve jerked awake. Their eyes met.

'Fuck me, Helen. How long have you been sat there?' He sat up, wiping the drool off his face with his sleeve.

'A few minutes.'

'I nearly shite myself, for fuck's sake.' He reached for the chip wrapper. 'That smells fucking brilliant. Any chips left?'

'No.'

'Aw, you bugger. You could've saved me some. There was nothing in the fridge either. Anyways, I only came over to see if you want to go to Ed's for a piss-up the night. Everyone's going.'

Helen shrugged.

'It wouldn't kill you to be sociable once in a while, Helen.' He stretched, showing his white paunch, and yawned. He shuffled over to the bay window and looked out. 'There's a big, bad world out there.'

She imagined pushing him so hard that his head would shatter the glass. Then another push and his rakish body would fly through it, arms flailing, severed arteries spraying blood. What sound would he make? A surprised squeal, maybe, or a long, terrified shout. Her brother would fall two storeys to the concrete below, and break his neck. *Mother decided your beginning. I can decide your end.*

'Helen?' Steve was standing close, now. 'Are you in there?'

She focused on his face, the black bags under his eyes, his teeth yellowing. He'd taken up smoking again. Another of his stupid habits.

He sighed. 'I'm away. I suppose I'll have to get some food before Ed's. Need to get to the offie too.' He waved his hand slowly in front of her. 'Are you all right?'

She nodded. He'd done nothing to hurt her, didn't have it in him. Steve was like an irritating yet familiar buzz in her ear, disconcerting if it stopped because she'd got used to it. She watched him go, shaking his head, tripping over his own feet. He'd searched for her, followed her trail when he finally learned he had a sister. He didn't exactly find the dream twin, but she was all he had.

'Steve?' she called out as he shut the front door.

He poked his head through. 'Aye?'

'How did you get the cut on your hand?'

He looked down at it. 'Oh, that. There was some trouble down the Porty last night. Jake was getting it from a couple of the new dockers, and so me and Ed, we stepped in.'

'Anything you want me to do?'

'Naw. Thanks, but I know what your help looks like and it isn't pretty. There's no' many I'd wish it on. See you, Helen.'

Too bad. The taste had returned and she was on a roll. But was another one too risky? The police would still be crawling after what happened at Arthur's Seat. There were always the back streets of Leith, the doorway prostitutes, those compliant women giving men what they wanted. Both parties deserved what they got, the obedient givers and the leaching takers. She could take a couple, stuck together like mating frogs, and slice them apart.

Or she could go to Ed's party.

She took a coin from her pocket and ran its edge along the middle of the coffee table. It made a shallow scratch in the faded wood, separating it into two halves. She placed the vase of fake flowers in the centre, so the line ran underneath it, and arranged the flowers so there were equal numbers drooping down on either side. Then she ran the coin up her arm, onto her chest, and up her neck and face, dividing her face in half, the cool metal on her nose, in between her eyes, and onto her forehead. Steve was right, there was a big, bad world out there. She was living in a tiny segment of it.

She threw the coin onto the floor. Oliver's love of probability had rubbed off on her. He loved to play games of chance, and it made life more interesting, she'd give him that.

Heads, Leith prostitutes.

Tails, Ed's party.

The coin rolled across the rug and onto the wood floor, then spun around three times before it finally dropped. Tails.

CHAPTER EIGHT

Lizzy Opens the Gate

Lizzy splashed her puffy eyes with cold water. Hazy memories were growing and spreading. She tried to push them away, but scenes from the past reared up. Her dad's raised hand was one of them. She hadn't even met him yet. She squeezed her eyes closed until orange circles came.

She hadn't felt too nauseated that morning, the fresher Highland air and the chill helping. She was almost at the twelve-week milestone, and so hopefully the morning sickness was on its way out. It had been the longest three months ever. It might have been more sensible to make the trip to Scotland a bit later, but as soon as she got pregnant, the desire to go back to her roots was intense. She couldn't let the not-quite baby get in the way of things.

'Hormones,' Alfie had said, like they were the answer to everything she did or said from then on.

She checked her phone, but there were no new messages. Alfie had texted her at bedtime. His meeting hadn't gone well. He had to go into work early that morning, and would call her later. She put it all down to his lack of ego. Alfie sounded full of it, most of the time, but she knew that underneath he fretted about work, and never thought meetings went well. Some suited ponce had probably made a comment that had made him feel inadequate. She'd give him a pep talk later, and he'd be fine. She'd much rather he was how he was, than one of those over-confident, brash twats, all public-school mouth and no substance. She hoped he'd worn his good suit, the slim one with the fitted trousers. It made him look stylish without trying.

She ran her fingers through her hair, feeling out the knots. There used to be a café near the High Street, an old-fashioned one with big bay windows and lacy curtains. Her mum had loved it, but when she was younger Lizzy had thought it was boring and stuffy. If it was still there, she'd have tea and figure out what do to about her dad. The easy option would be to avoid him, but she needed to sit and think about it.

He might know things.

As Lizzy made her way down, the creaking stairs announcing her to the world, Tilda poked her head around the doorframe of the dining room.

'Morning, dear. I've some fresh plain bread that'll go nice with scrambled eggs.'

Lizzy's eyes watered and her stomach heaved.

'Oh, I should have mentioned. I'm going out early this morning, so I'll skip the breakfast, but thanks anyway, Tilda.'

'No problem, doll. Saves me the bother.' She sidled into the hallway and lowered her voice. 'I was talking to some folk in the post office yesterday. I wasn't gossiping about you, nothing like that, you understand. I was asking who had known your mum and dad, was all.'

Lizzy stopped at the foot of the stairs and nodded. She knew this would happen, everyone knowing her business within a couple of days.

'Don't worry about it. What were they saying?'

Tilda's apron had an egg stain in the middle, her stomach sticking out so far that a yellow globule was threatening to drop from its ledge. She clenched her hands together, deep frown marks between her eyebrows.

'One of them, Judith, she nearly died when I said you were here. Oh, she filled up. She said you were best friends with her daughter Molly.

And what was the other thing I was to mind?' She put a finger to her lips. 'That was it. She said you're to pop by. She's still at number 11.'

'Thanks, maybe I will.' Lizzy started to edge towards the front door. Number 11, that was it.

Tilda called after her, 'Your old friend Molly lives not too far from here. And you know where she works, don't you? The newsagents.'

Lizzy pulled at the door, buttoning up her coat as she went, the morning air biting into her. She'd worn the old black cashmere scarf that Alfie gave her on their first Christmas together. He ribbed her about wearing black all the time, but it was a part of her. She wrapped it three times around her neck, grateful for its softness. She needed a cup of tea. Things were starting to feel too close. Molly at the newsagents? Life had moved on while she'd been gone, but in a straight up, linear kind of way. People had grown just where they were planted, slotted into place, handcuffed to their lives. They grew up towards the light to find their way, rather than spreading out their branches. She was grateful for it, because it meant she didn't regret leaving and making her own life in London. It hadn't been easy, but at least it wasn't the same old place with the same old people. *Stifling*.

༖ ༖ ༖

'Good bloody god, it's like a ghost just came in.' The woman taking the orders in Stone's Café put her floury hands to her face. She was a head taller than Lizzy, strong and solid looking.

Lizzy put her book on one of the tables and threw her bag on the floor. The smell of fresh baking was overwhelming: cinnamon mixed with dough and sweetness, but for some reason it didn't make her want to throw up.

'I know this place, and you, but I can't think of your name. I'm really sorry.'

'It's Maggie. Don't tell me you're Lauren's girl. And that book you've got. She used to read those lovey-dovey kinds of stories. A daydreamer, she was. It's Lizzy, isn't it?'

'Yes. You've got a good memory.' Lizzy gazed at her book. 'I didn't know about the stories mum used to read.'

Maggie scowled at an old woman, who was clearing her throat to get her attention.

'I'll be there in a minute, Flo. Keep your knickers on.' Then she turned back to Lizzy and grinned. 'She used to come in here to get away from that numpty Jessica in the shop. Take her break in peace. She'd have her nose in one of those books the whole time. Escape stories, she used to call them.'

She flipped open her note pad. 'What can I get you? It's on me today. I still miss your mum after all these years. Some lovely chats we used to have.'

'Thank you. That's the first time anyone's said that about mum. Usually it's all 'where did she go' and 'I think she ran off with the vicar.' I'd love a pot of tea and a scone or a pastry, anything stodgy.' Lizzy touched her fingertips to the cover of her book. Mum could have sat at this table, on this chair. She felt more like her as she grew older, as if she was becoming an old friend, with the same tastes. Mums who were alive grew older at the same rate, got further away, but hers would stay the same forever. One day they'd be the same age.

'I'll be right back. Have you visited your old house, Lizzy?' Maggie paused, a few paces away.

'No, I haven't. But I know *he's* there now.'

'That'll be tough for you.' Maggie swished past the other tables, three people waiting, holding up their hands and looking up expectantly. 'Hold your bloody horses, you lot, I'm seeing to an old friend,' she shouted.

Lizzy sat back, looking out into the street. The building opposite was boarded up, planks of wood over a cracked window. She saw a tiny bird flying out of one of the holes in the siding. At least someone was making use of the space. Next to it was a charity shop, an array of brassy ornaments and an old record player in the window.

Maggie came over with her tea, placing the pot carefully in front of her. 'I picked a big fruit scone, as they're still warm just now. They're looking bloody lovely, if I say so myself. My, but you're looking troubled, there. A penny for your thoughts.'

Lizzy smiled her thanks.

'Do you know Oliver? He lived opposite the shop when Mum worked there. They were friends, kind of.'

Maggie tapped her pencil against her teeth, 'Yes, he's been around for years, on and off. A bit of an oddball if you ask me. Keeps to himself. Haven't seen him in a while, though.'

'He's been away?'

'Aye, and I can't say I've missed him. He comes and goes, that one. I used to think he was good looking, but now he looks like something the cat dragged in. I didn't know he was a friend of your mum's.'

'Apparently.'

'Where did you get to all these years, if you don't mind me asking? One day you were there, all black eyeliner and boyfriend, and the next you were gone. Did that boy make you run away, doll? You don't have to tell me if you don't want to.'

'We ran away together. It wasn't his fault.'

'And now you're back.'

'For a visit, is all.'

Maggie disappeared off to the kitchen and Lizzy broke the scone apart. *There you go, not-quite baby. You can stop your growling now.* The scone was soft and warm inside. She poured some tea into her mug, enjoying the steam on her face. *No wonder you liked it in here, Mum.* She took out the picture frame, stuffed in the bottom of her bag, and placed it face down on the table. She unwrapped it, corner by corner.

Then she turned it over.

She lurched forward. Her face. It was exactly as she remembered, younger though.

She was smiling, the lines at the corners of her eyes showing. Straight hair framed her face, her cheekbones pronounced. She had her arm around Granny Mac's shoulders, who was laughing at something off-camera. They were both wearing heavy coats and scarves, like they were about to go out somewhere. Lizzy wondered who had taken the photo.

She wiped her tears away with a napkin, and sipped her tea. A hand was clenching her insides, squeezing, but no release. The crushing feeling might always be there, fading in and out, her past unreachable.

Miss you.

Outside, some sparrows were pecking at the pavement. Maggie had thrown some stale bread out front. Tiny beaks were scrabbling for scraps, just like her and Simon when they got to London. They had probably been more vulnerable. At least birds could fly away when danger came.

When Lizzy got up to leave, Maggie came over. 'Thanks for popping by. It's lovely to see an old face.'

'Thank you. I'll be back. You won't get rid of me now, after that scone.'

'I hope you find what you're looking for.' Maggie wiped her hands on her apron, then pulled at her bra strap.

How did she know she was looking? Lizzy paused. 'Do you know anything about what happened to Mum?'

Maggie gazed out the window. 'Now. There was a lot of talk. Like you said, everyone had a theory, a suspicion. But no one really knew, right? Mind you only pay attention to the facts, and don't listen to all the shite-ing gossips. I expect you already know that. And it goes without saying that you'll want to know what your dad has to say for himself.'

'I do. I'll see what I can find out.'

'Good for you,' said Maggie. 'Give him hell.'

◦◦ ◦◦ ◦◦

It was a short walk to the newsagents, around the corner and towards the mini island, full of weeds. Had it always been so neglected? The shop itself looked like it had been recently painted, a shiny sign across the door with blue capital letters. A vague image came of the old sign, in hand-painted script. Mc-something or other. Funny, but kind of sad, that Molly worked there now. When Lizzy began to bunk off school and spend more time down at the river with Simon, she and Molly had drifted apart. Then she'd left her behind without saying goodbye.

She hadn't said goodbye to anyone.

Across the road, behind the blackened railings, was Oliver's cottage. The paint was peeling, the place had an abandoned feel, and Lizzy shivered at the sight of it. The house was empty, no car in the drive, but she could feel him, his presence, radiating out. It had been years since she'd seen him in London, his dark eyes, the congealed blood on the side of his face. The white cottage felt like danger; she couldn't put her finger on it, but the feeling burrowed its way inside her.

She shrugged her shoulders a few times to compose herself, then opened the shop door. A bell tinkled. There were two women behind the counter, one of them older, with scraggly bleached hair, the other about her age, perhaps. They were bending over some stacks of newspapers, arguing over who was going to put them out.

'It's your turn. I did it yesterday, and the day before that.'

'I've just had my nails done. Don't make me ruin them.'

'Okay, but you owe me two days now, Jessica.'

Jessica. Lizzy paused at the door. Things were feeling stranger still. *Christ, she still works here. How can anyone breathe in this town?*

The two women had become aware of her staring, and they stopped talking. Lizzy couldn't move. The other woman must be Molly. Her eyes were hidden by a long limp fringe, her arms plump at the elbows.

'Hi. It's me, Lizzy.' She took a couple of steps inside.

Jessica made her way around the counter.

'Bloody hell. It's really you, isn't it? I'd know that hair of yours anywhere. Oh my dear god, Lizzy, where have you been? We all thought you were gone forever, so we did, didn't we Molly? You sound so different, though. You've an English accent, have you?'

Up close, Lizzy could see Jessica's fake tan marks. She always was the sunbed queen. The crêpe-paper chest that she had in her twenties had deeper crevices now, and her signature red lipstick bled into the lines on her top lip.

Molly stayed where she was, biting her thumb.

Lizzy shuffled closer. 'I was in a state when I left. You sold me some fags, Jessica, then you gave me a hug and a tissue. I needed that, I can tell you. I've never forgotten.'

Jessica scratched behind her ear, then inspected her fingernails. 'Your nose was bleeding. We were all feared for you when we realised you'd taken off with Simon and that Roy.'

Molly wiped whatever it was on the counter onto the floor, her frown deepening. She looked older than Lizzy, harder around the edges.

Lizzy spun the greeting card display—roses, poems in gold writing, photos of animals wearing silly hats, all whirling around. 'Everything had got really shit, right Molly?'

Molly shrugged. 'You never told me anything. I wouldn't have known what was going off.'

Lizzy cringed. 'We were all just kids then.'

Molly looked like she was close to tears. She didn't answer, looking up at the ceiling.

'I'm ever so sorry, all right? I was having a really hard time after mum disappeared. It'd be nice to catch up one day. I'm here for another week or so.'

'Aye, might as well. I've nothing better to do.'

'What about tomorrow?' Lizzy persisted. If anyone knew anything useful, it would be Molly. And she worked with Jessica, who was the biggest gobshite of them all. She smiled to herself at *gobshite*, which had just come to her. She used to say that all the time.

'All right', Molly said. 'I get off at two-thirty, then I get the kids from school. Come over at four-ish if you want.' She fiddled around with the till.

'Great. How many kids you got?'

'Three.' Molly sneaked a sideways glance at Jessica, who was smirking for some reason. 'I'll write the address down for you.'

Lizzy waited while she scribbled on a scrap of newspaper. She'd have a kid by the end of the year. One would be enough, let alone three.

'I miss your mum,' Jessica said. 'She never complained about anything, always bright and sunny.' She looked pointedly at Molly. 'Hardly missed a day's work.' She paused. 'Are you staying with your dad?'

Lizzy shook her head. 'No. I haven't seen him yet.'

'He hasn't changed much.'

'I was hoping he might have.'

'He's still . . . well. At least he's got Nicole, now.'

Lizzy couldn't listen to it. She grabbed the scrap of paper off Molly, still mute, and backed out of the shop. 'Nice to see you both. Got to go.'

Jessica called after her, 'Mind you come back later. We need a proper catch up.'

She made her way around the side of the building, where she wouldn't be seen. Sounded like Dad was still his charming self. Even Jessica was wary of him, and she wasn't exactly fussy. And who was Nicole? The name didn't ring a bell, but why would it? She'd never been a part of his life.

She leaned on the wall and regarded the cottage opposite. Piles of fallen leaves were lying on the pathway and the grass. The letterbox was held slightly open, a thick envelope not quite all the way through.

A tremor hovered in the air between her and the cottage. It was pulling at her, daring her to cross the road. So he wasn't there. Now was her chance to look for anything suspicious, or to at least have a nose around the back. It was all covered up with trees and bushes, so if she was careful no one would see her. The neighbours were nowhere to be seen, the street still sleepy. She peered back through the window, and saw Jessica and Molly bent over the shelving, putting newspapers out. Jessica must have agreed to help, then. A bloody miracle, her mum would have said.

She darted across the road, pulled open the iron gate, and strode down the side of the cottage. There was another tall wooden gate to get through at the back, with a pull latch. She shut it behind her, fast. The wind dropped, her blood making a noise in her ears. She was in. She pressed against the back wall, and slid across to the edge of the window. An invisible pressure was crushing her chest, like she was on a spinning ride at the fair, flattened against the sides. For a moment, she couldn't move, the hairs on the back of her neck prickling. *Breathe.*

CHAPTER NINE

Yellow Twine

I want to dart down and take you under my wing, fly us both away. But you're a strong woman now, Lizzy, not to be told even if I could. All I can do is watch while you're drawn to danger like it's a giant magnet. I'm not sure what you're looking for, wandering about his garden. All that greenery makes a wall between that place and the rest of the world. It's better that way, if you ask me. Keeps him separate.

And I can't believe you went to Stone's Café. Dear old Maggie, what a gem she is. Fancy that, giving you a free tea and a scone, just because you were my wee girl, and she knew who you were straight off. She's looking just the same as ever, still strong as an ox, with a mouth like a sailor. You were sat in that window. It was like looking at myself.

I used to talk to Maggie about all sorts. She was one of the few that I confided in about your dad. She hated him because of it. Granny Mac used to love Maggie, so she did, because she spoke her mind and didn't take any crap from her customers, or anyone else for that matter. A better woman than I used to be. When you pulled out the photo of me with Granny Mac, it brought home to me that the three of us will never be together. I hope it didn't make you feel too sad. You've so much ahead of you, with a new generation to come, and then another after that one day. The wean will make up for the broken bit of our family. It's about you now, making a new chain.

I would gaze out that café window and would see *him* walking past.

It happened a couple of times, the coincidence of him, looking over just in time for our eyes to meet. Except it was no accident, was it? It was calculated. He knew what he was doing and I fell for him. If I'd known what he was, I would never have given him the time of day. If I could have one wish, it would be that I'd kept my nose in my book and stayed in the land of knights and castles. It's better to be happy in your imagination.

Lizzy, I've had a terrible realization about how I went, after seeing the girls sorting out the newspapers in the shop. It dawned on me how much of a psycho that man was, and still is, no doubt. First of all, it was a shock, to see Jessica working there, lugging those papers around, still going on about her nails. Nothing changes, same old, her face covered in muck. She was always nice to you, mind, as she was today, and so I'll forgive her for being a skiver. And she said she missed me, the big softy. As for Molly, well, what a sight. With that puffy face and the bloodshot eyes, I'll be surprised if she isn't an alcoholic. I know one when I see one, poor soul. Who knows what she's been through to get like that. No doubt you'll find out soon enough.

But that isn't it. What bothered me were the newspapers themselves, the stacks they were arguing over. They were tied up with that yellow rope, thin and waxy. My hands used to get really sore from trying to pull it off. I found a way to cut it with big scissors by pulling at it using the blunt end, but it was still a bugger. That was the rope he used on me. It was the same one, I'm sure of it, cutting into my wrists. All those days and nights, waiting, fading until I floated away. I'm one of the lost folk, the ones that disappear and are never found. I was never a good story for the police or for the news. There were no clues left behind, and no witnesses. I just evaporated, and that's not interesting, is it? Stories only get told when a body is found, or scraps of clothing and clumps of hair. It would have been just withered flesh in my case.

He used to come into the shop every day for his paper. He'd be all flirty, with his good manners and his dark, brooding eyes. All of that was just a front. He used to ignore Jessica, and it drove her mad and tickled me pink. She was always asking if he'd like to go to the pub with her, and he never did, said he was busy. When he singled me out, asked me to dinner, I was so flattered. What an idiot I was. I hate myself for falling into his trap. And he was sick enough to use the twine that we had at work.

I didn't stand a chance. You won't either, if he comes back and catches you in his back garden. Get out of there while you still can. I hope you never find out what happened. You'd never get it out of your mind. 'Some things are best left.' You know who used to say that, don't you? Our Granny Mac, god rest her soul. She came out with the funniest things, and the longer I've been around, the more I've realised how true they were.

I'll never be found, Lizzy, wherever you look. I'm dissolved into the dirt now, mashed and swirled in with all the worms. What was the other thing Granny Mac used to say? 'Keep the heid.' Stay calm, Lizzy, and don't do anything rash. Take it from me. You don't want to know.

CHAPTER TEN

Helen's Party Trick

The party was kicking off when Helen arrived just after eleven, sober and alert—unlike everyone else there. It was a garden flat, with its own front door. Ed himself let her in, a can of beer in one hand, whisky in the other. The top of his head was shiny, like a hard-boiled egg without the shell on. He shouted a welcome that she couldn't quite make out, and motioned to the kitchen before he disappeared down the hallway, slopping his drink onto the carpet.

She went through, surveying the stacks of cans and half-drunk bottles of spirits and wine on the countertops. A young couple were snogging in the corner of the room, and she puttered around while they pawed at each other. There was a puddle on the floor by the fridge, and she stepped over it to get to the counter. She pulled out a six-pack from her bag and set it down, ripping a can from the plastic holder and opening the ring-pull in one fluid motion. She drank half of it before moving into the living room.

'Hey there,' Steve waved briefly. He was hovering over Jessie, showing off to her as usual. They were an item now, it seemed. She put up with his drinking and stupidity and he put up with her voice and bad skin.

Helen held up her free hand to him, then sat on a chair by the stereo, vibrating with the cranked-up bass, volume bars at maximum. Jessie wanted to move in with Steve, but he was resisting, said he liked his freedom. It was the only sensible thing he'd said in months. He was gesticulating and she was giggling, both of them drunk as skunks.

It was a good thing mind, that he was distracted.

A few folk were dancing around the coffee table, singing. Ed was one of them, a sweat stain on the back of his shirt. Helen didn't recognize the track, but that didn't mean much. She didn't have time for music.

No one except Steve had noticed her coming in the room, and even now she was invisible as usual, the one on the outside. She watched two girls laughing hysterically on the sofa, shoes kicked off, stocking feet waving up and down. Some guy was staggering over to them, absolutely blootered, a can of lager in each hand. He asked to sit between them. Did they want a drink? They both smirked and shook their heads, but he lunged in regardless, and his lager slopped on them.

'Come on girls, let me in,' he slurred. 'I'm a nice guy, really fuckin' nice.'

'Get lost, will you.' One of the girls wiped at a spill on her top.

'Aye, get te fuck.' The other one shot him a dirty look, then turned back to her friend.

'Fuckin' lesbians.' He turned away and stumbled towards the kitchen, tripping over his own feet and flying head first into the hall-way.

The two girls cracked up again. Helen got up and followed him. This hadn't taken long, then.

She felt in her pocket for the coin, and the syringe too, waiting in its plastic case. She looked back to see if anyone was watching. Steve was whispering into Jessie's ear. Ed and his cronies were only interested in each other. She tossed the coin, caught it with one hand and slammed it on the back of her other. *Heads, she stayed for a bit. Tails, she took the drunk out.* The drunk guy picked himself up and scrabbled around for his cans, lager fizzing.

It was tails.

She stood over him, her shoes but a few inches away from his fingers. 'Want some help?'

He looked up, eyes bloodshot, the front of his hair plastered to his forehead. A hopeful look quickly turned into one of disappointment.

'Naw. No offense, darlin'.'

She patted her coat pocket. 'I've got some gear. Want to go outside for a bit, share a toke?'

'Aye, I will, if you can spare.' He cheered up, crushed one of the cans and chucked it in the direction of the kitchen. 'Let's go.'

Helen darted into the kitchen and grabbed two of her lagers. She put them in her pocket, then cracked another and took it with her. Shame to waste them. She looked back. The snogging couple hadn't come up for breath. Didn't they get bored of it? There was a bowl of dodgy looking punch on the table next to them. Perhaps it would dampen the passion. She pushed the bowl so a wave of liquid tipped onto their laps, chopped lemon and shards of ice making a pleasing slushing sound. Then she made a quick exit, to squeals and angry growls, half drowned out by Ed's thumping music.

The drunk fool was waiting on the doorstep for her, singing softly and rocking on his heels. It was getting closer to midnight, a damp chill making dew as night was passing through to the early hours. Helen shut the front door softly behind her and moved closer, one hand in her pocket.

'Let's go for a walk, eh?' She nudged his arm.

His eyes were fixed on her pocket. He wasn't interested, just waiting for his free fix.

'We won't go far,' she said.

✂ ✂ ✂

Steve hadn't shaved. The remnants of what looked like a bacon roll with ketchup were stuck to the stubble on his chin. He'd let himself into the flat without knocking, as usual, and now he stood before Helen with a wild look about him. His clothes were crumpled, like he'd slept in them. She wondered if he'd passed out at Jessie's, then come straight 'round. There was a fusty smell about him.

'What happened to you last night?' He scratched his arse and snorted a thick and congealed clot back into his throat.

Helen was still in her pyjamas, feet up on the stool, chat show telly on. She wished he'd go away. Maybe she'd change the locks. That would throw him.

'Hello? Earth calling Helen. You didn't do one of your fuckin' freak-show numbers on pished-Eddie, did you? You left about the same time as him and he never showed up at home. His wife called Jessie the morn', in a right state.' Steve plunked himself down on the sofa and put his dirty boots on the arm.

'He has a wife?'

There was a woman on the telly with such big hair that it moved about in one single mass when she spoke.

'He's no' that bad. Harmless. Always pished, but never hurt a fly, not really. I was surprised to see you at Ed's, if I'm honest, but you didn't stay long. Something caught your eye, did it?'

'Got bored.'

He picked his teeth with his forefinger and examined his nail after. 'And what happened with the vodka punch? Sue and Minto said you threw it over them. Is that true? What the fuck?'

She sighed. Might as well admit to that one. 'They needed cooling off. Couldn't help myself.'

'Fuck's sake, Helen. I don't know what to do with you. So you're sure you don't know what happened wi' pished-Eddie? You can tell me. Just so's I know. I wouldn't say nothing.'

'I'm sure.' Out the corner of her eye, she saw pished-Eddie's wallet on the floor next to the leg of the coffee table. She got up and stood on it. 'Did you want tea?'

'Naw. I'm away home, get an Irn Bru and then back to my bed. There's a million hammers inside my poor heid. I'll see you later.'

'Bye.' She waited until she could hear his footsteps echoing down the stair, then bent to pick up the wallet. She'd taken the cash, just needed to discard the rest of it where it wouldn't be found. It was stupid to have brought it back to the flat in the first place. Steve could have seen it. But who did he think he was? He'd got high and mighty all of a sudden, like he was some angel. He was the chosen one, mister beautiful baby, the golden boy with all the choices. She was the booby prize. She hadn't been given much choice about anything.

Helen put on her coat and pushed the wallet deep into the inside pocket. A glimmer of sunlight was breaking through the clouds, through the bay window, and onto the coffee table. It showed up the dust, a dead fly, and the crumbs from breakfast. Under the sunshine was this filth. There were demons hiding everywhere.

One of her fuckin' freak-show numbers, did he say? They needed time apart, or she'd end up sticking him with one of her needles. She'd talk to Sue at work, confirm those days off. It was time to get away from it all, find some excitement someplace else. They said a change was as good as a rest.

She locked the door behind her and slapped down the stair, a faint smell of cigarette smoke lingering from Steve's exit. It wasn't exactly rest that she was looking for. But a change of scene might ignite a new spark. What she needed was a fresh project, meat to chew on. Pished-up blokes with rickety legs weren't exactly a challenge.

She saw a bus pulling up on Leith Walk and she ran for it. Wherever it was going, she'd get on, right to the end. Helen needed unfamiliarity, a sense of isolation, and of course a place to get rid of the wallet that was burning in her coat pocket. She hauled herself onto the bus just before it pulled away, and made for one of the empty seats in the middle. Her usual spot. There she felt balanced, able to think. She started to draw in the window steam, then rubbed it away. Last night was released, insignificant now. No need to linger on all things yesterday.

CHAPTER ELEVEN

The Addict

Lizzy handed a bottle of wine to Maureen as she followed her through to the kitchen. A pungent smell of browned-off mince filled the house, and her eyes started to water. Maureen opened the fridge and tried to find a space for the bottle. 'I've made a big chili for us all. It's the boys' favourite. Would you like a tinny for now? We're all having a wee lager.' She cracked one open and handed it to Lizzy before she could answer.

Lizzy pretended to take a drink. 'Thanks.'

Maureen had made an effort with the dinner, had even set the kitchen table with paper napkins, folded in triangles underneath the cutlery. There were four places around the square table, with a fifth squeezed into one corner.

Maureen shooed her out. 'Come and see Kai and Noah. We're still waiting on Kane. Once he's showed himself, we can eat. And if he's not here by seven, we'll eat anyway. Never can tell with that one.'

The lads were watching football, their filthy white Adidas trainers on the coffee table, a couple of crushed beer cans on the floor. Maureen cleared her throat, but they didn't look up, both wincing at a bad pass. She grabbed the remote and switched off the telly.

'What you doing, Ma?'

'Aw, Ma, we were watching that.'

Maureen scowled. 'Hold your wheesht. I told you Lizzy was coming, did I not? This is your long-lost cousin, and the least you can do is keep your eyes off the fitba for a bit and talk to her.' She put her hand on Lizzy's shoulder. 'Lizzy used to look after you, you know, when you were wee. Now. This here is Kai. The twins are twenty now, but you'll mind their wee pudgy legs, so sweet they used to be. And this one is Noah, the baby of the family, just turned eighteen. You probably changed his nappy hundreds of times.'

'Ma, for god's sake,' Noah said. He had long, dark eyelashes: the pretty one.

Lizzy grinned. They were swigging their lagers, their eyes on her. She could picture Kai and Kane as toddlers. Kai still had dimples in his cheeks. The twins had been all wispy blond hair sticking up at all angles. Kai's was thinning already.

She sat down on a sagging armchair as Maureen went back to the kitchen.

'You probably don't remember me at all.'

They both shook their heads. Kai tapped his ring finger on the side of his can. 'Ma said you ran away when you were thirteen.'

She shrugged. 'Not much choice, really. It was either that or get killed by a mental drug dealer.'

Kai and Noah glanced at each other.

'You were awful young.' Noah was wide-eyed.

She was about to tell them a story about Roy, when the door burst open and in stumbled a more disheveled, leather-clad version of Kai.

'What's the skinny?' Kane held onto the back of a chair while he focussed on them all. He came with a strong smell of cigarettes mixed with cheap deodorant and weed.

Maureen shouted, 'Is that you, Kane? Get in here, will you. I need to talk to you. Where've you been, anyway? No' the pub I hope.'

'Fuck.' Kane rubbed his forehead. 'In a minute, eh, Ma?' He leaned forward and took a good look at Lizzy. 'Christ, you're not bad looking for thirty, are you?'

'Fuck's sake, Kane, she's your cousin.' Kai rolled his eyes at Lizzy. 'Sorry about my brother. He's an arse.'

Lizzy shrugged. 'Bit of a cliché, isn't it. The bad twin.'

Kai scowled. 'Aye, the numpty twin.'

'Don't get your breeks in a twist, there Kai.' Kane blundered through to the kitchen, wiping sweat from his face with his coat sleeve. 'Sorry I'm late, Ma. I had to see a guy about a dog.'

'Cheeky bisem,' Maureen tutted.

Lizzy listened to the pair of them bickering, Kane winding up Maureen until she sent him away. He went off to the toilet, and she could hear the tap splashing. Perhaps he was trying to sober up.

'What is it you do for a living, Lizzy?' Noah crushed his can and put it on the floor with the other empties.

'I manage a shoe store. Not very glam, but I get cheap shoes, and I'm the boss so I can pretty much do what I want. Most of the time, anyway.' Lizzy tried to ignore the feral noises coming from the toilet down the hall.

'Aye, that's good. I'm trying to get into office work, but there's nothing much about just now,' he said.

Kai spluttered: 'Not much about unless you go down to Glasgow or Edinburgh, which you're too feeredy to do.'

'I am not. I'm looking closer to home first, that's all. I've an interview in Inverness, if you must know.'

'Aye, that's a long way. Need your passport to get there, do you?'

'Fuck off, Kai. It's more than you're doing.'

'Fuck off yourself.'

Lizzy was relieved when Maureen called them all into the kitchen for their dinner. She'd dished up the chili and rice, and put some taco shells in the middle of the table, balanced precariously in a tower.

Maureen fussed about. 'Lizzy, you sit there by Noah. I'll take the corner seat, and squeeze in between the two incredible hulks.'

They all sat down and immediately she felt Kane's leg pushing against hers. He put his elbows on the table, his wet face close. She could smell his sour breath and unwashed hair. His eyes were blood-shot and glazing over. He peered through his greasy fringe, his gaze running over her face and chest. As she tried to lean away, which was difficult at such a small table, he bent over his plate and began to shovel food into his mouth like he hadn't eaten for days.

'Slow down, Kane, you're no' a dog,' said Maureen.

He didn't stop, chewing loudly with his mouth open. Lizzy had seen a thousand men like him on the street. In her time as a runaway, she'd witnessed that kind of hunger, greed for what could come, for anything. His skin was pale and blemished, tiny spots around his mouth. Kane was an addict. And addicts took things, abused people, and hurt the ones who loved them most. She looked at the other faces around the table: Maureen's worry lines, Kai's dimples, Noah's eyelashes. She pushed her fork into the chili and moved it around, wondering how little she could get away with eating. Her appetite was gone.

Maureen talked about the weather, about old Mrs. Thomson down the road and her arthritis, and about how terrible shocking it was that only one of her sons had a proper job. Billy was doing well in Inver-ness, and had a nice girlfriend. Why couldn't they all be like him? Kai was glaring hard at the table. Kane looked up at the ceiling, his chair scraped back now he'd finished eating. Noah concentrated on his food, never looking up once. It was like having the radio on as back-ground noise. No one was really listening. Lizzy felt her phone vibrate in her pocket, and took a sneaky look down. It was a text from Alfie: 'Knackered, babes. Off to bed and wish you were in it. Call u in the morning. X'

Damn. She'd been looking forward to talking to him back in her room. As she slipped the phone back in her pocket, Kane leaned into her.

'That from one of your boyfriends?' He talked over Maureen's chatter. 'How many guys have you got stringing along? I bet you got hundreds, you dirty cow.'

Kai tapped him on the shoulder. 'Hey. Watch your mouth.'

Noah put down his fork in protest, but said nothing.

'Just having a bit of fun, that's all. Calm down,' Kane sniggered.

Maureen took a breath. 'It's not funny, Kane. Away and take the bin out, would you.'

Kane groaned. 'Come on.'

Lizzy pushed a pile of chili to one side of her plate during the distraction, hoping it would look like she'd eaten more. 'Don't worry about it. Heard it all before.'

'See? She can take it.' Kane leaned back, hands on his head, legs spread out. 'She fuckin' loves it.'

'Yeah, right. Dream on.' Lizzy winked at Maureen, not wanting any awkwardness. But her stomach felt like lead. She could hardly swallow.

Maureen flapped at Kane. 'Away. Now. You're embarrassing yourself.'

He grabbed the liner out of the bin and put it over his shoulder, water dripping from the bottom of it onto the floor. As he left the kitchen, he turned and, behind his mum's back, grabbed his crotch and stuck out his tongue at Lizzy. She opened her mouth and put her finger to it, giving him the universal 'I'm going to chunder' sign.

He left a heavy cloud behind him. All eyes were now on the table as a cold quiet fell. Lizzy felt a familiar unease crushing her insides. Little boy gone wrong. How easily it happened.

Lizzy left soon after dinner, to escape the mood. Kai and Noah were washing up, and Kane was slumped in front of the telly, sparks gone. Maureen seemed melancholy, quiet, and Lizzy felt bad for her. Noah offered to walk her back to the B&B, but Lizzy had insisted she was fine on her own. She wanted to take a detour, alone.

It was dark now, and she could see her breath in front of her face, the air cut with flakes of ice. She pulled up her hood and wrapped her scarf close, walking fast towards the High Street. It wasn't too far. Most places would be shut, but no matter. She wanted to see one building in particular, if it was still there. Her trainers were silent on the pavement; she was a ghost of what went before.

Past the back of the newsagents, a glimpse of the café, dark and lifeless. Nothing was recognizable in the light of streetlamps, but she could swear the place on the far corner used to be a Woolies. If so, the place she was looking for was further up, on the same side as the café. A tiny place, it was, with a red sign. Turned out many more of the shops were closed down, huge sale signs still in the windows, some boarded up. She stood in the middle of the road, looking, safe because there were no cars about.

Was that it? She peered closer at a blackout awning, filthy windows with wood bars nailed across them. In one window was an old CLOSED sign, with the hours and the restaurant name in chipped lettering underneath: *The Chinese*. Her throat squeezed closed, and she caught her breath. This was the last place her mum was seen alive. She leaned her face against the door, barred and dead now. Inside, she could see some scattered chairs, wires and rubble in the shadows. Any trace of past custom was long gone. She tried to imagine her mum inside, having dinner with some man, laughing perhaps, a glint in her eye. Alive.

She turned away, and trudged back down the street. None of it felt real. No one disappeared without a trace, with no evidence, no remnants of a life. And if they had, then it wasn't fair. She kicked at an empty can in the gutter and it hit the other side of the curb.

Where did you go?

❧ ❧ ❧

Her phone was ringing at last. Lizzy glanced at her watch on the bedside table while she picked up, thinking it was odd that Alfie had left it so late that morning. Perhaps he was calling on his way to work.

'Hi love, didn't wake you, did I?' His voice was deep and croaky.

'No, I've been up ages, eating crackers and watching the news on this ancient telly. Do you know what time it is? You sound hungover.'

Alfie yawned. 'No such luck, just didn't sleep very well.'

'How come?' She crumbled a cracker in her hand. Bloody things. Tasteless and claggy.

'You know that meeting I had to go to? It was about cutting costs. Turns out I'm one of the costs they've snipped away. Bad timing, but I'll get another job. Don't worry. Plenty of time before the nipper arrives to get myself sorted.'

Lizzy lay back on the bed. 'Oh, I'm sorry I'm not there. Are you okay? Do you have to finish off, or did they let you go now?'

He sighed. 'Finish off what? Selling things to idiots? Nah, they said I didn't have to go in, but they paid me to the end of next month. How did it go last night at dinner?'

'All right. Kai and Noah were nice enough. Kane has some problems. Bit of a twat, actually.'

'What kind of problems?'

'Nothing dramatic. I'll tell you when I see you. He's the wrong'un, put it that way.' She wouldn't tell him about the sleaziness, not yet. Alfie wouldn't like it, and there was no point in getting him all wound up.

'And your dad?'

'Haven't seen him yet. But Alfie, are you sure you're okay? What are you going to do today? Shall I come back early?'

'Don't be daft,' he said. 'I'll get myself down the Job Centre, and get myself a cracking new job. When you come back, I'll be a new man, all rich and irresistible.'

When she came off the phone, Lizzy turned to her mum's picture, now on the bedside table, and met her gaze. If only she was around to meet Alfie. He'd loved that job. He always had customers around him, like flies around a jam jar, agreeing to five-year warrantees and extended insurance plans like it was the most natural thing in the world. He'd get another job, no problem, maybe even a better one. He'd come through. She imagined her husband unshaven, sitting in his boxers at the kitchen counter, eating a bowl of sugary cereal. He had a firm chest and a flat stomach despite eating like a pig, and so the image wasn't a bad one. Still, there'd be a pile of dishes in the sink. He'd promised to do some tiling while she was away, make a backsplash, but the aquamarine squares would still be in the boxes by the back door. She couldn't blame him really. Tiling a backsplash seemed so middle-aged and dull.

She lay down and grabbed her iPod. She chose "The Caterpillar" and placed the earbuds on her belly for the baby. She'd try to be nice to it. *Here you go, baby. This is the closest thing I've got to a baby song. Are you a caterpillar girl or a caterpillar boy?*

She lay waiting for a response, which was silly. It was hard to believe there was life in there at all.

When the song finished, she switched off and heard voices outside, at the front door of the B&B. A man was talking loudly, almost shouting, and she could hear a woman chipping in here and there. Was it Tilda? Lizzy went to the window, but couldn't see past the roof line. What the hell was going on?

She got up and splashed her face with cold water, a headache threatening. A wave of nausea came and went. A constant reminder.

There was a soft tapping on her door. 'It's me, Tilda. Are you awake, dear?'

'Yes, I'm up.' She opened the door.

Tilda was wringing her hands. 'I'm awful sorry. Your dad's here to see you. I said it was too early, but he wouldn't hear any of it. Says he wants to see you right away.'

Lizzy swallowed. *Shit.* 'I don't know if I can, Tilda.'

'Do you want me to tell him to swing it?'

She held her heart and tried to think. 'No. Do you mind telling him to give me half an hour? I'll meet him at Stone's Café.'

'So I will, doll. Are you sure?'

'I think so.'

She leaned back on the door after Tilda had gone, and let all the air out of her lungs. So he'd found out where she was already. No secrets in this town. He wanted to see her right away, did he? He didn't seem so desperate for her company when she'd really needed him. A lifetime had passed since then. So now he'd have to wait.

She listened out for his footsteps on the street, and they eventually retreated, heavy and slow. He had gone, for now.

ojo ojo ojo

At least Maggie would be at the café. Lizzy imagined her holding up a floury rolling pin to anyone that made trouble. There was a fierce bite to the wind, and she was thankful for the wool coat that Alfie had made her bring. 'It's freezing up there,' he'd said, although he'd never actually been to Scotland before, or even north of Leicester.

She fluffed up her hair. She hadn't bothered tying it back, wanting to let her curls loose. She'd got the blonde gene from her dad, and she wanted him to see it in all its glory. For some reason, she needed to look her best, to show him what he'd missed. It was like meeting up with an ex-boyfriend. She put on her gloves as she walked, slow and steady.

She crossed the road at the charity shop and flinched when she saw her dad in the window, arms crossed, looking out for her. Maggie was taking orders at another table. He held up his hand in greeting.

Lizzy went inside and nodded at Maggie, who gave her a look that said, 'What the fuck?'

Her dad stood up and held out his arms. 'Lizzy. Bloody hell, just look at you.'

'Hi.' Lizzy sat at the table. She'd sounded casual, but if she hadn't sat down straightaway, her legs would have given way.

His whole body seemed to deflate at her rejection, his arms falling to his sides with a slap. 'Aye, well, it's been a long time,' he said. 'It's bound to feel strange.'

Lizzy looked around for Maggie, but she'd disappeared. 'So. You're living at Bryant Road.' She looked into his eyes. They were blue, paler than she remembered, like they'd faded over time.

'I paid for that house, darlin'. Your mum never came back, and so ...' he trailed off, and then shrugged as if his move was inevitable.

Lizzy said nothing, just raised her eyebrows. She'd resented him for so long that she was afraid to feel anything else for him. He was her dad, and a tiny part of her wanted to put her arms around his neck. But let him suffer.

He shifted his legs so they were sticking out from the table into the room. They were long and muscular, his jeans bursting at the seams and ripped at the knees. Pale skin and blond hairs were showing through. 'I saw you at the house. Did you hear me calling? I knew it was you.'

She nodded. A packet of sugar had burst, a trail of white crystals on the table. She pushed at them with her finger, making tracks.

He scratched his nose and fidgeted with his sleeves. 'I came up here that Christmas to see you, and you were gone. What year was it? Late nineties? We thought you might have gone down to Leeds to find me, and so I went back. Searched all over for you.'

'I would never have gone to Leeds. Why would I do that? You didn't want me.'

He sighed. 'I don't blame you, Lizzy, for hating me. Me and your mum weren't meant to be. So I wasn't there for you. I'm sorry.' He splayed his fingers out in front of him, like that was it, all he had. All his thoughts were out there.

Lizzy leaned forward, hiding her hands under the table because she didn't want him to see them shaking. 'That's it? That's all I get? Well, I was sorry too, when I was living on the street, when I was filthy and cold and surrounded by addicts. I was sorry when mum disappeared, and you didn't come and rescue me. You left me here for the vultures. I was *thirteen*.'

He looked shocked at her last statement. Didn't he realize how young she was then? She was just a kid. He should have stepped up, taken over. Been a proper dad.

He rubbed his hands over his face, a trickle of sweat finding its way down one side. 'I'll make it up to you. Anything. I want to be your dad, Lizzy. I need to be your dad. Please. I'm dying to know all about you. What you've been doing. You can come and stay with us, me and Nicole, for as long as you like. She's looking forward to meeting you.'

Lizzy drummed her fingers on the underside of the table. 'What's the point? I don't need you now. I've got Alfie, my husband, and we have a life in London. I scraped through without you, but it wasn't easy. Another family took me in, my best friend's parents. They didn't have to, but they wanted to. They wanted *me*. Who's Nicole, anyway, the woman you went off with back then? The same one, is it?'

He shook his head. 'No. But we've been together for ten years. She never had kids of her own.'

'So I can fill the gap?'

'No, nothing like that. But you're my blood. My girl. I want you back, Lizzy.'

She caught a glimpse of Maggie coming out the kitchen with her notepad. 'I might be your blood, but I'm not your girl. Never was. I was scared of you. When you came for your visits once a year at Christmas, I half looked forward to seeing you, and half dreaded them.'

Lizzy stood up, aware of a few eyes on her, but she didn't care what other people thought. Never had. 'I didn't come here to see you. I'd no idea you lived in our old house, and it's weird.'

He grabbed her wrist. 'I never meant to scare you. I'd never have hurt you.'

'Don't touch me.' She pulled away, her skin pulling under his grip.

Maggie was there in a second. 'What's going on here? You all right, Lizzy?'

'Yeah. I thought this would be okay, but it's not.'

'Did he hurt you?'

'No, I'm fine.' She glared at him. 'Just tell me. Do you know what happened to Mum? Had you seen her?'

He frowned. 'No. I was miles away, Lizzy.'

She gritted her teeth. 'Did you hurt her?'

'Yes I did, back in the day. But I didn't kill her. I was long gone.' He spoke softly. He looked her in the eye.

She nodded at Maggie and left the café, her coat still on. As she left, she heard Maggie telling her dad not to follow or she'd skelp him. Then she shouted at the rest of the folk in there. 'Show's over, you lot. Did you take notes, there, Mrs. Finnegan? See enough, did you?'

Her stride was heavy on the pavement. She could feel the place on her wrist where he'd grabbed her.

She knew he would follow. It wasn't long before his footsteps came up behind her, his voice low and whining. 'Talk to me. Please, Lizzy. I've thought about you every day.'

She felt a light drizzle on her cheek, soaking in, as she turned. 'Give me time. It's too much of a shock. You say you've thought about me every day. But I couldn't miss what I never had. I didn't miss you.'

He sighed, his head hung low. 'I'll come get you another time. Okay?'

She nodded. A tear threatened to emerge, but she swallowed it away. He'd let her down and he knew it. She half-ran towards the High Street, to anywhere, to get away from him.

As she turned the corner, she bumped into an old lady hunched over a walker, who tutted like Lizzy had done it on purpose. It felt like the old days, being a teenager with backcombed hair and an attitude. Presumed guilty. 'Sorry,' she shouted.

The woman gave her a toothy smile, her watery eyes shining. 'Never mind,' she said.

Lizzy took in her crazy hair, the big furry boots. 'You okay?'

'I would be if only it would stop bloody raining.'

'Right?' Lizzy grinned at her, and made her way to a large building set off from the main drag, with open garage doors and the faint smell of dirty vegetables in the air around it. It was the indoor market. Lizzy used to go there with her mum on Saturday afternoons. She burst into the bustle, and the chaos hit her with a cruel jolt of memories. They'd shop for fruit, try on boots, tease the guys on the stalls about their hair or their taste in clothes.

'All the latest fashions over here, doll,' a man was shouting from a nearby stall, racks of clothes forming a wall around it. 'Designer jeans, cargos, all colours.' He was wearing a white vest with CHILLAX written on it, in the same font as the old Frankie Goes to Hollywood ones. His arms were covered in messy tattoos, a huge gold sovereign ring covering three fingers. *Nice touch.*

She made her way into the thick of the market. There was a big stall full of cheap scarves, all different tartans. Caley Thistle football paraphernalia. FA Cups and ribbons. It felt warm and close, although it wasn't that crowded. She bought an apple from a young girl, and it reminded her of her days working on the fruit stall in Soho with Banana Dave. It had got her off the street, that job, and she'd made the most of it.

'Here's your change.' The girl held out some coins. Her nails, poking out through fingerless gloves, were black with grime from the market.

'Ta.' The girl's smile reminded Lizzy of her best friend Natalie. It was like going back in time, to two places. Everything was merging into one story. She felt dizzy suddenly, and grabbed onto the side of the stall.

'Hey, are you okay?' The girl came out and put her hand on Lizzy's shoulder.

'Yeah, I'm fine. Thanks. I felt weird for a minute.' She released her grip and put the apple in her pocket for later. Was it the baby, making her feel like this?

Opposite they were selling fake Uggs, in brown, pink, and blue. They were the kind of things her and Mum would have tried on and then had a good laugh. They were tormenting her, showing her what she couldn't have. The ceiling was getting lower, the humidity crowding her. It was like being in a giant tent where all of her memories were stored. The words of all the sellers reverberated around her, blending into one big noise.

'Sweet tomatoes, ripe and juicy.'

'Sparkles and stripes, not for the auldies.'

'Free scarf. If you buy two.'

Lizzy looked frantically for the doors, but was distracted by a face in the crowd that she recognized, along with the leather jacket and all that greasy hair. Kane. She saw him hand a small packet to one of the market workers, passed from palm to palm. She knew the motion well, the secretive nature of it, so obvious to her after years of seeing it, doing it. Lizzy trailed him, curious to see what he did next. She stayed behind him a few paces, and pulled up her hood. *I'm onto you.*

He headed for the exit and she followed him outside, grateful for the fresh air and space taking away her nausea. Kane was stumbling. He pulled out a cigarette from behind his ear and lit up, breathing in deep, a thin trail of smoke finding its way back to her. She didn't mind the smell. It was nostalgic, almost made her want to light up one for herself, although she hadn't smoked in years.

Kane went for the High Street, leering at a group of girls on their way to the market, handbags over shoulders, a cackling row of high-heeled boots and short skirts. Then he sat on a bench, head bowed between his legs. Just like Roy, back then.

She sat down next to him. He was her cousin, flesh and blood, and all this was going to be the death of him. It had been the death of Simon. She leaned back, hands in her coat pockets. 'Not many job prospects in dealing, you know.'

He looked up, incredulous. 'What did you say?'

'Been there, done that. It'll end badly.'

'Oh, it's you, Lizzy. Can't keep away, eh?' He reached across and put his hand on her leg.

Lizzy picked it up and placed it back on his own leg. 'Take it from someone who knows, that's all. Just looking out for you because we're related. Don't think I like you.'

'Some friendly advice, eh? Cousins can get married,' he said. 'Or just fuck.' He slid across the bench and put one arm across her shoulders. He pinched her cheek and pulled her face towards him.

'Get away, you freak.' She thumped his chest and tried to get up, but he was too strong for her.

'Give us a kiss. You know you want to, you little prick-tease.' He grabbed her breast and squeezed it hard, a spray of his saliva landing on her lips.

'Fuck off, seriously. Just fuck off.' She pulled her hands into fists and punched upwards, one landing on his jaw, the other in midair. His head was knocked back with a crack, and she broke free. 'What's wrong with you?' She took a few paces back.

'Plenty of time for all that, eh,' he said, stretching his arms across the back of the bench. 'I don't need advice from London-girl, by the way. Keep out of my road, right?'

She wiped her face with the back of her hand and glowered at him. Should have known better. She hesitated, trying to decide whether to squander any more of her breath on him, then decided he wasn't worth it. She walked away, trying to ignore his *here-kitty-kitty* clicking noises.

Two middle-aged men were going into the bookies opposite, looking back at her. The knitting shop owner was watching out her dirty window. Would anyone have stepped in to help if Kane had got a proper hold of her, or even dragged her away? There were plenty of folk scattered around, on their way somewhere, busying themselves. But trouble was invisible. And things would go away if they were ignored.

It was her against the rest of them again. Had it been like that for her mum? Was she dragged away somewhere, screaming maybe, while folk turned away?

Someone must have seen something. She just had to find them.

CHAPTER TWELVE

Jonno

Every day she came past the chippy, at five minutes after twelve. But I'm the only one who noticed her. Maybe it was because she was so old and small and dressed funny. Or maybe folk didn't pay as much attention as I did. Wendy was her name. I called her Weather Wendy.

She'd been doing it for over a year.

The morning had been busier than usual due to the road construction going on at the end of the High Street and all the workers being hungry. They said there's nothing better than my chips on an empty stomach. I had my *Guinness Book of World Records* propped up on the counter, but not much time to read it to myself, so instead I read individual facts out loud to the workers waiting in line. It was my entertainment to them.

The oldest confirmed amphibian is fifty-two. A giant Japanese salamander.

The next in line was a man covered in white dust that had mixed in with rain, and it dripped from his hard hat like cake icing. He didn't say anything about the amphibian fact, but asked me for a battered sausage supper with plenty of salt.

I served up the order and put mountains of salt on, then asked him for four pound.

Paleontologists discovered the largest clutch of eggs laid by a dinosaur. Thirty-four.

The next in line ignored my fact as well, and asked me for a poke of chips. He was older, his hands dirty and wrinkled, his thumbnails black.

And so it went on. I liked facts. No one else did.

It was so busy that when I next looked at the clock, it was three minutes after twelve. Two minutes to Weather Wendy. I told the last two in the queue to wait, and that I'd be right back. There was some moaning and sighing, but they did wait. Otherwise they wouldn't get any chips.

I went outside, and stood on the pavement. I held out my hand to the sky, just like I did every day. The rain was light, drizzly, and the clouds were pale grey. I sucked my finger to make it wet and held it up. The wind was cold, but weak.

Not a bad day. It had been much worse.

I waited.

Regular as clockwork, old Weather Wendy turned the corner and walked towards me, slow. She was hunched over her walker, but she lifted her head as she approached and I thought she looked very much like a tortoise. Her eyes were watering. She was wearing her furry boots and a rain mac, dressed for both the cold and the wet. Once she wore welly boots that looked like they were three sizes too big, and they tripped her up. In the summer, she once wore pink sandals with wooly socks.

She never looked directly at me, just straight ahead with her cloudy eyes. I didn't mind that because I didn't look folk in the eye much either. Her voice was always level, low, like she was talking only to me and I was the only person in the world.

'This bloody drizzle won't stop today,' she said. 'Goes right through you.'

That was it. She'd made her comment, her fact about the weather. She put her head down again, and leaned into her walker, her veiny hands clutching the bar. I felt a big grin coming. Weather Wendy was so funny. I looked around to see if anyone else heard. Two women were walking past, their umbrellas up, chatting, looking down at the puddles. A guy with a hoodie strode by, hands in his pockets, headphones in.

No one was listening.

I turned and went back inside. The next customer was tapping his fingers on the counter, looking this way and that. I knew who he was, what he was going to order, his full address, and that he liked to go to the betting shop on a Saturday morning.

I should have entered the World Memory Championships. It was a real thing. It existed. There was a German guy who memorized a deck of cards in twenty-one seconds, and 300 random words recounted in fifteen minutes. I reckoned I could give him a run for his money.

I've always seen things. Not everyone does. It's my special gift that no one knows about.

Because no one ever listens.

CHAPTER THIRTEEN

Oliver's Weeds

It was an early start that morning. I was on the road at first light, bags already packed in my roomy Volvo Estate, the flat scrubbed, linens washed and folded for my return. I almost wished I could stay once it had been decontaminated. The place was so clean and sparse, void of dust and the clutter of everyday life: scattered keys, a wallet on the kitchen table, the lingering smell of recently cooked food. All everyday objects were replaced by empty surfaces, a trail of disinfectant and the sparkling results of vinegar water. Ahh.

I had emptied the kitchen cupboards of perishables, many of which were edible on the road, meaning I didn't have to stop at any of the odious 'convenience' petrol stations on the way. Pit-stop cafés are ridden with germs and parasites, crawling on the grease from sweaty drivers' palms. One can almost see them. I had a flask filled with filtered water and another with hot tea, and hoped that I wouldn't need to stop more than once or twice to relieve my bladder, for there is nothing worse than a public toilet. I tried to avoid them altogether, choosing instead the trunk of a tree or some dense bushes at the side of a road, both preferable to the steaming stench of urinals.

The drive from Edinburgh was straightforward, although my eyes soon grew heavy from the strain of concentrating through the inevitable swish of my windscreen wipers. An end-of-summer downpour made the winding roads interesting, the thunder-cloud scenery like a high contrast black-and-white photograph. Once past Perth and north to

Pitlochry, the rolling hills and green-patch fields gave some colour to the land, although it remained largely dulled by the low skies. I kept my mind on Dalbegie and its inhabitants, the clean air, and my 'quaint' cottage there. My flat in the New Town had more grace and style than any of the downtrodden residents of Dalbegie could ever know, and yet my place there was charming in its own way, because it had a certain history.

It had seen things.

The whitewashing would need touching up that year. I'd wait until the leaves had fallen, to avoid any further brown stains left behind by sodden foliage. The back garden would be overgrown beyond belief, but of course I enjoyed the additional privacy that it gave. It was my hiding place. I tidied and weeded, raked and dug, but only where I needed to. The outer edges were wild, tangled shields.

When I eventually pulled up to my second home after a long and wet drive of some five hours, my watered-down enthusiasm disappeared altogether. The day was drab, the afternoon air thick with oppression. It didn't feel fresh like I had anticipated, but sour and dull. I climbed out of the car with heavy legs, a feeling of self-loathing flooding through me. There was a padded envelope sticking out of my letterbox. No one cared enough to push it through for me; it didn't matter because I didn't need anyone to care. But still, it got to me. I had a pang of longing for how things used to be when my favourite souls were still there. But they had flown.

The grassy island that separated my house from the newsagents was unkempt and ragged. The twee rows of flowers and trimmed grass had long been replaced by weeds, discarded wrappers, and empty cans. The shining iron fence was rusting, flaking, to reflect my mood. It was a neglect that had spiraled over the years, eating away to make ugliness.

I unpacked the car, since I had never cared for putting things off, and the sight of bags, bottles and empty wrappers on the passenger seat made me twitch. Once indoors, I shook out a fresh black sack for the bin, and turned on the kitchen tap for hot water to rinse out my drinks containers. My old Nikon Sport Optics were resting in their place by the sink and I touched their black sides with fondness. They had served me well. Tins went into cupboards, clothes into drawers and my double wardrobe. I hung up my shirts and trousers the way I liked them, hangers facing the same way, everything in colour-coded sections. Little pleasures.

Once things were in order, I began to feel better. I put the kettle on and ventured outside for a breath of air, my back garden a haven of privacy.

My garden tools had moved.

I left them in a straight line, leaning against the back wall of the house at a forty-five-degree angle, so the wind didn't topple them over. There was a substantial overhang from the roof, so things were sheltered there. But the large shovel and the compost fork had been moved. The shovel was at the far end next to the rake, and the fork was upside down.

Someone had been in my garden while I was away.

Patches of overgrown weeds around the pathway had been trampled. Those kinds of weeds usually sprang back quickly, and so they must be freshly crushed. My private space had been disrupted. I growled. Once I'd realigned the tools, I went inside, thrown by the violation. I rinsed a mug in scalding water then made tea. The house needed a thorough clean, but I was so unnerved that I decided to delay the scrubbing and bleaching until I'd double-checked that no one had been inside. Surely I would have noticed before, but still, I took my mug and inspected the kitchen, the living room, the pantry. I tapped my foot on the fake floor that covered the cellar, and dust flew up from the cracks. I went upstairs and gave myself another tour of the bedrooms and the bathroom. It became clear that the place was intact, with all the windows locked, and so I settled in the conservatory to finish my drink. If someone had been inside, I would have known. I knew every position and every angle of my possessions, from the furniture to the sole picture frame, to how I had left the shower curtain and bed linens. I was sure.

I pulled Bird from my trouser pocket and held her as I gazed at the photograph of my father on the mantle. His uniform was so smart. I picked up the watch that he gave me when I was a boy, his watch, that I kept next to his picture. The blue-and-red striped strap was ragged and faded, and if I'd worn it all the time it would snap. It was the only thing I had of him.

Nostalgia. It's a delicate thing, a weakness that takes us. I put the watch and Bird next to each other on the table and drained my tea. Damn them and their primary colours, their childlike status. I'd take my mind away from the past and go across the road to see that wench of a woman, Jessica. If there had been someone sniffing around the place, she would know about it. She had the mouth of a fishwife, chuntering on about things that weren't her business. But sometimes she came in handy.

I retrieved my trapper hat from the hook by the door, where it lived all year round, and braved the wind that had begun to whistle through the houses. The newsagents' door chimed and announced my presence. Sure enough, Jessica was flicking around that straw-blonde hair, flirting the very second I went inside.

'You're back,' she gushed. 'I saw the car earlier. How are you doing? Are you ready for me, Oliver?'

'Great to see you, Jessica.' *I'll never be ready for what you have in mind, my dear.*

There she stood, arms outstretched as though it was the most natural thing in the world to hug each other. I had no intention of going near her, of that hair brushing against me, and pretended not to notice the gesture. I looked about the place, hands on hips, as though I had missed it. She'd been trying to catch my eye for years, but she had never excited me the way Lauren did. Jessica wouldn't know what 'understated' meant. Another woman worked there too, a dank, squashy woman who smelled of alcohol. She tried to give me a smile, but ended up looking like the Mona Lisa had she been going through the menopause. It was a rather hideous effect.

I picked up a copy of *The Times,* shaking off a strand of yellow twine that had previously held the stack of newspapers together. The sight of it brought back a few memories. I'd used the very same twine. In a very different way. I took the newspaper up to the counter along with a tin of Heinz Tomato Soup that was not quite out of date.

Jessica followed me, nudging the other woman out of the way so that she could serve me. 'You'll never guess what.'

'Hmm?' I feigned a lack of interest, concentrating on getting the correct change from my wallet. Clearly she couldn't wait to tell me, and I knew she would spit it out from those blood-red lips soon enough. I asked a cruel question. 'Did you get married?' *As if anyone would stoop that low.*

'No, away with you,' she said, like that was the last thing that would happen. On that at least she was right.

She leaned in. 'Someone's back in town who you might remember. Lauren's girl. Lizzy. She was in here yesterday. I think you used to quite like our Lauren.' She said the last part with obvious disappointment.

The change dropped from my hand onto the counter with a clatter. The blood drained from my head all the way down to my toes. I gathered myself before I replied. 'Oh yes, I have a vague recollection of her. Lots of attitude. Her mother was friendly, I seem to remember.' *Her mother wanted me as badly as you do, you dirty whore.*

Jessica picked up my coins and dropped them in the till, brandishing chipped nail polish and ink-stained fingers. 'Lizzy's friendly too. And looking well. Glowing, actually. They must look after themselves in London. I've always wanted to go there myself. Perhaps I will.' She looked up and fluttered her eyelashes, daring me to beg her to stay here instead.

'Well if I see her, I shall say hello.' I was shaking. Lizzy was back in Dalbegie. *My girl.*

The other girl mumbled another snippet of information, but I couldn't tune into her strange tone. Her words circled around me and out the door, as though they were meant for someone else. I said my goodbyes and left with my newspaper under my right arm as usual. I wanted to ask if they knew where she was staying, how long she would be there, all kinds of questions.

The wind picked up, the whistle growing to a howl. Fall had well and truly set in here in Scotland, leaves swirling, making their way to the ground from all directions, the temperature taking a turn from chilly to frozen. Here the seasons were abrupt, falling from the heavens with a bang. I kicked at some leaves and a small piece of soil stuck to the end of my boot. The place was starting to get sodden. But even that didn't matter now. *She was here.*

An old man raised his hat to me, the one with the beige fetish who lived a few doors down the road. We always recognized each other when I returned to town, and had that pleasing relationship where one simply had to nod with each other's presence rather than engage in conversation. As he passed, I saw a bulge in his coat pocket, and a glint in his eye that I'd never seen before. It was a knowing look. I thought of the trampled weeds, wondered if he was carrying a gun, whether there was a surveillance team in the area who were onto me. I scanned the street before I went through my gate, my insides burning, the open sores on my scalp weeping under my hat. I was the watcher, but I felt suddenly that I was the one being observed. Had they sent Lizzy here as a trap? Perhaps I was being set up, the girl being thrown at my feet like a piece of meat. Why else would she be here? Coincidences were not a part of reality.

Back inside, I dealt with this newfound knowledge of Lizzy, of potential suspicion, by scrubbing the place to the bone, on hands and knees, bleach burning my hands. I didn't stop until every speck of dust, each grain of filth, was obliterated. I checked corners, ceilings, cupboard tops for cameras; if they were watching, I would find out. But there was nothing to find. Two of my knuckles bled, the tiny red gashes smiling, mocking me.

I drew the curtains, turned off the lights. I poked my binoculars through the blinds in the kitchen and surveyed the street. A couple of elderly women were going on their way, no one dubious. The old man who had raised his hat to me had gone. I focussed on one of the women, zoomed in on her zipped ankle boots and woolen tights. Harmless enough. Her face was set in a grimace, and I didn't linger on it, setting the Nikons down. For now.

Perhaps I was being paranoid. But paranoia wasn't one of my things.

I set up my laptop upstairs, my desk and chair in that pleasing state where the cables hadn't yet accumulated dust. The desk smelled faintly of wood polish, the chair brushed free of hair and lint. I logged in, and found the depression and anxiety forum that had previously caught my eye. I needed the distraction.

I set up a moniker for myself. It seemed that members were not allowed to use their real names, or anything that sounded like it could be a name, and so my new user profile would have to be completely innocuous. I sifted through some of the other members, noting the combinations of words and numbers. Kitten555 was a prolific user; MarigoldGirl was quite the advice giver; CloudyDay appeared here and there, her anxieties mounting. I decided upon the name OwlVerse; it was warm and inviting, to encourage empathy. Everyone of a certain 'type' liked owls and poetry, and so I would appear friendly without even trying. I found a thread about fretful thinking, and plunged in, introducing myself as a person riddled with fears, in a relapsed state of depression.

I like to work with birds–they're wonderful and I find their presence therapeutic. But I was recently fired from my job at the sanctuary due to lack of funding. Some days I find it hard to leave the house, to face the world.

Immediately I was offered a virtual hug by Kitten555, which wasn't surprising as she seemed to spend every waking hour on the forum. I was not alone, she insisted. I thanked her for the warm welcome and said I would log in the following day, promising to become a more active member. I stated that I was looking forward to mutual friendship and advice. *Easy.* I logged out, and sat back in the chair. The forum would be an interesting side project that could provide some mild entertainment to see me through the winter months.

But as my computer fell silent, the room shrank, and my chest tightened. The diversion had been short lived, and my mind turned back to Lizzy.

My favourite little bird had flown back to the nest. Even if she wasn't planted here, a trap, she must have come back for a reason. What was it? Was she homesick for this ghastly place? I couldn't help but dwell on the idea that she was bait, suspicions raised all these years later. I would have to circle her carefully, and wait.

On the other hand, perhaps life was simply pulling us together again. We were drawn to each other by some inexplicable force, like a migration. It could well be the right time, the one I'd been anticipating. It had been years since I last had the opportunity to pounce. A long time coming. I could soon be holding her, trembling in my hands, her tiny heart fluttering.

CHAPTER FOURTEEN

Helen on Holiday

The room was so small that she could sit on any side of the bed and touch a wall, even with her short arms. Helen tried it out, shifting from left to bottom then right to top. There was a narrow chest of drawers in one corner with a television on top, old and bulbous. She stood up and wiped her finger across the screen. Dust flew into the air and floated down to the thin, pink carpet.

She took a tiny step to the narrow window and looked out onto the street, strewn with fluttering leaves and twigs since the windstorm. The house was near the park, and a big council estate with a filthy looking high-rise. Not the best side of town, and so it was a good place for her to be staying. She wanted to go out, feel the cold on her face, but would wait until dark.

A couple went by, in their thirties perhaps, the woman's hand in the man's back pocket. She was wearing a white padded jacket, the furry hood dirty and matted. She walked lazily, her boots scuffing on the ground. The man put his arm around her and hurried her along. People looked so different up north, squashier or paler. Helen sat on the bed again, and picked absently at the old-fashioned quilted bedspread. A thread came loose and she began to wind it around her finger until her skin went blue. Time wasn't ticking along fast enough.

This was why she didn't go on holiday as a rule. Away from the familiarity of home, of the long-time smell of herself in the sheets, her body felt heavy, her head hazy and thick. It was like she was inside of a fuzzy television screen waiting to come back to the real world, to clarity. Change did this to her. It was disorienting.

She kicked off her shoes and lay down on top of the covers. She stared at the grease marks on the wall where a picture had been removed, then at the brass rings on the drawers, dulled and tarnished. At least the place was cheap and private. No group breakfasts or chatter. Helen had been given her own key and a kettle, which she'd have to plug into the shaving socket in the bathroom. It was low base, but she didn't have to clear up cat shit at the sanctuary for two whole weeks.

The owner of the house was clattering about downstairs. It sounded like she was transporting pots and pans from one place to another, over and over. She lived alone, which wasn't all that surprising, looking at the state of her. She'd told Helen her name, but it was forgotten now. Stay as long as you like, she'd said, as she wasn't expecting anyone else to come. Helen could settle up when she left. It was a good recommendation by the man in the bookies, who'd told Helen she wouldn't find anything cheaper or as cozy. And cozy it was—or small as some might say. And it was a good walk out of town, but never mind that. To be on the outskirts meant she could more easily look in.

The sounds continued to drift up through the floor, chinking and clanking. The owner was bony and brittle, with a deep throaty voice and the permanent smell of cigarette smoke. She reminded Helen of her first foster mother, chain smoking, pulling at her cardigan to cover her bony chest. When she opened the front door, Helen had taken a step back at first; the woman was so unnervingly familiar.

'I wanted to ask about your spare room,' she'd said.

The woman had kept one veiny hand on the door, both feet inside. 'Aye, I've one room going. Who's asking?'

'My name's Helen. I'm looking for a couple of weeks at most.'

'Right. Let's get you inside. Have a wee look and tell me if you want it. It's nuttin' sparkling, but it's clean, right?'

That voice. Words spit out like bullets. Helen went back, to her earliest days, when being an outsider had already become normal. The shouting was expected, those gravelly criticisms part of life. Her first foster mother had booted her out in the end, sent her to the next care home in London. But she'd remained a voice on her shoulder to disregard or to be influenced by, depending on the day of the week, the time of day. And proclamations from the dead could never be ignored.

ᴏᏟ ᴏᏟ ᴏᏟ

Little girl. She was using the worn-down crayons that were kept in the round clay pot in the kitchen. They were her foster brother's, little stubs with the paper torn right down to the bottom. He was only two, but he had more things to play with than she did. She'd asked for some pencils of her own, lots of times, but had never got them. Helen couldn't find any paper, so she got the free newspaper from the doorstep and opened it out onto the floor. She drew a house, with chimney pots and a pointed fence all around it. Not like the sagging wire one they had out front, with the sharp corners. This one was wooden, blue and cheery. The newsprint was ruining it a bit, but if she pressed hard, maybe the colours would stand out okay.

Since school finished, she'd been on her own in the house, and would be until everyone's work ended. As usual, she had to find things to amuse herself for a few hours, as telly wasn't allowed until after dinner. She sat on the kitchen floor and coloured, taking her time, working within the lines. The fridge was making that whirring sound. She'd looked in there earlier for a snack, and had found a blob of cheese and some peanut butter that wouldn't be missed.

The red crayon was almost gone now, what with the roof. She held it by her fingertips and scraped it across the last part of the chimney.

There was a dog barking in the distance. She imagined it was chasing away a robber.

Rain was ticking on the windowpane. *Tick, tick, tick.*

'What the hell do you think you're doing?' Her foster mother had let herself in the back door. She was holding a cigarette and blowing smoke back outside. Strands of white hair had come out of her ponytail, sticking up like whiskers.

Time had disappeared again.

Helen sat back on her heels. She'd gone over the lines. Red crayon had got onto the pale lino, and the sides of her hands were a mess from leaning on the newsprint. 'I'm colouring in.'

'I can see that, you stupid girl. Colouring in the bloody floor. Get up.'

She stood, and waited.

Her foster mother threw her cigarette stub on the back step, and pulled at her cardigan, the top button missing. She slammed the door shut. 'You're a pain in the arse. Get the scrubbing brush from under the sink and clean up that mess. Then you can get to your bed.'

'What about dinner and the cartoons?'

'I don't want to see your weird, greetin' face, d'you hear?'

Helen picked up the inner page of the newspaper, folded up the picture, and put it in her pocket. Then she got the brush and a bowl of water and set about cleaning the floor. The waxy crayon smeared into the lino and made a pinkish splodge. Her foster mother began the dinner, muttering to herself. The room filled with smells of cigarettes and bread, warm and doughy with an edge. The mess was getting worse. Helen put down the brush and ran upstairs, trying to ignore that voice calling after her, threatening her. She wiped the sides of her hands on her brother's white pillow, leaving red stains, then went to her own bedroom and lay down. Her stomach was rumbling already, and it wasn't even nighttime yet. She rolled a blanket around herself and shut her eyes, sinking into a different place, away from there. The smell of fried onions travelled upstairs and into the room, torturing her, so she put her head under the blanket too, and everything was muffled.

ᘔᘔ ᘔᘔ ᘔᘔ

She'd probably end up killing her, the woman downstairs. The pots and pans were bad enough, but the transference of hate from her first foster mother onto her would mark the end eventually. It was unfair, but so was life. The woman's demeanour, her cigarette-sandpaper voice, had stuck.

The sky dimmed from pale grey to charcoal. Night was coming. It would soon be time to venture out, when she could walk around unseen, and take it all in. Two weeks she had, in this faraway little place. Plenty of time to do what she needed to.

CHAPTER FIFTEEN

The Glow

Four o'clock and it felt like nighttime. It was already so dark, so cold. Lizzy didn't feel like going out again, but couldn't back out of the visit to Molly's now. Her old friend would only get more offended than she already was. Tilda had shown her where her house was on the map, and she was nearly there, her feet aching from all the walking that day. Molly lived on the other side of the High Street, towards the big park and the council high-rises. Back in London, Lizzy walked a fair bit, but there was always a bus or a tube to hop on when she got tired. Here, the streets never seemed to end, and the wind followed, needles of ice on her cheeks.

It was hard to know what to bring, and she'd settled for some iced almond tarts from the bakery on the way, and three tubes of Smarties for the kids. All kids liked Smarties, didn't they? Didn't matter what age they were. The plastic bag of treats kept banging on her leg, twisting so the handles cut into her fingers.

She could hardly blame Molly for being pissed off. They were tight when they were kids, but from the age of twelve Lizzy had gone off with Simon and discarded her. When her mum disappeared, no one but Simon really understood what it was like to be abandoned. Still, she should have confided in Molly more, included her at least.

Hopefully she'd get over herself. There'd been enough bullshit for one day.

She texted Natalie, who'd be finishing work at a big call centre in south London. Nat kept her mobile next to her for sanity. She'd be talking to some poor customer, reading off the spiel from her computer, looking at her watch to see how many minutes until she could put on her coat and run out the door. Lizzy couldn't do a job like that herself, but Nat seemed to take to it, could see the comical side of sales. She was like a fembot, she'd told her, and sometimes talked to the more difficult customers in the style of Siri from her phone. It made Lizzy laugh. She keyed in, 'Met my real dad. Wasn't expecting that. Wish you were here.'

Nat texted back after a few moments, 'I hope he isn't as stinky as my dad (your dad no. 2). You can do it. Love you.' Darren, Nat's dad, had become her surrogate father figure over the years. Him and his bad jokes. He was lovely, and had given her more support than her own dad ever had. She replied. 'Not as stinky. More of a pain in the arse, though.'

At last she came to the house, a tiny council terrace with a faded plastic slide and a broken tricycle in the front garden. There were leaves all over the lawn, sweet wrappers in the hedge. *Here goes.* She went up the short pathway, overgrown with moss and weeds, and knocked on the door.

'It's open!' Molly shouted from inside.

A young kid was crying and screaming. From the back, there was the monotonous sound of a football being kicked against a wall.

'For god's sake, Meg, give it to me. Stop your whining, will you.' Molly was bent over, wrestling a doll out of her daughter's grubby hands. 'I can fix it, but you've got to let go, silly girl.'

The little girl wiped her nose on her sleeve and coughed, her tiny body shaking from it. Her jeans were ripped at both knees, and she was barefooted and dirty. 'Craig pulled her arm off. I hate him.'

'I'll have a word with him later, don't you worry,' said Molly. 'Here. It's fixed. Now take it up to your bedroom and keep away from the boys.' She turned to Lizzy and sighed. 'There's always drama.'

Lizzy smiled. 'She's cute. Looks like you.' She held out the bag of Smarties and tarts. 'I got these. Wasn't sure what to bring.'

'Thanks. They'll go well with a vodka and tonic.' Molly went into the galley kitchen next to the living room. 'Sit down in there, if you like. Voddie okay for you?'

Lizzy sat on one of the armchairs after pushing some toy cars off it. It had packing tape covering a rip on the end of one arm. 'Actually, Molly, I'm off the booze at the moment. Antibiotics. A cup of tea would be good, though. I'm parched.'

She should tell her about the baby. It might make her feel special, to be included in the secret. But Lizzy didn't feel like talking about it.

'It's never too early for me.' Molly appeared with a pint glass, fizzing, and a plate for the almond tarts. 'I've put the kettle on.' She sat down on the sofa and took a big gulp of the drink. Her eyes seemed to soften in an instant. 'Listen, I'm sorry if I was a bitch in the shop yesterday. Jessica was doing my melt in, and it was a shock, seeing you. It freaked me out hearing your London accent, if I'm honest.'

'Don't worry about it,' said Lizzy. 'Jessica used to do my mum's head in too, when she worked with her. It's funny being back. It's like nothing's changed, but it has. I can't believe you've got three kids. Who did you get married to, anyone I used to know?'

Molly gulped at the drink, and shut her eyes for a second, trying to drown a memory. 'I married Duncan from the year above. He wore trousers that were too tight and had an older sister who did mean shite to him, like shave off his eyebrow or stick a sign on his back that said he was a numpty.'

'Shit. *That* Duncan. Is he at work? What's his sister like now?' She watched as Molly guzzled her vodka and wondered how much tonic was in the mix.

'We're separated and he stays at his mum's in the flats up the hill. They take the kids at the weekends. I don't know why I married him in the first place. He asked, I suppose. His sister's still a cow. She never liked me.' Molly got up as the kettle whistled, taking her glass with her. 'Back in a second.'

Lizzy looked at the shelf over the telly. There was a wind-up clock showing the wrong time, surrounded by photos in clip-frames of the kids in their school uniforms.

A boy of about nine appeared through the back door, letting in the cold. 'Mum, Craig stuck a rock up the drainpipe and it's getting blocked. And he kicked my ba' over the fence.' He traipsed mud across the carpet, stopping halfway into the room to regard Lizzy.

'Hi,' she said. 'I'm a friend of your mum's. We used to play together when we were about your age.'

He snorted as if he couldn't imagine that.

Molly shouted from the kitchen. 'Sort it out yourself, Ryan. I'm busy. Get the thing out of the drainpipe, and make Craig get the ball from next door. If the dog gets him, then he deserves it.'

Ryan frowned. 'Did she used to make you get the ba' when it went over?'

'Yes, always,' Lizzy said. 'If there was a dog, I used to take a treat for it, so it wouldn't bite me. Like a biscuit.' She watched as he mulled this over. Then he grabbed the biscuit tin from the side behind his mum, and ran outside. Lizzy hoped he'd take some for himself too, because he was stick thin.

Molly brought her a mug of tea and had filled up her own glass to the brim again. 'The boys get into trouble all the time. Wee shites, they are.' She sat down heavily, her belly hanging out over the top of her jeans. Some of the drink spilled on her chest, but she didn't seem to notice. 'I'll put them all in front of the telly if they don't shut up. The magic eye. And what about you, Lizzy? Don't tell me you married that Simon.'

The tea looked funny. The milk had curdled on the top. Perhaps it was off. Lizzy put down the mug and took a tart. 'I met my husband

Alfie six years ago. Snog at first sight, he says, silly sod. I left Simon when we were still kids. He got into bad drugs and he hit me one day, and I knew if he hit me once, he'd do it again. I got work on a market stall, sorted myself out. But the sad thing is he got himself killed on the tube. Fell onto the tracks when he was out of it.'

'That's terrible. Poor Simon. I mean, he was a bastard for hitting you, but still, no one deserves that. Any kids?'

'Not yet.'

'Don't. They're wee marriage breakers,' said Molly. She'd finished her second drink now, and was staring into the glass. 'If I could go back in time, I wouldn't have had them. I don't like sending the kids off to Duncan and his ma at weekends though. She's a cow. Chain smokes as well, in that tiny flat. The boys have to sleep on the floor.'

Lizzy shoved the last of the tart into her mouth and leaned back into the armchair, not sure what to say. Outside the dog was growling, a low, gravelly noise of a bred-to-fight kind of dog. Upstairs, the little girl was coughing again. The house felt empty.

Molly went to the kitchen again, mumbling about getting through the end of the day somehow. Lizzy shouted through, 'Do you have to send them every weekend?'

'Ach, it's complicated.' Lizzy heard the sound of ice cubes rattling in a glass. 'Courts gave them rights.'

There was a smell coming from beneath Lizzy's chair, like moldy food or a forgotten spill. If she'd stayed in Dalbegie, would she be living in this state? A few years on the street had been hard enough, but this seemed even worse, because it was more permanent. No way up or out. When you were homeless, you were free.

'Have you ever heard anything more about Mum? We did our investigating at The Chinese, remember? She'd been for dinner there, that night. Someone said she'd been with some bloke. I saw it's shut down now.'

Molly sat down, wiping mascara from under her eyes. 'Aye, that's right. But we never found out who the man was. I thought it was your dad, if you don't mind me saying.'

'But you don't know that for sure.'

'No one knows the truth. Lizzy, you've got to go with your gut feelings sometimes. I've learned that much over the years.' Molly gulped her drink. 'What do you think?'

'I don't think it was my dad.'

Molly pointed her finger. 'Then it wasn't him.'

Lizzy felt relief surge through. 'Thanks, Molly.'

Her dad wouldn't have done anything as bad as murder. She'd know if he'd been lying. Her mind turned to the white cottage opposite the newsagents, to the peeling paint and the pristine row of garden tools in the back that she'd disrupted. That smell of antiseptic that had filled Oliver's living room. It was a hospital smell, without the reassurance that usually went with it.

When she left, the kids all came to the door to wave her off. Molly poked them. 'What do you say for those Smarties?'

'Thank you, Lizzy,' they said in unison.

Craig had a finger up his nose, which Molly slapped out again. 'For god's sake,' she said, 'can you stop digging for gold?'

Lizzy waved and made her way down the street, thankful that it hadn't started to rain despite the black clouds gathering overhead. Molly had terrible dark rings around her eyes. She must love her kids, but the love was being smothered by the pressure of having them, of being alone with all that responsibility. *Wee marriage breakers.* Lizzy couldn't bear the thought of not being with Alfie. Now she'd found him, she wouldn't let him go. Not for some kid. Not for anything.

൦ඁ൦ ൦ඁ൦ ൦ඁ൦

It was too early for this. Tilda's front door was banging, loud and urgent. There was shouting, a man's voice. Lizzy knew it was her dad again, even before Tilda called up to her. *Here we go again.*

She'd been retching into the toilet for a while, but nothing was coming up. For a couple of days she'd felt the morning sickness dying down, but no such luck that morning. Waves of nausea made her head throb, her eyes watering and red.

She wasn't in the mood for him.

Already dressed, she slipped on her boots and marched downstairs. Tilda met her halfway, wiping her hands on her apron, white flour in her hair. She looked like an apparition, part of a haunted house. Lizzy sighed. 'That's him again, isn't it?'

'It is, darlin'. He says it's urgent. I'm awful sorry. I'd get Ken to warn him off, tell him not to come so early, but he had a few too many last night with auld Taff, and he's still in his bed with a hangover.'

This wasn't fair on Tilda. Lizzy stomped down the hall to the front door, where her dad was standing with his feet apart, arms folded. His cheeks were red, and there were damp patches under the arms of his shirt, despite the cold. His big coat was over his arm.

'What do you want?' Her voice echoed, and she didn't like the hollow sound of it. She didn't want him to think she was afraid.

'I want to see you,' he said. 'You're my daughter.'

Lizzy noticed he'd dropped the 'my girl' thing. Good. It had sounded too familiar, like they'd been close once. 'Why so early?'

'I couldn't wait.'

She stepped forward. 'Well, I'm here. You've seen me now.'

'Fancy a walk?' He dropped his arms by his sides and shifted his feet. 'We could talk.'

'Is it cold?'

'Aye.'

'I'll go and get my bag and my coat. I'll just be a minute.' Lizzy turned and left him there, feeling his eyes on her back as she went upstairs. She'd wanted to talk to Alfie first thing, and then she was meant to go to Auntie Maureen's, who'd found some things of Mum's for her. She wanted to tell her dad to come back another time, but the sight of him had got to her. He was pathetic, really. A sorry sight.

Soon they were walking to the river, side by side. Lizzy noticed they stepped at the same pace, their long legs striding. Genes were a powerful thing. The rain was holding off, but the air was damp, fine spray from the gushing water on her face. She hadn't forgotten about the river exactly, but when they got to the banks, it jolted some memories. It was one of her teenage hangouts, the long reeds hiding all the underage drinking and smoking. The lower banks were flat but muddy, not a popular kind of walk. Some kids had graffitied the low wall under the bridge—not the creative kind, but with black, ugly words and gang symbols.

She glanced at her dad. He should know how things had gone without him. She slowed a little. 'I used to come here with my boyfriend. Simon was the one I ran away to London with. We used to smoke down here and drink booze that he nicked off his mum and her boyfriend Roy.'

She didn't mention the kissing. Simon was good at that. He had tasted of lager and cigarettes, bubble gum and mints.

He stopped his stride and turned to face her. 'That's young to be drinking and smoking with some lad.'

Lizzy continued, leaving him to follow. 'It was. We did whatever we liked. Never went to school. Roy used to give us packages of drugs to deliver, and sometimes a packet of our own to snort.'

He shook his head, his face reddening. 'Where is he now, this Roy? Are they still here, the family?'

Oh, you wish. 'I don't know about the rest of them, but Simon died on the streets.' Lizzy looked up at the bank and wondered where exactly they used to sit. They would be surrounded by grasses, sheltered from the world, the sound of the river loud but calming.

'Jesus, Lizzy. That could have been you.'

'And you would never have known. No one would. We were lost kids.'

An image of Simon's face appeared in her mind, before he became a down-and-out, a mess. He was a handsome boy, gentle, despite his fierce tattoos and his shaved head. She'd let him down as much as anyone, in the end. He'd found her in the market, come to her in a mess. She'd helped him by giving him her day's wages and sending him on his way. What she should have done was take him back to her bedsit and scrubbed him. He'd needed her and she was too full of her own problems to help.

That was the day he died.

The guilt of it had stayed with her since, a heavy weight resurfacing once in a while to torment her. Simon was gone because no one had cared about him, not even her.

Her dad scratched the back of his neck. He took a deep breath and whooshed it out, as if he were building courage. 'I'm sorry I left you. I was badly in debt. My girlfriend at the time, Jeannie, was working down the bank as a teller and I was doing two shifts, one after the other, down the building site. We didn't have time for much else but keeping ourselves alive. But I should have taken you down south with me, when your mother disappeared. That's what I should have done. I know that now.'

Lizzy shrugged. 'Maybe. But it's all been and gone. I grew up fast and did the best I could.' Some heavy drops of rain touched her face and she put up her hood. 'Should we turn back?'

'Aye.'

They changed direction, her dad sniffing a lot, and looking at his feet. After a time, he asked, 'What does your Alfie do for a living? English, is he?'

'He's a salesman. Works in electronics. And yes, he's English.'

He nodded. 'As long as he's good to you, that's the main thing.'

It was an unexpected thing for him to say. 'He is,' she said. 'He's the best there is.'

The churning sounds of the river made up for their silence as they made their way back to the road. Lizzy had a sudden urge to hold his hand and swing it. He was so tall, and she felt childish next to him.

'When I was a kid, did we used to come down here?'

'No,' he said. 'I'd take you to the swings, though, with that Molly. A right one she's turned out to be.'

'I've seen her. She drinks a bit.'

'She lives in the pub, that one, or down the Social making an arse of herself. Keep away, I would.'

'Keep away? She was a good friend. I'm not going to get rid of her, just like that.' It was so like him to want to discard someone.

'Right enough, Lizzy.' He looked away. Like he knew.

When they parted, he held out his hand to her and she pressed her palm against his huge one. A pulse travelled along her arm as they touched. She'd been avoiding eye contact, but now their eyes met, the look running deep into her veins. She felt her anger subsiding, turning into a warm feeling that he would defend her at all costs, an animal protecting his cub. She felt it. His arms were thick as trunks, his chest rounded and hard. Powerful.

'See you soon,' she said.

As he strode away, she turned and watched his coat swishing at the back of him, the broad shoulders and that thick, powerful neck. When she was little, he was Superman, the ultimate hero. He could do anything, be anyone. A few times she'd seen the other side of him, the mean streak, and the halo would fade. It was there now, though, shining a little brighter than before, morphing into shape.

People learned from their mistakes, didn't they?

Lizzy turned back to Tilda's, past a row of bungalows with neat, clipped lawns out front. Some places were kept nice, cared for.

As long as he's good to you.

He was her blood and he cared. She put her hands on her belly and felt the small, hardening mass, the next line of blood to come. She was growing her son or daughter—and his grandchild.

As she trailed her finger along the low brick wall in front of the bungalows, a warm glow spread from her belly and into the rest of her. For the first time, it felt like the sun, radiating. A new beginning. Wanted.

CHAPTER SIXTEEN

Fairy Stories

Your dad's getting to you, wheedling his way into your heart again. I can see it all unfolding. Wee girls and their daddies; everyone knows they have a special bond. When you were too young to realize what was going on, you near on idolized him. He'd use it against me, say I was a terrible mother, and no wonder you'd rather he read all the bedtime stories, take you to the swings, sit with you at the Saturday morning pictures. He thought he was winning, that you loved him more than me. I didn't see him take over the three meals a day, all that cooking and clearing up, mind. I was good for all of that, wasn't I? I was working at the shop as well as doing all the laundry, the cleaning, scrubbing and washing his shirts, making sure there was a cold beer for him in the fridge.

I was a doormat.

If I could start all over again, I'd pick myself up, brush off the trampled-in dirt, and stand up to him. I'd throw him out before he had a chance to leave me.

It's what gets to me the most, that I never had the guts.

I kept your favourite book when I was alive, the fairy story that your dad used to read to you. I don't know why I saved it. Not because it reminded me of him, that's for certain. It was a piece of you, a memory. It's a terrible thing to say, but I felt relieved the first time you saw him kicking off. I'd protected you for so long and I was tired of it, the pretending. I wanted his bubble burst, for you to see him for what he was.

They say you should shelter your bairns, but I wanted you to hate him like I did, so I never had to see him again. As it happened, I didn't have to tell you anything. You saw it for yourself.

ᴔᴧ ᴔᴧ ᴔᴧ

He'd had a few. It was late. He wanted to go out, and I made some comment about the fact that he'd probably had enough. We were in the kitchen, and I was clearing up the dinner things, wiping the counters. You were in bed asleep, or so I thought. The telly was on in the front room, some news reporter or documentary voice, booming.

'You're getting at me again,' he said. 'You're a nag, aren't you? A right fuckin' nag.' He crushed his can of beer and chucked it into the sink, soapsuds splashing. 'If I want to go to the Dram, I'll go.'

'All right,' I said. 'Just go, then.' I wanted him out, now that he was getting annoyed. He was sweating and panting. Building up.

'Just go? I'm not done here yet. I'll go when I'm ready, woman.' He grabbed another beer out the fridge, cracked the ring pull and chugged it back. Some of it spilled down his front and he rubbed it into his jumper. He was drawing in.

'Don't you come near me.' I picked up the nearest thing, a wooden spoon. I held it up, pathetic, no use to anyone. I set my gaze on the clock on the wall, behind him. There was a stain on the rim that I hadn't noticed before. It was like having macro vision, but for the wrong thing. I didn't see what was coming, and it came fast.

He grabbed my head and pushed down. My nose cracked on his knee. Blood on the kitchen floor. Blood on my slippers. Then he pushed me back against the wall and held up the wooden spoon.

'You threatening me with this?' He jabbed the end of it into my chest. 'In my house? I paid for this fuckin' spoon and everything else in this place.'

I kicked, I pushed, but he was so strong. That's the thing. I couldn't get away. I screamed and shouted for him to stop poking me with that thing, but of course he didn't. It made him more furious. And the worst bit: I caught a glimpse of your nightie disappearing off down the hall. You'd seen it all.

I was covered in bruises after that. He didn't know his own strength, he used to say. Every time.

One night he punched me square in the face. My nose bled for hours after, dripping and swelling inside. I told you that I'd tripped on the stair. It was so awful, calculated. A punch in the face can't be forgiven. I'd been at work all day and I was dead tired, hadn't made anything for dinner. I was thinking we'd go and get fish suppers for our tea. But your dad had other ideas. He'd spent a load of cash in the Dram and didn't want to have to go out and spend more on food. I said I'd go and get them, but he said that wasn't the point. The point, I said, was that I was tired from work and didn't feel like cooking. I knew he wouldn't like that, me answering back, but I'd had enough that day. Jessica had been skiving off again, and my feet were aching, a headache creeping in. Then the punch came and I wished I'd never come home.

What a terrible thing to wish.

In those days, kids were left to fend for themselves, at whatever age. I'm trying to think how old you were then, when I was working all day and your dad was in the pub. Eight or so? These days you'd probably get the social services 'round, taking the kids away into care. I'd have been a headline for that. 'Mother leaves young daughter home alone.' Just because it was 'back then,' does it make it right? It was what we did, but then look what happened to you. You grew up too fast. You left.

It breaks my heart, to know that you miss me so much. I don't deserve it. Didn't deserve it.

But all of that was a long time ago, for you. Your emotions are all over the place. You're back home in Scotland; you feel closer to me, to your heritage. And Lizzy, you've got different eyes now you're going to be a mother. That sense of family gets stronger with each week of mounting hormones, raging in your blood, controlling your mind. Family is everything when you're pregnant.

I can't blame you for wanting to know your dad again, but don't let him get too close. Don't build him back up to the hero, because when that happens, things will start to go bad. And you know, you're not a little girl anymore, but a woman who answers back and knows her own mind.

That's his worst kind of a woman.

CHAPTER SEVENTEEN

The Jewellery Box

L izzy called Alfie as soon as she got back to the B&B. She lay on the bed, one hand stroking her belly. *He* or *she* was in there, cells multiplying, becoming a real person. It was amazing that they'd made a person, a miracle. Why hadn't she thought of it that way before? She looked at the photo on the bedside table. It would be a part of mum, genes rolling on from generations before. If it was a girl, she could call her Lauren.

Lauren. It was a beautiful name. Timeless.

Alfie was chewing something and slurping at what she knew was a cup of strong builder's tea. 'You saw your old man again, then? Did he behave himself?'

She held the phone away from her ear. 'Steady with the chimps' tea-party noises. Dad seemed sort of sorry for himself. I felt like holding his hand. Is that wrong?'

He gulped. 'Don't let him get away with it, will you? I know what you're like at the moment, you soppy thing. Promise?'

She lied. 'Promise. I'll never forgive him for what he did.' Now she'd seen him again, things were different. It was hard to explain. She pressed her fingers lightly into her flesh. 'I wonder what we're having.'

'What, the baby?'

'Yeah.' She shut her eyes and tried to imagine one or the other. *Lauren.*

'Doesn't matter, does it? They all look like old men in the beginning.'

'Alfie!'

'Well, they do. I dunno. A boy, I reckon.'

The conversation turned to Alfie's job search. He didn't ask how she was feeling, and she held off telling him she'd been sick that morning. He seemed to want to avoid talking about the baby. Maybe it would make it too real. He needed to find work before thinking about another mouth to feed, and so she didn't push, stress him out. All the things that were on her mind now would have to surface later.

But she was used to that, keeping things in.

☙ ☙ ☙

Later that morning, Lizzy walked to Auntie Maureen's, who'd dug out her mum's old jewellery box, along with some photos and postcards from the loft. Her fiftieth birthday was coming up, and she'd decided to have the party early while Lizzy was still there. The hall was booked for that coming Saturday, and 'everyone' was invited. Except for her dad and Nicole, of course. They weren't exactly flavour of the month in Maureen's world.

Lizzy offered to help decorate the hall on Friday, when Billy and his girlfriend were coming down from Inverness to set up the bar. Years later, and she was still doing all the skivvy work for Maureen. Still, it would be great to meet the rest of the family. It would save a few trips out, houses to visit. She could quiz everyone there about Mum in the one night.

On her way back, she passed by the Dalbegie Dram. It was lunchtime now. Inside would be the hard-core drinkers. She looked up at what looked like the original sign still hanging there, the blue paint cracked and dirty. The front door was vandalized, spray-painted with some random tag, cigarette butts littering the pavement and the gutters out front.

A woman staggered out of the front door. She was wearing torn spandex trousers and a tight top that barely covered her wrinkled chest. She must have been freezing.

'All right, all right, I'm going,' she muttered. 'And fuck the lot of yous.' She stumbled in her high heels.

Lizzy backed away as the woman leaned against the wall of the pub, and belched. 'Naebody fuckin' gives me a break,' she said to herself. 'All I wanted was another drink. Nae harm in that.' Her voice was deep, gravelly. She lit up a cigarette and noticed Lizzy. 'What you staring at?'

'Nothing.' She realised then who it was. *Shit.* It was Simon's mum. Her face was covered in deep lines, crevices almost.

'Well I'm no' a fuckin' show. Get lost.' The woman began to walk away, tripping on a broken paving slab.

Should she follow her? She could still be in the same house, where Simon lived, where Lizzy used to go all the time. Roy had lived there, too.

The woman hobbled on, flicking her ash into the wind. *Let her go.* She wouldn't be any use to Lizzy, not the state she was in. She didn't need to see some falling-down house that she used to visit. It didn't matter to her now. The woman made her way to the end of the road, still sucking on her cigarette. Her hair was matted at the back, the grey roots showing, a cheap plastic hair accessory plunked in the middle of a badly made bun.

Did she know what happened to her son? Would she care? The thought of Simon made her change her mind, and Lizzy jogged to the end of the road to follow her. She might find out about Roy.

They took a detour at the off-license, a rundown building on the corner, with barred windows, filthy and yellow. Was it the one where they used to nick voddie? Old haunts. Lizzy couldn't see what his mum bought from the owner, a huge man with overgrown sideburns, but it was a large bottle shoved into a brown paper bag. Then she was on her way again, lighting up another cigarette, a foot twisting every so often in her heels. She started to hum a tune, indecipherable, a throaty soundtrack for the rest of the journey. Lizzy kept a short distance behind, not worried she'd be noticed. That woman wouldn't notice a bus coming up behind her.

Finally, she turned into a street, not far from Molly's place, and Lizzy instantly knew it. There was a short curve at the beginning, scattered hedges, a lamppost on the left-hand side. The woman disappeared up the pathway of a semi-detached house with tatty net curtains. Simon's house.

She rang the bell while hunting through her bag for the key. 'Let us in, will ye. I'm bustin' for a piss,' she shouted.

Classy. Lizzy hid behind the nearest bush while the front door opened.

A man's thin voice. 'Where've you been, Lil? Did you get the bottle?'

'Aye, here ye go. Get out my road, eh, I'm desperate.' She barged into the house and disappeared. The door banged shut.

Lizzy held back. Lil was her name. It didn't mean anything to her, as she'd known the woman only as 'Simon's mum.'

Courage. She shuffled up the worn path and put one foot on the doorstep. If she could come here and brave Simon's mum when she was thirteen, she could do it now. She reached forward and rang the bell.

There was some muffled talking, irritated voices behind closed doors. Then silence. Perhaps they wanted to settle into an afternoon of uninterrupted drinking. Lizzy turned to face the street. A dog had begun a growling bark a few doors up, hurling itself against a metal gate by the sound of it. That part of town reminded her of where her old London bedsit used to be, where she'd slept on a mattress on the floor with no heating. The houses were cracked and crumbling, dog shit on the pavement, the roads chalked with swear words and hopscotch, tell-tale signs of kids' boredom and teenage angst. This was rough, even for Dalbegie, where there were no upscale areas, an absence of the middle classes. It was the bad end of a bad town. The high-rise loomed a couple of blocks away, rows of small, square windows and stairwells from top to bottom. It hadn't been there before, a new addition that wasn't exactly a step up.

Screw it. She rang the bell again, had come a long way to let this go. She heard raised voices, an argument about who should answer, perhaps.

In the end, the door opened a fraction, and the man appeared. 'What is it?' He had a ring of hair around his bald head, like a monk, and a three-day beard.

'My name's Lizzy. I used to be a friend of Simon's. I think his mum still lives here. Lil, is it?' She took a step back, keeping her distance from the door. The smell of stale cigarette smoke was overwhelming. There was also an acidic overtone that made her eyes sting.

'Lizzy, you say?' He shouted behind him. 'Lil! It's a girl, Lizzy, says she used to know your Simon.'

'Who?'

'Lizzy,' he shouted. 'An old friend of Simon's. Blonde. Skinny. Oh, shite,' he said, letting the door fall wide open. 'It's you. Lauren's girl. Is it you?'

He opened the door wide, his mouth open. Lil came up behind him, a cigarette between her lips, cracks around her mouth. Her top button had come undone, showing a leopard print bra with yellow straps. 'I mind who you are. I've a good memory for faces. You were the tart who took my Simon away. Fuckin' cheek you've got coming 'round here. What do you want, anyways?'

'Easy, there, darlin'. She's my niece. You better come in,' he said to Lizzy. He stepped back, barging Lil aside.

'All right, no need to fuckin' push me. I'm away into the kitchen to finish my fag.'

Lizzy put her fingers to her forehead. There was a lot to take in. Did he say she was his niece? She didn't have any uncles. Although she did once. Slowly it dawned on her who he was. Maureen's ex-husband. He was her uncle Brian. He'd aged a hundred years. He couldn't have been older than fifty-odd, but he looked like he was well on his way out. 'I didn't know,' she whispered. 'Maureen didn't tell me you were living here.'

'Aye, well she doesn't like it,' he said. 'Are you coming in, Lizzy? It's awfy cold.'

Lil had disappeared. Lizzy stepped inside. 'Okay. Just for a minute. I don't want to intrude.' They went through to the kitchen, where Lil scowled, dragging on her cigarette. A bare light bulb hung in the middle of the room. A draught was coming from the back door, a plastic blind rattling against the glass.

Roy had beaten half the life out of Simon in that kitchen. He'd punched Simon in the face, and the back of his head had hit Lizzy's nose and made it bleed. Then he gave her the package to take to Oliver, or she wouldn't see her 'fuckin' cunt of a boyfriend' again. He'd called her 'Princess,' but she'd felt like anything but. When she delivered the package and came back, she found he'd beaten Simon to a pulp anyway, just because he'd felt like it.

She hoped he was dead.

'I came back to find out what happened to Mum.' It was the first time she'd said that out loud. Somehow it didn't matter with these two. They didn't count. Brian was slumped at the chipped countertop, eyes shifting.

Lil pointed her cigarette at her. 'How the fuck should we know? Never mind your ma. You tell me what happened to my son. You were with him down there in London, weren't you? I got a call to tell me he was dead. I didn't even know where he'd gone. You all left me. Him, you, and that fuckin' bastard Roy.'

Brian leaned forward, head in his hands. Hiding. Lizzy felt a pang of hatred for him too.

She gripped the back of a chair. 'Roy never went with us. We were running away from him. Don't you remember what happened that day? Roy beat the shit out of Simon.' Blood had gushed from Simon's head, his limp body on the kitchen table.

'All I know is you and your ma thought you were better than everybody else, but you weren't. You were a wee slag, took away my boy. And she married a wife-beater and got herself murdered. Serves her bloody right.'

Lizzy scraped the chair across the floor. Every cell, every vein in her body trembled with rage. 'How dare you. Don't you say she deserved to be murdered. *You* killed Simon because you didn't give a shit about him. You were never there for him, always pissed, or off your face on drugs, you stupid cow, like you are now.'

Her eyes burned. She picked up the chair and threw it like it was weightless. It crashed against the back door.

Lil began to scream. 'Get out of my house, you fuckin' little bitch. Get out! Coming here, with all this shite.'

Brian motioned for Lizzy to leave. 'Sorry love. It's time for you to go.'

Lizzy clenched her fists. 'Don't worry, I'm going. Before I do something I'll regret.'

'Don't come back here, judging me. I was his Ma. You were a midden, a wee slag with your legs open for him. Simon didn't give a shite about you.'

'That's bollocks and you know it. I was the only one who cared about him.'

Lil took a long toke, regarding Lizzy through screwed up eyes. Then she turned to face the window, smoke billowing

Lizzy marched to the front door, Brian close behind. She turned to him. 'She's a monster. What are you doing here, with her?'

'Nothing's perfect, Lizzy.' He smiled faintly. He was still looking at his shoes, his hands, anywhere but her.

'Don't you smile at me.' As Lizzy left, she could still hear Lil's screams ringing in her ears. She'd always left that house in anger. She kicked a stone and it skittered down the road and into the gutter. *Fuck her. Fuck that woman.*

She'd get a Coke and a Twix from the shop on the way back. Some sugar would make her feel better. Lil had failed her own son and blamed everyone but herself. Seeing her made Lizzy feel less responsible for Simon's death, in a way. The guilt about ditching him in London was beginning to dissolve from the edges. His emaciated, filthy body was torn apart under that train. At least he didn't have to see his mum in that state again, worse now than she ever was.

Best he was gone from this world. It had never been kind to him.

CHAPTER EIGHTEEN

Helen's Vantage Point

Helen had ventured out in the early hours of the morning, and walked for miles around the outskirts of the town, surveying the place. The skies were low and drizzling, and she had her hood up, wooly hat pulled down to her eyes, tall wellies keeping her feet dry. It wasn't a bad look, actually, as it disguised her, made her even more bland. She was just some boring old woman, on her way.

There were puddles and sodden bracken in the outer parklands, and her boots got caked in mud. Even the ancient playpark by the block of flats to the east was flooded and empty, remnants of underage drinking scattered on the pathway and around the shelter. Cider bottles and empty fag packets, the odd used condom crushed into the ground. Everyone had their fun already. Now it was time for hers. She was on her holidays.

Helen's knees were aching after the recce, but she couldn't linger in a public place, just in case. So she climbed up a tree, a Scots pine. The first fork was wide and strong, thick enough that she could sit cross-legged and lean back into the trunk. It was quite comfortable, and dry too under the umbrella of foliage. She hung her rucksack on a short branch. It seemed out of place, this tree, a thick barrier against the barren concrete at the far end of the High Street. Must have been left over from all the trees they chopped while they built this eyesore of a place. But there it was, wallpaper to most people no doubt, and it gave her a good view of all the little scurrying bodies going about their business. All of them had their place in life, some kind of purpose. Ants. But what was it all for? She'd never been able to fathom the speed of the majority. *Slow down. Look around you, because you never know what's coming.*

Quite comfy. Mustn't fall.

When she opened her eyes again, there were more people about on the street and her legs were numb and tingling. She shifted, and rubbed her calves. She took a cereal bar out from her bag and ripped open the wrapper with her teeth.

Two middle-aged men came out of a bank a few metres away, stuffing their wallets into their trouser pockets. They were grinning. She heard one of them say, 'that's us to the pub, eh?' as he slapped his friend on the back. She thought of Steve and wondered if he'd be in the pub by now, slugging back a pint before lunch. When she was away from him, and didn't have to see his stupid face, she didn't mind the idea of his funny ways. What he did was up to him. She threw the empty wrapper down and it floated in the breeze away from the tree and into the gutter. It sat there, flapping, like a fortune-telling fish from a Christmas cracker. It was so shiny. She stared at it, her eyes glazing over.

What to do next?

She couldn't go back to that room yet, all the crashing kitchen noises. But she shouldn't be out in busy places in broad daylight. *He* might see her and that would ruin everything. She wanted to watch him, turn the tables, and find out what he got up to there. Because there was no way he'd stay in that place for months without a fix or two of something extraordinary.

✿ ✿ ✿

They were a great team, back in the day. The times they went out in the car, one of their favourite Friday night pastimes, picking up pished-up idiots and taking them where they didn't want to go. The young and useless took up the offer of a lift when there was a woman in the car, and especially when it was raining. Oliver couldn't have done it without her. But there was a patronizing undercurrent when he admitted that, a superior tone to his voice. He was the driver and she the assistant.

Well, times change.

ᘒ ᘒ ᘒ

More time passed. But it was still too light, too exposed to keep watch near his house. Helen decided to return to the playpark that she'd found earlier, and sit amongst the shrubbery. She wasn't interested in kids, but sloping, bored teens might come out of the cracks eventually. It was a place to smoke, to be away from school, to paw at each other or scrap with each other. Some scrubber of a girl might catch her eye. She'd have hoop earrings, hair slicked back into a ponytail with too much gel, a puffy jacket, too short. Like the worst girls she went to school with, all mouth and little to show for it. They thought they were hard stuff, but they were easy targets for her now.

She waited until the street was clear again. Some woman dressed in a long raincoat and fur-lined boots was wandering towards the café. An older couple trundled a shopper across the street. She jumped down, gathered herself quickly, then hobbled away, her legs getting used to moving again, following the curve of the street and back towards the council estate.

It would be her first conquest in this town. Catch of the day. No one of significance knew she was here, and being under the radar meant everything. No matter there were few places to hide. The important thing was to leave no trace—and never get caught.

CHAPTER NINETEEN

A Fish Supper with Jonno

They didn't have much, back then. This was all that was left: a cardboard box full of random objects that to anyone else was tat. Nothing but everything.

Lizzy texted Nat. 'Got some of mum's stuff. Tears.'

Maureen had given her the box, caving in on one side, with a layer of thick dust on top. It had probably lived at the back of her wardrobe since it was retrieved from 20 Bryant Road. The papers and photos Lizzy set aside for the moment, placing the jewellery box in the middle of the bed. It had once been a treasure chest to open on her mum's dressing table, not quite forbidden, but precious. When she was a kid, she was never allowed to wear any of the jewellery, just pick things up, touch them, and put them back carefully.

Nat texted back, 'Aw, good luck. Thinking of you. Talking to a right c-word at the mo.'

She smiled, imagining Natalie talking in her clipped Siri voice at a pain in the arse customer. Then she bent down and smelled the wood of the jewellery box, ancient and well-worn.

Deep breath. She opened it up.

There was a ballerina inside. She was supposed to spring up and twirl around, but the spring was bent and she was lying face down, tutu up. Thinking about it, the thing had never worked. There were a couple of high-pitched *tings*, when the metallic music strip was supposed to play a tune and turn the doll, but it didn't get going. Underneath were small compartments lined with velvet, all full of silver and gold pieces: some earrings, a couple of delicate necklaces, a few bangles on top of everything. She'd forgotten that Mum used to wear earrings, but it came back to her now; the pearls, the black studs. She pushed her finger through a tangle of chains and began to wonder what was missing, what Mum had been wearing when she disappeared.

The Scottish Cross.

The necklace that Granny Mac gave Mum wasn't there. It had been her favourite, long and gold, with a heavy Celtic blue-green cross. Mum wore it a lot in the days before she left, touching it while it was around her neck, all sentimental. Lizzy picked up a pair of earrings, delicate sliver droplets, and held them to her lobes. She'd never bothered having her ears pierced. Mum always said she would take her to have them done when she was older, but that day never came.

She put everything back in its place and shut the lid. She'd ask Alfie where to get a replacement music strip; he'd know about that sort of thing. She texted him, and he texted her straight back. 'Chin up. It's hard. I'll make it up to you, darlin'.' He always said the right things.

Now for the photos and the postcards.

They were bound up in a blue elastic band. She spread them out in a fan. The photographs were all of her, Mum, and Granny Mac, in different combinations. There was a familiar one of them all eating ice cream at the seaside. There were none of Dad. The postcards were silly cartoons, written to her and Mum from Granny Mac on her holidays. She must have been funny, Granny Mac, but Lizzy only vaguely remembered her infectious laugh. At the bottom of the pile was a children's book the size of a postcard, and barely thicker. It was a fairy tale, but not one she'd heard of, *The Fairy and the Miller's Wife.* On the inside cover were her initials, written in pink felt-tip pen. The pages were well worn, one or two of them torn near the spine.

There was ringing in her ears, a dull pain. Her pink, rounded writing, so innocent, contrasted cruelly with the rest of her miserable child-hood. She lay down on the bed, clutching the book to her chest. Tears ran from the corners, trickling down the sides of her face. She had many dimly lit memories of Mum, and the photos of her were so powerful that she could almost feel her here again. And there was a chance, a tiny one, that she might still be alive. Lizzy had never dared to think it before, but it was possible seeing as her body had never been found. Could she be one of those women kidnapped and hidden for years in some psycho's basement? There were enough stories like that on the news.

Are you alive, after all, Mum? Are you here, in Dalbegie, lost and for-gotten? Is that why I can sense you so strongly?

Dad used to read her bedtime stories when she was too young to read herself. She'd hold onto one of his forearms, playing with the little blond hairs, clinging to his every word while he told tales of old. He'd kiss her on the forehead, brushing aside her hair. *Good night wee bonny girl.*

She wrapped her arms around her own body as far as they would go. She could feel her blood flowing into the centre of her, nourishing, worshipping what was to come. It was thick with love, tenderness. Her own baby girl.

I hope you understand, Mum, why this is confusing for me. I haven't thought about Dad very much in years. It was like he didn't exist. But now, here he is, alive and kicking. He loved me once. We all loved each other. And I think he feels really bad about abandoning me. Maybe if I can push all the violent times to the back of my mind, if I focus on how he is with me now, in the present, I could forgive him.

It's not that what he did to you doesn't count. It does. But he's my dad and I think I need to give him another chance. One day, my daughter could stop talking to me, because of some stupid thing I did. And I'd hate to think she'd never forgive me. I get it, now more than ever.

I can still feel you here. I don't know what's worse. You being dead or you being alive in some terrible place, terrified of someone. I know where I've got to look, and I'm scared. But I'll go there again. Today. That's my promise to you.

She fell asleep on the bed, exhausted, and woke up half an hour or so later feeling better, ready. And starving. First she'd get some food, then business.

A fine, dewy mist had saturated everything, although the rain had finally stopped. Lizzy left the umbrella behind and put her hood up to save her ears from the wind, shoving her hands in her pockets. At the High Street, she scanned the shops along the road, and wondered if Dave's Discs was still around. She used to go there with Molly. Some of the signs were old and grimy; the electrical shop name was still hand painted, flaking at the edges. Maccy D's was still there of course, but she wouldn't eat in there, not with a baby inside her. It wouldn't seem right.

Where was that chip shop? It couldn't be far, if it was still around. Mum often picked up a carry-out on her way home from work. Fish suppers with pickled onions, trays on their laps, sat in front of the telly. That was the best dinner ever invented.

A woman came out of the tiny knitting shop behind her, its window crowded with dusty wool displays. 'Keeping out of the wind, there, are you doll? Once it starts raining again it won't stop for the rest of the day, I'll bet.'

Lizzy stepped closer. 'I wish I brought my brolly.'

The woman was wearing a multicoloured wool jacket with big pearl buttons. It might have been one of her own creations. 'Ach, you won't melt,' she said. 'You visiting, are you? I don't know your face, if you don't mind me saying.'

'Yes, and I'm looking for a few places I used to go to when I was a kid.' A tiny white cardigan with pale pink buttons hung in the middle of the window display. Lizzy pointed to it. 'I like the little cardy. Can I get all the stuff I need to make it?'

'Of course, dear. Come in and I'll gather it all up for you.' The woman went inside, trailing the scents of lavender and musty wool.

Lizzy followed, unsure. The inside of the shop was crammed full of different wools, racks of patterns, and knitting needles. She didn't even know how to knit.

'Is Dave's Discs still around? And is there a chip shop around here somewhere?'

The woman was packing up needles and white wool into a plastic bag. 'No, Dave had to close down years back. No one was buying, he said. Everyone was downloading. Cheaper for everyone, I suppose. His shop became a café that sells books, but I'm not sure if that's doing very well around here. Folk are more into the telly, if you ask me. But the chippy's still there, and hopefully always will be. Just a bit further up, turn left. You'll smell it before you see it.'

Lizzy ran her finger over a ball of Scottish Sirona green mohair. 'Oh great. I could murder a bag of chips. Is it still the same owner? I've forgotten his name.'

'The very same, and lovely boys they are. Jack still owns the place and his son Jonno is doing awful well in himself. He more or less runs it now, give or take a few wobblers. Do you know them, darlin'?'

Lizzy gasped. 'That was them, yes. I'd completely forgotten about Jonno. He used to sit and read books all the time, and he knew the answers to really hard questions that Jack used to shout out for him.'

'Still does,' the woman chuckled. 'He knows more than you think, that one.' She handed over the bag. 'That's a gorgeous cardigan you'll be making. Is it for someone special?'

'Yes.' Lizzy smiled as she gave her the money. 'A very special someone.'

She made her way further up the High Street, and before long the smell of the chip shop filled the air. Even though that fishy mix of salt and vinegar was universal, it was such a part of her childhood that her heart leapt. She used to sit and talk to Jonno, because no one else did, and because he was interesting. That knitting woman was right; he was 'knowing.'

There were three boys outside the chippy in baseball caps and filthy hoodies. One of them was holding a huge paper bag of chips, and they were spilling on the ground. The smallest one with ginger hair began to stamp on them.

Charming. As she got closer, she heard the ginger one calling to someone inside the shop. 'I'll pay you back tomorrow, promise.'

Another one pointed. 'That's a lovely hat you got yourself, Fish-Boy. Can I borrow it off you to wipe my arse on?'

They all laughed.

Lizzy got to the door and peered in. Jonno was behind the counter, clearly upset, pacing up and down, and wheezing in short, sharp bursts. She turned to the boys, who were still laughing, squashing the fallen chips into the wet pavement. 'What's going on? Didn't you pay for those?'

The one holding the bag flicked up his middle finger. 'Get to fuck, you nosy cow. Who are you, anyway? Mother fuckin' Theresa?'

'No, but I'm old enough to be your mother. Give him his money or I'll have a word with your parents. It won't be hard to find out where you live.' Lizzy stepped closer to him.

'Fuck off, you stupid bitch,' he said. 'Come on lads, let's away. Leave mumsy to dry Fish-Boy's tears.'

'You get back in there and pay.' Lizzy pointed at him, anger welling.

'No way.' He swaggered, a smirk on his face. The other two followed him, sniggering.

Lizzy contemplated twisting his arm behind his back, marching him into the shop and forcing him to pay. But she couldn't beat three boys like them. Instead, she went inside and shut the door behind her.

'Hello. You okay?'

Jonno stopped pacing. 'My name's not Fish-Boy.'

'I know. It's Jonno.' She stepped up to the counter. 'My name's Lizzy. I used to come here when I was their age.' There was a box of napkins on the counter. She pulled one out and gave it to him.

He wiped his brow, staring at her. 'They're from the estate up the hill. I don't like them.'

He had the same face, those inquisitive eyes that didn't stay on hers for very long, wavering here and there. He must have been in his mid-thirties now, overweight and pallid. The shop itself was immaculate, surfaces spotless, chairs and tables set out in perfect lines. On each checked tablecloth was a full bottle of ketchup, a malt vinegar, and a napkin dispenser. On the nearest table was a shiny *Guinness Book of World Records*.

'You're Lizzy,' he said. He studied her unabashedly, looking closely at her hair, her face, and momentarily into her eyes.

'You came back,' he said at last. 'You didn't write to me, though.'

'I ran away, Jonno, to London. I was living on the streets, and I couldn't write to you. I'm sorry.'

'On the streets like a homeless person?'

'Yes. For a while, anyway.'

'The world record for the longest pizza is a mile. It fed hundreds of homeless folk in California. You should have been there, not London.'

'Missed out on that one. Can I have a small fish supper please, and I'll eat it here. Maybe you could tell me what you've been doing.' She pulled out her purse and took out a twenty.

He put up his podgy hand. 'My dad says I'm allowed to give one free fish supper every year, to my best customer. My best customer is you.'

Lizzy laughed. 'I'm not sure that's what he meant, but that's really nice of you.'

'You told them to pay, and they were mean to you. They went away because of you though, Lizzy. You're my best customer now.' He grabbed a plate and piled it high with chips, then put a huge piece of cod on top. 'There.'

She took the plate and carried it over to the table at the window. 'Do you think I could have an orange juice? I'll be really thirsty after all this.'

'Coming up, Lizzy. My best customer gets a drink too.' He took a bottle from the fridge and brought it over. He stood next to her, watching her eat.

'Do you want to sit down for a minute? You'll want a rest before it gets busy.' She motioned at the seat opposite her.

'Yes, okay.' He sat down and put his hands in his lap, looking intently at the food on her plate. 'You were always my best customer, you know, even before you went away.'

'Was I? That's very sweet, Jonno. Do you want a chip? Or do you get sick of them, working here all the time?'

He patted his stomach so it wobbled. 'No thank you. I'm not sick of chips, but I shouldn't eat them all day long.'

'Where's your dad today? Jack isn't it?'

'He's gone to the bank to see the man who gives out more money.'

'Right.' She squirted ketchup over her fish and gave it a generous helping of malt vinegar. 'You make the best fish suppers ever.'

'Thank you. Not the biggest, though. The world record for the largest serving of fish and chips is 47.75kg.'

'That's big.'

'Mine are still the best, though. I put exactly the right amount of salt on.'

'Do you remember my mum, Jonno? She used to come in here a lot.'

'I mind her, a little bit, but not as much as you.' He shifted in his seat. 'And then she wasn't here anymore.'

Lizzy sighed. 'No. She never came back.'

He gazed out the window. 'I tried to tell them, but they wouldn't listen.'

Lizzy put down her fork. 'Tried to tell who? What did you try to tell, Jonno?'

'I tried to tell my dad and the policeman who talked too much. I wanted to tell them about the man with the hat. I shouted it out, twice. But they didn't listen. No one ever listened. They still don't.'

'The man with the hat? What do you mean?' *Jesus, did he know something?*

The bell on the door tinkled and an elderly couple walked in. 'Hello there, Jonno,' the woman called as she went to the till.

Jonno leapt up and went to serve the couple. Lizzy stared at her plate, in shock.

A workman came in next, and ordered a battered sausage, then a couple of kids asked for chips. Her legs jiggled up and down as she shovelled in some more food.

At last, Jonno came over, wiping his hands on his apron. 'I can take your plate away, if you're finished.'

'Oh thanks. But first, will you tell me what you were talking about earlier? You tried to tell your dad about someone, but he wouldn't listen.'

He scratched his head. 'It's too late, now. He was all around, then. But I don't see him much anymore. I tried to tell them about him. He was with your mum. He pushed her arm, I saw. I didn't like him.'

Lizzy could feel her heart pounding. 'Do you know who he was, Jonno? It's really important. Did you see them together?'

'Yes, I saw them. But I don't know his name. I'm sorry about that, Lizzy. You were my favourite person, and not everyone listens as well as you do.'

'So it wasn't my dad? His name's Rob. You know him, don't you?'

'It wasn't him. I don't like your dad, Lizzy, and I'm very sorry about that too. But it wasn't him that I saw.'

'I wish you'd told me, Jonno.'

He began to twist a napkin in his hands. 'I was going to, but I was scared of him. And also you stopped coming in as much, because you were with the bad men with the tattoos. And then you ran away.'

Jonno took Lizzy's plate back to the kitchen. He was humming tunelessly.

She gathered her things and made her way to the door. 'Thanks for the fish supper, Jonno. It was brilliant.'

He looked at the floor. 'I wish you still lived here.'

'I'll be back to see you before I go.'

'I'm sorry, Lizzy.'

'Nothing to be sorry for, Jonno. You're one of the best people I know.'

Lizzy stepped outside into the fresh air. Deep breaths. She could have pressed Jonno for more information, but didn't need to, not really. *The man with the hat.*

She turned back and pushed open the door. 'Was he tall and slim? Dark?'

Jonno shrugged. 'He was mean. Like a dark shadow. He wore black jeans and a long coat and he almost always wore gloves.'

Him. She felt a physical pull towards Oliver's place. She could break into his back garden again, and take a look through the windows. Maybe one would open from the outside, old and rickety, like the rest of the place. As Lizzy got closer the air thickened and the world went dark. *Dusk.* The truth sat, heavy in her stomach, a dangerous burden, waiting to be released.

CHAPTER TWENTY

Oliver's Shadows

She had come to me at last. I knew it was Lizzy as soon as I saw her slim figure in the shadow of the newsagents' awning, leaning against the wall. It could only be her. To anyone else in this town, I was a 'strange one' to be ignored; but to her, I was a fascination. We'd met under the most curious of circumstances.

I poked my binoculars through the kitchen blinds. It was nearly dark, but not enough that I couldn't see the stitching on her lapel, the blond curls escaping from the side of her hood, and those large, frightened eyes.

There. A frown was burrowing its way. She was pondering.

I kicked myself for going to the newsagents, for getting a warning from that fishwife that Lizzy was in town. It would have been the greatest surprise of all, to discover her standing before me, with no prior expectation, an angel fallen from the heavens. I would have recognized her straightaway. I would have known her even in silhouette, no matter how many years had passed.

As I watched, hidden in the half-darkness, she peered through the diminishing light towards my cottage, lifting her graceful chin as she studied the upstairs windows. My blinds were still down, lights off, and so there was nothing visible. But she would see my car in the driveway, and other signs of activity. She knew that I was back, and she wanted to see me.

After a time, she took a few steps forward. I held my breath as she appeared to stare directly through the binoculars into my eyes. But she didn't come closer. After a few moments, she turned away, her hair bouncing lightly.

My heart raced. I could run outside, pounce, and lure her back to the house. It was clear that she wanted to come closer, but hadn't found the courage. I grabbed my hat, but then stopped myself. I needed to think. I could easily put myself at risk by going out there now and exposing my desires. And whatever happened, she'd be back.

I took Bird from the mantelpiece, and cupped my hands around her, my thumbs stroking the soft fur. I wondered if it had been Lizzy who'd had the gall to enter my garden while I was away. Perhaps she moved my tools, and walked through the weeds to regard my compost. I rather liked to think it was her, trembling as she trespassed. Somehow the violation didn't seem so aggravating, but endearing and more than a little exciting. How long had it been since I set her free from my grasp? It must have been some thirteen years since she last saw me.

Unlucky for some.

Lizzy would eventually enter the house of the devil of her own accord, free spirited, just like her mother did during our 'romantic' night together. Lauren came to me despite herself, and now so would Lizzy.

Like mother like daughter.

Every woman knows the dangers of entering a man's abode, alone and vulnerable, and yet they continue to put themselves out to sacrifice time after time.

I scanned the street. A bad feeling continued to grip me, that someone had been sent to seduce me into giving myself away. I thought I saw movement coming from behind the shop, but it happened so fast. The street was deserted, the air curiously still.

When I could bear it no longer, I put on my hat and wool-lined leather gloves, and stormed outside. If someone was hiding out there, I would catch them. I darted around the back of the newsagents, but there was no sign of activity in the littered delivery area. I accidentally kicked an empty beer can and it clattered along the gutter amongst the wet leaves, making me jump. I felt a presence, someone there, and turned quickly, but there was no one. Despite the cold, I was sweating, with a sudden urge to pull off my clothes and cleanse.

It was despicable that I was so on edge. I knew deep down that my mind was playing games and hated myself for it. At the back of the shop were the deep, stinking bins, and I decided to pay them a visit, just like I'd done all those years ago. I lifted the heavy lid with my fingertips, wishing I'd worn two pairs of gloves. Inside was a mess of papers, cartons, out-of-date food, and black bin bags. At the far corner was a yellow strand sticking up out of the debris. I reached forward and pulled, and a substantial length of waxy twine unraveled, the kind that bound the stacks of newspapers together on delivery. This was the stuff of dreams. I couldn't wait to use it again, exactly as before. I did like a detail. Closing the lid, I ventured home with the tangle of twine in my coat pocket.

I could see outside of myself and knew that my clammy skin was a symptom of angst and pressure, and once I was safely inside, I washed only my hands under the hot tap as a penance for falling victim to my own emotions. With skin raw and burning, I sat before my computer screen, and became OwlVerse in the chat room for distraction. My throbbing fingers lingered on the keyboard, my vision slowly focusing on the screen.

I forced myself to concentrate, logged into the forum, and scanned some of the morning's entries. A new name had appeared: Parsley. I clicked on her entry and read the erratic deliberations of a woman in crisis. She was a middle-aged divorcee, the kind who lives with more than two cats. She spoke of her ex-husband, her childless existence, and drinking too much black tea. Who cared about black tea? It was hardly a drug.

I've suffered from depression for over ten years, since my husband left me. I have nothing to live for now.

Parsley sounded like the kind of desperate, easily influenced woman I was looking for. She was on the edge and isolated. Perfect. I noticed that Kitten555 had been straight in there with another virtual hug. The lovely MarigoldGirl offered her support, and told Parsley of her own experiences with divorce. I blundered in, wondering what proportion of women there were to men on the forum, and whether I would be seen as 'one of them.' I didn't say much, just that I hoped she would feel better. As an afterthought, I added some of my own 'feelings.'

My best friend moved away. It's hard for men to make new friends. I go to my local pub and sit at the bar. Sometimes I'm included in a conversation. I go to the supermarket and it's like I'm invisible. Depression is complicated. It shows itself here and there when we're least expecting it. Don't give up.

It made me sound quite sensitive. Someone even added a smiley face underneath my entry. It cheered me up, the audacity of my pretense, but my legs were still fidgety, my skin crawling. My ritual, a long-time procedure, would scrape it all away. I went upstairs and turned on the shower to its hottest setting. I threw my clothes in the laundry bin, and stepped into the steam, an act so routine and comforting that it sent me into a trance.

Soon I began to feel normal again, calm. As the water scalded my skin, and burned away the disquiet, I thought only of Lizzy. I scratched at my scalp with a pumice stone until the water ran pink, and the anxious thoughts flowed away. She had been mine from the beginning, and would stay mine to the end. *Ab initio. Ad finem.*

CHAPTER TWENTY-ONE

The Dram

L izzy made her way back to Tilda's, still sluggish after the huge fish and chips at Jonno's, her feet shuffling on the pavement like a worn-down old lady's. She needed a nap before going to Molly's place. As well as the tiredness, a blanket of tension had wrapped around her like plastic.

Oliver was back in town.

The overflow of mail had gone from his letterbox, and a car was in the driveway. He was lurking inside, behind closed curtains, she knew he was. She'd been drawn to his cottage since she got there. It taunted her, like a demon beckoning. She wanted it and didn't want it, repelled by Oliver, but attracted to the idea of finding out the truth.

She trudged along, wanting to feel the new life inside her emanating energy. But there was nothing inside her to feel, not a flutter or a sign. She tried to visualize her baby girl, but it wouldn't come, her mind too full of other, unwanted images. She should knock on his door and demand answers. But she'd never felt so defensive of her body, her own self. There was another, more important part of her now that needed protection.

The Dram loomed once more, its cracked walls drab and dingy in the low light and growing mist. Lil might be in there again, drinking her way through the afternoon with that smoker-voice of hers.

'Hey Lizzy, wait.'

It was *his* voice. *Shit.* Lizzy turned. 'Dad. I'm on my way back to the B&B for a nap. I'm knackered.'

He clapped his hands together. 'I'm going for a pint. Why don't you join me? I want to show you off. Come on, let your old man buy you a drink.'

He looked so pleased to see her. He was wearing a huge fisherman's jumper, and he looked round and huggable. Lizzy hesitated. 'I don't know. Maybe another time. I'm dead on my feet.'

'A quick half won't do you any harm. That'll be it, I promise, then I'll see you on your way to get a rest.' He motioned to the Dram. 'I bet you've never been in there.'

Lizzy nodded. 'Okay then, a quick drink.'

Inside, the ceiling lights were low and yellow, the windows frosted and dirty. There were about a dozen men spread out around the bar. The air smelled of bleach and the lingering stench of cigarettes, left over from the days when everyone smoked in pubs. The carpet looked like it had never been changed, the stains on the ceiling half-heartedly painted over. All eyes were on her.

'Who's this?' The lone woman behind the bar smirked, arms folded across her chest. She was wearing a t-shirt despite the cold, her forearms covered in tattoos. 'Not another one of your women, eh, Rob?'

A couple of the men sniggered, supping their pints and giving each other knowing looks. Lizzy glanced at her dad.

'This here's my daughter, Lizzy,' he said. 'Let's give her a welcome, shall we? Mine's a pint of the usual, there, Babs. What will you have, darlin'?' He put his hand on Lizzy's shoulder and gave it a gentle squeeze.

'Lime soda for me, please,' she said.

The barmaid smirked. 'Right.' She poured the pint first, then made a show of pouring lime cordial into a glass for Lizzy. 'Do you want a slice of lemon in your lime?'

'Yes, please.' She ignored the sarcasm and scanned the room. Lil wasn't there, thankfully. Lizzy didn't want a scene, although Lil had been in such a state the day before that it was possible she'd have forgotten what was done and said. Lizzy wondered how many of these paunchy men were there to escape their wives, which was what Uncle Brian used to do when he was with Maureen. And then she saw him, tucked away in a corner seat, supping his pint and staring at her. He looked like he never left that spot, set aside from the rest of them.

The man nearest to her turned on his seat and looked her up and down. He had white hair and a straggly beard, wet around his mouth from his pint. 'A daughter, eh, Rob? You're a dark horse. Where do you live, doll? Not around here.'

She gave him a stiff smile. 'London,' she said. 'I've been there since I was a kid.'

Her dad steered her over to a table by the window. 'Never you mind,' he said.

'Just being friendly.' The man shrugged and turned back to face the bar.

An older man with a huge belly held up his pint. 'Cheers to Lizzy. She's staying at me and Tilda's place. And a lovely guest she is, too.'

'Cheers to you, too,' Lizzy said, conscious of her accent, her stupid drink. So Ken was having a few pints while Tilda did all the work. *Typical.*

She sipped at her drink, the soda flat and warm. The formica table had a thin film on it, damp and sticky. 'Thanks for the drink,' she said.

'You're welcome. Next time we'll have a few real bevs, eh? Get ourselves greased up one night. Maybe have a laugh.'

She nodded. No one else was talking, and she had a feeling they were all listening in. A clock was ticking on the wall. Brian was staring intently and was starting to give her chills.

She lowered her voice. 'See Brian over there? Maureen's ex.'

Her dad glanced over. 'Is there a problem? If there is I'll tell him to get lost.'

'No, it's nothing,' she said, anxious not to cause trouble.

Brian downed the rest of his pint in one long gulp. He belched, wavered, then staggered over to their table. 'Lizzy. Sorry about what happened wi' Lil. Best stay away.'

'What'd you say? What did that skank do?' Her dad swiveled around in his seat, his face glowering. 'And don't tell my daughter to stay away. She'll go wherever she fuckin' well wants.'

Brian sniffed up the contents of his nose and then swallowed. 'All I'm saying, pal, is she's best to steer clear from Lil.' He pointed a finger at Lizzy as if it would help him focus. 'If she knows what's good for her.'

'What?' Her dad stood up.

'Are yous deaf?' Brian cleared his throat noisily, and made his way to the door, holding onto one of the tables on his way.

There was a collective sucking in of breath from all the punters.

Lizzy knew what was coming. Her stomach tightened. 'Let him be, Dad. He doesn't mean anything by it.'

'Get back here, you fuckin' piece of shite.' Her dad wasn't listening, already following Brian out the door. His fists were clenched.

Lizzy didn't see it but she heard it, the dull thump of fists on flesh, followed by a heavy fall to the ground. She started out, but before she could get to the door, a man grabbed her wrist and pulled her towards him. 'Are you that pal of Molly's, then?'

'Let go of me.' She pulled her arm away and glared at him. He looked about her age, too young to be a daytime diehard. His eyes were glazed, his skin pockmarked.

'I remember you from school,' he said. 'You were gorgeous then as well. I heard you were back. Wish I'd married you instead of my skank of an ex-wife.' He grinned at some of the other men at the bar, and there were some quiet chuckles.

'Duncan.' She felt her body slump with disappointment. He wore a lemon-yellow jumper, frayed at the cuffs. It looked like he'd had it twenty years.

'That's me.' He held his arms out wide. 'Did you miss me?'

'No. Looks like you're still a loser. Enjoy being in here, do you, and not with your kids?'

There was some swearing and shouting outside. Everyone was sat there, nonchalant, like it wasn't happening. Lizzy heard another thump. She winced.

Duncan wrapped his hands around his pint glass. He shook his head. 'I'm not allowed to see them in the week. I'm trying to get them back, full custody. She's an alchie, a fuckin' druggie. We get them for the weekend, me and my ma, and they're filthy and half-starved. Don't tell me I'm a fuckin' loser. I'm doing my best.'

'Maybe Molly's doing her best too.'

'I don't fuckin' think so.' He downed his pint and slammed his glass on the table. 'She's a liability.'

'Then get off your arse and help her.' Lizzy could have slapped him. He had a self-pitying manner she couldn't stand. 'Don't sit there and get pissed every day. Help your kids. And stop sniveling.'

That got another round of sniggers from the bar. Lizzy didn't care. She'd had enough. As she burst through the pub door, her dad met her eye with a brief look of shock, as though he'd forgotten she was there.

Brian was holding his nose. 'What the fuck, you crazy bastard.'

'That's for whatever Lil did. And for ordering my wee girl about. Now get to fuck back home.'

'Fuckin' psycho,' Brian mumbled as he brushed himself off and stumbled away, a hand to his face.

Lizzy backed away. 'Christ, you didn't have to hit him. What's wrong with you? I know he's weird, but he's my uncle.'

'Ach, it was just a tap. Let him know who's boss. He's not your uncle, not by blood. He's an ex-uncle, a nobody.' Her dad wiped his hands on the back of his trousers.

'You haven't changed one bit,' she said. 'Hit people a lot, do you? Do you still hit women as well? Do you slap Nicole about?'

Every time she took a step back, he took one forwards. His face crumpled, and he slumped down until he was sitting on the pavement, his feet in the gutter. It was raining again, not hard, but it soaked into Lizzy's hair, her cardigan, onto her skin.

'I couldn't help myself,' he said. 'I can't stand the thought of anyone hurting you, even if it's just words. I don't like that Brian, never have trusted him. I'd never hurt you, Lizzy. I'd do anything for you.' A trickle of rainwater made its way around his shoes and into the drain.

'I know. But I'm scared of you.'

She couldn't tell if the wet on his face was the rain or tears. He looked broken.

'I'm sorry,' he said. 'Please don't hate me anymore.'

She didn't hate him, but needed to get away from there, from him. Lizzy went back inside the pub to get her coat and her bags, waves of exhaustion pulling her down. The barmaid nodded with a new respect. No one said anything. Was there a silent rule? Don't get involved. Talk about it after, behind their backs, but don't jump into battles that weren't your own. She imagined the place full of bodies in the evening, drinks on all the tables, pop music on the jukebox. How many fights had this place seen over the years? The same people, in and out, some still here and some gone. Ghosts of what went before.

Before she left, she turned and opened her mouth to speak to the room, to the few curious pairs of eyes on her. But no words came. There was nothing to say, nothing to change. The door slammed shut behind her and echoed up the street.

Her dad had gone. She caught a glimpse of the bottom of a long grey coat sweeping around the corner of the street. He hadn't been wearing a coat, had he? She ran to the corner and turned, wanting to see him now that he'd gone. But it was some woman, short and squat, marching away. She should have felt pleased, but a wave of disappointment crept in.

He'd do anything for her.

There weren't many people in the world that could say that. She looked up and down for a sign of him, but both ends of the street were empty.

ols ols ols

On her way to Molly's, Lizzy started to wonder if there was a bit of truth in what Duncan had said about her and the kids. It was disturbing. Even Dad had mentioned Molly's drinking, and he liked a pint himself, hardly a saint.

Sure enough, Molly already had a large vodka in her hand when she opened her front door. 'I started without you. The kids were being terrible loud,' she said.

Lizzy followed her in, a strong smell of burned toast and a faint haze of smoke filling the hallway. 'Sorry I'm late. I got caught up in a pub fight.'

Molly chuckled. 'That's the old Lizzy back.'

She dumped her bags on the kitchen counter. 'Sticky buns for the kids. A bottle of voddie for you. I'll put the kettle on for me, if you don't mind. I've got a stinking headache now.'

'Suit yourself. More for me,' said Molly, who had parked herself on the sofa. Thick wool socks were pulled up over the elastic of her tracksuit bottoms. 'Although it's definitely booze o'clock now. Are you sure?'

Lizzy took out the carton of milk she'd brought with her and opened it up. She'd always hated black tea. 'Positive.'

Meg was sitting up at the table with a plate of blackened toast and what looked like a square of processed cheese squished between her fingers. The boys were outside kicking a football around, their plates more or less untouched.

'Can I please have my bun now?' Meg asked, looking at the bag intently.

'Is that all right, Molly?' Lizzy smiled at the little girl, who looked well overdue for a bath.

'Yeah, whatever.' Molly shouted to the boys. 'Boys, Lizzy's got sticky buns!'

Ryan and Craig came running in, and sat at the table, looking expectantly at Lizzy. Ryan was panting. 'A whole one each?'

Lizzy took out three plates and set them out. 'One each. Current buns with white icing on top. They were my absolute top favourite when I was a kid.'

All three kids cheered. They began to eat like dogs, chewing fast as if she might change her mind and take them back again. Meg went into a coughing fit, but she managed to cram in the bun before retreating back to her bedroom. Lizzy made herself a tea, while Molly drained her glass.

Molly yawned. 'While you're up, I don't suppose you can get me a refill?'

Lizzy took her tea through. 'Give me your glass, then. Do you want more ice in there?'

'Just voddie and a splash of tonic would be lovely. The tonic's in the fridge door. Have one with me. It could do wonders for your headache. It makes mine go away like a dream.'

'I'm fine.' Lizzy made the drink, going easy on the vodka. The inside of the fridge smelled of cheese or fish, or a rancid combination of both, and she shut it quick, trying not to heave. The boys were wiping their hands on their clothes. At least they'd eaten something now.

She sat facing Molly and sipped at her tea. 'I went to the chippy today and saw Jonno. I'd forgotten all about him.'

Molly chuckled. 'Aw, bless him. He struggles sometimes, but that's just the way he is. Old Jack hasn't got much choice because he can't afford to pay another person to work there, and he can't do everything himself any more what with his gammy leg.'

Lizzy sighed. 'When we were kids, we thought my mum was in love before she disappeared. Well Jonno told me he saw her with someone.'

Molly frowned. 'We always thought somebody must have seen something.'

'And it was Jonno. But no one listened to him.'

'Did he know who it was?'

'He didn't have a name or much else. Are you going to Maureen's fiftieth on Saturday? I'll be asking everyone what they know.'

She knew who he had described. It was Oliver. It was him. But she couldn't bring herself to say it out loud.

Molly laughed. 'Of course I'll be going. Half the town will be there. The kids will be running wilder than usual. But Lizzy, there's a lot of folk with funny ideas. You might hear a lot of shite about nothing.'

'I know.' She paused. 'Speaking of shit, I saw Duncan earlier in the pub.'

'You did, eh? What did he have to say for himself?' Molly's face clouded and she took a gulp of her drink.

'He was spouting off a few things about you, that you're a liability. What's going on, Molly?'

'I might as well tell you. We had another baby, after Meg. A beautiful wee girl.' Molly swallowed, and a tear ran down her face. She reached for a tissue on the coffee table. 'But she died of SIDS. I'd fed her three times in the night, and she was fine, then I slept in the next morning, exhausted I was. The other kids slept in too; they do unless I drag them out of bed for school. Duncan was up early for work, gone by six. And she didn't wake up, Lizzy. She never woke up again.'

Lizzy sat next to her friend on the sofa, and put her hand on her arm. 'I'm so sorry, that's awful. But Molly, that wasn't your fault.'

'The doctors all said there was nothing that I could have done. It was one of those things, unexplained and terrible. But Duncan saw it as my fault, for sleeping in, neglecting the baby. But I'd been up with her half the night, Lizzy.'

'That's awful, blaming you. You didn't do anything wrong.'

Molly blew her nose. 'Duncan and his ma don't think so. They make me feel like a bad person.'

There was a knock on the door, and Molly jumped. 'Who's that?'

Lizzy shrugged. 'Why? Is there someone you don't want to see?'

There was another knock, this one louder and more urgent. Lizzy sprung up. 'Want me to get it? I could say you're not here.'

'Fuck's sake.' Molly held a cushion on her lap, and swigged at her drink. 'There's a few people I don't want to see.'

Lizzy went to the door, wondering who Molly was afraid of. It could be the tax inspector, the landlord, Duncan perhaps, or even his mum.

But she wasn't expecting Kane.

He was shivering and wet through. 'Lizzy, now there's a surprise,' he leered. 'What are you doing here?' There was stale whisky on his breath.

She kept the door half closed. 'Molly's an old friend. I'm watching her kids for her. What do you want?'

'Is Molly in?' He put one foot in the door, jamming it open.

'No, she's out. You can't come in.' She held the door, her body blocking him.

'I'm soaked through, here. Could do with a cup of tea and a cuddle.' He gave her a creepy grin.

'Bugger off, Kane.' She pushed the door against his foot. 'I've had enough of you.'

He held his stance and leaned in. 'Look at you, with your hair and your fuckin' black jeans. I could have my way with you if I wanted, and you'd be begging for it after.'

'Nobody bloody wants you. Get out.' Lizzy scowled.

There was a battle with the door. Kane was much stronger than her, and she couldn't hold him back. He darted in, grabbed her hands and held them up above her head against the hallway wall.

He held his face close to hers and smiled. 'Tell your friend she owes me. I'll be back and next time she better have my money.'

Lizzy cringed. Pungent body odour crawled out from inside his leather jacket and filled the air.

'Let me go,' she said quietly.

'I'd like a kiss first.' He pursed his lips and closed his eyes.

His breath smelled like death.

'Fuck off will you.' She brought up her knee and jammed it into his crotch.

He bent over, grunting. 'Jesus, you fuckin' bitch. Frigid, you are. I'm going, all right. Fuck yous.' He blundered back outside and onto the pathway, cradling his groin.

She slammed the door. So it was money he was after. It was obvious why. Molly had fallen into that cruel trap of addiction. Duncan hadn't made that part up, then.

She went through to find Molly clinging to the cushion, weeping into another tissue, drink drained again. 'Has he gone?' Her hair hung limp and greasy around her face.

'He's gone for now,' she said. 'How much do you owe him, Molly?'

'More than I've got. It's stupid. I don't even like what he gives me. But I can't seem to stop. I feels good for a while, then worse afterwards, like I could crawl into a hole and die.'

Lizzy grabbed her hand. 'You've got to try and stop. I've been there; trust me. Addiction gets to you, eats into you bit by bit, until it reaches your bones.'

Molly wrenched her hand away. 'Don't fucking judge me, with your London fucking fancy life.' She was slurring now, shifting into anger.

Lizzy stepped away. 'My life isn't fancy, never has been. I lived on the street for years, for fuck's sake. I know what drugs do to you because I was in it.'

'Whatever. I still don't need you to tell me, so shut up about it.'

There was some crashing about outside, and Molly began a nervous wail. Lizzy went to the window and peered out. It was Kane, kicking the gate. The railings were bending, the posts on either side crooked. His face was contorted, full of hate.

Let him get it out of his system. She came away from the window, and turned to see Ryan and Craig standing in front of their mum.

'Who's that man out there, Ma?' Ryan looked distraught. 'Did he hurt you?'

'No, he didn't darlin'. Don't worry about me,' she said in a whisper.

Craig sat down next to her and put his hand on her arm. 'He's kicking everything in. We can't even get to our ba'.'

Lizzy took charge. 'He'll go in a minute. There's nothing to worry about, boys. He's not going to hurt anyone. I'll put the telly on, shall I? You two stay inside for now.' She locked the back door and switched on the television, turning it up loud. Kane had stopped kicking, but now he was swearing and thrashing about. She called for Meg, and the little girl ran down, clutching a doll. Her cough was rattling in her throat and she was hacking into her elbow. Each time she lifted her thin arm, it got covered in a spray of wet.

'Does she have any cough medicine I can get her?' Lizzy began to go through the kitchen cupboards, but found only tins and packets of sugar.

'Don't think so.' Molly shrugged.

'It sounds rough.'

'We don't notice it any more. She's had it forever. You can't fix us all, Lizzy.'

Meg coughed again, on cue, her chest wheezing. She was clinging onto the doll, her hands on a cushion. 'Can I have a drink of water?'

Lizzy got her a drink from the tap. *I'm not trying to fix you. I'm just trying to help.* When she took it to Meg, Molly was wiping her eyes and considering her empty glass. She snatched it out of her hand, and although it seemed wrong, poured her friend another drink. 'Here,' she said, 'at least there's some medicine for you. I'll talk to Kane, okay?'

'Thanks. I'm sorry for what I said.' Molly wiped her nose with her sleeve. 'I'm not myself.'

Not herself? Who was she then? Lizzy left it, not wanting to rile her friend up in front of the kids. You had to deal with what life brought you. No one owed you anything. She grabbed her coat and checked outside. Kane had gone. The boys' football was in the middle of the front garden, stamped on until it had burst. A parting gesture.

She slipped away to the sound of a cartoon roaring, three sets of eyes on the screen, bony knees hugged.

People had to help themselves, in the end. No point looking to anyone else. As Lizzy made her way back to her bed and a hot chocolate, Lil's angry accusations returned to her mind. Her ranting was a sure sign that she felt ashamed, just as Molly probably did, of neglecting her own children. Guilt never did fade.

Back at the B&B, Lizzy reclined on the bed, propped up by pillows. She spread out her new knitting supplies, the pattern and wool around her. Baby Lauren's cardigan. She studied the sheet, but it didn't mean much to her, the casting on and the pearl and the finishing off. She couldn't look up how to knit on the internet just now, because her phone wasn't one of those posh smartphones that everyone else in the world seemed to have. She'd lost two mobiles already, and had got a basic one for now. Calling and texting was all she was good for. Nat's mum Karen had a knitting basket at her place. Perhaps she'd show her how to do it when she got back to London. She looked at Mum's photo on the bedside table. *I bet you'd show me. If you were here.*

She picked up one of the balls of wool and held it to her face. It was soft and warm on her skin. She shut her eyes and tried to imagine a baby wearing the cardigan, tiny and golden, chubby fingers around hers. It was this image of her child that cleared her mind and sent her into sleep, her heavy head sinking down. Her own fingers softened, letting go of the ball of wool. It dropped to the floor and rolled away, barely making a sound.

CHAPTER TWENTY-TWO

Helen Plays

The girl had been the lairy, slutty kind, wearing high heels and a short skirt even though it was freezing out. Helen regarded her pale face, electric blue mascara smudged down her cheeks. Her eyes were half open, pupils withdrawn, the supposed windows of the soul blank and dull now.

Helen had waited in the shrubbery on the side of the playpark for over an hour before she had the opportunity to grab the girl. There were three boys and one other girl in the gang, chain smoking and swigging at a litre bottle of cider. They had a row about whose turn it was to get fags from the shop. The girl with the skirt lost. She went off in a huff, past Helen's bushes and out of sight of her friends. And so there it was. The needle went into her neck, and she was easily removed from the trail.

The rest of the park was too exposed to risk taking the body elsewhere. She should bury her amongst the shrubs and the leaves, right where she lay. They were cocooned inside the trees and bushes, a domed shrine. The girl wouldn't be found here unless they were searching hard. And something told her that this slut was never where she should be. No one would miss her, not for a while anyway.

Her body was amazingly light, nothing to her, and not much clothing either. Helen had taken off the girl's jacket while she played with the hammer and the nails, and now she pulled it back on her. Best everything was kept together. She took out a trowel from her rucksack and went about digging up some soil. It wasn't easy to make a hole as such, what with the roots and the rocks, but eventually she made a semblance of a pit and dragged the body in there, face down.

She squashed down the girl's feet and covered her up as best she could, with the dug-up soil, leaves, and bracken. She patted and smeared, scattered random twigs and sticks on top.

When it was done, Helen crouched at the edge of the grave, listening. In the distance, she could hear the 'gang', arguing again, probably pissed off they hadn't got their cigarettes yet. Tough luck. She stood tall and ventured out into the light. She'd go back to her room and clean up, hopefully avoiding the owner. Her hands were a mess of mud, blood, and scratches, her knees caked in much of the same. She wiped her sleeve over her face, and pulled up her hood.

She felt lighter, as if someone was carrying her rucksack for her, gently pushing her along, lifting up her feet. The glorious aftermath of a kill formed a billowing mist, emanating from within to the skies. The age of the girl had been perfect: aware and bolshy, yet fragile and childish. The push and pull years. Those kind of girls had become her favourite target.

ᐤ ᐤ ᐤ

Helen cleaned herself up, napped, and woke again with a raging hunger. She walked the streets, safe in the low light, making her way towards the chippy. There was some mud on the bottom of her coat, but no matter. No one would notice. She was a small, round ghost.

A car screeched by, headlights glaring, and splashed water from a puddle onto her legs. The oblivious driver was a white-haired man looking straight ahead, straining to see the road, his hands gripped to the wheel. As Helen turned towards the High Street, she saw a young woman, a mess of wavy blonde hair and skinny legs, coming towards her. The shape of her, the hair, and the confident way she was walking caught her attention. Helen stopped and backed up against the wall of the nearest building, the bricks cold on her back. Perhaps she'd be camouflaged there, her grey coat against the filthy wall.

Who was she? Didn't she know her from somewhere?

The girl looked angry, distracted. She was frowning at the ground, her hands thrust into her pockets. Black jeans, a black jacket, contrasting with her hair. *She was someone.*

Helen decided to delay her fish supper and follow the girl, long legs striding. She jogged a little to make up, then slowed her pace. The street was pockmarked with shallow puddles, and Helen tried to avoid them and walk quietly. The girl put her hands on her head, as if in pain. Helen strained to see the side of her face, but she was too far away. They walked in the direction of the bus depot, where Helen had arrived, past the rows of semis. The girl opened one of the gates, and went up the pathway. Helen waited until she'd gone inside, then drew closer.

It was a B&B. Interesting.

So the girl was from out of town. She might know her from Edinburgh, then. Or even from London. The memory was there somewhere, tucked away in her mind. It would surface another time, when she wasn't trying too hard to think of it. And then she'd know.

CHAPTER TWENTY-THREE

The Doorstep

It was the day before Maureen's Friday night bash, and Lizzy had arranged to meet Kai at the hall at eleven to decorate. Billy and his girlfriend Kayla were coming from Inverness, but apparently Noah couldn't be there to help because he had an interview in Edinburgh for a sales job. And there was no chance of Kane lending a hand; not that she'd want him there.

She'd been feeling dizzy that morning, and hoped she wouldn't have to stand on any ladders to decorate. She sat on the lower part of the wall outside the community centre to wait, wishing she'd brought her book along, as the surroundings weren't exactly pleasant to look at. This place was a dump. There were three rusty cars in the car park with steering wheel locks. No one would want to nick them, surely.

She pulled out her mobile and stared at the blank screen. Nothing to see there to distract her from the cold brick under her bum.

Two crows began to chase each other, squawking and flapping. She put her fingers to her temples. One crow picked at a bottle top, the other making off with a pink object, possibly a used condom.

This was where she grew up, where it all went bad. Ruthless and oppressive, so many people left wanting.

'Lizzy! Sorry I'm late.' Kai was calling out to her and waving.

'Don't worry, I was early,' she said as he got nearer. She got up from the wall and gave him a hug.

Kai reddened and looked away. 'Billy won't be here for an hour, I'll bet. Kayla will be painting her face and doing her hair even though the party's not 'til tomorrow.'

'Bit of a diva, is she?'

'You could say that.' He jangled some keys on a chain attached to his jeans. 'Let's get in there and make a start. We can set out the tables and blow up balloons, anyway. I'm hoping you'll have more of a clue with it all, Lizzy.'

She followed him. 'I'll do my best. We can dim the lights to cover up all our mistakes, and make sure everyone gets pissed really quick.'

Kai clapped his hands together. 'Now you're talking.'

They set to work, him moving the furniture as Lizzy directed, leaving a large space for dancing in front of the stage. Kai seemed more relaxed without the others around.

The kitchen had an opening into the hall, a makeshift bar, and they hung some balloons across the top of it. As if they needed to draw attention to it, Kai said; everyone would be queuing up as soon as they set foot in the place. Drinking was the family's favourite activity next to fighting.

A friend of Maureen's worked in the pound store, and she'd given them a load of plastic tablecloths in purple, with matching napkins and paper plates. It was Maureen's favourite colour, she'd said, although Kai guessed it might have been because she couldn't sell the purple. It was minging.

Lizzy sniffed, dust going up her nose from the tables. 'So where's Kane this morning? Sitting outside Maccy D's looking for clients?'

Kai spluttered. 'You've got him figured out then. Is it that obvious?'

'I was at Molly's when he came 'round looking for money she owes him. He had a fight with the fence when I told him to get lost. Does Maureen know he deals drugs to vulnerable single mums?'

'She doesn't know the half of it. You're not going to say anything are you?'

'Nah. But I'll kick his arse if I see him there again. He's not my number one cousin, put it that way.'

Kai smoothed down his side of the tablecloth. 'I've tried to talk to him. Me and Noah, we put up with a lot of shite from him. I wanted to leave home this year, but I'm feared for Mum, leaving her with him. I reckon he's been robbing from her purse. And it could get a lot worse.'

'That's rough. Sometimes you've got to be cruel, Kai. Kick him out if he does it again.'

'Aye, maybe. Easier said than done, though, eh? He's a hard fuck.'

Lizzy shrugged. 'He is, but I bet you're the only one he listens to.'

They'd already put everything out on the tables, and blown up most of the balloons by the time Billy and Kayla arrived. Billy was carrying a box filled with gold candlesticks covered in glitter. Kayla tiptoed next to him in high heels.

He set it down on the bar, and came straight over to Lizzy. 'You must be my long-lost cousin. Don't you dare say I've grown.'

She smiled. 'We'll leave that to the aunties, shall we? But you have grown, since you were four.'

They had a quick hug, his aftershave overpowering, even after she'd broken away.

'You've not grown much since you were twelve, upwards or outwards. You're looking great, there Lizzy,' he said. He stood back to look her up and down. 'Hey Kayla, come here and meet my cousin. Looks like she's been doing all the work.'

Kayla checked her nails as she walked. Her voice was fast and breathy, and Lizzy had to concentrate hard to understand her.

'Nice to meet you, Lizzy. Oh my god. Everything's looking great. I sat up all last night. Made some centerpieces for the tables. I thought gold went with everything. But they'll look fantastic with that purple. You wait. Hang on, I'll get one.'

She picked out a candlestick from the box and placed it in the middle of one of the tables. It was shiny and gaudy, like a Christmas ornament made in Kindergarten, and Lizzy could see a drizzle of glue where she'd stuck some tinsel on one side.

'Oh, they're lovely. Shall I help you set them out?'

'Yes, you do it, please,' Kayla said. 'I don't want glitter all over my new dress.'

Billy had crates of beer, wine, and spirits in his car, and him and Kai went to haul it in, leaving Lizzy and Kayla to fuss with the table arrangements. Billy had paid for all the booze on his credit card, and was hoping to sell most of it at the party at cost, or maybe even for a tiny profit, Kayla confessed.

When everything was done, they all sat on the edge of the stage. The disco ball was turning slowly from a draft in one of the top windows, projecting a faint series of silver sparkles on the floor in front of them. When it got dark, it would hopefully hide all the stains and scratches on the floor. Lizzy looked across at Kai, who was mesmerized by the lights, his expression childish and happy, like he was a kid again. She hoped Kane wouldn't spoil the party for them all. Everyone deserved a good time once in a while; a break in the long track.

As they all left, Kai offered to walk her to wherever she was going.

'Nah, I'm fine, thanks,' she waved him away. 'I'm going to visit my old school. Silly, really.'

'Take care of yourself, Lizzy,' he said.

'You too. What you up to now?'

He shrugged. 'Nothing. There's not a lot to do 'round here.'

'You should come and visit me in London. There's tons to do there.'

He brightened up. 'Maybe I will. I'll come as soon as I get a job and some cash. I'm glad you're here, Lizzy. I wasn't expecting . . . you know.'

'Did you think I was some posh London twat?'

'Aye, I suppose so.' He grinned. 'But you're cool.'

'See you tomorrow, Kai.'

'I'll be there. We all will. It's going to be a crackin' night.'

The school wasn't far from the centre. The noise coming from the playground at Dalbegie Primary was one wild, high-pitched scream where one kid couldn't be distinguished from another. It must have been the end of lunchtime, a bell ringing from inside telling them it was all over. The chain-link fence was battered and misshapen, one or two escape holes at the bottom where it had been pulled up and bent back. Lizzy put her fingers through it and watched as a gang of boys kicked their ball one last time, and some girls wrapped up their skipping rope. Kids were running and banging into each other to get to the main doors. That would have been her and Molly.

It was so long ago. Everything had shrunk. The playground was tiny, the school building low and compact. Her domain had been so small in those days. But at the time it felt like the world.

She put her hands to her core. One day, baby Lauren would be at a school like this, playing with her friends, giving someone a shove. She couldn't imagine it. The life inside her was only a half-creature: an orange, or an avocado stone. What if she was like Alfie? No, it wasn't possible. He was such a bloke, all hairy chest and scratchy stubble. She liked to rub her palm across his chin and make ape noises when he needed a shave. Then he'd pretend to get offended, and wrestle her to the floor, kissing her and rubbing his sandpaper chin on her face.

They'd spoken that morning and he'd sounded a bit down. There wasn't much on offer at the Job Centre and he had already started to worry about money, even though they had some savings and Lizzy had a decent job. She'd suggested he went to his brother's in Essex for a few days until she got back. He could see his nephews and have a laugh. His brother made him feel better about things. She was relieved when he'd gone for it.

At breakfast, she'd texted him. 'I'm eating haggis with toast!'

He sent a rude message back. 'You'll be wearing tartan knickers next. Cor!'

Funny old Alfie; he was fretting underneath all the jokes. Not long now, though, and she'd be able to give him that neck rub he liked. He was like a dog, really.

Where to now? She knew where she should be heading. But every time she thought of it—of him—her insides churned.

She turned towards her old street. There was something she wanted to do first.

Lizzy walked slowly up the road, towards her old house. Molly would pretend to be a plane while she ran down to the pavement to meet her for the walk to school. Socks wrinkled around her ankles, scuffed brown school shoes. Look at this place now. She'd ignore the peeling paint and the overgrown weeds, and take herself back, to her mum's furry hat in the hallway cupboard, the old tile around the bath, the two of them standing around the toaster waiting for it to pop.

The rain had started up again, and she put her hood up to stop her hair from going frizzy.

There it was. Number 20.

She touched the cold metal of the front gate and stared at the house. Frozen.

The front door began to open, slow, and a small, thin woman poked her head out. Lizzy tensed. The woman looked nervous, kept looking behind her. 'Lizzy, isn't it? You coming in, are you?'

'No, thanks. Are you Nicole?'

'Yes, love. Your dad's in the shower. Why don't you come in and wait for him?' She opened the door wide and stood to one side.

Lizzy could see partway down the hall. There were shoes in a pile by the telephone table. An old broom on the stair. Nicole had a northern accent that she couldn't place, her voice soft, barely there. Lizzy shuffled from one foot to the other. 'I think I'll come back another time.'

'Right you are. Your dad will be pleased you came, though. Will I tell him to meet you somewhere?'

Lizzy bit her thumbnail. 'Maybe.'

Nicole seemed okay, not the brazen type she'd imagined. And after all, she wasn't the woman he'd left them for. None of that was her fault.

'Where's his favourite café or whatever?'

Nicole frowned. 'Café? He's more of a pub sort of guy.'

'That'd be right.' Her dad appeared behind Nicole in his bare feet, hair still wet from his shower, a crumpled T-shirt on. 'I heard voices,' he said. 'Wondered who it was. Lizzy, darlin', what are you doing over by the gate? Come in. Nicole will make you a cup of tea. Did you not ask her in, Nic?'

'Yes, but she didn't want to, Rob.' Nicole scooted underneath his armpit and disappeared into the house.

'I'm not sure I can do it. Sorry.' Lizzy leaned on the gate-posts and looked down at her wet shoes.

Her dad came out and opened the gate for her. 'Come on, sit on the step with me for a second.'

He took her hand and pulled her down the path. His palm felt rough, his hand big enough to fit hers inside it. They sat on the doorstep under the short porch, knees up, backs against the front door frame. One either side. Lizzy looked into the front garden, and down the road, and imagined being twelve years old again. She'd had only school to worry about and whether she had enough money to buy records, sweets, and coloured pencils. Everything went wrong so fast.

'I'm glad you came. It's good to see you, even if I have to freeze off my toes.' He smiled at her.

'It's all a bit complicated, isn't it?' She hugged her shins and shifted towards him, a drip from the porch falling on her cheek.

'Aye, well. Nothing's perfect.' He reached out and wiped her cheek with his thumb.

'It was tough being on my own for so long. I couldn't help hating you.' She looked behind her shoulder. 'She seems nice. Nicole.'

'She's a good lass. We'll be all right, Lizzy.'

'Just please stop hitting people.'

'I'll try.'

He raised his arm and motioned for her to come closer. Lizzy sidled up to him and he rested his hand on her shoulders. She wanted to tell him, about the baby. His grandchild. But the words wouldn't come yet. There was a warm feeling inside her trying to reach him. She tried to relax into him, and tilted her head so her cheek was resting on his chest. He smelled of soap and deodorant. A dad's smell. It felt stiff, but it was as close to a hug as she was going to get.

It would do. It was about as much as she could handle. Dad and daughter, huddled stiffly on the step, in the rain. Nothing was perfect, like he said.

CHAPTER TWENTY-FOUR

The Face

At first I was all over the place. My body felt thin, sparse, like I'd been flattened with a rolling pin then nibbled at by the wind. Full of holes. I was with you, as much as I could be, in the party room, as you showed those boys what was what, and sorted out all the tables. Just as well you were there, Lizzy. Maureen claimed she'd brought the date forward so you could go, but I bet there was a part of her that needed your help too. The bisem. She was always one for squeezing folk for what she could get. God knows she used to have me running around after her, and I never got any help from her when you were born and I was sleep deprived and mental.

Maybe it was the reflections from that disco ball, spinning, that made me lose concentration, but I wasn't fully there. There was purple everywhere it seemed, covering the tables, on the walls, around the serving hatch. Maureen hated purple. I hope she changed her tastes, and that someone isn't having a laugh at her expense. Some of her friends were bitter and jealous. The worst of the town gossips.

Later, my body came back, skin tingling, as everything pulled together. My heart was almost pumping, although it has nothing to pump. You had that hard-set look about you that I know so well, chin out, striding long to number 20. I dreaded you going inside. I worried that you'd changed your mind about seeing it and willed myself to dissolve again so I didn't have to see it too.

But there you were, holding back. You stared at the flaking paint and the dirt-trodden front garden. You fidgeted, scratched your leg, took a step forward, then a step back again. You never went in, not even when you were asked.

In the end, something much worse happened. You and your dad had a moment.

I was dead jealous, I don't mind saying, as green as the front door used to be. You sidled up to him, looking all pie-eyed. His hand looked huge on your shoulder.

I used to feel that fist on my face.

I opened my liquid mouth and screamed into the universe. Silent pain that would never be felt. It should have been me sat there, with your head touching mine. I would die over and over again to be able to hold you.

And he got you.

What you didn't see was the thin face at the window, the shadowy cheekbones of that woman. She was watching you, with sadness in her eyes, bony fingers parting the curtains just enough to see out. She was longing for that kind of love, the sort that only exists for our bairns. Nicole's been with him for years now, by the sounds of it. And no kids of her own to speak of. I wonder why.

I've seen that face before, drawn and pinched, and lacking in happiness and hope. It's the face of a victim, Lizzy. I know, because twenty years ago, that face in the window was mine.

✧ ✧ ✧

I didn't listen to Granny Mac when she told me to keep away from your father. She didn't like the way he'd spoken to her at one of our parties, and then she said his eyes were set too close together, or some other such tale. I thought she must have it wrong, that he was nervous around my family or that he was putting up a front. He was so kind in the beginning, caring even. When we were on our own, he was the perfect gentleman.

I suppose that's how it starts. I should have broken away after the first 'incident.' By then, we were living under the same roof, married, with a future. But those things don't matter, places and belongings, signatures and promises. I know that now. He hurt me and I needed to leave. But I didn't, not for years.

Granny Mac popped by the house one day on her way to the shops, asked if I needed any messages. I'd had a row with your dad, and he'd gone down the Dram for a pint to get away from me, 'the nag.' The thing is, he'd given me a slap, not too hard, but enough to make one side of my face all red. I came to the front door pulling at my hair so it covered up the evidence.

'What's wrong with you?' Granny Mac said. She took a step forward and gave me one of her looks that said, 'I know you.'

'Nothing,' I said. 'I was cooking and I got hot.'

She stuck her head inside. 'I can't smell any cooking, Lauren. Are you sure that's why one cheek looks like a slapped arse? Walked into a door, did you?'

She knew. I knew that she did. But still I never told.

She put her hands on her hips and studied my face for a while. Then she left. 'I'll away and pick you up some ointment for that,' she called out. 'That's if they've anything strong enough.'

I got annoyed, like I'd been caught. Me. What a joke. I wonder how much of Granny Mac you remember, or if she's just a figure in an old tale to you. You don't hear the old sayings much these days. Whenever I had a bad day at school she'd say, 'failin' means yer playin'!' She made me feel better when I fluffed up. One day you scraped your knee badly at the playground trying to do a cartwheel. She wiped your eyes with a tissue that she had scrunched up in her pocket, gave you a minty lump and said it. You were all smiles, instant.

Why did I put up with your dad for so long? When you're constantly told you're useless, fat, lazy, a bad mother, a terrible person, you start to believe it yourself. I know they talk about 'low self-esteem' on the telly, but it's more than that. It's about becoming the victim, changing how you think and feel so that you'll stay alive, like a deer in the woods, constantly on the alert. You've no time to think about your ego, because it doesn't exist. It's buried, along with your real self.

You don't exist anymore; you're a shadow of a person, half a soul. It was the same with Maureen and that Brian. I saw how it was in the pub, and I hate to say it, but he deserved everything that came to him. I never told anyone, not even Maureen, when he came on to me one night at the Social. He cornered me when I was coming out of the loo 'round the back, tried to press himself against me. I'd had a few myself, but luckily I'd my wits about me and I kicked him right where it hurt him most.

But you don't know all of that, and nor should you. I can understand why you wanted to tug on your roots, Lizzy, but now you know what's there, you can go. Pull up a plant and see how ugly it is under the green and the flowers. It's just dirt. There's poison in puddles, everywhere. Regrets. They're a terrible thing. Don't feel sorry for never knowing what happened to me. Finding out who did it, and how they did it, wouldn't change a thing. It would creep inside you, settle in all the crannies of your mind, and it would never go away. It'd be worse than that, even. It would haunt you for the rest of your life. Best left, remember?

There was another of Granny Mac's sayings: 'whit's fur ye'll no go by ye'. What's meant to happen will happen. It's already done, and you can't mend it.

Which leads me to Oliver. He's a psycho, one of those men who has an air about him that unnerves you. He gives you the shivers and at first you mistake that feeling for attraction, or excitement maybe. I did. But it's fear dressed up. So you see, the whole town is bubbling over, an unseen volcano about to erupt. Because the dangers that you can't see, the ones that boil beneath, are the most deadly.

CHAPTER TWENTY-FIVE

Empty Chambers

I watched through my binoculars from behind the hedgerows as Lizzy edged closer to her father. I'd been following her since she left that ghastly community centre, a dismal building not unlike my old prison.

His beady eyes darted here and there like a weasel, and I could almost hear his brain ticking over, calculating his next move. There was a hard ball of sleep stuck on his bottom eyelash that nauseated me.

Lizzy was clearly reticent to go inside her old home, and I didn't blame her, for young women have a sentimentality that often overrides practicalities. I knew she wouldn't want to see it with other people's smells and clutter, habits and belongings. It was where she lived as a child with her mother, and she would want to keep the memory of that time intact. I could tell what she was thinking, the subtleties of her that he could not have appreciated.

He was there, in her old home, and I didn't like him.

Rob was his name. I'd seen him plenty of times around Dalbegie over the years. He was hefty and pushed his weight where it wasn't wanted, using his persuasive tactics all over town. I'd witnessed his scowls and bad temper. His partner was a wretched woman, bowing down to his every whim, shaking and quivering in his wake. He wouldn't be able to use the same bullying manner on Lizzy, though. She was too good for that, and he wouldn't want to risk pushing her away. He'd be working on her from a different angle, playing with her emotions, behaving himself on the outside.

Passive aggression. The worst kind.

He looked like a gorilla in negative next to her on the step. His feet were bare, toenails too long, white hairs on his toes. How could she stand him being so close? His skin was almost translucent, blue veins prominent on his hands, like a lizard.

I grit my teeth. Soon I'd be getting a visit of my own, when Lizzy would finally venture from the street all the way to my doorstep. She'd been edging closer to me, too. The anticipation seared into my gut, twisting like a knife. If she'd come to see *him* again, she'd surely pay me a special visit soon. When she came to me, it would make it all worthwhile, me receiving her gracefully rather than springing at her like an ungainly animal.

Then Lizzy put her head on his spongy chest. It was all I could do to hold back. He gazed into space as he comforted her, his daughter, and it seemed as though he was looking into my lens, taunting me. *She's mine*, he was saying.

He needed to go.

I'd have to rescue her again, like old times. I rescued her from Roy years ago by 'retaining' him in my cellar just as she fled to London with her scum of a boyfriend, Simon. Roy had it coming to him. It was perfectly timed, with everyone assuming they had all gone some place together. Later in London, young Simon also became a liability and so I engineered his 'fall' onto the tracks. Then of course I semi-strangled my long-standing colleague, Helen, when she tried to take my girl for her own needs. No one got dangerously close to Lizzy without rattling my cage.

And now this. What was the man doing with his hand on her shoulder? He wasn't her dad, had never been there for her. Where was he when Roy was making her deliver drugs, shouting at her, beating her boyfriend? I found her in London, and so anyone else could have done if they'd tried hard enough. But not him. He moved back into 'his' house with another doormat and settled for what he didn't have.

I put the binoculars away; I couldn't stand to see a second more of his sycophantic moves.

As soon as Lizzy had gone, and her pretend father had retreated back into his cave, and his sickly wench had removed her talons from the windowsill, I left. I caught up with Lizzy and followed her back to the bed and breakfast, stopping by the newsagents to pick up my newspaper.

Jessica straightened at the sight of me, a determined look on her crinkled face. I waited with trepidation for her latest news, not expecting what I was about to hear.

'A terrible thing's happened, Oliver.' She pursed her lips, pink lipstick smudged into the corners of her mouth and onto one of her front teeth.

I grabbed *The Times* and pulled out my wallet, anxious to get home and away from her cloying perfume. 'Oh?'

'Yes. Some girl's gone missing from the estate. She left her friends at the park yesterday and never went back. Her cousin was in here earlier, crying her eyes out, she was. Terrible. I hope it's nothing.'

My skin prickled. 'How old was she?'

'Sixteen, I think. Just a kid. They asked me if she'd come to get fags, but I never saw her, and neither did Molly. Shame.'

'Let's hope she turns up.' I laid down some coins on the counter and counted them with my finger. Jessica reached out to pick them up and her talons brushed against the back of my hand before I had a chance to pull back. My stomach churned and my blood fizzed as I turned to go.

She called after me. 'See you tomorrow. I'll let you know the latest, if she's been found.'

I gave her a short wave and half-ran home, the bathroom calling. I scanned the streets, the windows of houses, searching for someone or some sign that I was being watched. Was this part of their plan, to throw me off by feigning another abduction? I was being manipulated, played with.

There was a large stone on my driveway, and I became convinced that it had moved from one side to the other. I kicked it back, hurting my toes in the process, noting where it landed so that if it moved again I would know. As I put my key in the front door, I turned quickly to see if anyone had appeared, but there was only the patter of light rain and the slice of car tires on the wet road beyond.

I threw off my coat and ran up the stairs, almost forgetting to remove my shoes first, slipping them off on the second step. I filled the sink and plunged my hands into hot water, soaking my skin, ridding the germs from her touch. I thought of all the bacteria that lived under her overgrown fingernails and tried to visualize them being killed off by the scalding heat. I should have worn gloves like I usually did, and kicked myself for becoming so sloppy.

Lizzy had been the same age as the missing girl when we had our encounters in London. The stories that she accepted as a seventeen-year-old would now be playing through her mind, crumbling apart as she rejected them, one by one. She was uneducated, yes, but she wasn't stupid, and now all the naïveté of youth had gone.

I once told Lizzy that her mother had approached me in a dream and asked me to watch over her. It was my reason for being there, for tracking her, and turning up whenever she got into trouble. Of course the dead were not spirits, floating around the world giving out messages, but mere fragments of matter decomposing into nothing. Even if Lauren had come to me in a premonition, I would not have taken it seriously. To make out that I was looking after someone's daughter at the bequest of her dead mother was preposterous, the delusional whim of a madman. But at seventeen, I knew Lizzy would cling to the notion that her mother would be able to see her from heaven above.

That idealism would have faded as she grew older. Now she no doubt suspected that I had things to hide. And she was right.

Our last liaison in London was complicated. We were between two terraced houses, in broad daylight, but it was quiet, with no one around. Once I'd got rid of Helen, I decided to play a final game of chance with Lizzy, for in those days I was interested in Russian Roulette: firing the single unlucky bullet in a revolver with five empty chambers. It was a version of the game we played with our 'visitors' at The Audacious in Soho, at the end of every viewing session. Some got the bullet, some didn't.

So I had conceived an idea that involved choice, but nothing so crass as a bullet for my Lizzy. I chose a more symbolic route, offering her the chance to find out what happened to her mother. I told her I'd investigate on her behalf. Unbeknownst to her, if she chose yes, I would take her soul. And if she chose no, she would buy herself some more time alive. As a frightened teenager, she couldn't handle the truth, of course, and she unwittingly set herself free. I was left with the idea that I would eventually take her anyway, that I'd simply postponed my greatest prize.

And now it was my time to take it.

Once I was cleansed, I attempted to pull my mind away by climbing into the skin of OwlVerse. I logged into the forum and wheedled my way back inside the minds of the depressed. A dreadful environment, and only for the strong-hearted. At least it wasn't a lifeline for me, like it was for them. More of a deathline, if we can forgive the crass wordplay.

Having a bad day today. I applied for a position at a local vet, but my experience wasn't appropriate, apparently. I have no formal qualifications, only years of working with, and understanding, birds and animals. This isn't enough for them. They need certificates. Thinking of going for a long walk, but can't seem to get up from the sofa.

Three people agreed that today was a bad day, for their own reasons. Was it ever a good day for these people? MarigoldGirl hadn't even got out of bed for three days. I tried not to imagine the stale smell of her sheets. After a time, Parsley, my ticking clock, added her condolences.

I feel for you, OwlVerse. Life experience is more valuable than they can know. Their loss. One day a great opportunity will present itself to you. Today I am up and dressed, although sinking, heavy. The phone rang twice, but I couldn't face talking.

I told her that she could talk to us—to me—any time. She said she was grateful. I told her that we all need each other on our lowest days. I chuckled to myself, at my little game, like a side dish to serve along with my main course of Lizzy. I shut down my computer before I was tempted to leap inside Parsley's psyche too soon.

Usually, I was the tracker, but this time we'd been thrown together. Lizzy wanted to know what happened to her mother. I could see it in her face, the desperate need. And at last, I would show her.

I liked the premise of 'show not tell' when it came to selling a product, or highlighting its qualities. I'd learned to employ it over the years, when writing copy for online advertising. We wouldn't tell the consumer that a chocolate bar tasted good; we would show a woman nibbling on it and making sounds of pleasure. Perhaps she would close her eyes while swallowing, showing us her ecstasy; maybe she would crunch up the wrapper in her delicate hand, or roll it seductively in her palm.

This premise applied to my plans for the cellar.

There was more pleasure in showing Lizzy what happened to her mother than simply telling her. She had no other way of finding out, because in all those years, I'd never been caught. Only the egomaniacs leave clues to be found, a wall covered with press clippings highlighting their 'conquests.' Not my style. So if Lizzy had decided she wanted to know what happened, she would be shown. I owed it to her, after all that time. She'd thank me for it and feel closer to her mother in her final days.

My two best girls, leaving the world in the same manner. Other-worldly nonsense aside, there had to be some kind of spiritual closure in that. *'Tis true. The wheel is come full circle.*

CHAPTER TWENTY-SIX

The Party

L izzy pulled on some clothes and grabbed a hair tie, trying to ignore the lingering nausea that had haunted her body every morning for weeks. She grabbed her box of crackers and stuffed them in her bag for the walk. They'd have to do. She needed to get out before she changed her mind, before Alfie called, and before Tilda seduced her with bacon and sausages. Her sleep had been fitful, full of images and things said from years gone by, and she'd woken with a firm resolve. It was time to have it out with Oliver.

She'd been putting it off. No more.

She shut the main door as quietly as she could, the latch clicking gently. Weak early morning sun was trying to get through the clouds, but not quite making it. Lizzy felt the icy air through her coat, curling around all the fibres to find her skin. She shivered, pulling her sleeves over her hands and hunkering down into her scarf.

When the newsagents came into sight, she slowed her pace. He was close. There was an unfamiliar scent in the air, not natural, but a chemical kind of smell. Was it real or in her imagination? It didn't seem to be coming from anywhere in particular.

She glanced towards the window of the shop. Jessica and Molly were probably arguing over who was going to do the papers for the millionth time. They would be too busy to see her slipping around the corner, skirting Oliver's car, and striding up to his front door.

She'd done it. She was there.

The house was quiet and dark, all the blinds and curtains drawn. But that wasn't unusual. She lifted her hand to knock on the door, then brought it down again. Her body was trembling, tears pricking her eyes. She wrapped her arms around her middle and hugged herself, held her baby.

If he'd wanted to hurt her, he would have done it by now.

But those dark eyes. He was the one Mum was in love with. She knew it.

Oh, screw it. She bashed on the door, three times. Then she took two steps back.

There was no movement inside. Nothing.

Shit. She should have rung the doorbell. It was glowing, taunting her.

She lunged forward and held her thumb on it. It was an old-fashioned *ding-dong*, and it made her think of Granny Mac. She was saying, *get away, get away.*

She waited, but there was still no sign of activity.

Maybe it was too early for him. Minutes went by. The door handle was shining bright, polished immaculately. There was the sterile smell again, emanating from inside.

Silence.

She bent forward and held onto her knees, blowing out her breath. It was a relief, in a way, but frustrating. She'd have to go through it all again, later.

But later didn't come.

∽ ∽ ∽

Auntie Maureen had wanted the boys and Lizzy at the party early, to be there with her when the first lot of people arrived. She was fussing and flitting about the room, and her whisky and lemonade spilled on the floor when she threw out her arms with the excitement of it all. 'Ach away, I love it. It all looks brilliant. Shame about the purple, but I love the gold.'

Lizzy gave her a hug. 'I thought purple was your favourite colour.'

'Naw, reminds me of the inside of a chocolate box. I like red.'

'Not what I heard.'

'But Lizzy, there's nowhere to put all my presents. Could you get Kai to set aside a table against the wall?'

Maureen was clearly expecting to be inundated. Lizzy tried not to laugh as Kai and Billy moved the furthest table and removed the cutlery and gold candlestick ornament, to make room for the hundreds of gifts. Kayla's tinsel was already drooping, and when Kai held the centrepiece upside down, the top part fell off.

Lizzy took her gift bag over, stepping over the spilled drink puddle on the floor. 'I'll put my present on the table, shall I, so everyone knows what it's there for.' She'd bought her aunt a vase earlier, from one of the independent stores on the High Street. It was glass, with a purple tint to it, tall and slender. She placed it at the back next to the wall, hoping it wouldn't get broken.

'Oh thank you, darlin', is that for me?' Maureen put her drink down and lunged in for another hug.

'Happy Birthday, Maureen.' Lizzy planted a kiss on her cheek. The fabric of Maureen's dress was so static that it made tiny fizzing shocks when she broke free from her grasp. 'Open it later with all the others.'

Billy got comfortable behind the bar, setting out glasses and cocktail napkins. He was dressed in a pressed white shirt and a black bowtie, occasionally flipping bottles and catching them. Kayla sat on a stool to one side, enjoying the show, sipping at a gin and tonic. Her bare legs were tanned orange, a different colour than the rest of her.

She shouted over. 'Do you want a wee drink, Lizzy? You haven't got one yet.'

Balls. How to get away with not drinking all night? 'Yes please. I'm so thirsty right now though; I think I'll start with a Coke if you've got one, Billy. I need to pace myself.'

Billy chuckled. 'Don't be daft, Lizzy. I'll put a splash of rum in it for you, to get you going. Your first drink is on me.' He handed her a large glass with a straw in it. 'Cheers.'

She took a sip and tasted the rum instantly, strong and potent. 'Delicious, thanks. You make a good barman, just like Tom Cruise in that film.'

She'd pour away the drink at some point, in the toilet.

Nat and her parents, Karen and Darren, used to watch cheesy eighties films, like *Cocktail* and *Dirty Dancing*. They'd all have a good laugh together, eat popcorn and crisps, and stay up late, even before she moved in with them. She missed them, needed a 'Karen 'n' Darren' fix. She'd go and see them as soon as she got back to London. It had been too long.

The DJ finished setting up and switched on some flashing fairy lights around his table. He announced that he'd put the music on low for now, until things warmed up.

'Lovely,' said Maureen. 'Mind you play some of my favourites off that list that I gave you.'

Soon the crooning sounds of "Lady in Red" filled the room, and Maureen started to sway from side to side. Kai rolled his eyes and downed the rest of his beer, crushing the can while he made his way back to the bar. People were arriving, bustling at the door, squeals from the women.

Lizzy stood back, wishing she'd worn a dress, but she'd felt bloated around her middle and didn't fancy having to suck in her tummy for the night. She'd gone for black trousers and a sparkly top, but even they felt tight and restricting.

More people spilled into the room, most making straight for the bar, although a few stashed their own cases of beer on the floor underneath the tables. Maureen was grabbing everyone, and laughing loudly at anything they said. She was acting nervous, although Lizzy had never known her to be.

Now the DJ was playing "Tiger Feet" by Mud. It wasn't the seventies any more, people. It was the worst wedding music imaginable.

Kane eventually blundered in, eyes wild, his leather jacket open to reveal a stained T-shirt with a picture of a rock band that Lizzy didn't recognize. He wasn't walking straight, although he made it to the bar no problem, where he high-fived Billy and grabbed Kayla's knee. Kayla brushed it off and shooed him way.

A man with a white beard made his way over, holding out his hand. 'Lizzy?'

'Yes, hello.' She didn't recognize him. His face was red, with purple veins all over his nose. They shook hands.

'I'm your Great Uncle Jimmy, darlin'. Your Granny Mac was my sister. It's nice to see you, all grown up. Maureen told me the whole story.'

He put his hand on her arm. 'You probably did the right thing, getting away from this mad place so young. Although I wouldn't have chosen London, right enough. Terrible shock, that must have been, with the crowds and all those English.' He cracked open a can of beer and shouted over at Billy. 'Give us one of your beer glasses, will you son. I've got my own booze over here. Cheaper.'

Billy shrugged and gave a glass to Kayla, who passed it up to Jimmy. Granny Mac used to ignore Uncle Jimmy. He'd be the one slurring and staggering at family parties, or vomiting in the street. *Ace.*

'It's nice to see you, Uncle Jimmy.' Lizzy pretended to sip at her rum. 'I don't remember much about Granny Mac. I was really young when she died. But she used to talk about you. Whereabouts do you live?'

'Still at the same flat, but I don't think you ever came to mine. There's not much room for visitors, what with all the junk I keep in it. I've always been a hoarder, myself. But you're welcome any time, Lizzy. And I'm sorry about your mum, all those years ago. A terrible sadness, so it was. God rest her soul.'

'What do you remember about it all?' She may as well ask him now, before he became comatose.

He stroked his beard, and took a long swig of his beer. 'She was a quiet, sensible sort, your mum. That Rob pushed her about, and it took her a while, but she got rid of him eventually. Some folk said he'd come back for her. She wasn't daft, your mum, but they'd been married for a long time, and had you. She might have let him back in, you know?'

'You'd think she would have told me if her and dad were getting back together.'

'You were just a youngster, mind.'

'True.' Lizzy pushed him further, aware that he was finishing his beer and looking at his stash longingly. 'Anything else suspicious that you can think of?'

He wiped his mouth with his sleeve. 'Just this. If she were alive, she would have turned up at some point. She loved you too much to leave you high and dry. She's gone, and there's nothing we can do. Don't busy yourself with things that you can't understand, because you'll drive yourself up the wall. Okay, darlin'?'

'Okay.' He was probably right, but she hadn't come all this way for nothing.

The DJ put on "Sweet Caroline." Hopefully he'd get Maureen's favourites out of the way soon. No one was going to dance to that, not at the beginning of the evening anyway. She looked over to the bar. Kayla was chatting to Jessica, who was wearing a similar bare-legged outfit, but without the benefit of youth.

Molly showed up with her mum, Judith, who nearly cried when she saw Lizzy, said it was lovely to see her there with the rest of her family. 'There you are,' she said, 'where you belong.'

Lizzy didn't like to tell her that she felt like a spare part, an outsider.

Molly was obviously trying to avoid her, and darted off. Lizzy didn't really blame her. Perhaps she had been too self-righteous about the drugs and everything. But then Molly had been pretty rude.

'Judith, I want to say thank you for looking after Simon that time he'd been beaten up. We couldn't go to the hospital or the police, and you saved us.'

Judith linked her arm through Lizzy's and pulled her to one of the tables furthest away from the dance floor. 'I'd known you forever, Lizzy, you and your mum. I couldn't bear to see you hurt. If I'd realised what was going on, that you were going to run away, I would have tried to stop you, though. You know that, don't you?' She shrugged. 'But here you are, and you look absolutely gorgeous. Glowing.'

'You have no idea what it meant to us. Really. You should have been the first person I came to see on this visit, even before Auntie Maureen.'

'Oh, never mind that. Let's have a good look at you.' Judith reached out and held her face. 'You've your mother's eyes and her wise look about you.'

'Have I? I don't feel very wise at the moment. I came here to see everyone, obviously, but I also came thinking I'd find out what happened to Mum. But I'm not sure how I thought I'd do that.'

Judith folded her arms across her chest. 'We never did find out, did we? And that's terrible. You need to close the door on it all. Maybe coming back to Dalbegie and seeing all the folk you used to know is what you needed. How has your dad been behaving himself?'

'He's been okay. He feels guilty about leaving me.'

Judith rolled her eyes.

Lizzy sighed. 'Do you see them much? Dad and Nicole?'

'No. Only in passing. They have a crowd at the Dram, while me and all of your mum's old friends, we go to the Social. Nicole keeps to herself, quiet. I don't know why they don't sell up and go back to Yorkshire. They don't seem to have much going for them here.'

The music took a turn and the lights dimmed as the DJ played a louder and more upbeat track, although Lizzy couldn't quite place the song. A woman grabbed Judith and pulled her away. Billy couldn't serve everyone fast enough, despite the additional bring-your-own piles of cans here and there. People were still rolling in, and had started to take over some of the tables, picking at sausage rolls and crisps that some of Maureen's friends had brought with them.

Lizzy went to the Ladies and poured her drink down the sink when no one was looking. She texted Alfie. He'd be at his brother's house, hopefully getting spoiled. 'At the big 50th. Neil Diamond. The DJ is a corker.'

He texted straight back. 'Sounds a larf. Be good. Love on the Rocks.'

She took the empty glass back and put it on the side of the bar. The floor was throbbing now with the music and the jumping up and down.

Kai appeared by her side, with a can of lager in each hand. 'Here we go. Mum's on the dance floor. She loves Beyoncé.'

'Are you not going to join them, Kai?' she laughed.

'Not with that lot,' he said. 'Bloody scary, those women. They'll be pinching everyone's arses next, you wait. There's no way I'm going anywhere near them.'

Lizzy watched Maureen with her friends, drink in hand. Everyone was pissed up already, shouting over the music, singing and laughing. The noise was getting to her for some reason. Maybe it was because she was sober.

Molly threw her handbag on the floor and jigged about next to Lizzy. 'Hey, what are you drinking? Not still off the booze, are you?'

'I just finished a really strong rum and it's gone to my head.'

'Have another.' Molly waved at Billy and pointed at Lizzy. 'Listen, I'm sorry about the other day. I was a cow. Let's get blootered and have a dance. It's what parties are for. And I need to avoid Kane. He's still after me.'

'I tell you what, I'll go and speak to my shit of a cousin, and then I'll join you.'

'You're a doll.' Molly tottered off, her skirt riding up her legs, and joined Maureen and the rest of the women on the dance floor.

The DJ picked up the microphone and joined in with the barking bit in "Who Let the Dogs Out." Lizzy cringed and wondered when she could get away with going home. No one would miss her. Most of them wouldn't even notice she was gone. She could slip away, and have one of Tilda's hot chocolates in bed. She'd promised to talk to Kane though, and she spotted him near the bar chugging a litre bottle of cider. Some of it was dribbling down his chin and splashing on his T-shirt to add to the rest of the stains.

He skirted the edge of the dance floor, edging closer to Molly. She had her back to him, oblivious, when he grabbed her top. He pulled her towards him until her face was crushed against his damp chest, and slipped something into the back pocket of her jeans.

That was it.

Lizzy marched over. 'Leave her alone. She doesn't want your crap anymore.'

He laughed, eyes on her chest. 'Who, Molly? She's gagging for it, the stupid cow. Can't leave *me* alone. And what about you? Come over for a piece of Kane, eh?' He put his arm around her waist and pulled her close.

'Get lost.' She pushed him away, and he stumbled backwards into the ring of dancing women. They all squealed and tried to get him into the middle of their circle. Maureen started to clap.

Lizzy scanned the room for Molly and saw her disappearing into the Ladies. She followed.

She heard her crying in one of the stalls. 'Molly, it's me. Open up.'

Someone had graffitied *Sal is a bawbag* on the door.

There was a sniff, then the door opened. Molly was sitting on the closed toilet seat, a small package in her hand. 'He gave me this, Lizzy, and I want it bad.'

'I thought as much. Give it here.' Lizzy held out her hand. 'I'll give it back to him, tell him we don't want his shit.'

'No.' Molly clenched it tighter.

Lizzy leaned on the white tile, its grouting speckled with mould. 'What about the money you owe? It'll be even more if you accept that from him. And he knows it as well.'

'I know.'

'Well, it's up to you. I'm not going to go on about it. You already know what I think.'

'Fuck it.' Molly got up and lifted the toilet seat. She threw the wrap in there. 'Fucking arsehole.' She flushed, then sobbed. 'It's gone now. No one wins.'

Lizzy held her for a minute, Molly's hair tickling her neck. She used to be into pink, furry animals, girl bands, and strawberry bubblegum. What had this place done to her?

'Come on, let's get you a drink and then maybe we should get the hell out of here.'

Molly nodded, wiping underneath her eyes with her thumbs. 'I'll get us both a triple vodka and tonic, and a chaser.'

'Molly. I'm pregnant.'

She'd said it out loud, actually said it. It felt so strange to hear the words. They echoed about the room, mingled with the sounds of the cisterns.

'Oh my god, really?' Molly grinned. 'I wondered why you were being so fucking boring.'

They both laughed, and cried a bit at the same time. Lizzy grabbed some toilet roll and blew her nose. 'I wasn't supposed to say anything as I'm not quite twelve weeks, but you're my oldest friend.'

'Thanks for telling me. Come on, you silly arse.' Molly took her arm.

'I'll get a big bastard of a drink for me and a ginger ale for you, and meet you back here.'

Molly left her by one of the tables. Kane was at a safe distance, and Lizzy wrenched her eyes from him, not wanting to encourage him. She'd have one last drink, then go.

But the night wasn't over yet.

She wanted to walk out as the doors opened and her dad and Nicole walked in, but was so shocked that she couldn't move. Kai immediately went to Kane and Billy. One or two of Maureen's friends stopped talking and looked over. *Here we go.*

Lizzy felt the heat rising from her chest. They were here because of her. Dad would have felt pissed off about everyone being invited apart from him, when his own daughter was there. She knew what he was thinking. She could tell. He looked directly at her as he walked in. *She was his.*

Nicole was dressed smartly in a pencil skirt and blouse. There were bags under her eyes. She probably didn't want to come. Perhaps he made her.

He was coming over. Nicole followed behind, staring at the floor. Lizzy froze.

'We were at the pub, but it was quiet in there tonight.' His voice was slurring, his eyes bloodshot. 'Everyone's here.'

'You weren't invited, Dad. You know why.' Lizzy could smell the beer on him from a few feet away. He was stinking.

'I wanted to see you.'

'I know, but it's not the right time.'

Her cousins were standing together, Kai with his hand on Kane's shoulder, to hold him back. Molly was coming over, two drinks in her hands, looking angry. Maureen was oblivious, thankfully, still dancing with her friends while the music ramped up another few decibels. Nicole stayed a few paces back, clutching her handbag, her legs jiggling like a nervous animal's.

Her dad staggered closer and put his arms out. 'Why shouldn't I be here, fuck's sake. I want to be with my wee girl.'

Lizzy shouted over the music. 'I'll see you tomorrow. Just go, okay? It's Maureen's birthday. It's nothing to do with you and me.'

Kane crushed his beer can and threw it across the room. He pulled away from Kai's grip and strode over. 'Hey, you! Get te fuck out of here. You're no' wanted.'

Kai came too, rolling up his sleeves, Billy close behind. So this was what cousins were good for. It was like having three bodyguards.

Her dad growled, and tightened his fists. Even Molly put down the drinks and crossed her arms, standing in front of her, protective. Lizzy had to get her dad away before there was a fight.

She should handle this. It had to be her.

She stepped around Molly and took his arm. 'Come on, let's both go. I'm coming with you.'

'I'm not going.' He wrenched his arm away. 'This fuckin' place. All these folks who push me out. I'm from here, and I've every right to be here. I've had enough of all this shite.'

He shouted into the room, to no one in particular. 'What you going to do now?'

Kane stepped forward and pushed him in the chest. 'You're a fuckin' piece of work. Get out. You've been told.' His eyes were rolling back now, his face covered in sweat.

'Don't you touch me, you stinkin' druggie scum.'

Kane reached into his back pocket and pulled out a flick knife. 'I'll touch you if I want to. I'll fuckin' kill you.'

Things were kicking off, proper.

Lizzy pulled at her dad's arm. 'We'll go back to the pub now, okay? Together. I don't want any trouble, Dad.'

He didn't move. His eyes were fixed on Kane.

She squeezed. 'Let's go.'

Then everything moved fast. He pushed her off, Kane lunged in, and she got caught in between the two of them. The music pounded, the lights flashed. The stench of beer and sweat closed in.

There was a sharp pain in her side.

Lizzy slipped on a wet patch and came crashing down onto a crate of beer, her neck snapping back. She lay still. There were shouts and screams.

Everything was blurry. She caught a glimpse of her dad's face, red and furious, as he was marched to the door.

She held onto her stomach. *Please let the baby be okay.*

There was a warm sensation between her legs, and a burning in her groin.

No.

She felt a clammy hand on her arm. It was Nicole. She was looking at the floor, distraught.

Lizzy lifted her head, to see. A pool of dark liquid made an expanding shape. Another spill to end the night. Of what?

Then Molly was there. 'Get an ambulance right now,' she was saying. 'She's pregnant.'

Lizzy closed her eyes, willed it all to a dream. It was the beginning of it, she knew. And probably the end.

CHAPTER TWENTY-SEVEN

Lizzy Lost

ollow. That's how she felt, because there was no life inside her anymore. Just her own organs, blood, and veins, milling around with nothing to do. There was no one else to feed, to nourish, to love. She'd turned from a real woman creating a new life into a child, her little-girl sorrow drowning her. She needed to be looked after now, and she wanted Alfie.

But Alfie wasn't there.

They'd taken Lizzy to the neighbouring town's hospital, a small building with clean, bright rooms. She'd never been inside an ambulance before, but it wasn't what she had imagined. She thought there would be wires and pumps everywhere, a crowd of paramedics pressing buttons and pulling straps tight. Flashing lights. There would be a sense of urgency, of danger. But there was no thrill as they raced along the winding roads that joined up the towns, siren blaring. It was like being in a small white room, with drawers and tiny machines lining the walls. The two paramedics sat either side of her, calm and quiet. They gave her a sedative and she floated for a while, pale lights and voices spinning around the tiny orange stretcher. No one from the party had come with her in the ambulance.

And now she was empty.

'I'm afraid you've lost the baby,' the doctor had said, after examining her aching body, his gloved fingers pushing into her for the hundredth time. He wrote on her chart. What had he written there? *Lost Baby?*

Lizzy wanted to see, but also didn't. It wouldn't change anything. She didn't have her little girl any more.

He did this. He killed her.

Dad had let them all down, three generations of women, in the end.

She rolled onto her side and wrapped her arms around her numb body, the tube of the drip contorting slightly. Her eyes were closing, the drugs taking effect. She felt herself sinking down into the soft bed, her mind darkening into sleep. She wanted to disappear, and she dropped thankfully, into the abyss.

☙ ☙ ☙

'There's someone here to see you.' There was a soft voice coming from the end of the bed.

Lizzy blinked in the dim light. She'd been in deep sleep, but now her blissful ignorance was stripped away. She put her hand to her forehead, heart pounding as she looked up at the nurse. *Was it him?*

'Don't worry. It's only me.' Judith stepped into the room, hands clasped in front of her. Molly's mum. Her coat was wet at the bottom. She wrapped up her umbrella tight and hung it on the back of a chair.

Lizzy tried to smile, but her mouth wouldn't move.

Judith came to her side, and put her hand on top of hers. 'How are you feeling?'

She nodded.

'There's strict visiting hours, but they let me in because they thought you might want someone here first thing.'

The hospital was waking up, trolleys being wheeled, bandages being stripped off skin, machines beeping. Lizzy had been lying on her back and it was aching. She tried to shift up, but the dull pain in her lower abdomen stopped her. Whatever extras they had given her that night had worn off. 'I hate him,' she managed.

Judith patted her arm. 'You've every right to be angry at your dad. I don't know what he was thinking. After everything he's done, now this has happened. You could press charges, you know.'

Lizzy shrugged. *What good would it do?* Judith's touch felt like plastic, as if it wasn't real.

'Molly said it was Kane that pushed you. Billy said it was the both of them; they clashed together and you were in between. But I saw your dad raise his hand with my own two eyes.'

Lizzy stared at the ceiling. The details didn't matter.

A nurse arrived with a trolley. 'I've got a light breakfast for you. Let's try and sit you up, and I'll put the tray across the bed.' She pushed a button on the side, and Lizzy's head and upper body began to move up. 'I'll take your catheter out soon, and we'll make a trip to the bathroom together.'

Lizzy looked down at the tub of strawberry yoghurt, the applesauce, and the round carton of watery juice. The nausea was still there, although this time it was because of the anesthetic and not the baby. She took the juice and peeled off the tin-foil lid. It was pale yellow.

'That's the stuff, Lizzy. See if you can eat a wee something as well,' said Judith. She sat down on the plastic chair in the corner of the room. 'Darlin', we should try and call your husband. Maureen said she had your mobile number, but not Alfie's or the one at home. Do you want one of us to tell him, or do you want to call him yourself?'

Alfie. They didn't have a landline at home to save costs, but he was at his brother's anyway so she'd need to call him on his mobile. 'I'll tell him. Don't know where my things are. My phone and my clothes.'

Judith looked in the bedside drawer, but found nothing. 'I'll ask when the nurse comes back. They'll have put them somewhere for safekeeping, I expect.'

Lizzy wondered what Alfie would do when she told him. He could get himself hurt if he came up to Scotland, blazing. She was supposed to go home in two days' time, but might be able to get an earlier train. The doctor had told her she would bleed and have cramping for a few days, and would need strong painkillers. He recommended that she stay in Scotland an extra night or two, but to hell with that. She needed to be at home, with Alfie's arms around her.

'Would you like to stay with me, Lizzy? I don't think you'll want to go back to the B&B tonight on your own. Maureen's place is busy, what with the boys still there. It's just me rattling around the place.' Judith smiled. 'You'd be very welcome.'

'Yes, please.' She was so kind. Lizzy's tears dripped down her face and onto the tray. She let them go; they were coming so fast. 'I don't want to be on my own.'

'You're not on your own, darlin'. We're all here for you. I'm ever-so sorry for what's happened.'

Judith stayed for a while, holding her hand. The nurse came back and took her catheter out. Lizzy swung her legs around the side of the bed and stood up, but the sudden movement made her head spin. She grabbed the nurse's thick arm to steady herself. 'I feel a bit strange,' she said.

'Don't worry, hold onto me and take it steady,' said the nurse. She motioned towards the corridor.

But there came a stab of pain in her gut and a hot sensation in between her legs. A flood of red splashed onto the white floor, bright and stark.

'Let's get you on the bed, my dear.' The nurse helped her back. 'Nothing to worry about.'

Someone came to mop up the blood. Two nurses changed her bed-sheets and gown. Lizzy felt limp, like a broken doll, while everyone busied around efficiently. 'I need my phone,' she said to no one in particular. 'I have to speak to Alfie.'

'There's plenty time for all that,' said one of them. 'Let's get you sorted first.'

Plenty time to tell her husband that their baby was dead. Plenty time to get out of that town and never come back. Plenty time for regrets.

Lizzy held onto the place where her womb was wounded, willing it to stop bleeding. She squeezed her eyes shut, blocking out the hate. *I'd do anything for you.* That's what he'd said. Seeing her dad again had made her want the baby. But he'd taken it all away again. He was the bad guy, always was.

ი❧ ი❧ ი❧

Lizzy lay in Molly's old bed, propped up with pillows, a cup of tea on the bedside table. Why did she matter so much to Judith? Perhaps she just felt sorry for her, for all the loss. But they had history too. Lizzy had spent a lot of time there when they were kids, because it was a calmer place than her own.

They'd discharged Lizzy later in the afternoon, once her bleeding had subsided and she'd claimed to feel fine. She wanted out of there as soon as possible, away from the smells and sounds of the hospital. Molly had gone to Tilda's to pack up Lizzy's things for her. She seemed to have bucked up and become efficient in the middle of all the chaos.

It was a small room, with the bed next to the window, and she watched the rain and the clouds move across the sky. Judith was downstairs making something in a blender. It whizzed loudly in short, sharp bursts. Each time, a shockwave pierced her head. She picked up her pot of painkillers, and studied the label. 'One every four hours or when needed,' it read. She'd already taken two.

The doorbell rang, and Lizzy tensed. Hopefully *he* wouldn't know she was there. She listened for voices, and relaxed when she heard Maureen wittering on about the rain. Was she ready for Maureen? She pulled the duvet up to her chest and waited for the onslaught.

Heavy feet on the stairs.

Lizzy longed for her phone. It wasn't in her bag when they gave it back to her at the hospital. Must have been in her back pocket and fallen out somewhere. Alfie got a new contract and number since he was fired, and she didn't know it off by heart. His brother's number was in her phone too.

She wished the bed could swallow her whole, and she could sink into nowhere, murky and safe.

Maureen burst in. 'Oh, there you are, my wee darlin'. What the hell happened? I couldn't believe it when Billy said you'd gone away in an ambulance. There we were, all dancing and laughing away, and there was you going to hospital. We'd had a bit to drink. The party carried on, you know how folk are when there's still booze to be drunk. Me and Billy and the twins packed up all my presents and went home. We called the hospital, and they said you were stable, but had lost the baby. Baby? We couldn't believe it. What a shock that was. Visiting hours were at eleven the next morning they said; you'll have to wait until then to come in; well by then they were talking about sending you on your way. Poor thing.'

Had Maureen stopped talking now? Lizzy swallowed. 'Dad and Kane did it. I got caught between them fighting.'

Maureen was carrying a plate of biscuits, and she put them down on the end of the bed, taking one for herself. 'Kai and Billy told me what happened. Kane was trying to get rid of your dad. They gave him a bloody nose outside, so they did, and I can't blame them for it. I don't like violence, but he deserved everything he got, that one. Fancy that—pushing his own daughter to the floor. And you've lost the baby. I'm awful sorry. I suppose it was too early to tell us, was it?'

'Yes. I wasn't quite twelve weeks.'

Maureen nodded, like she'd known all along. 'Too early to tell folk.'

'What about Kane?'

'Kane?' Maureen took another biscuit, munching fast.

'Just wondered if he was sorry. He was high, Maureen, and drunk.'

'Oh my goodness, we all were.' Maureen flapped her hands, as if Kane was the same as the rest of them. 'Of course he'll be as sorry as anything. We haven't seen him mind, as he didn't make it home. But he'll be back soon enough.'

'He stayed out the whole night?'

'Yes, he does that sometimes.'

Lizzy sighed. 'Did anyone find my mobile?'

Maureen shook her head. 'Not as far as I know. I'll check with the boys when I get home. It must be somewhere, don't worry. I'll send Kai out, and get him to bring it to you later.'

'I texted Alfie in the loo just before it happened, so I definitely had it there.'

'We'll find it.' Maureen finally offered the plate of biscuits to Lizzy.

Lizzy took one. She had to ask. 'Has anyone seen him yet? Dad.'

'No. I should think he'd want to hide his face for a while. He won't know, about the baby, but still. He was rough and a lot of folk saw.'

'I don't want to see him.'

'Good. Don't let him get away with it, will you? I know you'd been seeing him.'

'I won't.'

⤙ ⤙ ⤙

Kai popped by a couple of hours later. He hadn't found her phone, but reckoned it would be in a pocket, a bag, forgotten for the time being. He'd keep trying, ask around. Alfie's brother was ex-directory and they couldn't find his details online. He wasn't on Facebook, same as Alfie. What was it with the Brown boys and their hatred of social media? She could contact Nat or Karen through Facebook on Judith's computer, but she didn't want anyone else to know there was a problem before Alfie if she could help it.

She sighed. 'Thanks for trying. Have you called my phone, Kai?'

'Aye, and at first it rang out. Now it goes straight to voicemail.' He grimaced.

'Shit. Maybe it ran out of battery. It was pretty low.'

'Could be that.'

'Please keep trying. I'll give you Alfie's gmail address, although he's crap at email and might not even look at it if he's at his brother's place drinking. You could give him Judith's number here.'

'No problem, Lizzy.' Kai looked close to tears. 'I'm sorry about what happened. I could murder Kane. I knew he shouldn't have piled in there.'

'Dad shouldn't have turned up in the first place. Don't say anything to Alfie, will you? Just that I've lost my phone.' Lizzy whispered, couldn't bear to think about the words. 'If that doesn't work, I'll have to call Nat in London.'

After Kai left, Molly arrived. She'd packed up all of Lizzy's things from the B&B. Tilda had sent best wishes and a Tupperware container full of cheese scones. Molly rolled her eyes, said it would have been better to give her some of her money back for the nights she hadn't stayed there, but Lizzy thought it was sweet.

Molly lay across the foot of the bed with her feet curled up. 'We never did get to the pub together, did we? When you feel better, let's go out and get hammered for old times' sake. We might not get another chance.'

'We'll see each other again, don't be daft.' The last place in the world Lizzy wanted to be was inside a pub.

'Another time, then.'

'Another time.'

Molly got up. 'I've got to go and see to the kids, but I'll be back to-morrow, okay?'

Molly's hands were shaking. She tried to hide them behind her back, but Lizzy saw. She smelled of stale booze. She was probably off to have a drink. She wondered how much Judith knew.

'Love those kids, Molly. Love them hard, okay?'

Her friend backed away to the door. 'Oh god, I'm sorry. I'm sorry this happened to you.'

'Keep them close.'

'I will. I'm trying.'

The door clicked shut, and finally Lizzy was alone again. She tried to think of the right words for when Alfie called, but the fragments wouldn't form. *Lost baby... dead before birth... unborn child.* The nurse said they should have a burial, to mourn. They would need to decide together. How did two people, parents, decide on such a thing? It made mourning sound structured, a process that happened once the traces of unborn baby had been buried, out of sight. Lizzy wanted none of it. Her grief was a private thing inside her and it would take its own path. Putting flesh into the ground wouldn't change that. Alfie would feel the same way.

ᴏⱱᴏ ᴏⱱᴏ ᴏⱱᴏ

It was getting dark. Lizzy could hear the telly on downstairs, moaning through the floor. She swallowed a painkiller and sat up slowly, reaching for the dressing gown that Judith had given her. It was an old one of Molly's apparently. Judith seemed to keep a lot of her things. Or maybe it seemed that way because Lizzy had never possessed a single item from her childhood. That's what came of being a runaway.

She could kill for a shower. The bathroom was just across the landing, but it felt like miles. She shuffled from the bed to the door, opened it as quietly as she could, then creaked across the floorboards. Her head felt muffled, each step resounding inward like she was inside a cupboard, her own noises echoing back at her.

Avoiding looking into the mirror above the sink, she threw her dressing gown onto a towel rail and turned the shower on hot. As the weak jets of water trickled across her skin, the steam rising, she watched a thin swirl of red disappearing down the plughole. There was less pain now, the remnants of the life wrenched from her body. The last of it.

Afterwards, she put her pyjamas back on, her damp hair springing curls, and went downstairs to find Judith in the kitchen making tea.

'Hi doll,' said Judith, pouring hot water into two mugs. 'I heard you in the bathroom. Do you feel better for the shower?'

'I think so.' Hers was a new voice, one that was empty. It didn't belong to her.

Judith handed her a tea. 'Can I make you a jammy piece?'

'No thanks, I'm not hungry.' She sat down at the table carefully, wiping away a few tears that had escaped without her noticing.

While Judith made herself some toast, the doorbell rang. They both jumped.

Judith put down her knife with a bang and looked at Lizzy. 'It's a bit late for a visitor. Will I answer?'

'I don't know.' Lizzy could feel her neck getting hot.

'I'll try and peek through the blinds in the living room. If it's *him*, I won't open the door.' Judith crept past the front door to the living room.

Lizzy sat, frozen. She could hear Judith rustling with the blinds and worried it would be obvious to the person on the doorstep. The doorbell rang again, longer, more urgent. Judith appeared and whispered, 'It's that woman. Nicole. Shall I let her in?'

Lizzy tried to process the information fast. What did she want? 'Shit. I suppose so. She did look after me when I fell over.'

Judith nodded and went to the front door. Lizzy kept very still and listened. 'Hi there,' Judith was saying, 'my god, you look terrible, Nicole. Come in, come in. We're just in the kitchen there. I'll make you a cup of tea.'

They both came through and Nicole stood next to the table while Judith went to fetch another mug. There were black circles around her eyes. Her thin hair was scraped back into a bun, a single pin holding it together.

Lizzy sat back in her chair. 'Did *he* send you?'

'No, love. I came myself.' She spoke in whispers, as if she were afraid to raise her voice.

'Did you hear about the baby?'

Nicole put her palms to the sides of her face. 'What do you mean?'

Lizzy spoke softly too. 'Did you not wonder what all the blood was about? I had a miscarriage, Nicole.'

Nicole sobbed, lurching forward to grab hold of the edge of the table, to steady herself. 'Oh god, I'm so sorry.'

Judith hurried over with the tea. 'It's not your fault, Nicole. Sit yourself down, dear. He's always been the same, that man. Violent and no good, I'm sorry to say.'

Lizzy leaned forward and touched her thin arm. 'I reckon you've seen the back of his hand yourself. Am I right in saying that, or am I out of order? You seem like a nice enough person, Nicole.'

Nicole wept, holding a tissue over her nose. 'You're right, okay? Most folk can probably tell that a mile off. But it's not as bad as you might think; it's not often, and he's so sorry afterwards. But Lizzy, I feel terrible he did that to you. Have you seen him? He hasn't been home since last night.'

'No. I haven't.' Lizzy looked at Judith.

Judith pulled out another chair. 'Where would he go? He's not got many friends around here, has he?'

Nicole sniffed. 'I checked the pub and even the Social. No one's seen him.'

Judith stared into space. 'I'll bet he's guilty as hell about what he did. I hope he jumped off a bridge.'

Nicole sobbed louder, and Judith apologized, patting her on the back.

Lizzy felt for her. 'He'll turn up, Nicole. But are you sure you want to be there when he does? Things could turn nasty.' At times like this, women had to stick together, no matter what.

'I don't know anymore,' she said. 'I love him and I hate him, you know?'

Lizzy knew. She'd seen it before with her mum. But after a while the love dissolved and they'd got on with their lives. It wasn't real love, but fear and compliance dressed up to feel like it. He was an addiction. 'Are you happy, Nicole?'

'Yes.' Nicole frowned, deep lines furrowing. 'No, not really.'

'Then change your life. Leave him. He's not worth your tears. He doesn't deserve either of us.'

✂ ✂ ✂

That night, Lizzy sat on the window seat in her bedroom and looked up the street, at the sparkling puddles lit by the moon. There was still no word from Kai about her phone, or a response from Alfie's gmail. Still, she'd be back on that train like she was supposed to, whether she was bleeding or in pain or not. At least Alfie would be meeting her at the other end. She'd leave all of this behind and all that would be left was her loss. Lizzy couldn't imagine it ever fading.

She turned to the box of photos and postcards that sat on top of her rucksack, slung into the corner of the bedroom. She opened the box and rooted through for her favourite, the one of her and mum and Granny Mac down at the seaside. The happiest days.

Where did you go, Mum?

Lizzy searched the sky for stars, clouds masking much of them, although the rain had stopped now. She found the one that stood for her mum, twinkling down, and fixed her gaze on it. Perhaps in time she'd choose another one, for one more life lost.

I should have known. It's my own fault for giving him a chance. All those years of his abuse, making our lives tense and unhappy, and then I go to him like a naive little girl. He seemed so down, but then he always was sorry for the things he did, wasn't he? Like he couldn't help himself, that nothing was really his fault. Well I'm sorry that I've let you down. It's just that I had a chance to have a dad again and I wanted to take it.

He did this to you, too, didn't he? After you'd been gone a while, I found some photos I wasn't supposed to see in your forbidden wardrobe. I let myself into the house to water the plants and get some of my things, because I was staying at Auntie Maureen's by then. I bought some purple irises, your favourite, and left them in a vase, thinking you'd get a lovely surprise when you came back. I still buy those flowers on your birthday.

You were protective of that wardrobe, and it was too tempting to resist, me being there on my own. I found the key, opened it up, and found your secret biscuit tin behind a load of shoes. Inside were piles of photographs and postcards, the same ones that Maureen gave me the other day. But there were also two baby scan photos, missing now from the stash. One was me. 'Lizzy 21 weeks', it said on it. And the other was 'Bobby, 13 weeks'. The brother I never had.

Maybe by not telling anyone about it, you were protecting my dad, in a way.

Forgive and forget, Granny Mac used to say. Well that's not going to happen. I'll never forget what he's done. And I'll never forgive him.

She mulled over the last few days. Jonno had seen her mum with 'the man with the hat' on the night she disappeared. She wondered what it felt like, to be so consistently unheard. She'd had a taste of being invisible as a grubby teenage street kid, blending in with the grime of the city. But that was temporary; nothing like what Jonno had to put up with.

The man with the hat.

Oliver. The last time she saw Oliver, it was Lizzy's seventeenth birthday. She'd been followed by a strange woman, a woman she'd caught staring at her in the market. The next thing Lizzy knew, there was a needle stuck in her neck and her drowsy body was being dragged into an alley. But then the woman was gone, and Oliver appeared. He seemed to have saved her from that woman, whoever she was. But where did he come from? Was he following her as well? And if so, why?

She remembered the details of their conversation through a fog of the sedative. He told her that the ghost of her mum had asked him to watch over her, and that he was her guardian, always nearby, protecting her from London scum. Then he asked her a question, and told her to answer carefully. He told her to take herself back a few years, to when she was living in Dalbegie with Mum, when she was happy. If she had the choice, he asked, would she want to find out exactly what happened to her mum—every detail? He said he could find out for her. Lizzy had been through so much already and felt so overwhelmed, that at the time she said no.

But Oliver already knew what happened. He'd been playing with her all along.

Her mum had come to her in dreams too, and so Oliver's account had been half-believable, enough for her then. No one else could understand the bond they'd had, even after her disappearance. Lizzy had never told anyone what happened in the alley that day; it was like Oliver had a hold over her, that she needed to keep it all to herself, to be loyal to her mum.

But it was all bullshit.

She could go to the police with the information and her suspicions, but it had been nearly twenty years since her mum disappeared. Case closed. It was in Lizzy's hands now. She owed it to her mum to uncover the monster who took her away.

Lizzy imagined dragging him out by the tail, exposing him, the truth finally uncovered. *The Dalbegie devil.* Oliver had no motive to hurt her mum. But then not all criminals needed a reason, acting on some kind of calling, a voice inside their disturbed minds.

Tomorrow she'd go to him. She couldn't be hurt much more than she already was. Her child had been ripped from her womb, and there was nothing worse than that. It was time to get some answers. She didn't need anyone's sympathy or help. What she needed to do was to climb inside the core of this place. And Oliver was at the centre of it all.

CHAPTER TWENTY-EIGHT

Oliver Pushes

There was always someone in my way. But the deviation that occurred at the party led me to a rather interesting situation, and admittedly it did spice things up. I had heard about the birthday gathering at the community centre via Jessica's dulcet tones as I picked up the morning paper. She asked, almost insisted, that I attend, and of course I declined. She'd never been one for subtleties and had been asking me out to that godforsaken pub for years despite my never showing the tiniest morsel of interest. She refused to give up. But later, once I was away from her dirty tidemark of a tan, I began to waver. Lizzy would be there. My idealized vision of her falling into my clutches on my own doorstep was starting to seem a little unrealistic. And so here was an opportunity.

I went along late. I foresaw the drunken faces, the blurred looks, and the raucous behaviour, and had decided that it was best to show up once the cogs were oiled, as it were. Everyone would stagger home at some ungodly hour, unaware of who remained, who had left, and indeed if they were ever there. The next morning would hold a huge hangover cloud over the town; late rising, head holding, and little interaction amongst all the attendees. It could be two days before a person was discovered missing. Everyone could be held accountable for the demise of a victim. All would be guilty of letting them down.

However, I did not foresee the stumbling block that would stop me from taking Lizzy for my own at last.

I arrived at the dingy hall, and stood at the far end against the wall, unseen and uninteresting to everyone else. I managed to circumnavigate Jessica, who was thankfully wrapped around another luckless man, his grubby hands around her waist. My eyes were mostly on Lizzy, although I occasionally glanced with disgust at the circus on the dance floor. The mess of stumpy legs, sprayed hair, and armpit sweat on cheap polyester was hard to ignore, and I prayed that I would get a chance to pull away before my headache really set in. The purple colour scheme was bad enough, my retinas aching with the tastelessness of it all. Even Lizzy's unfortunate friend from the newsagents had joined in the hilarity, stomping and slurping. I could see my dear Lizzy was vacillating, ignoring her drink, possibly wondering when she would be able to leave. *Soon, my dear.*

I waited. My whole body was tense, my toes stiff, my hands clenched. I'd wanted this for years, and the time had come to claim my long-awaited prize. She shone. She smiled.

The smell of body odour wound its way from the dancing animals across the room, teasing me, disgusting me, but I was focused. Lizzy pulled up the back of her hair momentarily, to allow the air to get to her slender neck. The sight of it was so inviting. But she was biding her time too. For what? I could only dream of what she wanted. For the first time, sexual feelings were stirring within me, and I flushed. She was different, of an age. I held a can of beer that I'd picked up from under a table to blend in, and it rapidly turned warm in my energized palm. I tried to suppress these unwanted feelings. This had never been about sex, and yet I wanted her. I needed to feel her skin.

That crass relation of hers in the leather jacket wended his drunken way to the dance floor, accosting the one from the newsagents. I wouldn't have bothered with her if I were him. She wasn't exactly a prize. To my delight, Lizzy went to give him a piece of her mind, her graceful hands on slim hips, her hair bouncing with each delivery of what I hoped were harsh words. But instead of recoiling, he grabbed and slobbered, reached and sucked at her until I could bear it no longer. I started towards them, seething, but then she was away from him, and making her way to the Ladies. I settled back. For now, he was safe, but he wouldn't get away with that, far from it.

The pace changed when Lizzy's father and his battered wife burst through the doors. I didn't like him in the first place, but that night he ruined all chance of surviving. I watched as everyone got riled, as he grew even angrier as a result.

It was down to Lizzy to get him to leave, it seemed. Her touch was gently persuasive, and yet he repaid her delicate touch with a brutal shove, just as the rancid boy in the leather jacket sprang forward, and as a result she was sent reeling backwards and onto the floor. There was a crash as some cans of beer rolled away, her face twisted with the shock and the hurt. I leapt forwards, a natural reaction, as did several others around her. Her father was pushed to the doors, shouting and flailing, his strength matched by three or four men on him.

I edged along the wall to get closer to Lizzy, ending up behind the pile of scattered cans and the crowd that was now forming. The battered wife was leaning over her, with a look of horror and fear merged into one. She may have experienced similar situations herself, judging by the dark shadows of recognition in her expression, her lack of surprise. I bent to pick up some of the cans, to stop them rolling, and saw what was certain to be Lizzy's mobile amongst them, black with a clear protective shield. Glancing around to make sure no one saw, I slipped it into my jacket pocket. All eyes were either on Lizzy or on the crashing doors. The music continued its dreadful noise.

The slutty girl who had been sitting at the bar tapped at her phone to call for an ambulance. Someone put a cardigan underneath Lizzy's head, and stroked her hair. An ambulance seemed dramatic, a drunken overreaction. My Lizzy was strong. She could survive a push to the floor without much consequence. But I let them do as they saw fit, their drunken hands on hearts, not realizing the true strength of the fallen. I walked away unseen, my role a different one now, my vengeance rearing.

Outside, her father was bent forwards, holding his face. Three men were kicking him and throwing punches, with a few more forming a ring around them. They were cheering every blow, some still holding onto their drinks, cigarettes clenched between hardened lips. I stood back, enjoying the rising fury, the sound of knuckles on meat. After a time the others backed away, slapping fists into palms, leaving one, the drugged-up reprobate in the leather jacket, his crazed eyes glittering in the moonlight. His punching was relentless, one hit after another, in the man's ribs, his back, his head. Spit was flying.

'That's enough, Kane.'

Someone had finally spoken out.

The siren that had started in the distance was getting closer now, an urgent sound. So Kane was his name. He stood back, leaving Lizzy's father in the middle of the ring, blood dripping from his face. I was amazed he was still standing, but he staggered, two men stepping aside to let him go. No doubt they all felt manly and brave, their testosterone released. I held my gaze on this Kane for a moment, and took in the contours of his snarling face. I would be back for him another time. The show was over, and I left to a grand display of whooping and cheering, high-fiving in a pathetic show of solidarity.

The siren was accompanied by flashing lights as the ambulance appeared. The police would follow shortly, no doubt.

I sauntered into the night, then once I was out of sight I broke into a jog to catch up with Lizzy's father, my rage building, my right eye pulsating so violently that I had trouble convincing myself it would stay in its socket. He had hurt what was mine, and he had ruined my plans for the evening.

He was going to pay for his actions twice that night.

It wasn't long before I caught up with his staggering. He was swearing loudly, although I couldn't make out many of the words except 'my baby girl,' but even on that I couldn't be sure. Any hint of delusion that he owned my Lizzy was enough to make my scalp itch.

He punched a tree on the way down to the river, shaking his hand afterwards. He'd obviously decided not to go home yet, which was most fortunate for me. He tripped and faltered, blurted and murmured, an intoxicated mess of a man. When he got to the lower banks, he shouted at the water, his anger joining the furious churning. I lowered myself into the reeds, hidden and silent under the gush of the river. He shook his fist at it, a ridiculous display. As he wobbled with rage, I crept closer, and when he began another torrent of abuse at nothing, I pushed. I came from nowhere, behind the roar of the wind and the water, a strong pair of hands against an unsuspecting body. He fell instantly, chest first, with a yelp of surprise. I watched him twist and turn, his body disappearing into the angry torrent. And then he was gone.

❦ ❦ ❦

As I sat with a glass of Macallan resting on the arm of my chair, I replayed the day I pushed Lizzy's old boyfriend Simon onto the tracks at Leicester Square tube station. It was undeniably satisfying to create an 'accident,' then not having to clear up one's mess, and now I'd done it all over again. Simon was an undesirable, a no-name dropout, and I did society a favour by getting rid of him. The assumption was, of course, that he'd jumped. I read about it in the local free newspaper, and he even got a mention on the six o'clock news. No one cared about the truth; a throwaway assumption was good enough for someone like him. And the same would happen with Lizzy's father. If his body was found, sodden and swollen, his eyeballs would be distended, parts of him rotting like putrid fish. Not a soul would lament his death, not even his downtrodden, stick insect of a partner. The river would wash away the evidence along with his mean spirit, a natural method of cleansing away my involvement. There would be plenty of heads shaking about his alcohol problem, about his violence coming to an end at last. *He asked for it. To hell with that man. Ach, I saw that one coming.* Everyone would imagine him stumbling in a drunken stupor to his death, perhaps even wracked with guilt about shoving his daughter to the floor, and yet no one would suspect or even care that he was aided in this. Even if they did, the attention would be on the men abusing him that night at the party.

Not me, the watcher, safe in the background.

I hoped Lizzy wouldn't be too disappointed that her only surviving parent was no longer around. But perhaps by the time he was found, she wouldn't be there to form an opinion, to mourn his loss, because she'd be with me at last. Everything was going to be just so.

My eyes rested on Bird, and I took her down and held her close to my chest. That night I'd been so close to Lizzy that I could feel the very soul of her, weighty and real. I sensed the tiniest crackle of static in the air, finding its way from her body to mine. She had been hurt, taken a fall, but would pick herself up and find her way again. I took a large sip of my whisky and felt the burn sliding down my throat and into my gut. It rested there, inside of me, alongside her.

∞ ∞ ∞

The next day, I began to have some tender conversations with Lizzy's husband via text on her phone. How progressive we were, speaking only in eight-word sentences brightened with a smattering of emoticons. How society's brains had shrunk, conveying our sentiments not through the careful choice of words or self-expression, but via yellow faces and balloons.

I quickly gathered that Lizzy hadn't been in touch for some time, because he was texting quite profusely, and leaving voicemail messages, although I didn't have the passcode to listen to them. His texts said he was looking forward to having her home. I replied, of course, on her behalf. I told him she would need a few more days to connect with family, to feel a sense of closure. In text speak, I said: 'Miss you, but might need more time here to get my head sorted.' I felt rather proud of myself, using a turn of phrase that Lizzy would use. 'Speak tomorrow,' I said. He replied: 'Miss you too, babes. Not too long I hope!' This came with a crooked smiley face. I supposed that meant he wasn't sure if he was happy about it or not. I replied: 'Nearly done.' I added a standard smiley face and a red heart. I wasn't sure if that was over-the-top, but at that point I was getting rather carried away. I almost missed him myself. *Alfie*. It was a name that immediately conjured an endearing, salt-of-the-earth character, a man with a sense of humour and a kind nature. He didn't want his wife away from him for much longer, nor could I blame him.

But then, Lizzy was not his. He had no right to make such demands.

Another text came in from Lizzy's old friend Nat. I was inundated. 'You okay?'

Ah, so Alfie had been in touch with the best friend, trying to get information. What a fuss he was making. I replied, for the hell of it. I said, 'I'm fine! Will explain when I see you.' It was hard to include the exclamation mark, but I did it, shuddering at the informality.

I decided to break free from the oh-so-compelling mobile conversation and go to the newsagents to get my *Times* and the latest in local news from the town crier. Jessica was alone, the other girl on her break, and she ramped up the flirting and the chest bouncing, even rolling the tip of her finger across her bottom lip in a 'come hither' manner that one might see in a low-budget porn movie.

After the usual bout of small talk, she hit me with the latest headlines.

'Did you hear about what happened on Saturday night down the community centre? Oh, it was terrible.'

'I'm sure you'd like to tell me all about it.' I smoothed the newspaper on the counter and added a packet of Polo mints to my purchases. I noticed there were tiny pink marks on the edge of the counter nearest the till, where Jessica had been painting her nails. There was a strong stench of it about the place, acidic and chemical. Cheap, slutty warpaint.

She pressed some buttons on the till, her fingers separated wide to prevent smudging. 'Well. Lizzy's dad pushed her over, quite violent, and she really hurt herself. There was blood all over the place, I'm not joking. Some of the boys took him outside and gave him a good seeing to.'

'And is she okay?'

'She'll never get over it, you know.' She leaned forward so that her breasts were squashed in between her arms, and whispered her secret. 'She lost her baby.'

I have to admit, I was taken aback with that information. I prided myself on noticing everything about Lizzy. I knew if her mood changed from day to day, if she was suffering from a headache. I used to know her inside out, every inch of her, and shouldn't have let her out of my sight for so long. She was a woman now, and I hadn't kept up.

I slammed my money on the counter. 'How pregnant was she?' It seemed like a strange question after I'd asked it, but Jessica was overjoyed to impart further information.

'Not quite the twelve-week mark, fortunately. But it's never easy to lose a child.'

I couldn't bring myself to reply to that. I decide to forgo my change, and put the folded newspaper under my arm, the mints in my pocket as I left.

Jessica called out. 'Your change, Oliver!'

'Keep it.' *Stuff it down your throat and choke on it.*

I heard a low coo from her, an approving pigeon-like noise. I wondered if she would ever give up on me. If she did, I would be almost disappointed for the loss of entertainment.

So Lizzy had lost her unborn child. I knew she would have appreciated me getting rid of the man who killed her offspring. I would be elevated in her eyes if she knew. In the meantime, she must remain strong. Her accident was a minor setback. A loss makes us tougher in the heart and in the mind. It would be for the good.

As I crossed the road to go home, an elderly man in a beige coat appeared. He was carrying a walking stick, but didn't have a limp. I wondered if it was a prop, designed to make him seem authentic, an unsuspecting old man. The stick could have a camera lodged inside its handle, recording, watching. I paused while he passed and he raised his hat to me. I glowered at him, and strode to my front door, the key rattling in the lock.

Was I being watched after all? Perhaps the past was catching up, just as the final curtain was about to fall.

Once I was safely inside, I stood poised at the kitchen window. The man had gone. He could have been any neighbour, going home. But I couldn't be sure.

I checked the skirting boards, the picture rails, every object and every surface, for signs of camera activity. I even punctured Bird with a small hole and thumbed through her fine stuffing from head to tail, but found nothing. The room felt colder, more empty than usual, as if its walls had been violated. Tiny pieces of the stuffing had scattered onto the floor, and I swept them up and threw them into the fireplace. I scratched at my skin, my scalp. Lizzy had been pregnant and I hadn't noticed. I was losing my touch, because of this feeling that I, the watcher, was being watched. There were sounds, muffled voices, coming from outside that were busying my mind. Or perhaps they originated from inside, my ever-present anxieties taking an audible form. I scratched at the bare wall facing the fireplace and felt paint particles and dust slice into my fingernails.

I logged into the forum, wanting to act, to move forward in some way, even if it was only virtual. White flecks of paint scattered onto my keyboard as I typed. I searched for Parsley and found her most recent entry, a response to someone who had just returned from a funeral. She was hopefully still online, her heartwarming message written only a few minutes before.

I didn't want to start a new thread and draw attention to myself, so I added my own post underneath hers.

I agree with Parsley. You shouldn't be alone after attending a funeral. Call a friend or someone in your family to talk to, or better still, ask them 'round. Sometimes you need to have someone by your side.

I had no idea what I was trying to say, but making sense didn't seem to matter on this forum. All people wanted was a response, a hand-hold. Any message of support would do, to make them feel life was worth living. Parsley added another comment immediately.

Good idea by OwlVerse. Call a special someone. I could do with a shoulder to cry on today, but I have no one.

The perfect response. I decided to go in for the kill. Sometimes you've got to take an opportunity, even if it presents itself at the wrong time.

You can cry on mine. No pressure.

I added a private email address that I'd previously set up for OwlVerse. She would see it, and hopefully note it down before my post was removed by the moderators and I received a virtual slap on the wrist. No direct contact was allowed. I shut down, hoped for the best. If I could get her on her own, 'talk' to her without inhibitions, who knew where the contact could lead.

The bathroom beckoned. I had to remove the grime from the day, from my fingernails, from my insides. But I wouldn't be truly cleansed until I had Lizzy here too, the pressure released from my chest, like a fine mist evaporating.

CHAPTER TWENTY-NINE

Helen's Penny Drops

It was the thumping music and the dull roar of drunken shouting that attracted her. It was the first time Helen had heard signs of full-on activity, of folk out having a good time, or a bad time, depending on how you looked at it. The pub seemed dour, a place for hard drinking and rucks, probably a selection of old-time tracks on the jukebox. The High Street was dead until closing, when the time came for battered sausages and chips, followed by a mass stagger home. Folk were comfortable here, set in. They went to the same places after drinking the same thing, night after night.

She'd circumnavigated the area around Oliver's place once again, but still there'd been nothing to see. His house was in darkness. Either he was hibernating or he was out. Helen's fingers were frozen and she couldn't stand the thought of hanging around, so she walked to the other end of town, surveying the houses that had lights on, sniffing the chill air, wondering what she was really doing. Perhaps it had been a mistake to think she'd figure out what Oliver did there. Maybe he didn't do anything interesting after all.

But then the sounds wound their way to her, the direction of the wind on her side. *There.* She followed the sounds and they led her to the community building some way off the High Street. As she drew closer, the doors burst open and several men poured out into the car park, swearing and shouting, bundling in to form a tight circle underneath a street lamp. She heard a yelp, someone getting hurt, and hurried to crouch behind the nearest car. They were kicking and punching the man in the middle, their shirt sleeves rolled up, grunting and panting. A few of them had lit up, and their cigarette smoke found her. It smelled of Mother's flat in Edinburgh, the lingering remains of her old, stinking habit.

Then she saw Oliver.

He was there, watching, on the periphery. He was easy to spot, tall and bold but always on the outskirts, his hat covering that manky head of his. His eyes were set on the man fighting. It felt like the old days at The Audacious in Soho, when they would enjoy a victim getting hurt in the middle of the room. But this wasn't premeditated. This was an impromptu party fight. What was Oliver doing there? He was out of place, too straight, too conservatively dressed.

She rubbed her knees, aching from all the walking, and kept very still. She was on the outer circumference of the circle; Oliver was in the inner membrane, and the others were in the nucleus.

The victim finally staggered away. One of the lads flicked his cigarette at him and another tried to trip him up.

'Get te fuck, you schemey piece.'

'Run before we fuckin' kill you, ye bass.'

There came the wail of an ambulance. Not for him, surely? No one in their right mind would call emergency for a pub brawl. The beat-up man was walking, holding his face, making his way towards the far end of the car park. Oliver kept his eyes on him, unwavering.

Helen shifted back. She couldn't risk Oliver seeing her there. The ambulance came right the way down and stopped outside the main doors. The paramedics ran inside with a stretcher and a bag. So someone else was hurt. Perhaps the beaten man had just paid for what had kicked off inside.

Oliver was moving away too, pulling down his hat, slipping on a pair of gloves. He glanced around the throng of men to check if anyone was watching him, then darted off in the direction that the beat-up man had gone. Helen knew the look on his face. It said, 'I'm going to get you.'

What had the man done?

She waited.

Then the doors were being held open and the paramedics came out with a woman on a stretcher. Oliver was out of sight now, so it was safe to come out of hiding. Helen pulled up her hood and crept forward, merging with the small crowd that was forming around the ambulance. She craned her neck to see the woman. She had wavy blonde hair that was spilling down the sides of the stretcher, her thin body covered in a blanket. She was crying.

That hair.

It was the girl she followed to the B&B, the one who had seemed so familiar. She'd been hurt. Helen smiled. Oliver didn't like it, would make the man who hurt her pay. *That was it.* She knew who she was now. It was that girl from the market in Soho, the one Oliver had a thing about. She was here, and he was watching her again, protecting her.

The back doors of the ambulance banged shut and the engine started up again. As it drove away, its lights flashing, Helen punched her chubby fist into the ether. Her trip had been worth it, after all. The nothingness of the last few days, the lack of stimulus apart from one measly body in the park, was worth putting up with if this was the grand finale. The girl in the bushes was a taste, a morsel compared to what could happen now.

That girl was Oliver's prize possession. She had been threatened and he was going to go into overdrive. He used to watch her in London, follow her. He protected her from the pimps and the scavengers, and finally from Helen herself in that alley.

She rubbed her hands together, slowly, deliciously.

As the sirens wailed into the distance, Helen put her hand in her pocket and rested her palm against the cold metal of her hammer. She imagined the sound it would make when it thudded against the woman's skull, cracking the bone, red soaking into all that hair. She looked like an angel, lying so fragile on that stretcher. Soon she'd be one, soaring up to heaven where she belonged.

Her hands tingled. She would pick someone else for tonight, to satisfy the burn in her blood. There were only men around, hawking onto the ground, the after-fight swagger. One of them would have to do. The one that was left punching at the end must be in Oliver's camp somehow, on the same side. He was sucking on a roll up, his leather jacket done up now, a sweat stain around the neck of his T-shirt. She saw him pass a wrap to one of the others, a palm switch. Lowlife. No one would miss him, then, unless he'd promised them a delivery.

The music coming from inside had slowed, and a few folk had started to spill out, talking in low voices. She stepped away from the dim light and waited for the leather jacket to stumble away. He was the kind who would go it alone. Wherever he was heading, he wouldn't get there. She was too fast, too alert for him. She would follow him at a distance, the hammer burning through to her skin, as if it were alive.

CHAPTER THIRTY

An Optimistic Discovery

Two mornings had come since the night at the hospital, and although the nausea had left Lizzy's body for good, she'd never felt so sick. She was sunken in, like an empty vessel. She sat on the sofa with the telly on low, a tartan blanket covering her knees. Judith had made her a cup of tea and it sat next to her, slowly turning lukewarm. She stared at the screen, the lights and colours flickering.

There were too many things unresolved. Her dad had disappeared, and now that she wasn't able to see him, she had a burning desire to tell him a few things. She hated him from the bottom of her heart and he should know that. She'd never come 'round to him again. He deserved to die in place of Mum. If she could switch their places, she would do it. She'd tell him all of that, if he crawled out of his hole and bothered trying to see her.

She had to go to Oliver. Today. She needed to pull her leaden body out of the house. But the idea of it was dragging at her, weighing her down even more.

Judith was making toast. The smell of it made her think of her mum, of slabs of butter, of how she used to brush her hair at night for her. She shut her eyes and lay her head back, wrapping her arms around a cushion. She could always come back to Dalbegie when she was stronger, to tie up all the threads. Right now they were flying around in all directions, an overwhelming mess of things. She couldn't even see them clearly, to hold them still.

Auntie Maureen came blethering in for a visit. She sat down on the other end of the sofa, put her stocking feet up on a stool and began to gossip about everyone in Dalbegie. Lizzy pretended to listen. Her aunt's lipstick had bled into the cracks on her top lip. Her stocking feet smelled of Parmesan. Kai had apparently given up trying to find her phone. How stupid she was to lose another one. Lizzy vowed to reinstate their landline when she got home, and learn Alfie's new mobile number off by heart. She hoped he wouldn't panic, that he would guess what had happened. And he still hadn't replied to the email. Still, she'd see him tomorrow. She could try other ways to make contact, but had decided it was better to tell him face to face. She'd tell Nat after.

Maureen went on to talk about men in general. 'They're all as bad as each other. I'm not sure what was worse, now I think about it. When my Brian was around, or when he was gone. I was left with four kids, but at least I didn't have him to look after as well.' She helped herself to a biscuit, and peered towards the kitchen, looking for her cup of tea.

'Was he that bad?' Lizzy pulled the cushion closer and sank into the sofa.

Maureen leaned forward, checking over her shoulder. 'Well,' she said, and paused for dramatic effect. 'He wasn't completely normal, I'll tell you that much.'

'What do you mean?' Lizzy sat up again.

'Ach'. Maureen waved her hands around, like she was dissolving the idea of it all. 'I'm not sure how to explain him. But four kids don't come by easily. You have to try a lot, plenty of trying, to get them. And he wanted to try every night, if you get my meaning. Every bloody night.'

'Gross.' The word slipped out before Lizzy could stop it. The image of Brian and Maureen at it every night was too much.

'And when I didn't want to try any more, after Noah was born, well. He said I was no good to him anymore. But I was tired, Lizzy, sick of all his fumbling and nonsense.'

Lizzy was unsure whether to trust her mouth by opening it. It was safer just to let Maureen carry on talking. She fixed her gaze on the crystal ornaments in Judith's cabinet. There was a hedgehog, a snail, and some kind of multi-faceted ball. Above them were two pewter beer mugs with engraving on them. One of them read 'World's Best Dad' and the other proclaimed 'Happy Father's Day.' She couldn't imagine Molly buying them.

Maureen had barely drawn breath. 'Eventually he found his alternative, didn't he? Someone who'd put up with his needs. I never mentioned Brian being with Simon's Ma to you before, because I can't bear to think of her. She's the lowest of the low. It's embarrassing, to think we were once married. I hope none of my boys have got his problem in their genes, because god help their girlfriends, is all I can say. My Kane has a flirty way about him, right enough.'

'Yes, I noticed.' *A flirty way?* The incident she'd had with him on the bench, and at Molly's, was more than that. *A pervert, more like.* She glanced at Maureen. 'Also the drugs.'

'Drugs? What are you talking about, drugs? My Kane likes a drink, but not the rest of it. My boys wouldn't have the drugs. I know them.' Maureen folded her arms.

'He deals drugs, Maureen. I'm sorry to have to tell you, but when I was at Molly's, he showed up looking for money. She owed him.'

'I don't think so. You must have that wrong. He's no angel, but drugs? Not my Kane.'

Lizzy was too weary to argue. 'You should talk to him about it.'

'I will ask him, I'll promise you that. When I see him.'

'What do you mean? Isn't he back yet?' Lizzy felt goosebumps rising on her arms. *Him too?*

Maureen didn't answer. She looked around the room, anywhere but at Lizzy, clasping and unclasping her hands.

She probed. 'Has he been home at all since the night of the party?'

'No, he hasn't. But I'm sure he's fine. He's gone off before, right enough.'

'He probably doesn't want to face up to what he did.'

'We all make mistakes. Especially him. Will I make you another cup of tea, dear?'

Mistakes? Lizzy curled her legs up. 'No I'm fine. I need to rest, now, Maureen.'

'Of course you do. I'll away.'

Maureen said her goodbyes, chatting away to Judith while she put on her coat. Lizzy heard Judith closing the front door on her a split second too early, while Maureen was still finishing her sentence.

Lizzy got up. The bleeding had almost stopped, her cramps now bearable. She told Judith she wouldn't be long, wrapped up warm, and promised to walk slowly.

Outside, her arms dropped by her sides of their own accord, and her legs plodded as if there were weights strapped to her ankles. Even the air felt heavy today, the clouds hazy and low. There was a faint rumble in the distance and she wondered if they'd be getting a thunderstorm. The air smelled of wet leaves, a pungent mass creeping up from the earth.

Her iron-chained legs were taking her to the river.

The distant hiss was approaching, the river's constant flow familiar and calming. She walked across the top banks and down through the reeds, her feet and ankles getting wet. She didn't care; her mind was shutting down, zoning out with the crash of water. This place was all about Simon, of cigarettes and stolen booze. She'd seen a side to him that no one else had. Underneath the tattoos and the attitude was a sensitive soul. She was the only real friend he'd had.

She sat at the riverside, where it twisted and turned northwards. She pulled out her iPod from her pocket and chose Joy Division's *Unknown Pleasures*, one of the most symbolic albums of their time together.

When she'd first listened to it, her life had taken a turn, her world spinning so fast she didn't know which way was up.

She'd failed him. Everyone in Simon's world let him down.

Her gaze softened as she watched the flowing water splash against rocks to the rhythm of the track, carrying leaves and twigs, bracken and scum. The earth moved with the bass line, deep, barely twisting, relentless. The notes reverberated, a pulsing good bye.

Above her was a line of trees at the top of the bank, and the edges of the town. She'd forgotten how much she needed time by herself. As an only child, she'd craved a bigger family, and yet these days she liked it when there was no noise of other people talking, questioning, and needing. She picked up a long stick and dipped it in the water, the strong current pulling at it.

The water was flowing too fast for reflections, but soon a pattern began to form next to the largest rock, water pooling, then gushing around the sides of it. She began to see a face there, a human outline, not her own but someone much younger. The girl had blond hair, straight unlike hers, and it was blowing in the wind. She was laughing, free. Lizzy's eyes filled. She waved her fingers and the girl waved back. She looked away, breaking the illusion, wiping her face with her sleeve.

But there was a glinting just under the surface of the water by the rocks at the water's edge. It was a real thing, moving and metallic. She pulled out her earphones and moved closer, crouching down on the slippery mud, careful to lodge her feet firm. It was a chain caught in between two rocks, the end of it being whipped by the water. She held out the stick and tried to hook the end of it.

She needed to get it. Lizzy put her hands square on the ground to steady herself, and stepped down onto the rocks. One of them wobbled, but she inched down, little by little, the noise of the water getting louder. She stretched out, her fingers in the water now, and felt the chain, cold metal covered with a thin veil of slime. A sharp tug and it came free. She found her feet and climbed up to the bank, not daring to look at it closely until she was out of danger.

It was exactly like her mum's chain, the one that used to have the Scottish Cross on the end of it. There was a place where the cross could have hung, a slightly larger link than the rest, bent and broken. She wiped off a piece wet grass and held the tarnished chain around her neck. It was exactly the right length and thickness. The cross would have sat on her breastbone, shining and blue. *I want it to be.* She touched it with her fingertips and gazed into the river, full of shadows and secrets, and broke down. Falling to her knees, she sobbed.

Were you thrown into the river, Mum? Is that what happened? Maybe you were attacked and discarded, your clothes and jewellery torn away from your body over the years, ripped and stuck in the river amongst the weeds and the stones, memories washed away. Were you brought here by him? Oliver. Dragged here? I want to know. I've come this far and I need to know.

My baby is dead and I have to know.

CHAPTER THIRTY-ONE

Lauren Floatin'

I wasn't thrown into that river, my wee darlin'. That's far from what actually happened, but if you want to believe that I drowned, dreamily, in the cool, soft water, that's fine by me. Better to think that I washed away, all floaty, than to know the hard truth. And if you want it to be, if it makes you happy, then let the necklace you found be mine. Let's just say that it's the one, passed down to me by my dear mother, the notorious Granny Mac. Although it wasn't exactly valuable, it was the most precious thing I owned. It was one of your favourite things, Lizzy; you used to sit up at my dressing table and hold it up around your neck. I'd tell you to take it off every time, terrified that you'd break it. Seems such a shame, now. I should have let you wear it whenever you wanted.

Beautiful things shouldn't be hidden away.

We think the things that are precious to us will somehow bring us luck, and it's not true. Even the real necklace didn't do me any favours. Look at me now. But if you want to live the fairy story, just this once, you deserve to be in it. God knows, we all need to live in our minds once in a while, as long as we're stuck on earth. Stick the chain in your pocket, touch it once in a while, and make believe it's looking after you.

Because right now, no one else is.

CHAPTER THIRTY-TWO

Lizzy Plunges In

The wind was picking up, whipping Lizzy's hair into her face. She wiped her tears with the back of her hand and forced herself to stand up. The chain was a sign, from her mum. It said, 'you're close.'

She went to him. The wet streets were streaked with oil, taking her where she needed to go. What was that thing Granny Mac used to say? It was 'listen to your innards' or 'watch your innards.' Lizzy was following her gut, and her gut said she should go to Oliver. Her heart was pounding, her head in turmoil. *Mind your innards.* That was it. She picked up speed.

He was there; she could sense his thunderous presence. Perhaps he could see her even now, watching her as she watched him. Lizzy felt an overwhelming sense of inevitability; that she was meant to be there.

It was all down to her now. *The truth.*

She was shifting in quicksand, her legs moving in slow motion, everything sinking to a lower and more uneven surface than before.

She sidetracked the newsagents, and stood against the blank wall underneath the awning, facing the cottage. There was no way she was going into the shop; she couldn't handle Jessica's over-the-top sympathy today. She wouldn't know how she felt; how could she? And neither did Molly, with her own three beautiful, grubby children she didn't seem to be grateful for. Some people didn't know what they'd got.

Perhaps she'd never have a kid of her own. Her body could be permanently damaged now, each fertilized egg rejected since that first one was wrenched from her womb. She stared at the cottage, her insides black like lead.

A voice made her jump.

'Is that you, Lizzy?'

It was Jessica. *Fuck.* She turned, one side of her body slumped against the wall.

'Are you okay?' Jessica came closer, smoothing down the front of her pencil skirt.

Lizzy shrugged. Jessica was wearing one of her tight acrylic v-neck jumpers in a ghastly turquoise. Her breasts were squashed together, her cleavage deep and wrinkled.

'I just popped out for a ciggy. Want one?' Jessica offered the pack, taking one for herself and half-throwing it between her red lips. She leaned against the wall next to Lizzy.

She was standing too close. Lizzy hesitated. She hadn't smoked in years and Alfie didn't like it. But what did it matter now, anyway? She wasn't even pregnant any more. 'Thanks.' She slid the cigarette out of the packet and rolled it between her thumb and finger.

Jessica held up her lighter. 'I heard about your baby. I'm really sorry.'

Lizzy leaned forward and lit her cigarette. The act of it seemed so familiar. She was a teenager again, with backcombed hair and DM boots, smoking behind the shop. She blew out the smoke above her head and watched it rise. 'Even more gossip to spread around, now, I suppose. I bet you're glad I came back. I've given everyone something to talk about.'

Jessica pulled away. 'That's not fair. I wouldn't wish that on anyone. I've lost two myself, you know.'

Lizzy looked up to see real tears in Jessica's eyes. 'Really? Oh shit, I'm sorry.'

'S'all right. You wouldn't know.'

'Were you married before?'

'No one marries the party girl. I went through a phase of trying to get pregnant, you know, pretending to be on the pill. And it worked—twice. But both times I had a miscarriage, like god was looking down on me and punishing me for doing it.'

Lizzy took a long drag. 'No. It's bad luck, and no one's judging.'

'I didn't deserve to have a baby, not the way I was carrying on. And now I'm too old, and all dried up. Life isn't fair, is it?'

'No, it isn't.' Lizzy sank down to crouching level. A buzz made its way through her blood and dulled her senses.

Jessica stubbed out her cigarette and put her hand on Lizzy's shoulder. 'I'm ever-so sorry for what happened. I know how you feel, honest I do. It's the same shite whether or not you've got a husband or a boyfriend, or if you're on your own.'

'Of course it is.' Lizzy felt horrible. She rubbed her eyes. 'I don't want to see Molly right now. Don't tell her I'm out here, okay? Please.'

'I won't. But she seems awful cut up about what happened. Molly doesn't like to show her emotions, even to the people she loves the most.'

Jessica tottered away, her high heels wobbling on the concrete. All the times Lizzy and her mum had laughed at Jessica's tight clothes. She was just trying her best to be liked. Or loved.

'Thanks for everything,' Lizzy called out. 'I'll come back again one day.' She flicked her stub into the gutter, and felt the remains of the cigarette in her lungs, the lingering smell of smoke. It was a disgusting thing to do after years of resistance, but it was what she'd needed, the drag of tar through her body, sticking to the rest of the blackness.

Don't be weak. It's time.

She glanced around, and waited for two women to disappear into the newsagents. She didn't want to draw attention to herself, or for

Molly or Jessica to see her as she ran across the street to the cottage. This was between her and Oliver. It was no business of anyone else.

As she lifted her hand to knock, the dread shot through her. It was crazy to be here. He was dangerous.

But she couldn't be anywhere else. This was where she had to be.

She tapped on the door three times, each one reverberating inside her. *No. No. No.*

It opened straightaway, as if Oliver had been waiting for her. He bowed, holding onto his hat, a grey fedora. 'Do come in,' he said, and retreated down the hallway. 'I'll make tea.'

The man with the hat. Did he wear hats indoors too, or had he just put it on? He was tall and very thin, like his trousers were stuck on two stilts.

Lizzy stepped inside, pausing for breath when fear cut through her. To follow him was insane. To not go in would be infuriating.

He looked back. 'Second thoughts?'

'No.' She shut the door behind her.

'Milk and sugar?' He swished through to the kitchen and switched the kettle on.

'Two, please.' She had tried to sound casual, like he did, but her voice trembled, too high and squeaky to be natural. *Keep it together.*

Oliver directed her into the living room. 'Your friend in the newsagents told me you were back, and I wondered if you'd come over. I'm pleased you did. I'm sure you'll have plenty of questions—so much time has passed since we last saw each other. Make yourself comfortable.'

He disappeared. He'd aged, must be well in his fifties now, but he looked older, his eyes bagged and black. His face was drawn and pinched, his skin blotchy. There were two burgundy lounge chairs facing the fireplace, and a large sofa against the wall that looked like it had never been sat on. The cushions were straight, the fabric immaculate.

She sat on one of the chairs, turning it slightly to face the inside of the room. There was a clock on the mantle, an old-fashioned one that was ticking loudly. Next to it was a small, yellow bird toy. It was bright and out of place; there were no pictures on the walls, photographs or frames. The smell of the house was the same as before: clean, almost clinical. The antiseptic smell reminded her of the hospital, of death. *Should I run?*

'Here we are.' Oliver brought in a tray with two mugs of tea and a packet of oatmeal biscuits. He set it down on the small round table next to Lizzy and turned one of the mugs so that the handle was facing her.

She looked at the tea, her hands frozen to the chair.

'You look cold,' he said. 'You've been standing outside for a while. Have you been contemplating the dangers of coming to see me? You shouldn't be worried. I've been looking out for you for many years now. You know that.'

Lizzy felt heat rising in her face. 'You said that years ago, that you were acting as my guardian. But nothing good ever seemed to come of it. Everyone seemed to disappear around me. Too right, I've got questions. Because nothing you've ever told me has made sense.'

All that crap about keeping their liaisons secret was stupid. She should have told Judith where she was going this afternoon, for a start. Why did she feel the need to keep the idea of him private? She didn't seriously think their odd relationship should be preserved, to keep the memory of her mum intact. Not anymore. *Idiot.*

'Alfie knows I'm here. I just texted him.'

He blinked. 'That's good.'

'I'm going back to him tomorrow. He's picking me up.'

'Of course.'

He took his tea and sat in the other lounge chair, his legs facing away from her towards the fireplace. They were like an old couple having an afternoon rest, putting things right after a quarrel. Lizzy felt sick, her whole body tingling now, as if it knew. *Get out. Get away from him.* But she was drawn to him, and she wanted answers.

She swallowed. 'Do you have tea like this with anyone else in this town? You've lived here for years.' His sideburns were tatty, with red scratches around them, and some kind of manky stuff under the rim of his hat. Was it dried blood? She couldn't help but stare.

He cupped his hand around his mug and looked into the fireplace, although that too was dead. 'I have no desire for idle friendships. Never have.'

She willed him to meet her eyes, so that she could see inside him. What would she find? A void, perhaps. 'What are you doing here? There's nothing for you in this place but rain and gossipy people and that crappy old newsagents. You hate this town. You hate the people. You hardly leave the house. Where do you go when you're not here? Don't you have family?' She was talking fast, her words tumbling into each other. Part of her wanted to rile him. The sides of her head throbbed.

He tapped his foot on the floor in time to the ticking clock. 'I've been here long enough that people know I prefer my own company. It's how I like it. When I'm not here, I'm in Edinburgh earning money. I don't have family.'

Lizzy took a deep breath in. 'I want to know.'

At last he looked at her, his eyes dark beneath the rim of his hat. 'What would you like to know?'

She picked up the mug of tea and held it in front of her. A small barrier. 'The last time we met you asked me if I wanted to find out what happened to my mum. You said you'd help me. You said I should think carefully about my answer. I've always wondered what would have happened if I'd said yes.'

'I would have helped you find out. But you chose not to, and a wise choice it was, I believe. You were young and vulnerable. I don't think you could have coped with the truth.' He leaned forward and sipped at his tea, his eyes remaining on her. 'And now?'

'Now I want to know. I'm ready.'

He raised his eyebrows, a faint smile appearing. 'Are you quite sure? You may not like the details when they're presented to you.'

Lizzy felt anger rise through her fear, hot waves of it filling her chest and head. He'd killed her, she was sure of it. He did it. She held back the tears and asked. 'You might as well tell me now. Because you already know, don't you? Did you throw her into the river?'

Silence. The clock ticked the seconds away.

'No, I did not.'

She gasped with the relief of it. Shaking, she gulped at the tea. It was hot and heavy, the steam dampening her face. 'Then who did?'

'My dear Lizzy. No one threw your mother into the river. But I did throw your father in there the other night, god rest his soul.'

'What do you mean?' A fizzing sensation made its way down her throat into her gut.

'He hurt you. I saw it happen. And I couldn't let him get away with it. He was drunk; he could barely stay on his feet. I hardly even touched him and he plummeted into the water like a ship's anchor. He more or less threw himself in . . . '

What was he saying? She was following his words, but his voice was becoming fainter and deeper, and the walls were bending.

Did he just tell her he threw her dad into the river? The ceiling caved so low that the pendant light lowered itself almost to the floor.

She tried to ask another question, but her mouth had turned to rubber. *The tea.* She shouldn't have drunk it. Her body had already felt heavy, but now it was iron, being pulled to the ground by a magnetic force.

Down she went, down and down. Plummeting.

And then there was the bottom of the earth.

CHAPTER THIRTY-THREE

Oliver's Desert

I had polished, wiped and dusted every inch of the house. I cleaned with unflinching vigour all through the night, a renewed enthusiasm giving me boundless energy. I hadn't worn my surgical gloves for a while, but had slid them on for the job, their familiar tightness a comfort to me. The whole place smacked of newness, ready to be used once again.

Once I had put Lizzy to sleep, I went straight to the pantry and pulled up the floorboards. The stench of death floated out of my hidden cellar, enveloping me. Previous experiments flashed through my mind. There had been some unusual responses, different reactions and lengths of time people took to die, and some of those subtleties came back to me then. Lauren, Lizzy's mother, whose smile I was attracted to while she was still alive, made for fascinating viewing, as myself and my subscribers watched as her face imploded, her cheekbones collapsing into themselves.

I climbed down the ladder and into my cave, the lone light bulb yellow and weak, the way I liked it. The platform in the middle of the room was bare, save for a large stain in the middle. I could catch most bodily fluids and expulsions, but sweat was impossible to collect or obstruct, weeping from every pore. My old experiments seemed rather basic, a kind of prelude to my more sophisticated endeavors, but they had been popular for their simplicity and for the length of time a subject could be regarded. Through the camera, my followers watched, enthralled with my experiments. I had already decided I would use the same camera, despite its heft and technological inferiority, for posterity. It had been with me for years, since before I had owned that particular house. There was charm in the whirr of its cranky mechanism, the pixilation of the less-refined picture.

I was an old romantic at heart.

There was going to be a special someone down there. I just needed to pick her up while she dreamed, my sleeping princess, and settle her in. I would peel off her clothes, touch her breastbone, feel the back of her neck. The softest place.

If the original camera was going to be there, then so should the old portal. I had restored NondescriptRambunctious.com, and tightened up the web site security and encryption so that layman internet users wouldn't find it. I would soon be confirming the password details with my most long-standing acquaintances. They had been with me for so long that I'd forgotten how I met some of them, how we crossed paths in the first place. A few were no longer in touch. One man tried to recruit two colleagues without my permission, and we had a serious breach of security, which was why I deactivated the site back then. And so, I was left with a few trusted watchers, all of whom were eager to revisit the entertainment we had enjoyed so much back then. Ahh, the dreamy early internet days of the nineties. It was so exciting then, on the World Wide Web.

I had already teased them about who was going to be the victim, asked them all to guess, and no one got it right. It was too good. I'd be paid well.

We were going back to our roots, Lizzy and me. This viewing would be a reflection of the past wrapped up in tissue paper for us all to keep. And then the website would be gone again, the camera packed away, as if nothing had ever happened. Over the years, I had become warier of online activity; in many ways, it was easier to hide in plain sight than it was online. We lived in a world in which no one looked around them, their orientation completely reliant on technology. People didn't speak to each other, but "posted" their thoughts, "liking" and commenting on subjects they knew nothing about, sharing posed photographs of themselves for a purpose that they couldn't really put their finger on if asked. Social media they continued to call it—a misnomer. The smartphone was merely a compact mirror, reflecting an image of ourselves for our own, egotistical admiration. We were all narcissists, whether we believed ourselves to be or not. And we were not, by any means, social.

Least of all me.

Although the pleasure of Lizzy's thirst would be great indeed, my fear was feeling empty after she'd gone, for she had filled my world for almost two decades. Eighteen years to be precise, from when she was a tender twelve-year-old girl. Was it ironic that her mother was body number eighteen? I liked to think of it as serendipity, a winding road that led us to our destinies, with perhaps a dead end here and there, minor stumbling blocks that gave the illusion that we were overcoming, shifting and changing, making decisions. But the choices were not ours. Things were given to us and we had to accept them graciously.

You can imagine how excited I was by my conquest; how eager I was to announce that I was ready to begin. There was one member of my circle who lived in Dalbegie, and I decided to start with him. I had the unique opportunity to tell someone face-to-face, to feed off their reaction, bask in the glory. It was dangerous to have someone involved who was so physically close to me. But he was one of my trusted members and we had little personal contact, certainly none that would be noticed by anyone else.

When he exposed himself as a potential colleague all those years ago, I was surprised at first, then wary. He first gave me a nod, making a subtle wink to his social needs, by meeting my gaze with those blackened eyes of his. His demeanor, and his pallor, fit the profile of the rest of my online followers, and it piqued my interest immediately, as it isn't often that I meet like minds. We had a short exchange, whereupon he made it clear what his needs were, and I offered to help him meet them. It was how I usually began my dealings. Partners in crime form alliances, the beginnings of a kind of faith. I suggested we meet the next day in Inverness, away from prying eyes, and make our way to Craigphadrig Wood. There was an abundance of housing estates on the way, rows of dirty and depressing white houses that were full of impressionables. We found our man after only half an hour. He was leaning on a lamppost, smoking, and looking like he'd do anything for money. Unfortunately for him, we didn't pay.

Following that first outing, we bonded, albeit superficially, and my Dalbegie contingent was born. He subscribed to my private website, paid his dues, and never gave me reason to doubt his loyalty and discretion. He was estranged from his family, one of life's victims and loners, and so he was an ideal addition. My circle comprised solely of those with societal failings.

I texted him with few words: *News. The river, 6pm.*

And it was there I waited, pacing the bank, the water churning so viciously that I couldn't hear oncoming footsteps, making it difficult to judge if and when he would appear. I hoped he hadn't changed his phone or was somehow incapacitated. I knew he drank, had seen him stagger out of the Dram on more than one occasion. The stereotypical Dalbegie wastrel. I threw sticks into the water, and watched them fly like I was a boy again. I glanced at my watch, too frequently.

And then he came.

'Oliver,' he said, his voice low and trembling as he climbed through the reeds.

'Brian. I'm glad you came. I've got some news that you might like to hear.' I extended my hand, not minding that his grubby paw would touch it, for I was wearing my extra padded winter gloves.

'Indeed, I would,' he said, clearly trying to be formal in my presence, forgetting perhaps that he was a bedraggled specimen of a man. The years had not been kind to him; his sallow skin sagged around his jaw.

He shook my hand for too long, his eyes not quite meeting my own. He was sweating although the temperature had dropped significantly, Mother Nature threatening to present winter prematurely.

I motioned to a clearing, where we could hear ourselves think, but would be hidden from any passersby. 'You recall the viewing you were privy to, many years ago now. I had taken a grotesque member of society away and put him in my cellar.'

'Roy. I'd never seen anything like it.' He rubbed his hands together. I couldn't tell if it was from glee or from the cold.

'And I hear you have been looking after his former lady-friend. Does it excite you?' I had to know. I loved to learn what made my members tick.

'Aye. She's no idea about any of it, still thinks he ran away with the kid. Not a bad woman, she is, but when she kicks off, it's satisfying to know that I witnessed her old flame deid.'

He was a small man with a hold over his woman. It was a hold that resided purely inside his own mind, but still, it was a smug knowledge enjoyed, even if she wasn't aware of it. Personally, I wouldn't have touched that disgusting hag, even to watch her die too, but each to their own.

'This time it's a woman,' I said. 'Someone you know.'

'Even better,' he said.

I could see the possibilities running through his psychotic little mind. Even though I knew he would have his own pleasures going on, I also understood that he was desperate for my next viewing. And I was right. His face lit up when I told him, his eyes finally boring into my own deep pools. Apparently, her dad had hit him recently, and so we would 'get him back.' Little did he know the dad was already 'got.' I could feel Brian's admiration and it inflated my ego, puffed out my feathers. No one put on a show like I did.

⌇⌇ ⌇⌇ ⌇⌇

That night, with Lizzy safely tucked away in my cellar, I sat in the conservatory and watched the rain dancing on the window. I could see my breath, and so I built a log fire, using the day's newspaper, lots of kindling, and some of the logs from the back garden. It roared up in an instant, the flames hungry and brazen. I was tempted to throw Lizzy's clothes into them, but the smoke might fill the room and I didn't want to draw any attention. Plenty of time to wrap them up and dispose of them elsewhere. Bird was safely tucked away from the flames. I had placed her on the floor next to Lizzy's platform bed to keep her company, to be there alongside her. My two delicate creatures, each as tranquil and fragile as the other.

Lizzy's wish had come true. She wanted to find out what happened, and now, after years of wondering, gossip, and speculation, she was going to. Just like her mother, she'd come to my house of her own free will, stepped into my living room, and accepted a drink from me. It was an easy abduction, and almost disappointing in its simplicity.

One only had to read or watch the news to know that the world was full of missing persons, and if they were discovered alive, they were usually within a twenty-mile radius of their home. It begged the question why every house wasn't searched within the immediate area of an abductee, but then the actions of the police were beyond ridiculous. And who was I to complain? The only significant visitation I received back when Lizzy's mother 'disappeared' was from a bumbling detective, who barely looked past the end of his nose. I wondered if anyone would come again, tipped off by someone with suspicions; maybe the old man with the cane. If they did, they wouldn't find the entrance to my cellar. It remained well hidden under a floorboard in the pantry, covered with a large rug and invisible from the outside of the house, below grade and under the radar.

Lizzy's phone rang again. There was no sound, as I'd set it to vibrate, but it was buzzing rather loudly on the table. I didn't answer, of course. I knew who it would be. Her husband Alfie—good old Alfie, love-you Alfie, smiley-face Alfie.

He seemed unable to leave her be, to give her some breathing space. He was all over Lizzy all the time, texting, ringing, worrying, asking questions. It must have been suffocating to have someone like him around, concerned about her every move. I was irritated with myself for letting her out of my sight for a few years, letting her get close to other people. It was inevitable that she would get married, as most women do, but for some reason I didn't expect it. In my mind, Lizzy had been waiting for me as much as I had been clinging to the notion of taking her. I hadn't imagined she would want to be with any man after being let down so badly by Simon, by her father, by Roy, by Spinner the pimp in the market. I had saved her from them all.

He began texting and calling more furiously. The phone gave a series of short vibrations. After a moment's hesitation I relented and picked up the device. He texted, 'Did u get on the train? What's going on?' No happy face, not even a zig-zag mouth accompanied that one. He must have been getting really concerned.

I put on my coat and wide-brimmed hat and went out with the phone vibrating in my pocket. There was hardly anyone out on the streets, the rain coming down strong, a gust blowing from the north and chilling my bones. My head was filled with visions of Lizzy, at twelve and devastated by the loss of her mother, as a defiant thirteen, angry at the world, then as a lost seventeen, consumed by the size and unpredictability of London. The resultant well-rounded thirty-year-old was pragmatic but bold, still rebellious in her own way. Her blond waves had never changed, and neither had her calm but stubborn character. She was an impeccable creature.

Lizzy. She was in my cellar. This was what I'd been dreaming about for over a decade, and yet my heart had tightened, my feet dragging.

In five, six, seven days at most, she would be gone. I would never see her again. What would I have to look forward to then? There would be all the other inhabitants of Dalbegie, the drudgery of it all, the same faces and sayings and small talk. No one else interested me there. My mind turned to Edinburgh, to the cracks and crevices of the streets of Leith, to the murky alleys and the dark opportunities. But it wasn't about the chance abductions, the ease of anonymity. It was about connections and motivations, discovering people who inadvertently drew me to them. People like Lizzy.

I walked until I found myself at the river once more.

As the water ravaged across rocks and mud, made angrier by the vertical rain, I marched along the lower bank, kicking the reeds and shrubs in my way, until at last I turned the far bend. There I stopped and threw Lizzy's phone into the river, watched it swirl and turn before disappearing into the scum and surf. *Goodbye-face, Alfie.* It only took a second to be gone, the relief of it too brief to curb my anxiety. I roared at the water, the sound masked by the elements. My presence was weak there, noiseless and overpowered.

I fell to my knees, the ground damp and gravelly, and howled like a thrashed dog. I wanted her, yet I didn't want to lose her. Without Lizzy, my world would be an empty place, bereft of desire. I would never again want anyone so vociferously, need anyone so acutely. I had won my trophy, but with that achievement came hollowness. Laid out before me, in the distance, was a barren land; a desert, hot and infinite.

CHAPTER THIRTY-FOUR

Lizzy Fights

A whirring sound was coming from near her feet. There was a sharp pain in her wrists and ankles, everything throbbing. Lizzy started to surge into consciousness, her sandpaper tongue stuck to the roof of her mouth. *So hot. So thirsty.*

There was a bare bulb above her, and she could barely open her eyes despite the light being dim. Her brain was expanding, filling her skull, and pushing on her eyeballs. She tried to get up, but couldn't move.

Her arms and legs were tied down. She was naked, lying on some kind of platform bed. Hard.

She moved her head from side to side, slow, the dull ache pounding every which way. There was nothing to see, darkness all around apart from the lone light dangling from the ceiling.

Her heart pounded, competing with her temples, as the reality set in. *Oliver.* She had been sitting in his chair, drinking tea, getting increasingly anxious as he became more relaxed. They were talking about the river.

She called out and her cracked voice echoed faintly in the room. There were no windows, no outside sounds. Was she underground? She struggled against the bindings, but they were tied tight, and the twisting burned her skin.

What's he going to do to me?

She sucked at the warm air. What was that mechanical noise? She lifted her chin and tried to see past her feet. There was a tripod with an old video camera on top of it, its red light on.

He was watching her. *Fucking freak.*

Squinting, she growled at the camera, at him. 'Let me go. You've no right. You sick fuck.' But the words grated at her throat, her face. She put her head back down. *Think.*

✧ ✧ ✧

Her best mate Natalie went missing from the market stall in Soho for days. When she reappeared, they found no evidence of sexual contact, not so much as a mark on her. And Nat couldn't remember anything about where she'd been. Amnesia, they said. It stopped her from coming up with anything useful for the police. But in the weeks after, she had terrible nightmares of pain, a white room, people watching while she was linked to wires, tormented. The dreams were too real and too terrible to have made up.

Was this how it started for Nat? Did they tie her up and watch while she squirmed? Perhaps Lizzy's own memories would be erased. If she survived.

✧ ✧ ✧

She tried to shout at the camera again, her voice weak and hoarse. 'Enjoying the show?' The effort sent waves of nausea and exhaustion through her, and she closed her eyes again. Her body was unwinding, pain coming in waves. Her mind tunneled down, and she went with it, relieved for it.

✧ ✧ ✧

She slept and woke again. More time passed. Her skin was itching, her lips were cracking, and Lizzy's thirst was raging. *How dare he.* He hadn't come to see her, to admit to what he'd done, or if he had, she hadn't seen him. Her head was a rock, hammers banging at it.

She was drying up.

Her stomach was tightening, cramping. She tried to lick her lips, but her tongue was like a lizard's, grazing her skin.

An image came to her of a bucket, with water spilling over the sides, the end of a hose inside it, hissing and spitting. The bucket toppled over, the water gushing over her body, cooling her skin, flowing into her mouth, her ears, her nose. She gulped and swallowed, letting it inside, replenishing her. She longed for anything liquid—a drop of condensation from the ceiling landing on her lips—a bead of sweat trickling down from her forehead. *Not a drop to drink.*

She managed to whisper, her eyes on the lens. 'You're disgusting.'

When she lost the baby, she wanted the ground to open up so she could lie down inside the cocoon of it and let the world disappear. But she couldn't die, not now. There were too many things left to do, another baby to make. There was Alfie, and the tiles in the kitchen, and her job and her friends.

The world needed to know about Oliver.

I'm not going to die.

A surge of energy came from within, and she strained at the bindings at all four corners of the hard bed. She pulled at them and shook them until the bed moved. She shouted as loud as her tender throat would let her. 'Coward.'

The camera was shaking now, as she heaved her body on the bed one last time. The far end of the platform bumped the tripod, and it teetered. She did it again, the twine on her wrists cutting through her skin, searing pain shooting through her. The bed hit it once more, and again, until finally the camera went crashing to the floor.

The whirring stopped. There was silence.

Lizzy let her body relax, her limbs burning. He'd have to come to her now, if he wanted to carry on watching. Warmth emanated from between her legs, soaking underneath her body. Blood was draining from the womb, from the depths of her. She imagined her organs shriveling, shrinking like prunes.

She had to stay awake, to force her mind to think, to count. To sleep would be to miss him, and she needed him to face up to her. If this was closure, it didn't count if all of her questions weren't answered. The main one, which had been shut away at the back of her mind ever since he claimed to be her secret guardian, was: why now? If all he wanted to do was capture her, why didn't he do it years ago? Instead, he'd been supposedly looking out for her. What was the point of it all?

If Oliver was a psycho, a freak, or just plain evil, then it was possible he didn't have a reason for what he did, and it would be a waste of breath trying to talk to him. But it presented a tiny glimmer of a chance that she'd get out of there alive.

Now come, freak. You come to me, and we'll see what happens when you have to look at me, all of me, skin and bones and blood. I'm here, exposed, all for the taking. I dare you.

CHAPTER THIRTY-FIVE

Lauren's Mirror

I'm pulling back together again, tumbling down to earth, to you. I'm dreading what I'll see, and I resist, screwing up my eyes, wrapping my half-there arms around my body like a barrier made of nothing.

On that terrible night when Oliver took me out, I put on the Scottish Cross along with a splash of my *Chanel No. 5*. It was our second time out together, and I wanted more than just his good manners, if you don't mind me saying. The first time, we'd gone down to The Chinese, nothing fancy, but it had been such a treat to be out with someone I found attractive. He listened to me, looked after me, and made me feel special. But he walked me home without so much as a peck on the cheek, and I worried that I'd had too much wine and put him off, so next time I suggested getting some chips and having a walk, all casual.

But it didn't end there.

After the walk, he asked me back to his place, and I jumped at the chance. The stupid thing was that I hadn't told you about him, just in case things didn't work out. I didn't want you to be disappointed in me if I screwed up. So no one knew where I was, or who I was with. If only I'd waited, got to know him better before jumping in, I would have stood a better chance of seeing through him. But there he was, pouring champagne into crystal glasses, impressing me. I have to admit, I was smitten.

Oliver got the Scottish Cross necklace, the most undeserving of them all. But it won't be tucked away in a drawer, a clue to be found. He's more sophisticated than that. He wouldn't need to keep it as a trophy of what he did, like you see in the films. It'll be long gone, melted down and remolded into some abstract sculpture. Or it'll be halfway around the world on the skin of another woman, or in some skanky charity shop five hundred miles away.

It's a cruel thing, to have come back here, to you. I want my pain to disappear into the depths of the universe. If I could find a black hole, I'd swim through the atoms and into it. And now my granddaughter has floated away too, to somewhere neither of us can know. My soul needs to pass on. Why can't I rest? If only I knew how to end the torture, I'd do it.

Keep me in your thoughts and I'll comfort you, like Granny Mac did for me. All that's left is love, and *he* can't get to that. It must be a terrible thing, not to be loved. Look what it did to him. Family will always be there, no matter where you are, near or far. Love slides over us like silk, subtle or obvious, cool or fiery. So think of me, and fold yourself in.

CHAPTER THIRTY-SIX

Kane's Wake

Helen threw his leather jacket on the back of the wooden chair in her room. She didn't usually keep items from her conquests, but it had taken her fancy. She'd always wanted a biker jacket, all the zips and the padded sections, and the pungent smell of it. This one had the added aroma of body odour, but she would scrub the armpits with a sponge and make it bearable. It was a generic enough jacket that no one would recognize or claim it.

She fished through all the pockets, and found three wraps of powder, a few coins, a tenner, and a small black comb. He didn't appear to have used the comb; his hair had been a matted, greasy mess. It was all crushed into the ground, now, along with his skull and skin.

She'd attacked him from the back, swinging the hammer into his head, and he fell over, face down, onto the pavement. She wasn't expecting it to be so easy, but then he'd seemed dazed in the first place, like he'd taken a pill that was kicking off wrong. She'd timed it when he was near to the foot of the alley winding in between some houses and out towards the bus depot. She dragged him in there, easy. He was muttering, swearing in a confused tone, like all of it was an inconvenience.

She'd needed it, the feel of pounding on flesh, the crack of bone. The release.

The woman that owned the house had said she could do some laundry, even offering to take it from Helen and put it in for her. Helen had insisted she do it herself, thinking of the blood, and possibly even tiny chunks of flesh, on her clothes. 'Suit yourself,' the woman had snapped, apparently not gracious about anything in this world, even escaping the housework. Helen put everything in a bin bag and took it downstairs to the basement, where the washing machine, dryer, cleaning liquids, and mops and brushes lived. There were cobwebs in the corners, and piles of lint on the floor from the dryer. She stamped on an earwig and ground it in. She put everything into the machine and slammed the door shut. There. It was all gone, now.

That night, sleep came to her quickly, pulling her down into the bed, her muscles used up, and all the tension let go. She floated there until morning came, and then everything began to simmer again.

Because while she'd been hard at work, someone else had been busy too.

She fired up her laptop to check email, click on a sicko site maybe. It would be a break from breakfast telly, seeing the same old faces saying the same superficial things. She waited expectantly for her email to download. The wifi there was CLARTY777, whatever that meant, and it was a bit spotty. The usual junk was popping up, with two interesting messages in between. She opened the first, recognizing Oliver's style of subject line. Apparently, he was firing up the old site, and would send out passwords separately. Everyone was going to be excited about this 'little extra,' as he called it. The old site? It had been years since he'd used it. She bit her fingernail, and scrolled up to the next email. This one was from a different email account, but she knew it was Oliver again. 'She's here,' it read. 'The daughter of number eighteen.'

She had to think back. Number eighteen. There had been so many, the deaths blurred together. But whoever. It was irrelevant. The point was he'd got the daughter. And it was obvious he was talking about that girl—the blond—the one who went off in the ambulance. It had always been about her. She'd wanted to hammer her before he could get to her. *Damn it.* Helen slammed the laptop shut. She tore off her pyjamas and put on some clothes, tearing a hole in her sock as she jammed her foot in it, her toenails long and craggy.

It wasn't supposed to happen like this. She put on her boots and kicked the end of the bed. *Fuck you.* Clods of mud fell onto the carpet. Then she grabbed her bag and stomped down the stairs. The picture in the hall rattled.

That woman poked her head out of the living room door. 'What's wi' the banging up there? Quieten down, will ye.'

Helen ignored her. She would see to her later.

'Are ye deaf? Hey, I'm talking to you.'

She barged through the front door, slamming it so hard that it made the house vibrate. A crow squawked and flew out of a nearby tree. The street was empty, as usual, the morning ghost town. She got to the end of it, and made a sharp turn. She knew where she was going, but not what she was going to do. Not yet, anyway. But she couldn't let Oliver win.

CHAPTER THIRTY-SEVEN

Oliver's Experiment

I dusted off my old logbooks, well hidden behind the brickwork, and studied some of the entries. They started well before I moved to this town, only the last two victims selected from the Dalbegie locals. Some casualties died early, unable to cope with the lack of water. Some hung on for over a week, sunken and parched, their hearts fluttering just enough to keep them alive. One woman writhed in apparent ecstasy, making low moans that titillated her audience even more than they already were.

Thirst. It's a terrible thing. In some ways it was predictable, and yet the effects remained fascinating.

I read the entry from November 1998, the day Lizzy's mother left this earth. She lasted until day 7. *The body is deceased. Decay has begun prematurely and disposal should be imminent. The skin is extremely withered and yellow in colour.* Oh dear. Death was such an ungainly affair. I imagined her daughter would be more delicate, more refined in her departure. A quiet and serene end to her life seemed appropriate.

Lizzy fell to the floor after she'd drunk my special tea, her face white, her eyes rolling back. I picked her up in my arms and carried her like one would carry a bride, her head back, limbs light and frail over mine. She was strong, and still young, but then she'd just been though a physical ordeal, what with the lost baby. I bet on six days. That was my prediction.

I sharpened my pencil and licked the end, the taste of it pleasantly reminiscent of the last time I used it. I hadn't felt the urge to log conquests since the odious Roy, but it was a must this time, going back to the old methodology. I began the entry, quite possibly the last. This was the grand finale, as it were. The word *finale* comes from the Latin nominative *f n lis*, pertaining to boundaries. I imagined the end of the world, the edge, looming.

∿ ∿ ∿

Notes — Experiment Number Twenty
Start Date: Wednesday 23 Sept
End Date: (tbd)
Place: Dalbegie, Scotland
Age of Body: 30
Est. Weight of Body: 140lb
Name of Body: Lizzy

∿ ∿ ∿

Day 1, Wed 23 Sept: Rohypnol was administered in a hot cup of tea and body number twenty has been in a state of unconsciousness for some hours. Everything is prepared: the camera, the customary yellow twine scavenged from the newsagents, the catheter, and the lights. Everyone is waiting for her to come around, to waken. This time we have the added interest of a young woman finding out firsthand how her mother died.

∿ ∿ ∿

It all seemed effortless, flawless. But I had become overly confident. Things soon began to go wrong because of my complacency; I'd never seen anything like it. We'd had all kinds of reactions to our starvation program, however due to the lack of water, most people caved in quickly, their energy waning early on. Yes, there had been anger, but indicated only by the quietest of muttering, the slightest movements during times of delirium and semi-consciousness. But Lizzy proved herself unique with her energy and spark. I'd known her to be a livewire, but this was an unexpected viewing to say the least. Her lips were cracked, eyes yellowing as dehydration set in. My little birdie was getting thirsty, but it didn't stop her from batting her wings in fight. I was fortunate enough to be watching as she rattled the bed and crashed down the tripod, her eyes glinting from the other side as if she could see me.

I'd set it too close to the platform. The camera had been disconnected and I would have to go to her. My subscribers were impatiently awaiting the return of their picture, but I let them hang on awhile. I needed to reflect. I scratched at the arm of my chair and stared into the ashes, the remnants of a roaring fire from the night before. I should have built another one, the air damp and chill, but I didn't want to get dirty again, having spent an hour deep cleansing in the shower. Medicated soap and a scrubbing brush helped, but I still felt contaminated.

My scalp was bloodied, my scabs from previous cleansings open and oozing. I wore hats when I went out or in the company of others so they were spared the sight of my encrusted hair and skin. But at home I could let my head breathe, allowing oxygen to heal the wounds and freshen my mind. I touched the side of my head, just above my ear, and felt the raised bumps, scratches and scars, some of them part of my history and some new and raw.

Just before it came crashing down, she'd spoken to the camera and called me a coward. The worst thing.

On the day Lizzy's mother passed into death, I believe I heard her say that same word as her last breath left her. *Coward.* I hated that word.

But I may have misheard or misrepresented the sound she made when she was finally made to rest in peace. It was barely detectable, what she had been trying to say. But the way Lizzy shouted it out; it was unmistakable. She called me a coward, a distinctive declaration, and I didn't know what to do with that.

It wasn't what I was. I was many things, but not that.

There was the time my mother declared I was a coward for running away when she came after me with a frying pan, like a Tom and Jerry cartoon chase. I knew if I stopped running, she'd hit me across the head until I fell. Cowardice implied fear and reticence, and I wasn't capable of such feelings.

Wind howled down the chimney into the fireplace, shifting some of the ashes, dislodging more memories. I gripped the sides of my chair.

The last time I saw my father, before he left.

The day my mother received the telegram from the Royal Navy, to tell us that my father had been killed in service.

The last time she came at me. I didn't stop running until I'd reached the depths of the city.

I regarded the photo of my father, a stranger now. Just like my dear Lizzy, I ran away from home, and so I didn't know my errant mother for long either. I'd always been near to Lizzy, even during periods when I wasn't watching her closely. Now she was starting to wither away. What would I have left? The circle of acquaintances who relied on me for kicks were scattered across the country, and were certainly not friends. All of them were social deviants, recluses in some instances, and not worthy of my attention. My mind was in turmoil, thoughts whirling around like tiny tornados in a trainset scene. My head was bursting, thoughts so thick and thunderous I could almost see them in the room.

If I left her be, to cave in, to implode, she would be gone from my life forever.

If I cut her bindings and set her free, I would put myself in danger. When she called me a coward, it made me want to watch her die. When she called me a coward, it filled me with admiration.

I went to the bathroom again, itching, burning. As I passed my computer on the way, it dinged. I glanced at the screen. Parsley had emailed me following my social *faux pas* on the forum, and I felt a sudden violent need to look at it. They had since 'removed' me from the site, which was inevitable, but I had got what I had wanted. Direct contact.

I sat down at my desk and shook away the tornadoes. Parsley told me she was grateful for the shoulder to cry on, and was sorry that I had been banned from the site because of it. She was apologizing to me, which I found vaguely entertaining, some of my thunder dissipating. Bad things happened to good people, she said, and she was feeling particularly down because of it.

I replied, anger seething behind my words as I was all too aware that I was hiding behind some half-baked web forum. I decided to cut ties with Parsley, to go for the jugular. I was not a coward in cyberspace, but a commendable and devious antagonist.

Parsley. My real name is Joseph, by the way. Thank you for the kind thoughts. I agree with you, that the best of us don't always have our kindness returned. I'm wondering if I would be much happier in a different realm, away from this earth and its darkness. Perhaps one day we'll meet someplace else, where the air is fresh and the meadows are full of buttercups.

I sat back and waited, my legs twitching up and down, my hands at my scalp, scratching and pulling. I was rewarded with a message a few minutes later, short but significant.

I think that sounds lovely, Joseph. I wish for it too. My real name is Penny. For now, I'm going to sleep, and hope that tomorrow will be a new, better day.

A good reply. I blundered in. *I'm sorry you've had such a terrible few* days. *I've had the same feelings here, and I can only send my best wishes that you will come out of this better than I will. I'm thinking of ending my never-ending unhappiness by removing myself from the world.*

She came straight back at me. *Never-ending unhappiness. That's how I feel today. This isn't going to get better. I have nothing, nobody, and no sense of an end to it all. I'm pleased you're there to talk to. Don't leave me alone, will you Joseph?*

I wanted to finish, to consume this side dish of an experiment and focus on what was happening under my feet. Penny had to go away, for Lizzy's survival.

Would you like to do it together?

Do what together?

I'm going to drink two litres of vodka then cut my wrists in the bath. It's my time. I can't do this anymore. Sorry to leave you, Penny. Unless you want to join me in another life, that is.

I waited, confident.

I'm going to join you. Let's do it tonight. I hope we meet again, in a better place. Thank you for being here for me.

10pm. I'll be thinking of you.

And that was all it took. It was an anti-climax, the finality of it after such a short time. I had wanted her dead. And she was gone. I resolved to check the site the following day, to find out if 'Parsley' had vanished. Bye-bye, Penny.

I cleansed, Parsley out of my mind as soon as she'd popped into it, debating with myself about what to do about Lizzy while I showered and scrubbed. But when I came out of the bathroom, steamy and relaxed, my next move was forced upon me.

Someone knocked on my door.

It happened so infrequently, I admit I jumped at the sound of it, my mind racing with the possibilities of police, investigators, Lizzy's relatives, conspiring and prying. I had 'taken' too many souls at once, been too slack. I peered through my spy-hole to see only the grotesque Brian, biting the skin around his thumbnail and perspiring from every pore. The audacity of the man, turning up like that.

I opened the door a fraction, and hissed at him. 'Are you insane? Go away.'

'What's going on? Is it all over?' He was drunk, his sourness wafting its way to me, clouds of pungent stench. He put one arm out and leaned on the porch wall to steady himself.

He was too far away to reach, or I would have stuck out my arm and pulled him inside, got rid of him quickly and quietly. His neck looked scrawny enough to snap in half. All it would take was one person to see him there, and the whole town would be gossiping.

I growled. 'It's all over for you now. Get lost, and don't ever come back here.'

'What you sayin'?' He bent forward, hands on his knees.

I raised my voice a touch. 'Go away or you'll be sorry.' I slammed the door, resisting the urge to let him in and let him learn.

'Fuck yous, you can't do this,' he slurred. He then lifted my letterbox and shouted in. 'You better get it sorted. I've paid good money.'

I crouched on the floor, and smashed the door with my fist. 'We'll talk about your money another time. You can't be here.'

'Aye, well you better had.'

I hit the door again, and I heard him stepping back. *Idiot*. What did he think he was doing, drawing attention to me, to us? I looked through a crack in the curtains and saw him zig-zagging across the road in the direction of the pub. If it was the money he was worried about, of course he'd get it back. All the subscribers would get a refund. I didn't care about that. All I was concerned about was the bond between Lizzy and I; it was too special to break, and so it was important our remaining hours were private.

We didn't need an audience now.

I put on my coat and hat and went out, the blood rushing to my head, the cold air biting my face. I would go for a walk, then go to the Dram and wait outside for him. He had started off as a vulture, scavenging from my skillful captures. Now he was going to be the victim, the flesh to be stripped. He had overstepped the line, crossed me. And I couldn't risk him jeopardizing my set-up. I passed the Dram, the faint smell of stale beer and urine emanating from the front door. He would be entrenched at the bar, drinking, staring, and whining about the world; when he came out, I would really stop his complaining. I would be back.

I made it to the High Street, past the dead Chinese restaurant and the unnecessary wool shop full of old ladies and dusty bric-a-brac. The owner was fussing in the shop window, and she stared at me, unsmiling, as though I shouldn't be there. Further up the street, the mentally deficient chip-shop boy was also watching from his doorway, his fat face blank and staring. I glanced briefly towards him, thankful that it was only him, someone harmless. He shook his head, as if he were disapproving of me, his double chin wobbling. I looked him up and down, taking in the grease stain on his apron, the swollen ankles, then turned away slowly, to let him know that I didn't care for him. I doubled back on myself, and walked to the café, glancing inside at the table by the window, like I used to. An older couple were sipping tea, their gazes soft and pensive. Lauren used to sit there and read romantic novels. Whenever I went by, she'd inexplicably look up and meet my eye. She had little else to occupy her mind, but still, I liked to think she was drawn to me. But those two glared like I was disgusting.

What was it with everyone today? I paused for what seemed like a fraction of a second, but it was just long enough for the Godzilla woman in the café to notice me. She thundered out of her front door and stood with her pudgy hands on hips, looking every bit like a dirty wench from medieval times.

'Everything all right, Mr. Oliver? Do you want me to take a photo of my customers, so's you can look at them whenever you like?'

I was taken aback. I wasn't sure of her meaning at first.

'It's just you're staring at them. Are you coming inside?'

I began to walk away. 'No, thank you.'

'Wait a minute, I haven't finished with you yet.'

'Yes?'

'We're missing a young lass called Lizzy. You mind her Mum used to work in the newsagents? Lauren was her name. Any idea where she is?'

'Lauren?'

'No, Lizzy, her daughter. She's disappeared as well. Keep up.'

I touched my hat. 'No idea, I'm afraid. Good luck with the search.'

The wench watched me go, her eyes narrowed. That woman had a problem, body issues that she shouldn't take out on others. I whistled faintly, then stopped when I realized that's what guilty parties do when they're trying to appear innocent. I wasn't quite out of earshot when she shouted after me.

'I'm watching you.'

I pretended I hadn't heard her. She could watch all she liked, but she wouldn't find Lizzy.

I stopped at the post office, where I bought a book of stamps and a padded envelope. Everyday objects for a regular working man. *Nothing to see here.* It was there I felt the buzz of the town, the repercussions of an occurrence that was out of the ordinary. They hadn't had a proper disappearance since Lauren's. And news travelled fast. Whispers, nods, and knowing looks all presented themselves at the post office. Often a morgue of quiet, the place had become alive with theories, questions, and opinions.

'Depressed, she was, very down. Judith said she had trouble getting out of bed.'

'Lovely girl, but what a hard life she had. I'm not surprised she got hurt by her dad again.'

'What a shame for her. First her mum and now this. She lost a baby, you know.'

'Depression. It's a terrible thing.'

It would keep them all going for months to come, years possibly. When Lauren 'disappeared,' the echo of unfounded theories resounded time and time again.

A roll of thunder in the distance gave my exit the dramatic edge that it deserved. The sky was low, the air oppressive. I looked up and saw a flock of birds fly overhead, a perfect v-shaped formation. They were free. I was not.

As I approached the newsagents, I saw an unfamiliar figure outside talking to Jessica. At first, I thought it was a plainclothes policeman, but his stance was all wrong, too loose. Jessica looked up and waved, and I slowed down, disinclined to stop and talk. They both watched my approach. It was too late to turn back, or take a sudden change in direction.

'Oliver!' Jessica beckoned. 'This is Alfie, Lizzy's husband. He's come up from London to find Lizzy.' She said 'London' as if it were a faraway, magical land. 'She's gone AWOL. Maureen and the boys have been looking everywhere. Her dad's never appeared since the party either.'

Alfie stared at me, unmoving. *Smiley-face Alfie. Where's the smile?*

I stopped a few paces away, and nodded my greetings. 'Good to meet you.' I turned to Jessica. 'They haven't found her father either? That's strange, isn't it?'

'I think it's suspicious. I've never liked him.' She turned to Alfie and put her talons on his forearm. 'Don't you worry, Alfie, we'll soon have her found.'

'I know we will,' he said. He was looking at my head, as if he could see the carnage beneath my hat.

I felt I should offer some other morsel of consolation. 'Perhaps she's taken some time for herself and will be back before we know it.'

Alfie widened his stance. 'Not a lot goes unnoticed here, does it? You lot are in each other's pockets by the sounds of it.'

'It's a small town,' I said. 'Now, I must get going. Good luck.' I skirted around them, made my way to the Dram, dying to look back to see if they were watching me, but resisting. They'd gone quiet; even the sounds of Jessica's chatter had dissipated.

Let them think what they liked. I brushed the encounter aside, and tucked myself away behind the Dram to wait.

Over an hour went by. My hands went numb, and I shivered both with cold and frustration. Night was settling in, wrapping a blanket of ice around me. It might be hours before Brian swigged his last ale and blundered out, retching. I was anxious to go back and see Lizzy. But then, the pub door screeched open and Brian stumbled out. He muttered to himself, perfecting the Dalbegie stagger as he made his way, his square body weaving from one end of the street to the other. I was torn. Alfie was here in town, suspicious. I'd already got rid of Lizzy's father, and his body could turn up any time. Did I need to add another?

Let him drink himself to death instead. Brian was part of the dregs of society at the bottom of the social scale, the outcasts. Conversely, many of the women I had taken were attractive, wanted, with person-alities that shone. I hadn't realised that about myself until that moment. I took the worst of the men and the best of the women. I'd forget him. For now, at least.

The roads were quiet now that darkness had fallen, the moon hiding behind the clouds. I went home, where Lizzy would be waiting for me. *I'm coming, little bird.* It was time to venture down to my cellar again, to regain control. And to rescue her one last time.

I'd decided. I didn't want *us* to end.

I felt her beckoning, sparks in the air, as I was pulled along the street. I had an urge to press our fingertips together, to feel the current that ran between us. Electric.

CHAPTER THIRTY-EIGHT

Lizzy's Dream

All her strength was shrunken. Lizzy kept quiet to conserve her energy, her eyes closed, everything falling. The room was so silent that she could hear only the weak pump of her own blood, her whispering breath. Minutes were hours; hours were days. Everything had turned into a dream, where time didn't exist. Although her mind tumbled and turned, she somehow knew that she wasn't awake but waiting in some dark place for death.

Perhaps she had already gone there.

The time that didn't exist ticked on.

But now there was another sound, a presence. There was someone else in the room.

She tried to open her eyes a fraction, but everything blurred. A shadowy body at the foot of her makeshift bed, watching. She tried to speak, but all that surfaced was a croak. Her throat was sand, her voice dried up.

Him. He'd been after her for years. And she'd given herself to him, let herself fall. Why didn't he say anything? Her heart was fluttering, her chest struggling to pump air. *Speak to me. Touch me.*

A cold hand on her foot. Her whole body recoiled. It was collapsing in on itself. She was drying up, withering like an apple core in the sun, or a piece of worn leather. She'd been through a miscarriage, lost blood, and she wouldn't last much longer. She was thinking these things as if they weren't really happening. It was too terrible to be real. *Let me go,* she wanted to say. *Water.* Still no words came.

Her throat was closing. She would stop breathing soon. Lizzy let her eyes clamp shut, no use fighting it. She drifted. *Let go.*

Then came a dream. She floated up to the ceiling and looked down on herself. Her face morphed, twisting and reshaping, until it settled. It was her mum below now, her eyes closed, her body sinewy and wrinkled. There was a drip from the ceiling, water coming from a pipe. The drips became more frequent, splashing on the bed, on her mum's body and on the floor. Then it began to trickle out, then faster, and faster, until it was like an open tap. Her mum began to move, her eyes opening, her mouth wide to catch the spray and the splashes. Someone, faceless, sexless, was scooping water into her mouth with cupped hands.

The realization came, slow, whirling. *This is what happened to Mum.* He took her out for the night, brought her back here, drugged her, and kept her down there to starve to death.

No food, no water.

She tried to cry out, but it was a quiet, dream-muffled cry. No one had figured it out in all these years. She'd been a few metres away from the newsagents, suffering, and all anyone could talk about was whether or not she'd got back with Dad, or been dining with some weird boyfriend. She wouldn't have done that. She wasn't stupid.

This is where she died. This is how I'm finding out.

She watched herself, or her mum, or the both of them, begging for more water, more. She swallowed and gulped, wept.

After a time, the flow of water stopped. She was lifted up and held, her body limp. The face of her rescuer was still a blank. Perhaps because it wasn't true; there was no knight in shining armor with a happy ending. Just a dead room, in a dark place.

CHAPTER THIRTY-NINE

Oliver Sinks

When I got home, my eyelids were like lead, my legs stiff and cumbersome. Waiting for Brian had tired me; my head was pounding with cold and my feet were aching. I wanted to be on top form for Lizzy, and I went straight upstairs for one of my scalding hot showers, scraping my skin until it bled and throbbed the way I liked it. It warmed my body through to the bone, and I stretched out my back until I felt flexible again, ready.

Had I not been so eager to get to Lizzy, so chilled from waiting for odious Brian, itching so intensely for a cleanse, I might have noticed the open window downstairs, letting in the cold.

Dried and clothed in a fresh shirt, I went to the window and parted the curtains. The moon was shimmering, almost full, light glinting on the railings around the patch of weeds outside. I rested my forehead against the cold glass. I'd been looking forward to orchestrating Lizzy's death for so long that I had been blinded by it, the right pathway hidden behind a thick fog of desire.

I couldn't let her die.

I pattered down to the kitchen to get some supplies: a jug of water, a cup with a straw, some cucumber and strawberries perhaps. Watery fruits and vegetables. I had some sachets of electrolyte in the cupboard and I mixed one up and poured it into a small pot with a lid. I put everything on a small tray that I could hold in one hand, not wanting anything to spill on my way down the cellar steps. I was going to water her, feed her, until she bloomed again.

Except she wasn't there.

As I crept down the cellar stairs, carefully, so eager to see her, I discovered the bed was empty. I stepped the rest of the way down, my eyes smarting and head reeling. It was such a shock that I wasn't on game, didn't think properly about what I was doing. The bed was empty and I was drawn to it. There was a small amount of blood on the lower edge. It had turned black, like tar. I bent to put the tray on the floor. That was my next mistake in a long line of mistakes.

A sharp pain in the back of my head.

A dull thud, flesh shifting.

Not her, I thought. *It couldn't be.*

CHAPTER FORTY

Lizzy's Heaven

L izzy came to with a cold towel on her forehead, a soft pillow beneath. There was a warm light emanating from one side, and she could hear chirping from the trees. She shifted. The warmth and light gave way to horror. Her hands were bound together in front, frozen and stiff.

A sharp pain in her wrists seared through gristle. She pulled her knees up to her body, turning her feet into each other. They were free, at least. She opened her eyes a crack, and looked through her eyelashes. She was still naked, but covered with a cotton sheet, cool on her skin.

This was a different place. She'd moved.

She was afraid to open her eyes fully. Was she in heaven? Alone even in death.

She'd had a dream about water, about Mum.

Gradually she took in the room. It was tiny. There was a small lamp on the floor, plugged into the wall by the window. A strong smell of dust and old things filled the fusty air. A plastic cup full of water sat on a low mahogany table by her head. There were ice shards, a lid, and a white straw, like the one she'd had in the hospital. *Water.* Her body seemed replenished, less weak, her throat cooled. Still, the thirst was raging. She shifted her legs until her feet were over the edge of the bed, then sat up using her elbows. She reached out for the cup, her bound arms moving slow, until her fingers were linked around the base of it.

It wasn't heavy and she lifted it towards her, the straw finding her lips, and she drank. And drank.

There was a bucket in the corner, lid on. Perhaps she was expected to use it as a toilet.

She lay flat, her eyelids heavy again.

Was she still in the dream? It seemed so real, but where was this? Her head sunk into the pillow, a cloud of softness and warmth. Sleep came again, quietly, and took her away.

CHAPTER FORTY-ONE

Helen's Hidey-Hole

There was a lovely calmness about the place now that she'd silenced that bitter, scrawny woman down the stair. Usually the owner would be crashing about the place like a cranky old witch, but now she was conspicuously absent.

Helen yawned. Perhaps she'd have a long nap after lunch. She had full control of the telly in the living room now, feet up on the coffee table, a fish supper on her lap. She'd kept it in the paper, and put the paper on a plate. There was no ketchup about the place, but she'd asked the mental guy in the chippy for extra salt and vinegar so it was okay.

She'd put a few of the chips on a plate for Blondie and left them on the table beside her. Hopefully she'd eat them when she woke up again. They'd keep her going for a bit longer. Skinny shrimp she was, hardly anything of her. She'd been easy to carry over her shoulder, at least.

The wretched little owner woman was in the garden now. No friends had knocked on her door since Helen had been staying; she couldn't have been popular. She was so frail; her bones almost cracked when Helen threw her to the ground. Undernourished. There was an ideal patch of dirt in the far corner, overgrown with weeds, but fairly soft. She'd dug a hole last night, and placed the body inside it, curled up like a sleeping fox fur. It hadn't been difficult to cover it over and hide the freshly turned dirt with leaves, twigs, and shambolic weeds. Ground cover. The rest of the garden was a mess, and so it didn't stand out too badly, a hidden, makeshift grave. It was her third one in this town. Not bad going.

Soon there'd be a fourth. And then it would be time to leave.

She turned up the sound on the telly and wiped some grease from her hand on the arm of the sofa. There was a framed photo on the side table, a family with two kids. She pushed it over so she didn't have them looking at her. Fake smiles and frilly eighties blouses. Why did folk keep such memories? She imagined having a picture of Steve and their old Ma on her shelf and chuckled to herself. *Ridiculous.*

After her programme finished, she went up and looked in on the girl. She was still sleeping, her hands tightly bound in front of her, so it looked like she was begging in her dreams. The chips were still there, but some more of the water had been drunk. Helen smirked. It had been Oliver's desire for them all to watch his precious girl starve, while he basked in the glory of his ultimate abduction. NondescriptRambunctious.com had served him well in the past, but now it had let him down. Served him right for being too cheap to buy a new camera. Well now the viewing was hers. She imagined his contorted face, the scabs reopened on his scalp, the rage. He shouldn't have been so self-righteous, so sure that he'd get what he wanted.

She'd give him his very own torture, in three easy stages.

One, two, three, it was you then me.

She locked the door, then lay down in the dead woman's bedroom. Very comfy it was, too. Last night was the best sleep she'd had in days. Might as well make the most of the excellent mattress, the silky eiderdown. The pillow had smelled of bitterness, but she didn't notice it once she'd turned it over. She turned onto her back. The ceiling had that bumpy plaster that looked like the surface of the moon. There was a white plastic light shade in the centre of it, like a space ship.

She went on a trip through the solar system, travelling through time, weightless.

Hours passed.

It felt like afternoon when she came 'round. She'd climbed under the covers in her sleep and now she was sweating, her hair damp about her face. She listened for any sign of movement in the bedroom next door, but the house was silent save for the clicking of a radiator. She got up and went to the bathroom, then put her ear to the other bedroom door before going in. The girl was lying on her side now, still sleeping, her bound hands in the prayer position in front of her face. Helen took a few steps in, and regarded her bouncy hair, the pale skin. She wondered if Oliver fantasized about her, if he'd wanted to fuck her once she was dead. She would make a beautiful corpse.

She shook the girl's foot. 'Wake up, will you.' Her voice sounded strange, having not spoken for a while. Her Scottish accent seemed more pronounced, somehow.

The girl barely stirred. Her eyelids fluttered and she gave a faint moan. She was still under the effects of the drugs, and weak too. Helen's eyes rested on the plate on the bedside table. The chips and the water were all gone. 'Hello?' She slapped the girl's arm, but still didn't get a reaction. She'd leave the filming until later, or even tomorrow, when the girl would be capable of knowing what was happening—and of screaming in a way that Oliver wouldn't like.

Because it wouldn't be him making her scream.

Helen left the room, locked the door, and made her way downstairs. As she reached halfway, she heard the police sirens in the distance. She sat on the bottom step and waited, biting a hangnail on her thumb. There were bits, hairs, all over the carpet at her feet. The sirens were definitely getting louder, closer. She grabbed her coat and put her boots on, then waited by the back door. Just in case.

Through the square of glass in the door, she could see the hillock in the far flowerbed, her handiwork. There was a small patch of heather next to it, dull purple under the darkening clouds. But still, the colour of it stood out against the freshly dug earth. It was more noticeable than she'd thought.

The sirens went past the house and on towards the park and the estate. They'd gone, for now. Sirens made her uncomfortable. 'We know what you've done,' they whined. A walker, or their dog, might have found one of the other bodies. Her killing spree might have been a mistake, for what worked in the big city wasn't the same deal in a small place like this. All those people on top of you. Noticing. Knowing each other. She threw her coat on the kitchen counter and kicked off her boots. They wouldn't catch her if she acted soon, and got out of there fast. First she'd pack up her stuff. Shouldn't take long. Then she'd get on with stage two, whether the girl was drowsy or not. After all, she'd had enough energy to eat those chips. If she screamed, or if she moaned in a half-sleep, it would be enough to make him suffer.

CHAPTER FORTY-TWO

Jonno Speaks

I always wanted to be a paleontologist, but I never made it. I was really good at wrapping up fish suppers and keeping track of the money, and so I never left my dad's chippy. And it never left me. It was what I knew. The good thing was that when Lizzy finally came back, I was right there for her.

She never wrote me a letter in all those years. But she came back, and that was better. My dad always told me that no one wrote letters any more, but she could have sent a postcard to let me know where she was. Postcards only take five minutes to write, and I was one of her friends. She used to come and see me in the chippy all the time, and she asked me proper questions, and never laughed at me like some of the others did.

The longest letter in the world was written in 1952, by a lady in New York. She wrote it to her boyfriend who was in the army in Korea, and it took her a month to write. But I got nothing. I forgave Lizzy, for not keeping in touch, because she was nice and because she came back. Also, when she lived on the streets of London, she didn't have stamps, or even a pen. I understood her, same as how she understood me.

I'd been waiting until she was eighteen so that I could ask her to marry me, but the waiting didn't count in the end, because she wasn't even there. After Lizzy had been gone for a few years, Dad told me that no woman was worth waiting that long for. She might never come back. I'd saved up enough money to buy a ring in a box, but I ended up spending it on computer games. I needed to buy a lot, because I got to the advanced levels so quickly. Dad said marriage wasn't all it was cracked up to be, anyway. It was much better to have only yourself to worry about. He knew that because my mum left us when I was wee. The most expensive wedding ever was Prince Charles and Lady Diana's in 1981 at St. Paul's Cathedral. There were twenty-seven wedding cakes. It cost over $20 million pounds. I'd never be able to save up that much in my whole life.

Lizzy didn't smell of smoke anymore, like she did when she was thirteen, and so I liked her even more. Also she didn't put black stuff around her eyes like she used to. I knew it was her straightaway. She had the same blonde hair and the exact same smile. Her face had a few wrinkles on it, but they looked nice, and they were in the right places, so they didn't make her look grumpy. Mrs. MacTavish down the road had wrinkles in between her eyebrows and down the sides of her mouth and they made her have an angry face.

I didn't mind that Lizzy had got married to someone else, even when her husband came in the chippy. He was with a group of policemen, who were asking questions along the whole street. It was a quarter past twelve. Weather Wendy had been and gone already. She was wearing her big anorak and a knitted hat that could even have been a tea cozy. It was a dry day, but she said that it wouldn't last, that the rains were coming.

The husband said he was very worried about his wife Lizzy because she'd disappeared. He asked if I knew her, and when I last saw her.

Oh dear. Oh no.

Of course I knew her. I'd known her for a long time, first in real life, and then inside my head, and finally in real life again.

I didn't know she had gone missing. No one had told me. If I'd known, I would have gone to look for her myself. I banged at my forehead, and I walked up and down behind the counter. Those things usually made me feel better, but that time they didn't make any difference. I got even hotter and sadder.

Lizzy's husband was very calm, and he put his hands flat on the counter while he talked to me. He was wearing a shiny gold wedding ring. He said that I didn't have to worry, because the police were going to find her. A policeman put his head in the door, and asked if everything was all right, and he said yes it was. He would be a few more minutes. The others seemed in a rush, but he made me feel like there was all the time in the world.

Soon I finished with the pacing. He told me his name was Alfie, and I liked that name, and after that I stopped banging. He seemed like a nice man, and I was pleased that Lizzy had married him and not the man with the hat, who had been watching her since she was thirteen.

He was a bad egg.

I'd seen him the day before, in the street. He was back in town, and I was supposed to tell Lizzy if I saw him, but now she'd gone missing. He looked angry. The man with the hat inspected my shoes and then all the way up my legs to my face, and I didn't like the way he looked at me, as if I was the worst person he'd ever seen. He was the most terrible person I knew, so he had it the wrong way 'round. I would never forget his face; it was cracked up and sore. He used to walk the streets and hide in corners, watching Lizzy like she was someone off the telly. One day he caught me staring at him, and he came into the chippy when my dad was out the back. He grabbed my arm, and his fingers pinched my skin. He told me to stop looking or he'd really hurt me. I was much younger then, and I was too scared to tell Lizzy about seeing him and her mum. I didn't want him to come back and hurt my skin. But I wasn't afraid of him anymore, because I'd grown into a man and I was bigger than him. I'd just crush his hand if he tried to hurt me again, and then I'd tell the police.

Alfie said I must care about Lizzy very much. He had that right. I don't know what it was about him, but I wanted to tell him everything. His eyes were kind and they smiled at me. I opened my mouth and the words came and didn't stop like they usually did. I told him that I'd known her ever since she wore all the black make-up, and that when she came back to see me I was so pleased I gave her a fish supper for free. I told him that she rescued me from the estate boys, and he smiled. That sounded like his Lizzy, he said. I told him that she wasn't 'his' Lizzy, but she was her own person and didn't belong to anyone. He didn't get cross with me.

I had a 'yes' and a 'no' list that I kept inside my head for all the people I met. Lizzy was at the top of the 'yes' list. Her mum was also on there, even though she was *presumed dead*. *Presumed dead* is when someone has been missing for so long that they must be in heaven. Her dad was on the 'no' list because he was one of the ones who ignored me when I was right in front of them. I didn't like his face either; it was mean. At first Mrs. MacTavish was on the 'no' list because she always looked cross, but when she was kind to me and I realized the cross look was because of her wrinkles, she flew over to the 'yes' side.

Alfie's name went straight onto the 'yes' list. I put him underneath Lizzy's name. He asked again if I knew anything about where Lizzy was. I said yes I did, and that we'd talked about the man with the hat, who had been with her mum the night she disappeared. I told him about how I'd tried to tell my dad and the inspector about the man with the hat at the time, but no one had listened to me.

'Tell them about who?' he asked.

I spoke slowly, and I said, 'the...man...with...the...hat.'

'I think I know who you mean,' he said.

I said, 'you would know if you met him. He gives you a sick feeling in your stomach.'

Alfie had a funny look on his face. He said thank you very much. I'd been very helpful.

'But there's someone else too,' I said. I told him about the tiny round woman in the grey coat. She wasn't from the town, and I would know, as I'd been there my whole life. She'd been in and got a fish supper every day for a week. Seemed like she only ate fish and chips for her tea. The British eat 382 million portions of fish and chips every year, which is an average of six each. She already had her share. She always came in late, just before closing. The quiet time. She was always on her own and she was really dirty. My dad would have said she'd been through a hedge backwards, but he was never there as I finished up the night shift. She must have been staying up towards the park and the estate, because that's the way she walked after. It was where I lived with Dad, and once I saw her walking down my road towards the town. I told him the name of the road. Brushwood Drive.

As I was talking about the round woman, more police cars whizzed by, all the sirens going. I'd never seen so many of them in one go. I got distracted and went outside to watch. So did Alfie, and so did some of the other folk in the street. It was a spectacle. Not the kind that you wear, but the kind that's amazing.

Alfie shook my hand and thanked me again for all the information. He'd listened to me. Really listened. I got the feeling that he noticed things too, same as me.

'Look out for the both of them,' I said. 'The man with the hat and the round woman in the grey coat. They're the bad people.'

I had to shout that last part, because he was already running towards the estate, to where the police cars were going. I was feared for Lizzy, more than when she was gone the first time. I got a bad feeling in my stomach, the same as when I had to go to the dentist. It felt like a terrible thing was going to happen. I watched until all the police were out of sight.

Whatever it was, I hoped it hadn't happened yet.

CHAPTER FORTY-THREE

Helen's Lens

Her laptop was resting on the chest of drawers in front of the bed, webcam ready. The old telly was discarded on the floor to one side, a bulky thing that didn't fit under the bed. She'd chuck it out in the hall. The room was too cramped as it was. Helen sidled around until she was out of sight, crouching on the floor with her tools next to her. Oliver would know she was there, and that was enough.

The girl was awake now, her eyes wide, her body trembling. She must have known what was coming. Or thought she did. She hadn't said anything yet. Her throat would be parched mind you, dried up like a strip of sandpaper.

Helen had the syringe ready, set to one side. She double-checked the strength of the bindings around the girl's wrists, tied now to the bedposts, separated and splayed. The pillow was thin, so she added another underneath, to prop the girl's head up. She lifted it for her, by the hair. 'We're going to talk to Oliver, through the camera,' she said. 'You can tell him what you think of him.'

The girl looked straight ahead. Vacant. Her body was limp, hands hanging from the bindings. Although she didn't have much energy, she would surely want to say a few parting words to the man who had captured her.

'I'm going to count down from five.' She held up her hand in front of the girl's face. 'And then you can speak to the camera. To him. He killed your mother. Did you know?'

The girl blinked. She was deflated, a wilted flower.

Helen stretched up and switched on the camera. She rested the hammer on the end of the bed, along with her tub of nails. Ready for the next stage. She could hardly wait for it, a tremor circling through the whole of her. The girl began to pant, eyes rolling back a little.

She held up her hand. 'Five…four…three…two…one…' She gave her a nod of encouragement. 'Talk to him.'

'Where is he?' The girl's voice was but a whisper.

'He's on the other end of this webcam. He can see you.'

'Why?'

'He was going to let you die, but I took you away. Don't you have something to say to him?'

The girl looked blankly at the screen. 'Why?'

Helen leaned forward. 'You were his top prize, girly. But you're mine, now.'

CHAPTER FORTY-FOUR

Lizzy's Monsters

The room smelled of stale sweat and vinegar. It was small, close, and with that woman and the whirring computer in the room, she could barely breathe. The damp walls and the ceiling were all closing in, radiating thick, musky heat. This wasn't a dream. This was real.

Lizzy knew the woman. She was no rescuer, but another beast who was keeping her captive for her own means. She'd been giving her water and scraps of food. One level better, but she was still on the bottom rung. She was the same woman who'd scavenged about the market in Soho, the one who tried to take her away that time in the alley. Lizzy could never forget her bowl-cut hair, the odd way she stared. It was like she didn't belong to this world, living inside her own dark mind. An outsider.

A searing pain travelled from the base of her spine, all the way up to her neck. Her arms were tingling, her fingertips tiny slices of ice, the blood flow cut off by the tight rope around her wrists. Her legs were free, but they felt suspended. Her body belonged to someone else. She kept her limbs soft, weak, so that she'd seem malleable, but her mind felt strong and her wits were alive. She wouldn't let on.

The woman was panting like a dog now, or a wolf, her breath rasping. She seemed desperate for her to talk to Oliver, tell him what she thought. But there was no point. It didn't matter. Whatever she thought of him, she was still going to die. She could tell by the energy in the room, the antic-ipation flooding from this woman. The suspense.

She wouldn't give her the pleasure. Or him.

Lizzy didn't move. She stared ahead, and shut out the breathing, the webcam light, and the stench. She turned her mind to Alfie, of home, of the smell of popcorn. She forced out the thoughts of death, and replaced them with purple flowers and family movie nights at Nat's with Chunky Monkey ice cream. Freshly buttered toast.

Out of the corner of her eye, she could see a hammer and a square box at the end of the bed, just within reach of her feet. A rush of fear flowed through her.

'A few words,' the woman was saying. 'Go on.'

But wait. There were voices out on the street, below the window. Walkie-talkies beeping and crackling. The police were in town; she'd heard all the sirens. Perhaps they were right there, trawling the streets.

She might only have a moment. One chance.

Lizzy clenched her stomach muscles, pulled together all her strength. The woman was crouched on the floor, still waiting for her to speak to the camera, to come up with some hate. She took a deep breath in, as if she were about to speak. Twisting at the waist, she managed to turn her body a fraction, then she kicked at the box. It wasn't as heavy as it looked, and it flew up in an arc and crashed into the window. The box exploded open, nails bursting out, making a large ring of taps and scrapes on the glass. It was like abstract art, an installation at a posh gallery that might present itself in time intervals.

Bang, chink, clink—an ugly but beautiful display.

Then she screamed, her voice surprisingly loud, cracked but piercing. She'd managed to form the word 'help'.

The box and all the nails fell to the floor. The art of it finished in a second.

The woman reached up and put her damp hand over Lizzy's mouth. Their eyes met briefly. Inside the woman it was empty, soulless. Her insides were the same as Oliver's. They were from the same place. Only this was a woman, and so it was worse. Or was it?

The voices were getting further away. *Nothing to see here.*

Lizzy twisted her head from side to side, her wrists burning, toes throbbing from kicking the box. The woman took her hand away briefly, and scuffled on the floor. Then a needle came at her, just like before. She kicked out again, wrenched at the bindings. But the woman was too strong for her, and pushed down until the needle was pricking at the thin skin on the side of her neck.

This was it.

Lizzy held her breath, felt her face reddening. There was a noise coming from downstairs, a low knocking. It was the front door maybe. The woman pulled away, distracted. She began to mutter to herself as she sidled over to the window.

The needle had gone in a bit. Some of the drug must have got in her vein. Lizzy was looking through a cloud. Hearing through cotton wool. Everything was thick, viscous.

Another crash, muffled and deep.

The woman went as if to leave the room, but paused, staring into space. Her eyes were glazed over, her arms hanging by her sides. What was she doing?

The room spun, and stopped when it was still tilted to the right. Lizzy blinked, sinking. The woman was shuffling across the floor to the bedroom door, going out now. It was like she was in a trance, moving through treacle, although it could have been Lizzy's mind playing tricks.

She peered out of the haze, shimmering. That red light was still on. Was he watching all this? Now she was screaming again, or trying to, the sound deeper and slower. What would Oliver say, if he could speak through the screen? *They can't take you away from me.*

I'm not yours to keep. She may have said it inside her mind, or out loud. It wasn't clear to her which.

Where was he? Why was he watching this? None of it made sense. She stared at the webcam, into him. He would be staring back at her. Black eyes, and dark thoughts that she'd never understand.

Someone was touching her wrist, her forehead. A policeman. Blue uniform. A badge. 'Lizzy. Can you smile for me?'

She pulled up the corners of her mouth. Her eyes stayed dead.

'How many fingers?' The policeman held his hand close.

'Three,' she whispered.

The woman downstairs was being told not to move. Anything she did say might be given as evidence. Lizzy had never heard that statement except on the telly, on crime shows. Or in this hallucination. She pointed at the laptop, at the red light. 'Oliver's watching,' she said, or she whispered.

The policeman turned his attention to the webcam. 'Jesus,' he said.

More police. Shouting. The paramedics appeared with a stretcher. She was cut free, then strapped down tight again before they lifted her. There were sirens, flashing lights, police radios, and the buzz of adrenaline in every voice.

Then she was out, carried through the living room to the front door. She had survived him, beaten them.

There were people looking through the house, gloves on, studying the walls, pulling out chairs. As they went outside, she saw, through the mist of daylight, the red-blue lights of the ambulance and some worried faces standing behind the blockade of police. They all gasped when she came outside. One woman was crying. Another was comforting her. Dalbegie was tight, a close place. It had a dark edge, but it also had a golden heart. Fresh air seeped into her lungs, the taste of it natural and beautiful after the stale stench of the cellar, and that room.

When she ran away with Simon all those years ago, she thought she had no one. But plenty of people had cared about her. Auntie Maureen was wrapped up in herself, but she'd given her a home. Molly and Judith, Maggie in the café. Jonno. Even Jessica. She'd been missed, loved by folk in their own funny ways.

There was a man standing at the edge of the crowd, an illusion. He looked like Alfie. Couldn't be him. He was back home in London, tiling the kitchen. She wasn't seeing straight.

They lifted her stretcher onto a bed with wheels. That man was climbing into the ambulance. *It was Alfie.* It made sense, now. Who else would have sorted out this mess, been there for her at the end? He was solid, invincible.

The paramedics were putting a needle in her arm, squeezing a bag above her head. They got Alfie to sit next to her. Hold her hand, they said. Talk to her. They knew; he would make everything better. He had that look about him.

'I wondered why you hadn't texted me back,' he said. He touched her hand.

She searched for him, for his eyes. *There he was.* Felt like two months, not two weeks, since she'd seen him. 'Sorry,' she said. Her voice was deep, muted, like she was underwater.

'That's okay,' he said. 'I can see you were busy.'

'How'd you know?'

He tapped the side of his nose. 'I know everything, me. But that Jonno's a good lad. We owe him one. They're onto the psycho that lives opposite the newsagents. And we were looking for that woman; Jonno told us what street she might be in. They'd found a body near there. Then the bang at the window. And the weird scream.'

She screwed up her eyes. There was another thing.

'I know about the baby,' he said. 'We'll be all right.'

They spent the rest of the journey to the hospital in silence. Alfie kept his hand resting on hers, his eyes locked onto her own. His expression said he loved her. The monsters, all of them, were perishing.

When the ambulance pulled into emergency, she thought of something she'd seen at the beginning of her visit. 'Oliver's back garden.'

'Is Oliver 'the man with the hat'?'

'Yes. His compost.'

'What about it?' He frowned.
'Get the police to look in it.'

❧ ❧ ❧

I'm back here in hospital again, Mum. I was lucky, they said, to be alive. I had spasms in my neck and I've got a fracture in my knee. There are lots of bruises, or 'traumas' as they call them. And I'm severely dehydrated for obvious reasons, but nothing that a drip can't sort out apparently. I suppose I was lucky, in a way. But you make your own luck, don't you?

Alfie was with me in the hospital until they kicked him out. He's staying at Tilda's; how funny is that? I can just imagine how he wolfs down her huge breakfasts, and how much she likes feeding him. She'll be fussing all over him, like a mother hen.

I'm supposed to be sleeping, and I can feel the pills taking effect now. My mind is finally relaxing. I got what I wanted, in a way. I didn't ask to lose my baby, or put my body through all of this. But the one thing I longed for was to find out what happened to you. Oliver grabbed me by the scruff of my neck and showed me—whether I wanted to see or not. I'm grateful for it, and I know that sounds strange. If I hadn't experienced it myself, I would have died of sadness to think of you lying in his cellar, shrinking, hurting, and drying up. But I know about the spiritual side of death, now. I had dreams. I was floating in some other world, delirious and free of pain. In the end, part of me died, to be with you, and the other part of me stayed here, to be with Alfie.

I hope they get him. If he was on the other side of that webcam, he would have seen the police, and done a runner. That woman might shop him though; she hated his guts. He took away your life, and my childhood, and we'll never get them back. But I feel closer to you than ever. I'm up there next to you; I can feel your breath on my skin, your hair silky soft next to mine. I'll cherish the photos of you, but I didn't really need them.

As if I'd forget your face. You're my blood, and it runs thick, as Granny Mac used to say. Deep in the core of me, there's always been the pull of a cord that runs to you. Oliver tried to sever it, imagined he could wrench away our souls for his own, but he didn't manage it. Our wounds are just scratches on the surface, because what lies underneath can't be touched.

I'm sinking now, into sleep. The edges are rounded off, welded together. Bonded.

Replenished

Everything is as it should be. The tunnel that leads down to you is closing, no longer needed. My light's waning, and it'll switch off soon, I'll bet. You'll need to replace it with another, for your own wee girl, the beginnings of a new generation to come. Keep it all going, you know? You'll have another go, at filling that wee wool cardy you wanted to knit. I know you will.

Turns out Oliver did have some keepsakes stashed away, after all. You were right about that compost of his. It reminds me of that game they used to have at the fair, wee wrapped presents hidden in a bucketful of sawdust. You pay your money, plunge your hand in and pull out a prize.

They found a few prizes in his back garden. A selection of bones, all bagged up now and taken away. One of those boggin' pagers from the nineties, rusted and broken. A gold chain, like the ones the schemie guys wore down the market. Your black scarf covered in mud; he didn't wait long to push that in there. And a tube pass from years ago, crumbled up in a plastic sleeve. But best of all, they found what you were looking for. The Scottish Cross, the real one, still on my necklace, salvageable. I never dreamed it would be so close. When they're done with it, I hope they give it to you to keep.

And he's hidden away too, left to rot in his own cellar. Oliver got what was coming to him. You don't know it yet, but that funny woman saw to it he wouldn't be able to get off that hard bed of his. And she nailed down the floorboards that hid the cellar. She's not right in the heid, just as psycho as him, but I can't help but be thankful for her a wee bit for what she did. Is that wrong? When they find him, he might be hanging on, or he might be gone. Either way, he's got.

∽ ∽ ∽

I turn to face away from the earth, my arms spread out, my face in the sun. I can see a pale vision of you, smiling, hair spilling about your face. You reach out to me and our fingertips brush together. Then I float upwards, away, just like I was meant.

What happens to us as weans always comes back later in fuzzy pictures, snippets of conversations, or wrapped up in smells or feelings. We remember everything in our own funny ways.

When we're all grown up, we fret about the past almost as much as we worry about the future. What happened we can't change, but we're confined by it. It stops us in our tracks. But the barriers have been taken away, Lizzy, and you can take whatever road you like. Let the past go, free fall, make your own way. You're unhindered by history now. I hope you know what I mean by that.

One last saying: 'There's a lang road that's no' goat a turnin'.' Don't lose heart in the bad times; things can't go on in the same direction forever. The way changes. You've done it, Lizzy. You're free. Go where you want to go. Be who you want to be. And don't look back.

∽ ∽ ∽

Notes — Experiment Number Twenty-One
Start Date: Saturday 26 Sept
End Date: (tbd)
Place: Dalbegie, Scotland

Age of Body: 56
Est. Weight of Body: 170lb
Name of Body: Oliver

The body may not last long given the additional trauma to wrists and ankles to ensure a secure capture. Dehydration will undoubtedly set in prematurely, given blood loss. This time we have the added interest that this victim has—until now—been the victimizer. At last, he feels what the others felt. And someone has taken his place.

—H

ACKNOWLEDGEMENTS

A special thanks to Erin Macnair and Fiona Winning for reading this book in its early form. To Nikki Jobson for insisting that Helen wasn't actually dead. And to my editor Jenn Farrell for making it all better. Finally, thank you Brian Kaufman and Karen Green at Anvil Press for making it all happen. This is the end of a trilogy of books that has been a real journey in so many ways.

ABOUT THE AUTHOR

Jackie Bateman lives with her family in North Vancouver. Her first novel *Nondescript Rambunctious* won a national first book competition in Canada, and grew into a trilogy of psychological thrillers. The second novel in the series, *Savour,* was shortlisted for the 2015 Relit Awards. *Straight Circles* ties up all of the disturbing threads in a grand psychotic finale. The trilogy has been optioned for a multi-episode TV series.